P9-CDU-431

The Cracks in the Kingdom

THE COLORS OF MADELEINE

BOOK TWO

JACLYN MORIARTY

NEW HANOVER COUNTY
PUBLIC LIBRARY
201 CHESTNUT STREET
WILMINGTON, NC 28401

ARTHUR A. LEVINE BOOKS
An Imprint of Scholastic Inc.

TO CORRIE STEPAN AND RACHEL COHN
FOR FRIENDSHIP ABOVE AND BEYOND

Text copyright © 2014 by Jaclyn Moriarty

All rights reserved. Published by Arthur A. Levine Books, an imprint of Scholastic Inc., *Publishers since 1920.* SCHOLASTIC, the LANTERN LOGO, and associated logos are trademarks and/or registered trademarks of Scholastic Inc.

No part of this publication may be reproduced, stored in a retrieval system, or transmitted in any form or by any means, electronic, mechanical, photocopying, recording, or otherwise, without written permission of the publisher. For information regarding permission, write to Scholastic Inc., Attention: Permissions Department, 557 Broadway, New York, NY 10012.

Library of Congress Cataloging-in-Publication Data is available.

ISBN 978-0-545-39738-4

10 9 8 7 6 5 4 3 2 1   14 15 16 17 18

Printed in the U.S.A.   23

First edition, April 2014

Book design by Elizabeth B. Parisi
Title page image © bethsp/istockphoto

From *Memoirs of Sir Isaac Newton's Life*, by William Stukeley, 1752:

On the day that Oliver Cromwell died, there was a very great wind, or tempest over the whole kingdom. That day, as the boys were playing, a set of them went to leaping. Sir Isaac, tho' he was little practis'd in the exercise, & at other times outdone by many; yet this day was surprizingly superior to them all, which they much wondered at, but could not discover the reason; which was this: Sir Isaac observed the gusts of wind, & took so proper an advantage of them, as to carry him far beyond the rest . . .

From *The Kingdom of Cello: An Illustrated Travel Guide*, by T. I. Candle, 7th edition, © 2012, reprinted with kind permission, Brellidge University Press, T. I. Candle.

The People of Cello

There are plenty of people in Cello, so that's good news.

Most of these people sleep at night, and love their royal family, and get about by walking on the ground. Nevertheless, in the course of your visit to Cello, you may well meet a Night-Dweller. Or come across a Wandering Hostile. Or bump into an Occasional — actually, you probably *won't* meet an Occasional Pilot. That's about as likely as finding a toad living underneath your fingernail, to be honest. (Although considerably more pleasant — Occasional Pilots are a total blast, whereas a toad under your nail would surely irk.)

In any case, this section is designed to prepare you for such a meeting, and to help you avoid any awkwardness should one take place.

The Cracks in the Kingdom

PART 1

1.

Maximillian Reisman can stand on his head for thirty minutes if he wants to.

Today he doesn't want to.

His head is too busy, for a start.

It is trying to recall some advice he was once given, about how to revive wilting lettuce leaves. At the same time, it is constructing an advertising campaign for organic oatmeal. It is composing a humorous speech to deliver at a colleague's farewell drinks; it is holding a cell phone underneath Maximillian's chin; and on that very chin, it is quietly growing a beard.

Maximillian kicks the fridge closed on the wilting lettuce leaves. He snaps his cell phone shut without leaving a message.

"*Tabernacle,*" he says. This is a curse word. He says it because he has realised, abruptly, that he (and his head) are trying to do too much.

Maximillian is fifty-two years old. He is lighting a cigarette. He is walking to the window. He is opening the shutters, leaning out into the warm evening air. He is blowing smoke across Place d'Youville, watching it fade into the shadows of the Musée d'archéologie.

It is 6 P.M. on Saturday, August 22, in Montreal, Quebec, Canada.

Maximillian is thinking.

A smile forms around his cigarette.

It's the beard! The growing of the beard! *That* is the thing that has taken him over the edge into too busy.

He heads to the bathroom to shave.

The heat wakes Sasha Wilczek, as it does every morning, with its weight and its feather lines of sweat.

It is 6 A.M. on Sunday, August 23, in Taipei, Taiwan.

Sasha's bedroom is not much bigger than Maximillian's bathtub.

Pale murmurs drift through the open door. The tap of a fingernail against a fan of cards.

Those are Sasha's flatmates. A boy and a girl, both American students. They play gin rummy through the nights.

"You have a dry sense of humour." That's the girl's voice, suddenly clear.

Sasha waits for the boy's reply.

"What does that mean?" he says eventually.

"It means your tone doesn't change when you're making a joke," replies the girl.

Sasha Wilczek is forty-nine years old. She is lying in a narrow bed. She is considering the girl's definition of dry humour, turning it over in her mind. She is looking at the dust-smudged bedroom window, at its criss-crossed patterns of masking tape ready for typhoons. She is looking through the dust into her mind, into her schedule for today.

She teaches an 11 A.M. Zumba class at a local gym. Also 2 P.M. Hip Hop and 3:30 P.M. Freestyle dance.

Outside her bedroom, the boy flatmate yawns and wonders aloud why he's so tired.

That boy does not have a dry sense of humour, Sasha thinks suddenly. He has no sense of humour at *all. That's* why his tone never changes.

Maybe she could recommend a 5 P.M. Sense of Humour class.

Monty Rickard is laughing so hard he has to fall down on the carpet.

It is four o'clock on Saturday afternoon, August 22, in Boise, Idaho, USA.

There are five people in the room. Two of them are laughing as they unplug a computer and lift its cords and keyboard into the air. The others, like Monty, are letting their laughter knock them sideways.

Everything could be lost! *Everything!*

It's not really that funny.

For the last six months, in their spare time, Monty and his friends have been designing a computer game. Gianni (one of the people falling about) is always going on about how they need to back it up.

Just now, Gianni spilled a can of Red Bull all over the computer.

There's no backup copy.

They're laughing so hard their throats are hurting.

Monty Rickard is eighteen. He has just started a dog-walking business. He chews his knuckles. He plays seven different musical instruments including saxophone, drums, and mandolin. He's not especially good at computer programming, but his friends are, especially Gianni.

A dog jumps onto Monty's stomach, not sure how else to join the hilarity. A guitar, leaning up against the wall, slips to the floor with a *twang* that makes the laughter rise an octave.

* * *

In Berlin, Germany, it's midnight. Chimes are splitting Saturday, August 22, from Sunday, 23.

Ariel Peters is studying her new tattoo. It's on her arm. It's a dragon. Her room vibrates with the backbeat from the dance floor downstairs. There are sudden thudding footsteps outside her door, then they're gone.

Ariel is fourteen. She lied about her age to get the job behind the bar downstairs. Also, to get this room. Also, the tattoo.

It needs more. The dragon needs to breathe fire. It needs to be carrying a basket of eggs in its claws. A saddle so she can ride it. Maybe a cover for rainy days. An espresso maker.

She'll save up her pay and return to the tattoo parlour soon.

Finn Mackenzie, eight years old, is watching a snail climb a window.

Eight A.M., Sunday, August 23.

Beyond the snail is Avoca Beach, which is an hour north of Sydney, Australia.

Finn sees a couple walk along the beach. They're carrying their shoes, skirting seaweed. The woman wears a long woollen scarf. She crouches down to fold up her jeans, and the scarf drapes along the sand beside her.

Finn has solemn eyes and a head cold. He wipes his nose on the back of his sleeve. "You're heading in the wrong direction," he says. "Snails don't belong in the sky." He thinks he might watch *Toy Story 3* again today. He thinks that the colour of the woman's scarf is exactly like a raspberry slushy.

These small events across the world, you'll be wondering why they're here.

You'll be right to wonder: They are profoundly inconsequential.

Except for two things.

First:

Time slides around the world so strangely that all of this is happening at once. Summer dusk in Montreal is midnight in Berlin is winter breakfast time on a beach to the north of Sydney. Maximillian shaves while Sasha dusts her mind while Monty scratches behind his dog's ears. Ariel imagines a new tattoo just as little Finn raises the window and flicks the snail from the glass. He watches it fall into the garden.

Second:

Maximillian Reisman, Sasha Wilczek, Monty Rickard, Ariel Peters, and Finn Mackenzie are not, originally, from this world.

Those are not even their real names.

They all come from a kingdom called Cello.

They were brought here to our world against their will, through cracks that were sealed tightly behind them. Now they laugh, fry eggs, take showers, send texts — and sometimes even stand on their heads — in a world that, to them, is as strange as time itself.

2.

"So there's a kingdom called Cello and it's lost its royal family."

"Right."

"Careless."

"I know, right? I said the same thing. But they were abducted and brought here to our world. That's what they think anyway."

"That's what who think?"

"I don't know. The police or security force or whatever in Cello."

"So who's in the family, like, a king and a queen?"

"Yeah, and four kids. Three of the kids are missing: an eighteen-year-old prince, a fourteen-year-old princess, and another prince, a little boy. He's eight."

"And you know about the Kingdom of Cello cause . . ."

"Because I found a, sort of like, *conduit* between our world and Cello. In a parking meter. I've been using it to write letters to a boy named Elliot Baranski."

There was a long pause.

Belle, who had been asking the questions, turned and looked at Madeleine.

Madeleine shrugged. "I *get* that it sounds sort of —"

"Unexpected." Jack's voice drifted out from the bathroom where he was cleaning the toilet.

"Like bollocks." Belle plunged a scrubbing brush into the bucket beside her. "Unnecessarily complicated bollocks," she amended thoughtfully. "And who needs complications in bollocks?"

Madeleine, Jack, and Belle were in a flat in Cambridge, England. The flat's owner, Denny Michalski, was one of their home-schooling teachers, but he'd gone to see a doctor about his asthma.

He'd left them a Geography assignment to complete.

Denny's real work was in computer-hardware repair, and his place was overrun with toolboxes and motherboards: You couldn't take a step without stubbing your toe on an open PC carcass.

"It's a health and safety disaster zone," Jack had said.

"Dust and dog hairs everywhere," Belle had added. "No wonder he's got asthma."

"I'm not really *moved* by tectonic plates," Madeleine had reflected, looking at the Geography assignment.

So they had decided to clean the flat instead.

While they cleaned, Madeleine was telling her friends about the Kingdom of Cello. She'd never mentioned it to them before. Why now?

The cleaning fluids must have muddled her brain. She turned on the kitchen tap to wash the suds away. Could you get water back into the tap once it was down the drain?

No, she thought philosophically. You could not.

But you could try.

"Forget it," she commanded. "I was just making the whole thing up."

"But to get it straight," Belle said, "you've been sending letters to a boy named Elliot Baranski who lives in a kingdom called Cello?"

"I get that it sounds crazy," Madeleine repeated. She found the broom leaning up against the fridge, and started sweeping. "I thought it was a hoax at first, and that Elliot Baranski was just somebody's invention. But one time I went *into* the Kingdom. For a fraction of a moment. A splinter of a second."

"What was it like?"

"Sunny."

Belle nodded, approving of Cellian weather, and Madeleine continued.

"Anyway, Elliot's dad disappeared ages ago, and turns out he's been captured by a terrorist organisation. So Elliot wants to be rescuing his dad, but his Kingdom want him to help find the royal family."

"Conflicting priorities," Jack called sympathetically. "Why'd they want his help in particular?"

"They found out he has a contact here in the World."

"Cool. Who's his contact?"

"Well. Me."

She swept over a small object on the floor three or four times but it didn't shift, so she gave the broom a disappointed glance and crouched down to dig it out herself. It was just a little bolt, stuck between the floorboards. Or was this called a nut? Who knew.

Madeleine looked up. Belle was watching her. Jack, in the bathroom, was silent, except for the swish of a cloth along the bath tiles.

"I mean, I *get* that I must have been *hallucinating* when I went into the Kingdom. And I *get* that it doesn't *really* exist —"

"Can you stop getting things?" Belle interrupted. "It's materialistic. And what do you mean it doesn't exist?"

"Well, obviously — and you just . . ."

"I said it *sounds* like bollocks," Belle said irritably. "Not that it is. Why should there *not* be a kingdom called Cello?"

"I always thought there might be." Jack sat himself cross-legged in the doorway to the bathroom. "I mean, I thought there'd be another world. Not that it would be called Cello. How could I have known its name?"

He rested his head against the doorframe.

"For all I knew," he said, "it could've been Violin or Double Bass. Not even necessarily strings. Could have been the Kingdom of Trumpet."

"Who said it had to be an instrument?" said Belle. "You tosser."

Jack ignored her. "There's probably more than just the one kingdom in your parking meter." He looked at Madeleine respectfully. "There's a whole brass band of them."

Madeleine twisted the broom between her hands, and turned to Belle.

"You *believe* there's a kingdom in the parking meter?"

"Not *in* the parking meter. Wouldn't fit, would it? Jack doesn't know what he's talking about. And anyway, I thought you said the meter was like a conduit or mailbox or something?" In her exasperation, Belle sent a spray of water flying across the room. It splattered onto the bedspread. "Oops," she said in a formal sort of way.

At that moment there was the sound of the door slamming downstairs. All three of them paused, gazing around at the mops, rags, buckets of sludge brown water, and half-hearted piles of swept-up crumbs and wire snippets.

There were slow footsteps on the stairs, and pattering claws.

"If the royal family's here in our world," Belle said suddenly, "who's running the Kingdom of Cello?"

The door opened. Denny walked in, his dog, Sulky-Anne, slipping past as if she'd remembered something urgent. She ran straight to the bed, leapt onto it, got herself comfortable, and fixed them with a penetrating gaze.

Denny's own eyes had the wild bright look they always got when he'd just had asthma treatment. Now his face changed shape with emotion.

"You kids," he said. "You've *cleaned*."

"We didn't do any of the assignment," all three confessed rapidly, under cover of his enthusiasm.

"You've even done the *bathroom*!" Denny was ducking his head into that room. He emerged again. "And you've got that donkey-shaped mould stain off the wall!"

"Plus we got rid of the junk you had along the other wall,"

Madeleine pointed out. "Those bikes with missing wheels and the half dartboard and that? We chucked them in a bin."

"I feel like they might have been useful at some point." Denny's voice turned suddenly mournful.

"That seems unlikely," Belle said caustically, then to Madeleine in an aside: "Seriously, who's running Cello? Or is it the sort of rubbish monarchy where the royals are just for dressing up and getting pregnant?"

Madeleine reflected. "Yeah, no, I think they've got proper royalty. And there's one princess sister left behind. She's only fifteen or something, and *she's* ruling the Kingdom."

"Nice," said Belle, impressed, and Madeleine felt a surge of pride, as if she herself were the ruling princess. Belle was almost never impressed.

"I see you've reorganised my trays of screws and things." Denny's voice was swinging towards doubt.

"I just re-classified," Jack explained. "That's all right, isn't it?"

Denny settled on recklessness. "How could it hurt! Hey, you know what, guys? Who cares about Geography! Let's go out and celebrate the fact that I can breathe! And that I have a clean" — he paused, looked about — "a half . . . a *quarter*-clean flat!"

Everyone agreed, including the dog.

3.

Princess Ko, reigning monarch of Cello (by default), was rolling a mint along the table.

She was in the upper-level boardroom of the White Palace, and the Commissioner of Finance was addressing her.

The mint spun quietly. It hit Princess Ko's right palm and she batted it back to her left.

"I've briefed the Queen on all of this," the Commissioner was saying. "By which I mean, of course, that I sent the proposals to her in the Southern Climes a fortnight ago. How is your mother getting along there anyhow?"

The Princess stopped the flow of the mint with a turn of her hand.

"Like a starspin!" she exclaimed. "At least, when I spoke to her last night, that's how she sounded. The southern chocolate just *does my mother in*! Of course, she might have run out by now and gone into a tailspin. Don't look so bemused! That was humor! I'm sure she's still got plenty of chocolate!"

There was a pause, then, "O-o-oh! You mean, how's her *work* getting on. Well, I understand it is utterly important — her work — and I really cannot fathom how glad I am. That she's doing it."

The Commissioner blinked.

"Marvelous," he said, and scratched the back of his neck. "And did she mention whether she'd — received my proposals, by any chance?"

"Did she ever! She was turning somersaults of ecstasy about them! As Finance Commissioner, you, sir, rock this Kingdom so hard you put it to sleep! Those were her words! But there's no doubt or consequence in my mind either."

"In that case, perhaps I could trouble you, in your mother's absence . . ."

Princess Ko kept her left hand pressed over the mint, while she reached, with her right, for the Royal Stamp. Carved of sandalwood, tall as a wine bottle, this stood beside a stack of folders.

Ca-clamp.

She blew on the ink.

The Commissioner nodded his thanks and pushed back his chair, glancing toward the nearest window as he did so.

"That view." He shook his head. "You must never tire of it."

Politely, the Princess turned to look.

Snowfields drew the eye across a dazzle of blue-white, silver-white, and white-white. The only interruptions were splashes of azure blue (lakes) or galloping specks (bears or wolves — or possibly werewolves; it was hard to tell the difference these days) — and, in the vast distance, the crags of a drifting mountain range.

"Does a scarecrow tire of turning cartwheels!" Princess Ko exclaimed.

The Commissioner bowed to hide his bewilderment, and quickly withdrew from the conference room.

As the door closed behind him, the Princess put the mint in her mouth. She swiveled her chair 180 degrees.

A man and a woman stood shoulder to shoulder against the wall behind her. These were her security agents.

"One down, seventeen to go," said the Princess.

The female agent nodded briskly. "Mmhmm."

The man stared hard at Princess Ko, as if trying to sort through her mind.

"You two always look as if you're lined up before a firing squad," Princess Ko observed. "And yet my efforts to persuade you to sit down never come to more than a whipplespit of horse dung."

The man allowed himself a smile.

"Too much?" she said.

"The image of the Queen turning somersaults of ecstasy *might* have gone a little too far," he replied.

Princess Ko smiled faintly. "The Commissioner of Finance," she mused. "He's questionable on interest rate policy, but on tax matters he's sound. Fiscally speaking, he seems astute even if, in other ways, he's almost as moronic as *I* am."

Both agents snorted.

Before the conversation could continue, the door opened to an announcement: "The Commissioner for Public Transport, Your Highness."

Princess Ko reached for the second folder in the pile.

The day carried on.

Three junior PR officers wanted to express their distress about the Queen's preferred brand of sunglasses. The Army General needed an advance on next year's budget. Skirmishes with Wandering Hostiles in the province of Nature Strip. The Assistant Chair of the Illumination Society was excited about a potential breakthrough in Color bending. The Royal Chef, a tall redhead wearing crimson lipstick, needed approval of the menu for the Welcome Banquet.

"Welcome Banquet?"

"Yes, Your Highness. The Royal Youth Alliance. Its inaugural convention is next week — surely, you . . ."

"Forgotten! Had I forgotten! Why, I'm tossing and turning in my *sleep* with the excitement. Or I would be if I were asleep."

The Chef smiled. "It's a pity your sister, Princess Jupiter, will not be here for the feast. We're serving delicacies from each of the participant's provinces — and there's one boy coming from the Farms. . . ."

"Elliot Baranski," said Princess Ko.

"Is that his name? All right. Well, so there'll be pecan pies, pumpkin pies, sugar pies, and cinnamon pies in honor of Elliot's province. Fortunately our dessert chef is Farms-trained. Anyway, my point is, we all know how fond Princess Jupiter is of pastries!"

"I *know*! She'd be scaling the walls of that rehab center if she — oops. Just try to *unhear* that, would you? Princess Jupiter is nowhere *near* a rehab center! As everyone knows, she's in a mathematics college, enhancing her knowledge of that — field of — subject."

The Chef widened her eyes in confusion and thrust the menu at the Princess.

Ca-clamp! Ca-clamp! Ca-clamp! went the Royal Stamp.

Some visitors were formal and straight-backed, wiping sweaty palms on trouser legs. Others affected nonchalance, leaning back or reaching to pour themselves iced water from the silver jug. Some had trouble hiding their amazement at the Princess's stupidity.

All made reference to the view.

The final meeting of the day was with the Social Secretary. He was a short, droll man who liked to wear shirts with upright collars, usually in shades of green. He always rocked back in his chair, both hands in his pockets, then drew the hands out to point to the next item on his list. After which, the hands would return to his pockets. It seemed a wasteful ritual.

Eventually he rocked back, drew out his hands, and tapped firmly on the final item. "I have saved the best for last," he declared.

"You have," agreed Princess Ko, and paused. "Have you?"

"An invitation that arrived just this morning, Princess. I've already forwarded the details to your father — to the extent that you can forward things to a ship crossing the Narraburra — and I've given a heads-up to all *manner* of departments. Diplomacy, Security, Foreign

Relations, Armed Forces, not to mention Etiquette and Protocol. Can you guess what the invitation is?"

He twinkled and the Princess twinkled back.

"No," she admitted after they'd exchanged several more twinkles.

"It's from the King of Aldhibah! He has invited your father to attend the namesaking of his son, in the role of . . . wait for it! . . . Candlemaker! Also known as Light Guide! That is to say, the King of Aldhibah is asking *your* father to be the *role model* for his firstborn child throughout his life! Now, you'll already know about the rather *strained* relations between our two Kingdoms — to put it mildly — and hence you will know, Princess, that this invitation is . . . !"

He paused, flourishing a white card the size of his palm.

"Quite small," murmured the Princess.

"HUGE!!" cried the Social Secretary, undeterred. "Am I right?!"

"Is the sea the same color as a scallywag?!" Princess Ko got into the swing of things.

"Well, no, it's not, actually. Scallywags are pale apricot, whereas the sea is — but I see from your demeanor you agree with me! It's *massive*, right? When I mentioned it to Foreign Relations, they practically knocked me over with their excitement. It's better than the offer of a peace treaty! It's more than an alliance! It could mark the end of *centuries* of conflict!"

"It's a rainbow of fantastic," agreed Princess Ko. "And in Jagged Edge the scallywags are blue-green like the sea. Just for your reference."

"Thank you. Your father *will* be home from the Narraburra in time, won't he? Or if not, he'll cut the trip short?"

"Of course he'd cut the trip short if he had to — but you haven't said: When is it?"

The Social Secretary flipped the card over.

"Exactly three months from today."

"Reply at once," Princess Ko declared. "Let's not wait for my father to respond from his ship — that could take days, and seem like an insult. Send an answer saying that he's honored to accept and —"

Behind Princess Ko, there was a sharp sound like the flick of an elastic band. Ko and the Social Secretary turned. The security agents stood motionless, gazing at a middle distance.

"Are they *real*?" whispered the Social Secretary.

"I don't know. How can you tell?"

They both studied the agents awhile.

"Whoop!" cried the Social Secretary. "He's trying not to yawn! He's got a yawn all caught up in his cheeks, see that? Do you see?"

"So he has. They *are* real." The Princess swiveled back again. "That's a relief. Of course, the yawn was probably boredom on account of *everyone* making that joke, but yes, please accept on Dad's behalf, and say he can't hardly wait, and the honor, and our two great Kingdoms, and blahdy blah, hooray! You know the words. And get Diplomacy to check it — and all those other official channels you were on about. Where shall I stamp?"

Ca-clamp! Ca-clamp!

The Social Secretary gathered his files.

"*You*," he exclaimed, "are the best princess in the room! And far smarter than you let on."

He spun around to gaze through the window.

"But *this*!" he exclaimed. "It's almost as dazzling as you are! Would you *look* at this view?! Ah, snowfields at twilight — ooh, there are dragons in the distance. See the light picking up their scales? And the sky is just ablaze with tangerines and silv — wait, is that an actual *Silver*?"

The Princess, still seated, studied the view.

"No," she said. "Not a Silver, just a sunset. But certainly it *is* a headspin of a view."

"Ahh," murmured the Social Secretary. "Lucky you!"

Then he bowed, tilting a sly grin toward the security agents, and Princess Ko tilted and grinned back.

The door closed behind him.

The Princess took a mint and rolled it around on the palm of her hand.

The security agents watched her.

"We have exactly three months," she said, "to get my family back."

Then she stood and strode to the window, unhooked the cords from around the drapes, and *whoosh*ed them closed. The room shook itself into dimness.

PART 2

Two weeks of summer in Bonfire, the Farms, Kingdom of Cello, and the heat was creeping underneath collars.

The sun stretched its legs across dry gray fields, and pressed its elbows hard onto the searing roofs of barns.

Elliot Baranski was sitting in the corner of a barn, surrounded by papers and open drawers. This was the space that Elliot's dad used to use as a workshop — back before he disappeared — whenever he brought appliances home from his electronics repair shop downtown.

Music was playing. His dad's old soundplayer was still on the bench, and Elliot had scraped away the cobwebs from the speakers. As he leafed through papers, he was tapping his hand on his leg now and then, in time to the music. Simultaneously, ever so faintly, his whole body was moving — foot trembling, fingers vibrating — but that was in time to the agitation in his mind.

This was the craziest feeling. He'd spent a year living with his dad's disappearance — either taken by a Purple or run off with a woman — but in the last few weeks, that year had toppled sideways. There were people up high, with low-down voices, who knew *just* where his dad was. Or practically anyway.

In a Hostile compound, they said. Most likely in the province of Jagged Edge. A prisoner, but healthy, well-fed, taken care of — they had *intel* that confirmed this — and these people, with their voices and cuff links, were working on how to get him out.

It was as if a giant had lifted the blue right off the world like a lid, guffawing as it did: "You thought *this* was the sky?!"

Elated, terrified, and dazzled all at once, that's how Elliot felt.

He had looked through his dad's papers before. They were work records, invoices, manuals, specifications. Some personal stuff too: Elliot's own school reports, a recipe book, birthday cards, a handful of photographs. There'd never been anything relevant before, but now he had this whole new slant.

It seemed — the smooth voices had told him — that his father had been working undercover for the Loyalists, and that's why the Hostiles had taken him.

So Elliot was looking again. Seeing if these papers might have shifted themselves, might be singing in a different key.

Tricky to concentrate with the jitters, though. The figures and diagrams swayed. Heat squeezed his shoulders. Everything was different and the same.

Ah, how could you know which words were clues and which said exactly what they said? He'd have to leave it to those voices. Well, not *leave* it to them. He'd make them delegate to him. He needed to be helping, working, moving.

He packed up the papers, ready to return them to the filing cabinets. That recipe book made him smile. Like all good Farmers, Abel Baranski could bake up a storm, and he used to relax by reading recipes, often with a pencil in his hand so he could make adjustments. Add nutmeg or raisins, orange peels or cloves. This book looked to be standard Farms fare — there were recipes for plum cake and lemon meringue pie, blueberry muffins and pecan-maple brownies.

Ah, pecan-maple brownies. Elliot's eyes ran down the ingredients, breathing in an imagining of his dad back in their kitchen — his mother shouting as she stamped up the front steps — the oven door opening — that deep, round smell of roasting pecan, the sweet, high maple —

He closed the book, smiling.

Then he opened it again.

Reread the recipe. Turned a page. Read another. Turned another page.

He laughed aloud.

He stood in the corner of that sweltering barn and laughed and shook, the crazy feeling just about doing his head in. He felt like swinging from a rope into a river. Driving fast through a rainstorm, music pounding. Kissing a girl.

He checked his watch.

For crying out loud, it was that late already? He looked down at himself. His jeans were dust-covered and torn at the right knee. Dirty, beat-up sneakers. His oldest T-shirt, the one with the collar that looked as if he'd taken both hands and given it a good wrench to the side.

Ah, well, he'd do. He stuck the recipe book in his back pocket, and ran from the barn.

If he took the truck, he'd make it — nope. That's right. His mother had the truck. She'd driven a load of blueberries to the Sugarloaf markets.

He'd have to take his bike.

Fifteen minutes later, Elliot's bike spun into the parking lot of the Watermelon Inn.

He got off so fast that he tripped a little; steadied himself against a car, which burned his hand. Sun on metal.

A couple of guests were sprawled on the sun lounges in the front garden, getting some river breeze. Elliot's little cousin, Corrie-Lynn, was jumping back and forth over the sprinklers.

"Hey," she said when she saw him. "You look like your skin's melting right off your face. But I guess that's just sweat. Come over here."

He obliged her. She held up a sprinkler, and he stood still. The splash hit his face and closed his eyes.

"More?" she offered, and he said, "Hang on," holding up a hand. She waited while he took the recipe book from his back pocket, and set it on the front steps of the Inn. "Go for your life."

Now she aimed the sprinkler until he was well drenched.

"Corrie-Lynn," he said, "that was beautiful," wringing out his T-shirt. "I've got to meet some people" — indicating the Inn, then looking at his watch — "right now, so I'll see what's up with them, then we can talk more."

"You mean the Central Intelligence agents?" Corrie-Lynn asked. "They got here late last night, and we put them in 7B and 7C. They both had the waffles for breakfast — nothing else, just the waffles — well, with maple syrup, of course. And housekeeping say they've both used two sets of towels already, so I guess they're super clean."

"Good to know," Elliot said. "See you soon, kid."

He ran up the stairs of the Inn.

They were eating apple pie.

The CI agents had their backs to Elliot. They were sitting on a two-seater couch by the picture window, and Hector and Jimmy — County and Deputy Sheriff — were facing them in separate armchairs. There was a low table between the men, and this was scattered with a coffeepot, mugs, plates of pie, notepads, and pens.

Hector and Jimmy were both talking at once, both leaning so far forward in their chairs they were practically standing.

As Elliot approached, it seemed to him that the agents were the cabin of a front-end loader, while Hector and Jimmy were the scoop.

Hector spotted Elliot and raised a hand, so the agents turned to look.

Now he could see their faces. He studied them a moment.

They were built on different scales, one much bigger than the other. But you couldn't say one was fat, the other skinny. It was more a hardcover book and a paperback. Neither wore glasses, so Elliot could see their eyes, which now were caught in serious-listening mode.

But as they took in Elliot — his wet hair, water-stained T-shirt, dripping jeans, muddy sneakers — their eyes lit into grins.

Neither agent said a word. They let Hector and Jimmy do the welcomes and introductions — the big guy was Agent Tovey, the smaller one, Agent Kim — only nodding or reaching to shake Elliot's hand at the appropriate moments. Agent Kim sipped from his coffee, Agent Tovey sat back and watched. But those smiles didn't leave their eyes, as if Elliot had brightened their day somehow, turning up in this bedraggled state. Maybe they'd have liked to get wet and muddy themselves, instead of sitting here in suit pants and button-up shirts.

By the time Elliot had dragged over a chair, slapped his dad's recipe book on the table and poured himself a coffee, the agents were serious again.

Agent Tovey looked hard at Elliot and started talking. While he spoke, Agent Kim sketched in a notebook.

"Here's the situation as I see it," Tovey said. "Just over a year ago, your father went missing and so did the local physics teacher. On the same night, your Uncle Jon was found dead on the side of the road." He paused, and turned to look through the picture window. "That's Uncle Jon's little girl playing there now," he said — not a question, but a fact — and they all watched Corrie-Lynn, who had moved from the sprinklers and was climbing one of the mulberry trees.

Tovey turned back again.

"I hear it was you who found him, Elliot," he said. "That must have been tough. I also hear the coroner concluded it was a Purple that killed your uncle. So you've been searching for your dad in Purple caverns a lot of this last year. That makes you the bravest kid I've ever met."

He was stacking up facts like counters, and that last fell into place with the exact same click. Just another fact. He paused, picked up his coffee, hesitated, replaced it on the table.

"We know," he continued, "that your dad and uncle were working with a Loyalist group. We don't know what they were doing. We know that the teacher, Mischka Tegan, was an undercover Hostile. We think that, on the night in question, your dad and uncle realized this truth and confronted her — and that's how Jon ended up dead and your dad, a prisoner. We don't know why they're holding him."

As Elliot listened, he thought how voices were different. There'd been other CI agents in town the last few weeks, and they'd all had the same educated tone. But Tovey's voice was more than smooth. It knew its way around a room. It was a voice that could find paths through a labyrinth of furniture while all the time it looked you in the eye.

At this point, Hector interrupted. Elliot smiled to himself. The Sheriff's voice would shove tables aside and trample right over the couch.

"Abel Baranski is a good man," Hector declared. "Whatever he's doing with those Hostiles, he's not working *with* them if that's where you're headed."

Tovey studied the Sheriff's face.

"From what I know," he said, "I agree with you one hundred percent." He swung back toward Elliot. "To get your father out safely, we want to know more. We want to talk to the townsfolk, but people don't relax around government agents." He swung his thumb toward Hector. "It's my belief they'd relax around this guy."

Hector warmed to him at once. "I'll get them singing for you," he said. "I'll get them playing the fiddle!"

"Don't mind a bit of live music," Tovey said mildly.

"Now as for my deputy, Jimmy, here," Hector continued, "you know that his skills at missing persons are legendary?"

"Ah, now," Jimmy began, but both agents were smiling.

"I've been looking forward to working with the missing-persons legend," Kim said, and he turned the notepad around so they could see he'd sketched a perfect likeness of Jimmy's face. It was not clear why.

"Just like to sketch." Agent Kim shrugged.

Tovey turned to Elliot again. "You and your mother might explain your dad's papers to us, but we'd also like to chat more broadly. Get a real sense of your dad."

Hector interrupted again.

"Now I know that Elliot will do his best for you," he said, "but he might not be available *all* the time."

"Sheriff," said Elliot.

"No, let me tell them! This boy has got himself selected to the Royal Youth Alliance! Had you heard? The Princess Sisters chose *three* young people from all across the Kingdom — just three, that's fewer fingers than I have on this hand — and Elliot here was one of them! From all across the Kingdom! A Bonfire boy! He'll be going along to a get-together in the Magical North next weekend."

The agents looked across at Elliot.

"We heard," said Agent Kim. "Congratulations."

"It's only for the weekend," Elliot shrugged. "Otherwise, I'm around."

Tovey stared at Elliot, as if trying to figure something out. He curled his hand into a fist, held it to his mouth, then drew it away abruptly.

"What's with the recipe book?" he said.

Elliot raised his eyebrows. The book had been lying on the table all this time, unnoticed, he'd thought. He'd been meaning to mention it when the time seemed right. Now he picked it up.

"It was in my dad's filing cabinet," he explained. "The recipe for pecan-maple brownies calls for two and a half cups of ginger."

"And?" Tovey tilted his head.

"That can't be right," Hector and Jimmy spoke at once.

"It's way too much," Elliot explained. "I looked through and turns out *all* the recipes have one or two things wrong. Four cups of cardamom.

Five pounds of butter. That kind of thing. I'm thinking, maybe the book's a sort of code?" He shrugged. "Either that, or the publishers were trashed when they printed it."

Those laughing smiles were forming in the agents' eyes again.

Tovey took the book, flicked through, then shrugged broadly, indicating that he didn't have a clue what recipes should look like. He passed it over to Kim.

"We'll get our code crackers onto it," he said. "I knew you were good value, Elliot, the moment I saw you. Hector and Jimmy told us earlier what a popular kid you are: something about the famous *Elliot Baranski* grin. Lights up the town like a carnival, they say, only nobody's seen it in a while. Listen, we plan to do everything we can to bring your dad home. I've made it my primary objective to see that grin."

Kim put the recipe book into his briefcase, and ran the side of his thumb over his empty pie plate. "As fast as possible," he agreed, "but I wouldn't mind a reasonably long stay in a province that bakes like this."

"And you haven't even tried Jimmy's cinnamon-and-apple brioche yet," Hector declared. "Not to mention Elliot's blueberry muffins."

Jimmy and Elliot took the cue and told the agents all about Hector's famous oatmeal cookies. They moved on to the specialties of various townsfolk — including Alanna Baranski, who ran this Inn, took care of Corrie-Lynn, *and* made this here pie. There was a lot of laughter, but Elliot caught Tovey glancing sideways, out through the picture window. Corrie-Lynn was clambering through branches of the mulberry, collecting handfuls of leaves. A sadness snapped the edge off Tovey's smile. He might find Elliot's dad, but there was nothing he could do for that little girl or her pie-baking mother — that's what his face seemed to say.

Seeing this, Elliot felt a surge — an almost terrifying conviction — that the one person in all of the Kingdom — the *only* person, in fact — who could bring his father home was this man. Agent Tovey.

He went by the high school later that night, around eleven.

There was a sculpture in the middle of the schoolyard here — an old TV with its back missing, wedged onto a pile of cement — and this was the location of a crack just big enough for letters to a girl in the World. Her name was Madeleine.

The stars were out and the night was hot. Insects in the streetlights. Elliot looked around awhile before he checked the sculpture. It was a capital offense to communicate with the World.

There was a pale, buzzing silence. A voice called in the distance, then was quiet.

He looked at his watch. It was just before eleven.

He took out his flashlight and shone it into the open back of the TV. There was a tangle of red and white wires in there, circuit boards, metal plates. He waited.

A curl of white slipped through a crack. He reached for the paper, and read it.

Hey, Elliot. You there?

Elliot took out his notepad and wrote a reply.

Yep.

A moment later another piece of paper emerged.

It's Madeleine.

Elliot raised his eyebrows.

I kinda guessed.

Another few moments, and then she wrote again.

Okay, I've searched high and low. I've looked in the cupboards, under the baking dish, inside saucepans, behind the curtains, everywhere. Still can't find your royal family.

He smiled.

Ah, well. Thanks for trying. How's your mother?

Madeleine's mother had almost died from a tumor in her brain. There was a long pause, then Madeleine's answer.

She's okay – the tumour's not coming back, but she's insane. You'd think a miraculous survival would make you appreciate the small things in life like sunlight on rusty hubcaps or whatever, but she's always (a) arching her back to try to touch her heels (yoga), (b) copying out inspirational phrases about Live in the Moment and It Is What It Is (Reiki/Buddhism), (c) smashing the alarm clock with a hammer (radioactive waves), (d) drinking filtered water and eating mung beans (purification), or (e) lying with her face in the sun, eating supersize McDonald's fries and coffee laced with whisky (cause we're all going to die, so you may as well die happy). And meanwhile her moods swing from dreamy to intense to manic to basic cranky.

Elliot thought about this.

What's McDonald's fries? Ah, that's not the point. I guess it makes sense that nearly dying would mess with your mother's mind.

Yeah, I know that already. Stop being so wise. Listen, I told my friends Belle and Jack about you. About you and the Kingdom of Cello, I mean. That's okay, right? You're not a secret, are you? Nah. Why would you be.

What did they say?

They totally believe in you! But don't let it go to your head. Jack's into horoscopes and Belle's into auras, so, you know, credulity is not really an issue for them.

Before Elliot had a chance to reply, another paper came sliding into the TV.

But seriously, do you want us to try to find your royal family? You really think they're here? Belle and Jack want to help. Or more specifically, Belle wants to meet the Prince and Jack wants to meet the Princess. We're not that interested in the King and Queen, although I'm sure they're nice. And I'm happy to watch Pixar films or build Lego spaceships or whatever with the little prince while Jack and Belle are getting it on with the older ones.

Elliot hadn't even finished *reading* this note when another message arrived.

I hope that's not treason or something in your Kingdom. To talk about getting it on with the royals. I mean no disrespect.

And then, while he was figuring out how to answer that:

But we need more information. Not sure how things work in Cello, but in our world if you want to find someone you (a) ask the police, (b) Google (but in the reverse order, obviously). And if you're me, you also (c) see if Isaac Newton has anything to say about the issue.

I think the police might be confused. Sorting out their confusion could take years. Google is also confused. I typed in the King's name and it gave me a computer game called EcoQuest in which King Cetus is a whale. And Isaac Newton invented the reflecting telescope, so he excelled at looking for things so you'd THINK he'd be helpful. But I guess the relevant events are unfolding right now. After his time.

Elliot raised his eyebrows high.

Madeleine, you talk faster and make less sense than a coked-up Jagged-Edgian. Take it easy for a minute now and let me think.

Then he turned a full circle, checking again that the darkness and shadows were empty, before he sat on a nearby bench with his notepad and wrote.

Okay, I'll know more once I hear what Princess Ko wants from us. I'm seeing her next weekend at the "Royal Youth Alliance" meeting. That's just a cover so we can talk about her lost family, but I sure wish I didn't have to go.

The missing royals seem kinda irrelevant to me. There are fake news stories about them all the time, so it doesn't seem real: I sometimes even forget it myself. I can't tell my buddies about it 'cause that'd be treason, and sometimes it seems like an issue isn't real until Cody, Gabe, Nikki, and Shelby have given their opinion on it. Or shouted their opinion. Or expressed the opinion in the form of a sculpture, a motor-scooter street race, or a high-powered explosive in the middle of a paddock.

But mainly it's irrelevant 'cause I just want to be looking for my dad.

Madeleine's reply came a moment later, and this time the handwriting seemed calmer.

Sorry I didn't ask about your dad earlier. I shouldn't have been making jokes about missing persons behind curtains and that. Even though you sort of know where he is now, it must still be scary. Have you got any more news about him?

No need to be sorry. Yeah, there are two agents in town, Tovey and Kim. I like them.

Well, their names sound like they know what they're doing. Tovey and Kim. Total agents. Tell me what happens. I feel like I should ask about your farm too, cause I don't think I've ever done that before. But not sure what to say. Um. How are the cows?

Elliot laughed.

We don't raise cows.

Okay. Grow anything lately?

Well, if you really want to know, nobody's growing much of anything these days. Farming's still in crisis. Listen, I should get home 'cause I've got an early start. I'll write again when I get back from the RYA meeting.

Okay. Sweet dreams. Say whassup to the Princess for me.

Elliot laughed again. *Say whassup to the Princess.* What was she even talking about? He watched the open TV awhile, in case she had more to say, but it stayed black and still.

So he folded all her notes together and wound an elastic band around them. He'd take them home now, and burn them.

PART 3

1.

His boots were scuffed and cracked.

That was something Elliot had never noticed before, but here he was in the Reception Room of the White Palace, looking down at his worn-out boots. He had a sense that something was wrong just above his eyebrows too. He touched his forehead. That's what it was: He was still wearing his woolen hat.

He swiped it off; ran his hand back and forth over his hair.

"It looks perfect."

The girl beside him jutted her chin toward his hair, then winked slyly, as if they were sharing a secret joke. This was a technique she had used several times over the last ten minutes: a reassuring statement followed by a meaningful wink. "Don't worry, you're not late" (wink); "Relax; it'll be easy" (wink); "The restrooms are just around the corner" (wink). In his experience, winks were meant to negate the statement. So he *was* late. So it *wouldn't* be easy. So the restrooms were *not* around the corner? In which case, why tell him that they were?

He didn't get the joke.

The girl was in charge of him. Or anyway in charge of looking *after* him, which here, in a palace, sort of meant the same thing. He'd forgotten her name, but that was her fault: She was so glossed-up and smart-suited, so full of winks, it was impossible to take in what she said.

There were crowds of people in the room, a general swirl of big talk and laughter, with concentrated regions of smaller, more intense talk. Now and then, the whole place was lit up by a camera flash. Princess Ko's voice and giggle rippled up and across the room from one hefty concentrated region to another.

The other two members of the Royal Youth Alliance were in the room too, but Elliot had only caught glimpses of them so far. One was that girl over there. She always seemed to be facing away from him, so all he knew was that her hair was very short and a golden-orange-red color, like firelight. Her clothes were variations on gray, and crazy tight.

The other was a plump boy who smiled a lot in an alarmed way, and who seemed to have dressed specifically to show up Elliot's jeans.

Elliot had worn his best jeans. He'd even ironed his shirt. (His mother had suggested this.) But that plump kid was nothing but ruffles, collars, and shine.

Elliot was handed a glass of bubbling teakwater. Now he was holding his hat in one hand and the glass in the other. A stranger approached to congratulate him and to ask how he was finding this great and snowy province, the Magical North. Tricky to answer as he'd only arrived half an hour before, and as he was trying to figure out how to deal with the stranger's outstretched hand.

The winking girl slipped his hat away smoothly, so now he had a hand free for shaking.

He fell in love with her for a moment.

Next thing, the Princess's voice was striding out from a raised platform across the room. There was a hush, and the camera flashes increased.

"Do I even need to *tell* you how ecstatisfied I am?!" Princess Ko exclaimed. The crowd murmured various reactions: laughter, approval, confusion, speculation.

"Well, I *am*! It's the first ever Convention of the Royal Youth Alliance! Welcome, everybody, but most of all *welcome* to the three members of the Alliance! Keira Platter of Jagged Edge! Samuel Jurgend of Olde Quainte! Elliot Baranski of the Farms!" A spotlight swerved around the room, seeking them out, and the cameras flashed faster. Elliot noticed several people writing in small notebooks.

"My royal parents can say it better, so I will now read out a greeting from the King of Cello." A brief exchange between the Princess and some guy in a suit, a rustle of paper, and she was talking again. "My noble father, King Cetus, sends us this message direct from his good ship, the *Onion Ring*!"

There were shouted whispers from close by the Princess — "The *Unwin Wing*!" — and she continued smoothly, "He wires this from his ship, and who really cares what it's called, right?" Bewildered laughter. "Just listen, okay, guys? Here's what he says: 'My heartiest congratulations to the members of the newly formed Royal Youth Alliance. I wish you great joy in your weekend together at the White Palace, and I have no doubt that you will bring the vitality and intelligence of the youth of our Kingdom to some of the larger issues facing us today.' "

There was a mild round of applause.

"That's my dad," grinned the Princess, looking up from the paper. "Goes on a bit, but so *wise*, right? And *now*, if we can get the technology to work, we have a surprise! Guess who's on the line waiting to address us *right now*?!"

Nobody could guess.

"It's the Queen! Queen Lyra! My great mother! She's in the Southern Climes, as you know, doing important, totally urgent work, but she especially wanted to address you tonight, because she loves the idea of the Royal Youth Alliance. Of course, that's if the Magical North will let us get away with this for once!" There was obliging, knowing laughter. "She should be coming in over the speakers now — um, hello there? Royal mother? Can you hear me?"

The air crackled and a woman's voice — faint, distant — seeped into the room.

"Good evening, everybody, and welcome. Welcome, especially, to the young people of Cello —" Then the static was back, loud as rainfall, followed by silence.

"I guess the Magical North did *not* want us to get away with it!" the Princess exclaimed while Elliot's companion explained to him in a rapid whisper that technology — especially telephone lines — rarely worked in this province because of the untamed ripples of magic.

"I've heard," Elliot nodded.

Well, so had everybody heard. It was common knowledge. He fell out of love with her, and started wondering if she couldn't circulate a little — share that wink of hers around a bit — and let him do his own thing.

The cocktail reception was followed by a photo shoot and a Welcome Banquet, and Elliot continued to drift through it all in his scuffed, cracked boots. The noise never seemed to stop. Even during the banquet there was entertainment — dancers, musicians, clowns, mimes, and somebody who wanted to sing a tale about each of the provinces. Conversation shouted and rushed around him, up and over the crack and crunch of foods being broken, twisted, and consumed. Delicious, sure, but weird, a lot of that food.

Much later he found himself closing the door of his guest room.

The clamor still sounded in his ears, and he looked around at the pillows, drapes, cushions, paintings, mirrors, rugs, tapestries, ornaments, ornamental fireplace (with busy, cracking fire), and it seemed like there was a *showbag* on the bed, alongside cellophane-wrapped chocolates, and a fax machine — *why a fax machine?* — on a table in the corner, and alongside *that* some complicated device that seemed to be hung with *coffee cups* — what the — well, so maybe it was a coffeemaker.

Also, there was an ornate telephone, which seemed pointless given the situation with phones in this province, and there were blues, golds, crimsons, whites, rich mahogany browns, and words like *gilt*, *marble*, *silver* jangled at Elliot's head, all of it seeming to blaze and bustle at him, and he thought, *Ah, for crying out loud, would you all just quiet down a minute?*

Even the floorboards were noisy: They were that polished, they were shouting to be noticed.

Okay, take it easy, he said to them. *I see you there. Still not planning to do anything more than walk on you.*

He sat on the edge of his bed and wrenched off his old boots, feeling sorry for them. Used to be, he loved and trusted them but now it seemed they'd let each other down, him and his boots. Things would never be the same between them again.

He reached for the showbag sitting on his bed, and looked inside. There was a bunch of papers in there, as well as a name tag with a pin stuck behind it:

Elliot Baranski,
Bonfire, the Farms

The papers included a map of the Palace, a list of its recreational facilities, a Note on Room Service (apparently, fax machines were the only technology that could reliably bypass the magic, so if you wanted a cheeseburger in the night, you should fax the kitchen — at least that explained the machine on the table), some souvenir royal soaps (he'd bring those home for the Sheriff, a certified royalphile), and a Schedule of the Weekend Ahead.

The Schedule was printed on white cardboard, thick as a chopping board. Well, maybe not that thick. Still. And it wasn't so much white as shining with a pale silver gloss.

The writing was beautifully manicured, he thought. Then he closed his eyes a moment. That wasn't the word. There was another word. Stenography? Ah, he was too tired to think. *Calligraphy*. That's what he meant. It curled all over the place, the writing. Flounced around like a drunk girl on a dance floor.

He got past the calligraphy and studied the actual meaning. Cardboard sheets like this had been handed out to reporters tonight, so it must be the "official" version of the weekend ahead.

He skimmed the Friday schedule — cocktail reception, photo shoot, banquet: that was all done, at least — and read on to Saturday and Sunday.

Saturday

10:00 A.M. *Session 1 — Green Conference Room 1A*
Round table discussion: Is Cello a united Kingdom? Can the rifts between provinces be healed? What steps can the Young People of Cello take to heal them?
Session to include getting-to-know-you games and team-building activities

LUNCH

2:00 P.M. *Session 2 — Blue Conference Room 3B*
Round table discussion: Cello's Environment: revegetation of the southeastern Nature Strip; should the Moving Mountains be anchored?; desalination of the Inland Sea; mining of the Undisclosed Province; the crisis in the Farms. How can Young People help with the Crops?

How can Young People help with the Crops? He thought about his buddies back home and how they'd honk, shout, snort, and shriek their laughter at that. Nothing like the laughter here, which was like trying out the high notes on musical instruments (for the women) and beating a bass drum in slow, careful rhythm (for the men).

He turned the schedule over and read on. More of the same "themed" sessions, interspersed with various Activities and Tours of the Vicinity. All the meetings took place in conference rooms with different colors — What were they doing, showing off about how much paint they had around here? Had there been a sale at the local hardware store? — right up to a final session on Sunday afternoon which asked: "What can Young People do about the Future?"

That struck him as pretty funny too.

He couldn't stop laughing for a while.

Then his mood turned grim again.

Get through this weekend, he thought. *Then* the future can begin.

The next morning he woke to a quiet tinging, and opened his eyes. A woman dressed in a black uniform was in his room. She seemed to be building up the fire.

"Good morning," she said without turning. "Did you sleep well?"

She straightened up then, and adjusted a tray table so it was suspended over his bed. It held a silver jug, a plate of pastries, a glass of juice, and a bowl of fruit. The woman opened the drapes, and bright stripes of snow-light dazzled his eyes, splashing color and shadows about the room.

"I did sleep well," he said, surprised.

In fact, he'd slept the deepest, darkest sleep he'd known in years. This bed, he realized, and these sheets — he sat up, feeling them. It was like they were *drenched* in softness.

Now he felt the side of the silver jug and it was hot. He breathed deeply and smelled rich chocolate. Touched the pastries: They were warm and golden.

Well, he thought, scratching the back of his head. It was just a couple of days after all. Might not be *so* bad.

2.

The Green Conference Room was painted white, not green, and the table was rectangular, not round.

Princess Ko stood at the head, a pile of folders and papers before her, alongside a silver bowl of mints.

Two security agents stood against the wall behind her. Just beyond them was a closed door, so Elliot had the impression the agents were lined up waiting for the bathroom. It struck him that they were feeling very solemn about their bathroom wait, those agents.

He looked around the table.

Beside him was Samuel, the smiling kid from Olde Quainte, still dressed in ruffles, and with collars the size of sun hats. He seemed to be about twelve years old and had pale pink cheeks and a kind of stilled agitation — like a contestant on a game show ready to pounce on the buzzer.

Opposite Elliot was Keira. She seemed older than Samuel, maybe closer to Elliot's age, and today her red-gold hair was hidden beneath tight black netting. He remembered reading that those hair-net things were fashionable in Jagged Edge. Her face was all angles and perfect skin, and she was wearing a loose-woven sweater in an earthy color — it had a ragged look, but might have been made from the yarn of a capelbeast, in which case it was super expensive. There was tension about Keira too, but hers was more controlled. She leaned back, gaze fixed on the window.

There was one other person at the table — a slight boy with dark hair and fine cheekbones, who grinned at Elliot and raised a hand, as if they were old buddies. Now who was that? He was definitely familiar but in a weird sideways way, like someone Elliot might have seen as an extra on a TV show one day.

"Welcome, everybody," Princess Ko began, and that startled the room because her voice — even her face — were so different from how they'd been last night. All of it lower and calmer. Elliot had only met the Princess once before, briefly, and had almost forgotten how she was when she wasn't performing.

"I, for my province and my happiness, call your royal self a good morning, and welcome *you* in turn!" cried Samuel in a tumbling Olde Quainte accent, his ruffles and collars agitating in time with his voice. "Of course, you are *already* here — this is your home! — so welcome is perhaps not to order. However, as to a turnkey in a battleship, if I may begin the discussion? I, for one, believe within my heart, and its vessels and capillaries, that the Kingdom of Cello is *far too* divided, but I — in turn — believe that we, the young people of Cello, *can* heal the rifts! We can do it!"

There was a silence.

Keira leaned toward him. "I'm thinking maybe the schedule is fake?" she said.

A shudder ran across Samuel's face. His voice rumpled with almost-sobs: "Of course it is! I knew that! I was so taken up by its *perfection*, Princess Ko, of your —"

"It's all right, Samuel." The Princess knocked her fist against the folders. "It *is* confusing. Even I feel nonplussed at times by my own farce. Thus, let us move directly to the real reason we are here."

She drew out a pile of stapled papers and handed these around.

Elliot flicked through it. There were lists, pie charts, flowcharts, and bar graphs. He remembered that one thing he'd noticed when he'd met her before was that the Princess seemed to know what she was doing. He relaxed a little.

"We are here," said the Princess, "because my family has been abducted. I believe they have been taken through cracks into the World. The rest of the Kingdom does not know this. To them, *you* are nothing more than a public relations exercise. In fact, I have invited you here to help. These are my objectives."

She swung around, pointing to a whiteboard behind her. The female security agent took a sideways step, and pressed a button.

Writing emerged on the screen: a list of bullet points.

Elliot looked down. The list on the board was replicated on the first page of the notes. Overkill. He shrugged. Okay, so this would be like school.

"*One*, I must rule the Kingdom.
"*Two*, I must conceal the fact that my family is missing.
"*Three*, I must conceal the fact that *I* am running the Kingdom.
"*Four*, I must find my family, find whoever is responsible for stealing my family, punish them, and *bring my family home*."

She turned back, just as the writing on the board began to jumble — provincial magic getting under the skin of technology again — and gazed at them.

"Did you consider making item Four into items Four, Five, Six, and Seven?"

Princess Ko blinked, and looked at Keira.

"What?"

"It's just, it's actually four items in one, right? *Find* your family, *find* who's responsible, and so on. Or is it like a *four-pointer*? Like, you have to get all the components if you want the full mark for that question?" There was a beat. "In the exam," Keira added.

Elliot was watching Keira. Her face was solemn but he caught a glint in her eye, and he turned to see how Princess Ko would take this.

"Be *aware* of items One to Three," Princess Ko said to the room — so she was going to ignore it — "but your focus is on item Four. On all its components. Find my family and bring them home — in under three months. I will now introduce you."

She pointed to Samuel, who bowed so low that his head *thunk*ed against the table. When he looked up, he was trying to hide his wince. It must have hurt, though. His eyes were tearing up.

"Samuel has extensive knowledge of Cello's history with a special interest in World-Cello interaction. He's a member of every historical society in the Kingdom, and on the board of half of those societies. His school history teacher wrote a reference letter that was a firefly of dazzle."

Samuel blushed and bowed again, this time being careful to stop in time.

The Princess waved a hand at Elliot.

"Elliot was chosen because he found a crack in his hometown of Bonfire, and has been exchanging letters with a girl in the World."

This made an impression on the room. Samuel gasped, and swiveled so he was facing Elliot. Keira adjusted her headnet.

"Incidentally, it was the Deputy Sheriff in Elliot's hometown who deduced that my family had been taken to the World," the Princess continued. "To him, they were anonymous missing people, not the royal family. It was impressive — but that is not the reason Elliot was chosen. It is simply interesting trivia."

Princess Ko now indicated the slight, dark boy across the table — the one who seemed familiar to Elliot.

"This is the shadow member of our team," she explained. "He is not formally on the Alliance and you will not mention him to anybody. Nor will you acknowledge him if you see him around the Palace. However, you may remember him. He is my stable boy, Sergio, and he played the role of my sister, Princess Jupiter, on the royal tour when the three of you were chosen."

That explained the familiarity.

Sergio had bright eyes. He bounced around a little as if in time to a silent beat, then placed his elbows on the table. Now he looked ready for a cracking good game of cards.

There was another silence.

"As pleased as I am to see him," faltered Samuel, "might I ask, Your Honorable Princess . . . might I ask *why* your stable boy is here?"

Princess Ko looked just over their heads. "He's my best friend," she said.

Well, that took courage, Elliot thought. To say that.

Still, why exactly was the stable boy here?

But she had moved on to Keira.

"Finally, Keira has been chosen because she has expertise in technology and excellent vision."

Keira cracked her knuckles so loudly that both the security agents flinched. Elliot caught the flinches from the corner of his eye. He looked at Keira's hands and saw that she bit her nails. She dragged her sweater sleeves down, covering them.

"My province," Keira said, looking at her sweater sleeves, "is crammed with technologists who see well. It's a night-dwelling thing, the vision."

"You are also a motocross champion," Princess Ko shrugged.

"So, what, you want me to ride into the World and throw your family on the back of my bike?"

The windows shadowed for a moment.

"If you could," said Princess Ko steadily, "then certainly," and she pulled out her chair and sat down.

"If it might please for you for me to ask for you a question?" Samuel said.

Everyone disentangled this, then Princess Ko nodded.

"You can ask a question."

"As to a wisecrack in pajamas, I note that the Queen — your good mother — addressed us, ever so briefly, on the telephone last night. *Now*, can you not simply follow the *line* of that telephone — I admit to being entirely unsure about the technology, but I believe there *are* telephone lines — and so, follow it, Princess, hand over hand, so to speak — until you *reach your mother*?"

There was another silence, during which various people sighed deeply.

"That was not real," Princess Ko explained carefully. "Samuel, as you know, we have spent the last year tricking the Kingdom into believing the family is still here. That was an old recording of my mother."

Samuel gasped in admiration. *"Ingenious,"* he whispered, then gathering his voice again: "And your own conduct in public — some might even say — call yourself a forgiveness, but some might say you are *stupid*! Is that also trickery? If so, I am somewhat in the wilderness . . . but of course, a magician must not reveal —"

"I cannot have people suspecting that I'm running things," Princess Ko interrupted. "Nobody would suspect someone that stupid. Let's get on."

She reached for a mint. Elliot noticed that her nails, unlike Keira's, were perfectly painted — manicured, this was where *that* word belonged — her hands, perfectly steady.

3.

The second meeting took place in the Blue Conference Room, Level 3.

It was identical to the Green Conference Room except that the Blue Room had green cushions on its seats. Confusing.

Elliot was first to arrive.

Apart from the security agents, of course. They must have already screened the room or whatever they did, and now were standing against the wall.

"Hey," he said to them, holding up the bread roll he'd grabbed on the way out of Lunch. The agents blinked and nodded *ever so* slightly — as slightly as a bread crumb — in response.

Elliot raised his eyebrows at that, and moved over to the window, taking a bite of the roll. You could see the Palace moat from here — it was permanently frozen, he'd heard, and a few people were skating on it now. Staff, he guessed. This place seemed overrun with staff. Beyond the moat, a snowplow was reversing through the Palace gates, while a couple of guys in parkas directed it.

A shape appeared beside him, and Elliot startled. It was Keira. She sure knew how to move stealthily. That was a night-dwelling thing, he guessed.

"Snow here never melts," she reflected.

Elliot had been thinking the same thing. Most of Cello had wandering seasons, so you never knew when summer might give way to spring, or how long autumn would keep blowing down the leaves. Here in the Magical North, however, it was always winter.

"It's beautiful," Keira said thoughtfully. "But they miss out on that cracking, snapping time when the whole world breaks into pieces."

"And everything starts fresh," he agreed.

He looked at her. She kept her gaze on the window, and crinkled her eyes into a dreamy smile, as if she was recalling the thaws of her past. He realized that her skin was not perfect after all. It was coated in makeup that barely concealed a serious outbreak of zits.

They moved to the table to sit down, and it felt like something was unfolding — sitting down itself, maybe — in Elliot's chest. If he was honest, he'd been thinking that Keira was a supercool Jagged

Edge snob — even if she had a sense of humor — and that Samuel was a baby-faced, sycophantic nerd, and Sergio, a friendly-enough but seriously-what-was-he-doing-here? dancing stable boy, and Princess Ko, sort of impressive in her organizational skills and with the whole running-a-kingdom-without-your-family thing going for her, but her stupid act was so annoying it made you want to suffocate yourself, and the fact that she'd roped him into being here in the first place was worse than a stone caught in the tractor brakes —

Well, that was sort of brutally honest.

But still. There it was. That's how he'd been feeling.

Except that now, that glimpse of something real from Keira — her sentiment about thaws; her bad skin — it had shifted things for him. He felt calmer.

The others arrived and the calming continued. Lunchtime seemed to have brought out the glow and the *point* to them all. Samuel had finally removed his jacket, and it's true that his shirt was ruffled, but frills on a shirt were one thing: Frills on a *jacket* had been taking it too far. Also, the suspenders added some pizzazz to his look, and the kid's face was maybe less manic than usual. Maybe a little plumper too. He ate a lot at each meal, that Samuel.

Sergio seemed to shoot a line of energy into the room when he arrived with his bright eyes and his skip-dance-jog from the door to the table.

Then Princess Ko was standing at the head of the table again, her hair as yellow as a quince. Even yellower than before. Was that possible?

She pulled the whiteboard forward, and words appeared:

King Cetus — Sandringham Convention Center, Ducale, Golden Coast (*Stepped out of a formal function for a brief meeting with the Commissioner for Foreign Relations — disappeared between cloak room and conference room).*

QUEEN LYRA — Department of Finance, Ducale, Golden Coast (*disappeared while perusing finance reports in a second-level office*).

PRINCE CHYBA — Cast Iron Restaurant, McCabe Town, Nature Strip (*disappeared en route to the restrooms*).

PRINCESS JUPITER — the Harrington Hotel, Ducale, Golden Coast (*disappeared from penthouse suite*).

PRINCE TIPPETT — the White Palace, Magical North (*disappeared from his bedroom; nanny had stepped out for two minutes to fetch a tissue*).

"There was not a single witness to any of the actual disappearances," the Princess said. "Nor were there reports of any suspicious activity in the vicinity. Each took place in such short time periods, and in such confined spaces, it seems possible that the abductors came *through* a crack from the World then took their captive back with them."

"Nobody's supposed to know about the abductions?" Keira said. "So how exactly did the security people investigate or ask any questions?"

"Nobody does know," the Princess agreed. "Apart from the two agents you see in this room, five other handpicked agents, and the head of the Security Forces. The people interviewed were all given plausible explanations for the questions and led to believe these were standard security procedures."

Keira seemed about to speak again, her expression skeptical, but Elliot interrupted. "Wait. If you know exactly where they disappeared," he said, "can't you just go to the WSU and get a detector, locate the cracks, go through, and get them?"

"The royal family has no authority over the World Severance Unit," the Princess said, shaking her head. "And yes, they have detectors, but those are only accessible to the highest-ranking WSU officers."

"Could you not humbly request a loan?" suggested Samuel.

Again, the Princess shook her head.

"It would be refused. The WSU guard their authority fiercely. Moreover, we would be forced to explain our request, which would mean revealing the disappearances, a risk that we consider not worth taking. A detector would illuminate a crack, sure, but what then? We would need to know how to *unseal* the crack, in addition to the secret to going *through* the crack. There is no chance that the WSU would ever give us that — assuming they even know it themselves. They would not permit communion with the World even to try to retrieve the royal family."

The Princess pressed a button and the words on the screen disappeared.

"At this session," she said, "I want to try something called *brainstorming*. Here's how it works. I throw out questions, you throw back ideas. *Nothing* is stupid. Nobody laughs. The crazier, the better." She paused, then added defensively: "I read about it — it's a way of cracking a problem open and finding a creative solution."

Elliot glanced sideways at Keira and felt her glance at him too. Brainstorming was something teachers were always doing at school. Had Princess Ko missed that somehow? He remembered that she and the other royal kids switched between boarding schools and tutors a lot, so maybe she *had* missed it. Or not paid attention, being too caught up with princessing.

It was sort of cute, her not knowing. He smiled briefly, and noticed Keira do the same.

"Now, here are the questions — answer whichever grabs you. Who took my family? Why? Why take them to the World? What's happening to them there? Have they found each other? Or are they still alone? Are they okay?"

Samuel's mouth fell open. He stared.

"How could we possibly *know*?" he whispered.

"Samuel," said the Princess. "That's the point. We *don't* know. I want you to come up with *possible* answers — use your imagination. Go wild."

Sergio had not participated in the previous meeting, but now he spoke, and his voice was strongly accented. Elliot couldn't place the accent.

"The Hostiles took them so they can take power over this Kingdom," Sergio said. "Only, why make such without *you*, Princess? Why leave a princess behind? The bandits of Sorranjin will steal a herd of wild white horses from the compounds of Mount Dkia." He paused, eyes intense. "But *never* have I heard they leave *one* of the herd behind. Such a thing can I not even imagine."

"Right," said Elliot uncertainly. "I guess the bandits of Sorranjin don't plan to take power in the compounds of Mount Dkia — so, there's that — but anyway, the thing is, all this time has passed and no Hostiles have made a move."

"Good. Great." Princess Ko was scribbling on the whiteboard as they spoke. *Hostiles*, she wrote, followed by a question mark and an arrow that flew across the board to the word *World*. Beneath that she wrote: *But not Ko?? No power taken???*

"Someone else?" she said, turning around.

Surely she had seen this done at school.

"Very well," Samuel murmured, then in his own schoolboy voice: "Perhaps it was an enemy kingdom."

Ko wrote *enemy* and put a circle around it.

"Or villains!" cried Sergio. "It is that villains wish something Cello has! The sapphire mines? The milk of the Hovers on the Golden Coast Swamp? These are such that I imagine. A horse, it will nuzzle you! It will nip at you! If it knows you have the sugar or the apple in your pocket. But a *villain* — a villain has more — how you say? — *resources* than a horse, and so it will steal a royal family."

Ko wrote rapidly. "Only, why have they not issued their demands yet?"

Nobody spoke for a moment.

"That question about why they took all the family except you, Princess," Keira said. "Maybe they don't see you as a threat."

"They took Prince Tippett," Samuel pointed out. "How might a seven-year-old be a threat but not his older sister? Of course, he would have turned eight by now, but he was seven when taken, so, as to a blister in a clam shell."

"His older sister is incredibly stupid." Keira shrugged.

There was a slight movement from the security agents, which was a little like a pair of potted plants twitching.

"It's all right." Princess Ko frowned at the agents. "This is brainstorming. People must be free to say whatever comes to their heads. And I assume that came into your head, Keira."

"It did," agreed Keira.

"She started putting on the stupid act *after* they went missing," Elliot pointed out.

Keira nodded slowly, studying the palm of her hand.

"When people go missing," Elliot said, to change the subject, "it doesn't always mean they were taken. They could've just upped and left."

The Princess turned back to the board.

"All of the family?" Keira demanded, her words touched with contempt. "At the same moment?"

Elliot had clearly been too quick to revise his opinion of Keira. Getting sentimental about a thaw didn't mean you weren't an ice queen. "Could've been planned in advance," he said mildly. "Maybe they'd just had enough of being royals?"

"And left Princess Ko out of their plans?" Keira's contempt was building, then she stopped and reconsidered. "Well, in a way that makes sense."

The Princess's back was turned and she was scribbling recklessly, the words barely legible. She turned, a blush threading across her cheeks.

"I don't think your family ran away," Elliot said. "I think they were taken. I'm just doing the brainstorming thing."

The blush flared briefly and then faded.

"Thank you." She nodded at him curtly.

Something seemed to light in Samuel's eyes. "It's a prank!" he cried. "A hoax! There was a club, if you will know it, inaugurated in Olde Quainte in 1327, and its name, be it known, was the Pranksters. Hear ye this, it had twelve members and they concocted the most elaborate pranks! A storm of giant cucumbers! The theft of the royal mint! Detachment of the Undisclosed Province! Why, snaffling the royal family is *exactly* like to this club!!"

Sergio looked surprised. "They *completed* all this? With the cucumbers and the mint and the so on? Beautiful!"

"Of course not." Samuel frowned. "How could they? Where would they have found giant cucumbers? How could you *steal* the royal mint? It's a building. And you certainly cannot *detach* an entire province. Continental drift might do the trick eventually — an earthquake perhaps — but pranksters could not do it."

Princess Ko was looking from Samuel to Sergio and back again, rolling the marker between her palms.

"This club still exists?" she asked.

"Why, no," said Samuel. "It was disbanded in 1328 without ever having performed a single prank. They had a lark, however, imagining them."

"Aren't we wasting time?" Keira asked.

"But!" protested Samuel. "I was *brainstorming*! How is it that *Elliot* can . . ."

Elliot widened his eyes slightly. Maybe he'd revised his opinion of Samuel too soon too.

"Samuel," Princess Ko said gently. "You just illustrated the reason I selected you. You have extensive knowledge of Cellian history. Now I want to add something and need your help. Can you tell us about the tradition of Cellian royal blood?"

Samuel brightened. "There is a theory," he said, "as to a sliver of orange rind, widely held in the fifteenth and sixteenth centuries, but since somewhat slipped from popularity. Call yourselves to my attention for it is this: that the blood of the royal family is superior to that of ordinary Cellians. Thus, the theory goes, if the royal family were removed from the Kingdom, it would so destabilize the Kingdom — in a fundamental sense, not merely political — that a foreign power could walk in and take over."

Sergio raised his eyebrows, and his foreign accent (probably southern, Elliot thought, but he still wasn't sure) seemed to grow stronger: "The Kingdom *is* destabilized!" he said. "It is the Color attacks! It is the farmers and the crisis! The *beautiful* crisis, it is everywhere! So! Yes! But what is it that they wait?"

"Perhaps," mused Samuel, "it is like to a tellybird that plucks twigs from the nest of a yellowcrest? Once it has plucked, the tellybird hovers out of sight, awaiting the moment of truth. That is to say, perhaps the enemy kingdom is waiting for Cello to plummet from the cliff edge to the mudswamp far below."

"What use is a Kingdom in a mudswamp?" Sergio wondered.

"The tellybird swoops on the eggs as the nest falls," Samuel explained gently.

"Let's not get off track," said Princess Ko.

Elliot was trying to figure out what was going on.

"Are you saying this royal blood thing is true?" he asked the Princess. "That royals have better blood than the rest of us? 'Cause I kind of don't get how it would work. Don't royals marry regular Cellians all the time and have kids with them? So if royal blood really had this sort of magical power that makes Cello *function*, well, wouldn't it get diluted over time?"

"I'm not saying it's true," the Princess explained. "Only that there are people who *believe* it to be —"

"Have they done scientific studies?" Keira interrupted.

"I'm not saying it's true," the Princess repeated.

"Is there genetic testing?" Keira persisted.

"I think maybe —"

"If your blood is so *superior* to us ordinary Cellians, why don't you share it around?"

"You don't —"

"You're right. I don't understand. If your blood is so much *better*, do you *donate* it regularly? Do you arrange for transfusions all across the Kingdom so the *commoners* can get some of your *super*powers?"

"Keira, I don't —"

"Why don't you cut yourself right now and rain blood on our heads?"

Keira's words seemed to reconfigure the room.

Sergio stood up so fast his chair crashed to the ground, his small face ferocious. Samuel buried his head into his arms. The security agents stepped forward, hands on their holsters.

Princess Ko was so pale you could see the veins in her cheeks.

"I have a suggestion," Elliot said, speaking slow and easy, the way he might if he'd accidentally stumbled into a paddock of bulls. "Could be dumb as all get-out but for what it's worth — I found this book a while back, that tells you how to find a spell at the Lake of Spells. I was going to use it to get a Locator Spell and find my dad, back before we knew the Hostiles had him."

Princess Ko's eyes focused on the opposite wall for a moment.

Then she looked at Elliot.

"You can't choose what spell you catch at the Lake of Spells," she said.

"I know," agreed Elliot. "But I've got this book, says you can."

"But we know where my family is," she said. "They're in the World."

Elliot shrugged. "Don't know *where* in the World they are," he said. "Maybe the place where they disappeared will tell us which part of the World they were taken — if anyone knows how the World and Cello link up — but they could still be anywhere by now. If a spell can tell us where, I can ask Madeleine — my girl in the World — to track them down. The World's a big place, is my impression."

The Princess's eyes stayed fixed on him a moment.

Abruptly, she gathered up her papers.

"It's not a terrible idea." She straightened the edges, and walked toward the door. "Put your weapons away," she added irritably, without looking back.

4.

They had to pretend to be friends right after that, which struck Elliot as funny.

The schedule called for another photo shoot, and they slung their arms around one another and beamed. Reporters joined them for their Tour of the Environs, so they kept up the act, helping one another climb into the husky-drawn sleigh, checking that the rugs and furs were evenly distributed. Elliot felt laughter building inside him. *Ca-click, ca-click, ca-click*, went the cameras.

The sleigh rattled off across the snowfields, and the guide called out that he *guaranteed* a dragon, but that werewolf dens were anybody's guess. They slid past Sergio, tramping through fresh snow, leading three horses, a stable boy again. The guide handed out foil-wrapped chocolate peppermints and they struggled to unwrap them with their bulky gloves, gave up, and slid off the gloves, holding these for one another, crushing the foil, smiling eyes around as they chewed on the chocolate. They all teased Samuel — gently, as new friends would — for flinching when a dragon swooped too close, and they asked one another if that smoke meant fire or just the dragon's breath misting in cold air. "Maybe she's smoking a cigarette," joked Keira, and they all laughed aloud, Princess Ko the hardest.

The reporters laughed too, and chatted with them about things like how they thought *this* generation differed from the previous one. *Ca-click, ca-click, ca-click.*

Even when the reporters had gone, and it was just the three of them — Keira, Samuel, and Elliot — touring the Palace with the Princess as their guide, he felt the laughter in his chest. They kept standing back and saying, "After you," at doorways.

Now and then they had to run a few steps, to keep up with the Princess as she strode through ballrooms, games rooms, tea rooms; past fountains, sculptures, strutting peacocks, sleeping white wolves — those last were plain pretentious, he thought, but still funny.

Walls rose high, halls ribboned forever, and staircases stretched so wide it made Elliot think of concertinas — but as far as he could see the only reason for any of it was to show off how many paintings they had, and how many fax machines sitting on curly-legged tables, and how many handwoven stair rugs.

Then Princess Ko turned down a dimmer, quieter hallway, led them around a corner or two, and opened a door.

"This is Prince Tippett's room," she said, and waved them in.

It was a big room, sure, with a giant televisual screen on one wall — but otherwise, in a lot of ways, it was just like any kid's bedroom.

There was a basket overloaded with stuffed teddies. There was a rumpled bed covered in toys, as if he'd just been playing there — including a racing car track with a loop that was not properly linked up. You could see exactly where the toy car had crash-landed when it hit the break. *You need a hard surface*, Elliot thought at the kid, *not a mattress, for a racing car track.*

Scattered on the floor were socks, a crumpled undershirt, an inside-out sweater. There were Color combat games, remote-control choppers, Aldhian pirate ships, a souvenir hovering Hideum from Golden Coast, dress-up capes and masks. Also, now that Elliot looked more closely, a whole lot of frogs: ceramic frogs, stuffed frogs, posters depicting species of provincial frogs and toads, a homemade frog mobile. These were hung on walls and wardrobe doors, and pasted to the sides of chests of drawers.

Elliot remembered that Prince Tippett was known to have a passion for frogs, and it came to him slow and sharp, like someone hanging posters up and adding pins *here* and *here*, that a child was missing.

A little boy. Ko's brother.

The pins kept jabbing at him, getting in behind his eyes, his nasal passages, his gums. Had the little boy cried out when he was taken, or just felt confused? Did he have time to speak? Was it somebody he knew? Had they fooled him into thinking they were buddies? Or had they bound him up and knocked him unconscious?

Right now, that kid was somewhere. Terrified maybe, or tired of being terrified. All these months later, his tears were probably all used up. He might have found a way to enjoy his new life, or he might be dead.

That was why that stupid brainstorming session had been so bizarre.

The whole royal family could be dead.

"This is where he was last seen," the Princess was saying in her cool guide's voice. "Housekeeping have not been through: We had to leave it just as it was. Let's continue the tour."

5.

The next session was the second to last.

They arrived in turn and made their way to the table carefully, smiling briefly at one another as if they had all recently been battered by a hurricane.

The exception was Sergio, who strode in, narrowing his eyes at Keira as he swept back his chair. Keira held his gaze. She seemed sad today; the kind of sadness that has settled in, and that makes other people's narrow eyes irrelevant.

Princess Ko stood in her usual position at the head.

Then she surprised them by stepping around the table and taking a seat alongside Elliot.

"At this session," she said, from her new position, "we are going to hear from two people. You will know them well by now. Agents Nettles and Ramsay."

As she spoke, the security agents stepped away from the wall. It was almost as shocking as if a bookcase had marched toward you, breaking itself into two separate pieces as it did.

You will know them well by now was overstating things a little. You didn't usually get to know a bookcase, did you? They dressed identically and seemed completely humorless was about all Elliot had on them.

He hadn't even known their names until this moment.

It turned out that Agent Nettles was the woman, and she was the one who addressed them. While she spoke, Agent Ramsay shadowed her silently, his posture much as if he were still up against the wall. But there was something different about him.

That's what it was. He was allowing himself facial expressions.

His expressions were mostly of an open-necked, shrugging, what's-to-lose? sort, even when that didn't particularly match what Agent Nettles was saying. Now and then, he'd switch to a more intense, soulful gaze, and he'd twist his lips, a world of profound thought apparently going on behind his eyes.

If it was unexpected to be hearing Agent Nettles speak, what she had to say was a kick in the teeth.

"Okay," she began. "Cutting to the chase, we have three messages today. Number one: *The royal family is NOT missing.*"

Dramatic pause.

The royal family is not missing? Elliot assumed this was for effect — that she had some point to make — and he waited for the explanation. Predictably, Samuel gasped. "They're not *missing*? But that is like to a wonder of —! They're not — but in that case, why . . . ?" and so forth.

"As far as the *entire* Kingdom is concerned," Agent Nettles qualified, "they are not."

There it was.

"Aaah." Samuel blew the air out of his cheeks.

"And that's how *you* have to see things too. Tell yourselves that. Believe it. When you go home, *convince* yourselves — however you do your convincing — meditation, yoga, self-help audios, whatever — but *convince* yourselves that the royals are fine. Because *that's* the impression you *must* give to every person in your lives. Mothers, fathers, sweethearts. No exception. And if you don't, we'll track you down and break your fingers." She smiled, as if this were a joke, but carried the smile for so long that the joke seemed to turn a corner toward truth.

Eventually, it ran right into truth. She *would* break their fingers if they told.

"The fact is," she continued, letting go of the complicated smile and picking up her words again, "it's *not your responsibility to find the royal family.*" She indicated herself and Agent Ramsay. "It's ours. And the handful of agents who know about the disappearances. Second."

Another pause, and then she said the teeth-kicking thing.

"We do *not* believe that the royal family is in the World. That's one theory, sure, but it's the theory of some small-town cop who's as clueless as — well, as a small-town cop."

"Hang on." Elliot could feel his temper, which mostly stayed out of his way, clambering up on him. "You're talking about Jimmy Hawthorn. He's Deputy Sheriff in my town, and there is no way in —"

"I know, I know. You respect him. He's a genius! He's got a great reputation with missing persons cases, yada yada yada. But trust me, we have a world more expertise on these issues, and your Jimmy did *not* have the facts." She shrugged. "He wasn't even told that the files he was studying were members of the royal family. Princess Ko believes him. She believes her family has been taken to the World. And, hell, it's *remotely* possible. But we are exploring several far more likely options. Anyhow, yada yada. All you need to know is that we're taking care of this. Your job is to help the Princess follow her chosen path: a path we believe leads nowhere."

They all looked at the Princess. She was scratching at a mark on her sleeve, and did not seem remotely bothered.

Elliot was plenty bothered.

It was like they'd spent a weekend trying to solve a hornworm infestation in the tomato crop, and turned out the issue was the carrots. What was he even doing here?

Keira was smirking. Samuel, of course, was openmouthed and aghast, and Sergio's eyes had narrowed again.

"*You must not*," Agent Nettles went on, shaking her head slowly as if her enunciation was insufficiently emphatic — which, it seemed to Elliot, was not the case — "*get in the way of the true investigation*. Now, that, in a nutshell, is message number two. Before I move on to three, do you have anything to add, Princess Ko?"

"No, no." The Princess twisted her lower lip thoughtfully. "Just, I suppose, everyone should listen to the agents — I trust and respect them completely. I mean, I *do* believe my family is in the World." She shrugged. "In fact, I've been thinking about Elliot's suggestion that we go to the Lake of Spells and try to catch a Locator Spell. It might work, and a trip there would be just the thing the Royal Youth Alliance might do, so it's perfect as a cover."

The Princess reached across the table and got herself a mint.

"We have one more meeting before everyone goes home," she continued, weighing the mint in the palm of her hand. "I'll give you the arrangements for the expedition then. Go on, Agent Nettles. You're doing great."

Agent Nettles nodded.

"Thank you, Princess. And here is the final message."

Agent Ramsay handed her a stack of thick manila folders. She raised the top folder, then paused for so long that most of them began to frown or fidget.

During the pause, Elliot studied her. She had thin shoulders, pearl earrings, and a number of pins in her hair. The skin around her lips was dry, and she seemed to have a nervous habit of stretching out her mouth suddenly so that her eyes widened and brows lifted, before just as quickly relaxing both, like a twitch.

Elliot sighed, bored by her pause. He'd never liked theatrics.

"THESE!" she shouted suddenly. Naturally, they all jumped, and Elliot felt even more irritated. The agent's voice lowered. "These are files on each of you."

The room straightened up, curious, looking from the folders to Agent Nettles's face.

"You may not realize this," she continued, "but we do not allow people to have access to the Princess without first finding out *every single thing we can about them*."

She slapped the folders onto the table.

"You," she said, pointing at Samuel so he flinched. "You *live* in one of the most Hostile towns in the Kingdom. We're *appalled* by your presence here!"

"But . . ." Samuel protested, his hands fluttering, his eyes pooling with tears.

"And you," she said, next turning to Sergio. "You're from Maneesh."

So that's what the accent was. Maneesh was a small island nation, adjacent to the Southern Climes. Elliot had never met anyone from there before, and knew almost nothing about the place. Something about civil war, years before? Or a clash with a neighboring kingdom?

"It's not clear to me why we should be trusting a foreigner at this time of crisis," Agent Nettles was saying, her eyes fixed on Sergio, "when every foreign nation *must* be suspect — no disrespect nor racism intended, yada yada — but more to the point, it's not at *all* clear what skills you bring to the table."

Sergio looked back at the agent, his face impassive, unreadable. Then he shrugged, ever so slightly and held up his hands, meaning, Elliot guessed: *no skills at all.*

She turned to Elliot.

"As for you," she said, "we absolutely did *not* want you. You communicate with the World? You have a contact there? You know about a crack and you have not reported it? These are *serious* capital offenses, and even the slightest hint that the Princess knew about this would be catastrophic for the royals. So, Elliot Baranski, know this —"

She leaned forward — again with the dramatic pause. He thought about asking if he could go get a cup of coffee and come back when she was done with it.

"Know this," she repeated at last. "The World Severance Unit currently has more manpower, more weaponry than the armies of all the

Kingdoms combined. They have crack teams who live, breathe, and dream about locating cracks and killing people who conceal or use them. Yes, that's what I said. Their preference is to kill, rather than risk losing at trial on a technicality, and they're adept at finding loopholes to justify homicide. Indeed, if a suspect is classified as a Flagrant Offender, they are legally *obliged* to execute on sight. They *will* find you, Elliot. You *will*, at the very least, be arrested and condemned to death. And when that happens, do you know what the Princess will do? What she *must* do for the sake of the Kingdom?"

Another pause, then: "She will *wash her hands of you*."

Ah, what was this, an action thriller? The woman had seen too many movies.

"Thanks," Elliot said dryly.

Agent Nettles was holding up those folders again.

"If there is even the *slightest* hint of you kids doing *anything* that might hurt the Princess or her family," she said, "we will not *hesitate* to use this information, and hang you out to dry."

At this point, she looked at Keira.

Keira looked back.

Neither said a word.

There was a long silence, and this time it didn't feel like an effect, it felt like something was creeping slow and steady into the room, climbing up the sides of their chairs.

Agent Nettles drummed her fingers on the topmost of the folders. She kept right on staring.

Keira's eyes dropped.

"Okay, that's it for us," Agent Nettles said.

She and Agent Ramsay stepped back, resuming their positions.

PART 4

1.

It used to be, the world was a fried egg.

Madeleine woke.

The light suggested late morning. She had an odd sense that something important was trying to make its way into her thoughts. Roaming the perimeters of her mind, running its hands along the railings. If she stayed perfectly still — lying on the couch, facing the ceiling — it might edge its way in.

There was poised suspense. Her eyes flickered, but her breathing was deliberate and slow. She thought of what Belle called "soft focus," where you look around in an *un*looking way — receptive, listening — and she tried to still herself further, listen with her eyes. Let the world *in*, let herself into herself.

It was something to do with the thought that had just woken her, she realised:

It used to be, the world was a fried egg.

That thought made no sense.

She was being a half-wit. She shifted, ready to sit up, but then right away lay down again. As if someone had grabbed her shoulders and forced her back.

All right, she thought, I'll go along with this. The flat was empty:

Her mother had a morning appointment at the hospital, she remembered. So there was nothing stopping Madeleine from staring at the ceiling for a while.

She tried to return to her trance-like state. She imagined she was a fried egg in a pan. You'd just lie there, wouldn't you, perfectly still, as a fried egg in a pan. Stray thoughts would weave their way into you.

Into your yolk.

She nodded, pleased with the thought. Your yolk could be your soul. This seemed Belle-esque.

It'd be hot, though. In the pan.

She changed it to an egg on a plate.

I am a fried egg on a plate.

That was no good either.

She'd get eaten in a moment.

Ah, she was useless at this. Maybe the idea was to think of nothing at all.

She'd have to be quick with her nothing thinking, though. She had a lot to do today. There was the French translation, the essay on *Macbeth* — or anyway, *finding* her lost copy of *Macbeth* so she could read it and think about an essay — and she had to buy batteries for the remote, and Clearasil, and she had to take back those biscuits that were past their use-by date. That felt embarrassing, taking them back. They were only a couple of quid, so why not just chuck them out?

Quid and *chuck*. Her language seemed to have transformed.

Anyway, the point was, she and her mum almost never bought biscuits these days. They were a treat, a luxury. And Sainsbury's should not sell stale luxuries.

Or were you supposed to check use-by dates yourself? Did everyone else squint closely at the products they picked up from supermarket shelves?

Her upbringing had left serious gaps. None of her fancy boarding schools or governesses had ever flown her to England for a guided tour of a Sainsbury's.

Anyway, the point was — here, she returned to the wandering thought, and addressed it — the point was, she was very busy with schoolwork and shopping today.

Not to mention finding the royal family of the Kingdom of Cello. Where was she supposed to fit that in?

Ha-ha. Well, that was a private joke with herself. There wasn't much she could do about that right now. She was waiting to hear from Elliot when he got back from the Magical somewhere. North. That's where it was. The meeting with the leftover Princess.

Belle and Jack had been very enthusiastic about it all for a minute. Jack had even sat down, opened a notebook, and said, "Right, then. So Madeleine's found herself a kingdom. Nice work, Madeleine. Anyway, as I see it, a kingdom needs its royals. So let's find them. But how? Go to shopping centres and railway stations and make an announcement: *Attention, all members of the Cello royal family, please report to the stationmaster's office*?"

"That'd take years," Belle had reflected. "Longer even."

So that had been that. They'd gone to Gardies for burgers instead.

Still. Even without having to track down a royal family, Madeleine had a lot on today.

She shifted a bit. The sheet was sliding off the couch, and her T-shirt nightie was riding up, so her back was on the scratchy cushions. She stood and fixed her couch-bed, turned the pillow over, and lay back down.

Strange, lying in the stillness, staring at the ceiling, while everything was busy being Saturday outside. Even up here in the attic flat she could hear the street noises clearly. Footsteps hurrying past, or running past, and someone shouting, "Come on, then!" and people laughing. Even the laughter was running along. Cars slid by, over and over, each with its own thoughtful, superior drone, rising up and down, definitely busy getting on with things. People pedalled by on bikes, and some of them were *brrring*ing bells. That was *sharply* busy, to be ringing bells. That was moving around and through, moving people out of the way!

Something was happening to Madeleine now. She had the sense that her stillness was about to pay off. The thought was going to present itself, and it had taken the form of an egg being cracked against the side of a mixing bowl. Not that motion so much, as the sensation of the egg *itself* cracking, sliding, glugging out of the freshly broken shell.

What's with all the eggs this morning? she thought.

But she didn't answer because it had come to her, the meaning of her waking thought: that long ago, everyone had thought that our planet was sitting flat and still. A big fried egg. In the centre of the plate.

They'd seen the rest of the universe as a sort of children's mobile, put there to entertain the egg. There'd been a series of rings in the mobile — moon, planets, sun, and stars were all dangling from the rings — and some benevolent giant hand set these all to spinning, gently and harmoniously, while the fried-egg earth sat and watched, feeling chuffed.

Imagine that, she thought.

Imagine you were lying on your scratchy couch, and you honestly believed you were living on a giant fried egg, while the universe was a decoration, slowly rotating around you. And then imagine someone came up, stood at your shoulder and said, "Actually, you know this world? It's not so much a fried egg, it's more a *boiled* egg, and this boiled egg is actually flying around out there, part of the universe, spinning as it flies."

It'd set your head to turning circles, wouldn't it!

No, actually, it would not.

You'd just go: Rubbish.

If you could be bothered, you might point out that the floor wasn't moving, which it would be, if it was. Then this person at your shoulder might go on about scale and perspective, and how it's calibrated so we can't see it happening, and you'd stop listening. You'd go: Whatever. Or maybe: Look, would you mind popping somewhere else for a bit?

No *wonder* it had taken ages for people to come to terms with the idea of the revolving, rotating earth! Even Aristotle — and he was a smart one — he'd laughed his head off. He'd gone, "Watch this," and he'd thrown a chicken or something straight up in the air. "See?" he'd said. "It landed right where I threw it. If Earth was *moving*, the chicken would have landed over there!" What's more, Aristotle had said, warming up, there'd be winds like you wouldn't *believe*. We'd never get anything done, what with holding our hats down.

Everyone had laughed, pleased, and that had been that with the idea.

Madeleine had always had a sense that people used to be a bit daft. Whereas *now*, they were smart. *Now* we walk around going: Well, of *course*, the world's not sitting there being an egg. It's spinning and flying! It's getting the shopping done and doing its homework and meeting up with its friends, it's a *kite* of activity with its tail going mad, is what the world is, and aren't I clever? For knowing that?

We're not clever, though. We're just stating the new obvious.

She sat up suddenly.

She was starving.

That's why all the thoughts about eggs.

An hour later, she'd had her cornflakes and she'd bathed, dressed, and brushed her hair and she was out there in the Saturday.

She still felt odd, but not remotely like a fried egg. Now she felt like a girl.

A busy girl. But she went by the laneway anyway to check the parking meter — and there it was.

A letter from Elliot of Cello.

A long one, but she sat down on the edge of the gutter and read it anyway.

Dear Madeleine,

I once saw the mating dance of the carbuncle-bats of Nature Strip. If I hadn't seen that, I'd be saying right now: The weekend I just had was the weirdest experience of my life.

(But seriously, those carbuncle-bats. Must be one of the twelve wonders of the Kingdom they ever reproduce at all. You wouldn't believe me if I told you.)

Anyway, I got back a few days ago. Haven't had time to write, and still don't, actually, but I will anyway. 'Cause I've got to give you a message from Princess Ko. And 'cause I might go mad if I don't tell *somebody* about it. Can't tell my buddies, or even my mother.

I'll start with the people.

There's Princess Ko. She's okay, I guess. Super pretty and super organized, anyway, what with her flowcharts and diagrams.

There's Keira from Jagged Edge. She's a beautiful techhead with a personality like sandpaper, and an attitude could start a fire. She's got some fierce secret reason for hating the Princess. Or maybe she just hates her randomly. Either way, I feel like ducking for cover whenever those two exchange glances.

There's a kid named Samuel from Olde Quainte who's a walking panic attack.

There's a nice enough stable boy named Sergio.

And there's me.

We sat around all weekend talking about how the royal family has gone to the World, and coming up with absolutely no solution to that situation.

Then there's the security agents. Completely irrelevant except when they stepped up near the end of the weekend and said, actually, the royals have NOT gone to the World.

Then Princess Ko's back again, painting her fingernails (well, that's how it felt), as if the agents hadn't spoken, and planning a trip to the Lake of Spells, to track down a spell to find her family in the World.

(This part was my fault, 'cause I tried to diffuse a situation by suggesting we go to the Lake, never expecting they'd take me up on it. I'm an idiot.)

It's a total waste of time. You can't choose what spell you get at the Lake — for a while I thought you could 'cause I wanted it to be true and I had a book said you could, but then I came to my senses. Tried to explain this, but it was too late, the Princess had got stuck on the idea.

And more to the point, I DON'T WANT TO DO ANYTHING ELSE ABOUT THE MISSING ROYAL FAMILY. *THOSE SECURITY AGENTS CAN TAKE CARE OF IT.* I WANT TO BE LOOKING FOR MY DAD. I WANT TO BE WORKING WITH TOVEY AND KIM (THE CI AGENTS).

SURE, IT'S GOOD WE SORT OF KNOW WHERE HE IS, BUT HE'S IN TROUBLE. YOU DON'T WANT TO BE A PRISONER OF THE HOSTILES. WHAT IF THEY TURN ON HIM BEFORE IT'S TOO LATE? WHAT IF HE TRIES SOMETHING HIMSELF BEFORE THE CI GUYS FIND A WAY TO GET HIM BACK???

Anyhow, so that's one part of the situation.

The other part is, the Princess gave us assignments. It's a lot like school, this whole Royal Youth Alliance thing.

Keira's job is to read six boxes of documents. The documents are covered in tiny, tiny print. It's XML code, apparently — some kind of computing language? — which most techheads in JE can read. There was a lot going on in the facial expressions between Keira and the Princess, and I think what they were saying was that Keira was getting shafted.

Samuel has to look through the archives of World-Cello interaction. He also has to research how the World and Cello link up so we'll at least know which part of the World the royals went to first, since we know exactly where they were taken.

Sergio has to go work at the WSU headquarters, which are in Olde Quainte, and see if he can get ahold of a crack detector.

The security agents went a bit ballistic when Princess Ko gave Sergio this job. He's a *stable boy*. He has no *training* in undercover work. He'd be in serious *danger*. Etc., etc.

But the Princess just said that Sergio's a great actor, and then she turned it back on the agents by saying she was sure they had the proficiency to get Sergio false papers, and the contacts to get him a position in the WSU as a junior clerk.

And my job is to work with my "contact in the World" (you) to figure out how to break open this crack and get people through.

So, I guess, do you want to talk about that sometime? If you get this today (Saturday), maybe midnight tonight?

I leave for the Lake of Spells in two weeks.

Catch ya,

Elliot

Madeleine looked at the parking meter.

It wasn't just the earth not being centre of the universe. It was every time someone picked up the truth and gave it a good shake so that things we thought we knew crashed into splinters. There'd always be a clamour of disbelief. What, the *moon* causes the tides?! Don't be such a tosser. What, there's *gravity* somehow holding things in place via invisible strings? Oh, yes, *certainly* there's a thing called space-time that gets bent out of shape when a planet passes by. No question.

The thing was, just because it went against everything you'd believed before — didn't mean it wasn't correct.

There's a whole other world called Cello just beyond a crack in that parking meter? And now you're going to help a boy there figure out how to *open* that crack?

Madeleine stood on the street, holding Elliot's letter in one hand, let the summer breeze rustle it a little, let the traffic and voices and footsteps slide back into her head.

2.

Elliot arrived at the high-school grounds a few minutes before midnight.

The sky was high black and star-studded, and the air seemed frozen into silence. His boots scuffed through snow from that afternoon's fall, still powder white, and he lifted up his collar and pulled his coat tighter around him.

Seemed unfair that it was winter here in Bonfire soon as he got back from all that snow of the Magical North. People said he must have brought it with him, which, now that he thought about it, was actually quite possible. He'd flown from MN to the airfield in Sugarloaf, then taken the train home from there. Seasons sometimes hitched a ride on fixed wings and express trains.

It was the sort of cold that tensed your neck and shoulders, made your face hold panic-still. Which was all wrong. He tried to loosen up: shook his arms, stamped his boots. Then he examined the sculpture.

The base was a great hunk of concrete formed into a little hillock, and the old TV was wedged on top of it, its back open, internal workings exposed. All he knew was that there must have been a crack hovering here in the schoolyard, and the sculpture had somehow caught ahold of it.

He thought through what he knew about cracks. They were invisible and intangible. That was something. And they came in two types. First there were the minor cracks that opened now and then. Small things, like pencils, matchboxes, receipts, operating instructions for toys, shopping lists, would blow through, mostly drifting away unnoticed. It was only if someone happened on an object that jarred as being Worldian that these cracks got discovered. Anyone who found a Worldian object — or even *suspected* something had links to the World — had to notify the WSU immediately. They'd swoop in with their detectors, locate the crack, and seal it up.

The second kind were the major cracks, and these were big enough for people. You couldn't just walk through a major crack, even if you knew where it was (which was tricky in itself, their being invisible) — there was some secret technique. The WSU had sealed up the old ones, and major cracks never opened anymore.

Obviously, this one in the schoolyard was a minor crack. Could he stretch it into a major crack?

Ah, who understood the science. He'd never paid much attention back in World Studies. Maybe they'd had an entire class on constructing cracks?

Although, that seemed unlikely. That'd be like a class on how to rob a bank or manufacture heroin. Worse, actually. Closer to selling state secrets to a foreign power. There was probably some rule against teaching kids to commit high treason.

He'd have to look into it, read up, ask around, whatever. He seemed to remember that Mr. Garenstein, the World Studies teacher, had actively discouraged discussions outside the classroom. Wasn't it Mr. G who'd once clapped a hand over Elliot's mouth when he'd started to ask a question on the way out of the classroom? And pointed to his own right foot, just past the door frame, bellowing, "Look! I'm outside! I have immunity!" before thundering away down the corridor.

Elliot smiled, remembering. He'd only been going to ask Mr. G if he knew what time his wife — Clara Garenstein, she ran the grocery store — if he knew what time she was closing up that night. He'd had a delivery of quinces for her.

Of course, even if he got Mr. G to talk, he'd have to be careful how he phrased his questions. He'd need some plausible reason why the sudden interest in the World.

Tricky.

He checked the back of the TV. Still nothing from Madeleine, but it was not quite midnight.

He stood back and examined the sculpture as a whole again.

The obvious thing would be a chain saw.

Or anyway, a shovel or a pick.

Break open the crack. Dig through, cut through, tunnel through, tear his way into the World.

He could get Madeleine to start up with a jackhammer on her side, and he could bring in a bulldozer, and they could meet in the middle.

Maybe not the most subtle approach, if you were trying to avoid the attention of the WSU.

And, actually, even without having listened much in World Studies classes, he had a feeling the cracks might be a little more complicated.

A flash of white caught the light, and there it was, a note from Madeleine.

Hey, Elliot, you there?

She always started off like this.

And he always replied:

Yep.

A few moments passed and another paper appeared.

It's me. Plus Belle and Jack are here. They wanted to meet you. They say hi, and pleased to meet you and that, and they'd shake your hand only there's the whole issue of you being in another dimension or whatever. They're keen to help solve this issue so the royals can get back through once we find them, and they extend their honour and greetings from our world to yours, cause they're polite like that, they say (not something I've particularly noticed, but anyway).

A brief laugh of surprise shook the cold out of Elliot a minute. Strange: Even though she'd talked about her friends, a part of him had half thought that Madeleine was all that there *was* to the World.

He replied:

Tell Jack and Belle I said hey, and my Kingdom extends greetings and honor right back at 'em.

Madeleine's reply was fast:

Belle and Jack are totally psyched to see their names in your handwriting. They're star-struck by you. I told them they'd get over that and you're just regular and nothing special.

Much appreciated.

There was a lengthy pause, then Madeleine wrote again.

Did you hear that?

Elliot startled. Maybe there *had* been a rustle from the trees over there just now? But it was just the wind, right? And wait, how could *she* have heard it over in the World?

Hear what?

Don't worry. I knew it wouldn't work. Belle's just been bellowing your name into the parking meter. Luckily this laneway's empty, so nobody can see her and get her sectioned or whatever. But she's totally going to wake somebody up any moment.

Elliot was still reading this, and reflecting on it, when another note appeared.

See, Belle and Jack say if there's a "crack" you should be able to hear sounds through it. Or feel our breeze or our rain or whatever. And smell our low-grade fuel. And Jack says if letters can get through, what about tiny little organisms and germs and stuff? I told them they make no sense, but actually it DOES make sense.

This was followed up by another shorter note.

Jack says we need to figure out the nature of the crack if we're going to crack the crack. Also, as an aside, he asks if crack is the freebase form of cocaine in Cello?

Elliot wrote a reply.

I think your friends are right that we need to figure out the nature of the crack.

I just want to say that it wasn't just Belle and Jack saying that about the crack issue; I've been thinking the exact same thing.

What's your point?

When you praise them, praise me too.

Elliot decided not to get into that. He wrote a new note:

I've been thinking: So far we've only sent letters to each other — apart from those healing beads I sent for your mother. So maybe we see what other objects can get through? Start small and then work our way up to bigger things?

And see if we can sort of stretch the crack?

Elliot nodded in the cold night air.

Right. Go from marbles to oranges to apples.

Are apples bigger than oranges over there? They're about the same size here. Sometimes oranges are bigger.

That might be sort of off topic.

The oranges and apples might disagree with you on that. But then we'll move on to watermelons, right? Watermelons are bigger than apples?

And after watermelons, a head.

There was another delay. It felt to Elliot like the pen might have glued itself to his hand, it was that stiff with the cold. Then Madeleine's note appeared:

You mean, like a severed head? Where would you get that from?

I mean my own head.

Attached to your body, though, right?

Yeah, no, I was thinking I'd cut off my head and send it through.

Belle and Jack are laughing *their* heads off right now. They think you're a riot. But that's still them being star-struck. You're not that funny.

If I could get my head through, maybe I could kind of pull the rest of my body through? Don't know. I need to ask the World Studies teacher about how these cracks work. So, you want to talk again this time next week?

Wait. Belle and Jack want to try some stuff. (Me too. I mean, if these things work, I want the credit for them. If not, they're Belle and Jack's ideas.) Just wait.

A gust of wind slapped Elliot's face. He stamped his feet in the snow.

3.

For the next two hours, Madeleine, Belle, and Jack experimented with the parking meter. They slapped it around, and kicked it. They hit it with closed fists (which hurt). They leaned in close and blew air at it, threw their shadows and jackets over it, grabbed it with both hands and shook it from side to side.

Belle had some of her mother's cheap perfume in her handbag and she sprayed this all over the meter. She chewed some peppermint gum and breathed hard on it. Then she lit a cigarette, took a drag, and blew smoke.

"You're doing that in the wrong order," Madeleine reflected.

Jack offered to take off his running shoes, as that would be as strong a smell as anything that could be produced in all of England, and there was a minor scuffle when they tried to stop him doing that. He won the scuffle, as he had the interests of science and World-Cellian relations on his side. So then there was some screaming and rearing away from him while he waved his shoes around the parking meter.

Every now and then they sent a message to Elliot:

Don't tell me you didn't hear that?

or

You felt a sort of shaking sensation just now, right?

or

Are there any wisps of smoke tendrilling towards you from the crack there?

or else:

Come on, you MUST have smelled that. (You've got noses there, right?)

But Elliot's replies were always "nope," and they started to see him as a bit of a nuisance. A wet blanket, even. Eventually, they forgot about him altogether, as they joined hands and danced around the parking meter, and chanted nursery rhymes, prayers, multiplication tables, the periodic table, and French irregular verbs. Madeleine found a stick and beat the side of the meter with it, because maybe he would be able to *sense* the rhythm even if he couldn't hear it, and Jack recited a lot of Byron's poetry because maybe only *beautiful* words could get through.

By now it was almost two o'clock in the morning and they were drunk on sleepiness and on their own laughter, and Belle was getting into the noise thing again, announcing that he *must* be able to hear this, he's just not *listening* hard enough. She got them all singing Florence and the Machine at the top of their voices, then she gave one of her own high-pitched whistles, the kind that could cross a city. It was so close and so alarming that Madeleine and Jack screamed in shock and then fell into wailing hysterics.

At that point, a window was thrown open in a house along the street and a stream of words came flying out at them.

The window slammed shut.

"Nice," Belle murmured, impressed.

They quietened, untangling their breath from the laughter and from the echoes of the shouting just now, and then gazed at one another in subdued silence.

"People live in those houses," Jack reflected. "All this time I'd been thinking they were sort of decoration."

Belle was looking at the parking meter.

"There's another note," she said. "How long has that been sitting there?"

Madeleine drew out the paper and held it out to them.

Are we nearly done? I'm freezing my balls off here.

Belle grabbed the pen and notepad from the path where Madeleine had left it, and wrote:

You have balls in Cello?

There was a long pause. Then Elliot's reply.

We might be talking about different things.

Belle smiled, and wrote again, pushing Madeleine aside with her elbow as she did so.

I think we mean the same thing. This is Belle here, and I have questions. Is there censorship of the cracks between Cello and the World? And how filthy is your language there generally? And you speak English, right? Is that all over Cello or just where you are?

As Belle wrote this, Madeleine was watching over her shoulder, agitated. She wanted the pen back, but she also wanted to see what Belle would say.

Jack was spring-jumping from the street to the kerb and back again, his hands in the pockets of his jeans.

Elliot's reply came a few moments later.

We don't speak English, we speak Cellian. What's English? Anyhow, this is what we speak all over the Kingdom but different provinces have their own accents and slang, and sometimes — like in Nature Strip — the accent's so strong it's like another language. Also, I just remembered that there are parts of MN and OQ where they have their own dialects. And the Wanderers speak a version of Southern Climean. (In the Undisclosed Province they speak with their eyes.) But maybe we could have a discussion about linguistics another time, 'cause I'm not sure if I'm just exhausted or hypothermic, but either way, I'm about to pass out.

Belle glanced over her shoulder at Madeleine. "Your boy needs to toughen up," she said, and wrote again, speaking her words aloud as she did so.

I don't get why you guys speak the same language as us.

She folded it, posted it, and pulled her jacket tighter around her. "Cold here too," she said. "You hear us complaining?"

"But this is summer," Madeleine pointed out. "He's got winter there. We don't even know what the temperature is in Cello."

"Still cold here."

Jack stopped jumping and looked at them both.

"How do we know we're speaking the same language as Elliot?" he said. "There could be some kind of inbuilt translation device inside the crack, and it's instantly converting the messages."

Another note appeared.

I don't get it either. Are we done here?

Madeleine was watching Belle.

"Why are you asking him these questions?" she asked. "Are you thinking it's not real — do you think it's all, like, a trick?"

"No." Belle tapped the notepad with the pen, distracted. "Just thinking —" then her head swung up and her eyes widened. "But *you* do."

They held each other's eyes a moment.

"I know what it is," Belle said slowly. "You're believing and not believing at the same time. You can't do that. It's like you're on a train track and one foot's on one — wait, what are those things called? Those tracks that trains run on?"

"Tracks," Jack said.

"Right, and you're trying to run along with a foot on each track, Madeleine. It won't work. They'll go off in different directions."

"No, they won't," Jack said. "They run parallel. That's how train tracks work."

"Well, still. They're too far apart. You've got to choose one of the tracks, otherwise you're just, like, doing the splits all the time."

"Could get uncomfortable," Jack agreed.

Belle sat down on the edge of the kerb and rubbed her arms. Jack and Madeleine sat on either side of her. They stretched their legs out and contemplated three pairs of shoes.

"You guys really think the Kingdom of Cello is real," Madeleine said eventually. "I mean real like *real* real — not like your auras and your horoscopes."

Jack and Belle snorted simultaneously.

"I don't mean auras and horoscopes aren't *real*," Madeleine said quickly. "I mean in *your* minds, they're totally — I mean . . ."

"Ah, it's all right." Belle squinted at the space around Madeleine's head. "Your aura's gone all complicated trying to get out of that one. It's like it's crowded with tiny china figurines. Calm down, Madeleine's aura, it's not her fault she's a bit simple."

"A bit unevolved," Jack suggested.

"Well, all right." Madeleine shifted back so she was leaning up against the parking meter now. "It's like this. You guys remember when I first came to Cambridge last year, and I kind of thought I was too special for this life? Cause I was used to being rich and travelling the world and everything, right?"

Belle and Jack nodded.

"And I was a bit of a loser, and I had to, kind of like, *learn* I'm not superior?"

They nodded again.

"You're allowed to jump in at any point and say I wasn't that bad."

Jack reached back and squeezed Madeleine's knee, which could have been interpreted either way.

"Get to your point," Belle said.

"If I believe in Cello, I also have to believe there's a place nobody knows about except me. Out of all the people in the world, *I* discovered it. So wouldn't that make me special? Which is the opposite of what I learned, and therefore can't be true, and so Cello can't be true either?"

Jack stuck his little finger in his ear and gazed at Madeleine with interest.

"Ah, you've got everything upside down," Belle said. "You were just the only one tosser enough to stop and look at something jammed in a parking meter. Everyone else would've gone, *bit of old junk in that parking meter*, or wouldn't have bothered to think anything. Whereas you walk around all sad and missing your dad and thinking about the sky and it's cause you *want* to believe in magic, Madeleine. So, you know, go ahead. Believe."

There was another thoughtful quiet.

Jack took his finger out of his ear and studied it.

"Believe that there is wax in my ear," he said.

"The way I see it," Belle continued, ignoring Jack, "if you want to make a connection with your Elliot, you've got to let go of the doubts and overthinking. And just go with it."

Jack clicked his tongue loudly. "Now you're doing the Star Wars thing."

"What are you on about?"

"It's *the force is with you* thing. The whole, *if you just believe the spaceship will do its own precision shooting, it'll do it.* It's the whole *let go* and *feel it in your heart* and *trust your instincts* and *don't think* and *just BE* and *stop thinking with this*" — he thunked the top of Belle's head — "and *think with this instead*" — he touched his own chest. "It's just lazy is what it is. It's bollocks." He paused. "I tried it myself playing football once."

The girls laughed, and Jack did too, but a bit grimly.

There was a faint rustle behind them, and they looked up at the parking meter.

"I forgot all about him!" Belle said. "Ah, well, that's what you get for living inside a parking meter."

Madeleine reached for the paper and read it.

Going home. Night.

They all stood up, yawning.

"Hang on a minute," Jack said. "You told us you went *into* the Kingdom once before. Well, how did you do it that time? That's what you've gotta figure out."

Belle thwacked his head.

"He's got some brains in there," she said, "along with the wax."

"He has," Jack agreed. "Can we go home now?"

They trailed slowly towards their homes, Madeleine looking back just once at the parking meter. A dark hulking shape, a shadowy figure, and it seemed to her that it was bending forward, lost in thought itself.

4.

Over the next couple of weeks, Elliot got himself so tangled in busy he couldn't see his way around the knots.

The snowfall melted overnight and summer veered its way down Main Street. Seemed Elliot was always sweating now, as he ran from breakfast to the greenhouse to school to deftball practice, and from there to his friend Nikki's farm. They were harvesting the macadamias, and he and his buddies always pitched in with that. Sure, he needed the extra cash, but now was not an ideal time.

He'd rush home late to catch Agents Tovey and Kim — they dropped by the farmhouse most nights to keep him and his mother up-to-date, and to ask any questions — and there they'd be, sitting in the porch light. Drinking whiskey, sometimes shelling peas, and he'd grab a cold drink and join them.

"I don't know what it is," Elliot's mother said one night, then she paused. She and Elliot were leaning on the porch railing, watching Tovey's car slide down the driveway. Way down at the gates, the indicator flashed orange for a moment. She and Elliot both smiled at that. City boys. Then the car turned left and disappeared.

"I don't know what it is," Petra repeated, "but whenever those two talk it's like they're taking a coat off my shoulders. A heavy coat I didn't want to wear 'cause it's so hot, is what I mean. You see what I'm saying?"

Elliot knew exactly what she meant.

Tovey had eyes that seemed never to stop thinking; he'd stop and rub his chin, turn a question upside down, shell peas at super speed. Agent Kim was different — you couldn't see his eyes so much, they were always lowered to his notebook. He sketched everything: Elliot's mother's profile, fences cutting through fields, a half-full whiskey tumbler.

But whatever the agents said — even when they slipped off topic and started swapping Central Intelligence jokes for farming anecdotes — there was always a powerful sense that they could make things happen: that they were steadily, methodically, patiently working toward the rescue of Elliot's dad.

Once the agents had gone for the night, Elliot would open up his schoolbag and try to stay awake through homework. Teachers were piling it up on him now, to make up for the school he'd missed over the last year. They used to be quiet and cautious with him, back when nobody knew just what had happened to his dad.

But now the truth was out, and it was a solid, heroic story with a couple of solid extra characters — Tovey and Kim — who'd ridden into town to sort things out. Surely, the teachers seemed to reason, this must free him up for schoolwork?

On top of that, Elliot was a minor celebrity in town, since he'd been selected for the Royal Youth Alliance. That lightened the mood even further. Teachers had switched from quiet to riotously noisy.

It was all kinds of noisy, to be honest, thanks to that Royal Youth Alliance. Everyone wanted to shout questions at Elliot, about Princess Ko, and the White Palace, and werewolf colonies up north. Kids kept showing him his own photo in the *Cellian Herald* — waving articles in his face in a weirdly triumphant way, as if they were giving him a treat. He was never sure how to react to that. It didn't *feel* like a treat. He'd already seen most of the articles, for a start.

Teachers had questions too, but they tried to disguise plain curiosity as something more dignified — educational, even — and they'd take slow, thoughtful pauses between questions, which sent him insane — he could have written a whole essay in some of those pauses (his essays were pretty short) — and then they'd smile generously, as if it was a privilege for him to be chatting with them.

They were too accustomed to being able to command words from students, that was their problem.

Outside school was not so bad — his friends had already asked what they wanted to know, which wasn't too much — but the Sheriff was the worst. Great guy, but obsessed with the royals. He kept using his police skills to track Elliot down and then asking things like, how did the Princesses take their coffee? And how did they feel about the breeding of thornless roses? And did they prefer fizzy or still water — ah, the Sheriff didn't *know* what he wanted to know, he just wanted.

Elliot had to dig through his weekend at the Palace for answers that were true — or at least plausible — to keep his interrogators happy. They weren't satisfied, he'd noticed, unless he said something tangible, preferably funny — words like *beautiful* or *sparkly* or *super nice* didn't cut it.

On top of all this he had to find time to brush his teeth and scratch mosquito bites.

Two days before the trip to the Lake of Spells, he woke up at ten past his usual waking time. From that point on, the day kept sliding from his reach.

He pulled on his running shoes, tied the laces fast and hard, and they snapped in his hands. They were already broken in three places — he kept knotting them back together. Who had time to buy new laces and rethread them?

The school assembly ran overtime, which meant he couldn't get moss growing in the petri dish in Biology like he was supposed to. So now he'd have to do that at home. He was running to the Mathematics lab to do another makeup exam when the alarm rang for an emergency drill — they'd been doing a lot of those on account of increased Color attacks, but seriously, how many different ways were there for everyone to get into the gymnasium?

Then the yearbook editor sidelined him for an interview about the royals.

Then his buddy Cody reminded him about the performance artwork he was about to reveal in the stairwell of the admin building.

That meant he was late for his History group meeting — they were doing a presentation on the origins of the 1422 Cello-Aldhibah War of Attrition, drawing comparisons with the recent Cello-Aldhibah Missile Crisis. Half the group were pissed at him for being late. The other half hadn't done their share of the work, so they stayed quiet.

Then, just as the school day was finally winding down, the warning bells rang for real — a Charcoal Gray, Level 11 — and who had time to be trapped behind security shutters while a Gray shook, rattled, and juddered through town?

It was not as bad as Charcoal Grays can be, and only lasted a few minutes, but word got around that the Watermelon Inn had taken a beating — half the pipes dislodged, and the rooms in the northern wing a shambles.

So he headed over there to see how he could help his Auntie Alanna.

He was standing on a bed in an empty guest room, refitting the curtain rod, when his little cousin, Corrie-Lynn, came in with a fresh-squeezed juice for him.

She had a book under her arm: *The Kingdom of Cello: The Illustrated Travel Guide.*

"Listen, Elliot," she said, holding up the book. "I was just reading about Occasional Pilots, and what I'm thinking is, I think you might turn out to *be* an Occasional Pilot. 'Cause of how you're a hero all over the place and you can jump so high in deftball. So I'm going to read it out to you while you work."

"Why are you always reading that book?" Elliot set down the empty juice glass, and turned back to the curtain rod. "Why not read books about woodwork? Seeing as you're so talented at it."

"Why does it bother you?" Corrie-Lynn countered, ignoring his question.

"Don't like the guy who wrote it."

She turned to the cover.

"T. I. Candle. You *know* him?"

"Nope. Just don't like the way he writes. He's a tosser."

"What's a tosser?"

That was a word he'd gotten from Madeleine-in-the-World. He should be more careful.

Ah, who cared. Nobody would get the connection.

"Well, he doesn't like the Farms. He thinks our province is boring."

"So? It kinda is."

Elliot laughed. "If you want to read something to me, maybe find the bit about the Lake of Spells."

Corrie-Lynn nodded, approving. "For your trip on Saturday."

Elliot kept threading the curtains back into place while Corrie-Lynn read in her clear, strong voice, tripping over strange words now and then:

"The Lake of Spells is shaped like a battered handbag. It is, as the name suggests, replete with spells. You can dive, fish, swim, or prospect for spells. You can spin or skip pebbles to gather surface spells, snorkel for spells, net them, trap them, or simply wash your hands through the water — the spells will wind themselves around your fingers like slithers of seaweed."

Corrie-Lynn sighed.

"You are so lucky. Will you bring me back a spell, Elliot?"

Elliot promised he'd do his best.

"But a lot of people don't catch any spells at all," he warned her.

"You will," she said, confident.

Elliot shook his head, and told her to keep reading.

"The Lake of Spells has its own microclimate, separate from the constant winter of the Magical North: Here, the seasons rotate, and with every season, additional methods for spell collection arise. In springtime, spells grow on brambles around the edges of the Lake, like berries. In the summer, you can sail or windsurf for spells. In the fall, gather those that fall from surrounding trees. In winter, ice fish or skate for spells — risk skating on thin ice to get the most valuable spells. Spells can be frozen for later use, but like most things, they are best if used fresh. Oh, the nights I have spent with my friend (Vincent) around the campfire — feasting on spells for song, for love, for ghost stories, for games . . . these are the some of the fondest memories I have. If only I had not grown up and found myself excluded from the Lake!"

"See," said Elliot. "He's a tosser."

"You're a tosser," Corrie-Lynn said amiably. "There's a whole other section here on types of spells. You want me to read that?"

Elliot gave her a look, so she shrugged, closed the book, and collected his empty glass from the bedside table. "Missed the third loop," she added, thumb pointing over her shoulder as she headed out of the room.

"Ah, for crying out loud." Elliot saw he'd have to start afresh.

He cycled home from the Watermelon Inn, the day dripping off him in slides of sweat. Not even a breeze.

He passed the high school, and there was the sculpture, black with shadows. Nobody was around, so he slipped in and checked it. A new letter from Madeleine. It looked like a fat one. He put it into his pocket to read later, and carried on.

With all that had been happening, he'd hardly even thought about Madeleine since that night she and her buddies had kept him up trying their dumb experiments. He'd written to her a couple of times, once because he'd remembered Princess Ko's request — or command, more like — that he get ahold of some current maps of the World. And the second time to thank her for the maps.

But that was it. He'd done nothing about figuring out how to open the crack.

Well, seriously. How were they ever going to find the royals in the World? Setting aside the somewhat blinding fact that they probably weren't even *in* the World. Security agents generally knew what they were talking about, as hyperorganized as Princess Ko might be.

But the next day Elliot was walking by a notice board at school, and there was one of the newspaper articles about the RYA. Princess Ko's face dimpled out at him, and he turned away, thinking about the steel bone structure that seemed to lie behind those dimples.

As he turned, he realized he was almost side by side with Mr. Garenstein, the World Studies teacher. Right ahead of them, a crack ran along the brickwork, left there by yesterday's Charcoal Gray.

You couldn't get a better opportunity.

Mr. Garenstein was raising a paper bag toward his mouth, and had just taken a bite from a pastry in there, when Elliot said his name. It must have been a hot pastry — you could see it was burning his mouth, the way his eyes opened in mild panic even as they turned toward Elliot.

Elliot swung his thumb toward the crack in the brickwork.

"Do Charcoal Grays ever open up cracks through to the World?" he said.

Mr. Garenstein swallowed the bite of pie, and wiped his mouth. "Not that I've heard."

"How *do* cracks open anyway?" Elliot said, like he'd just thought of it.

"They just do."

Not especially forthcoming, this guy. And he was opening his mouth again, ready for more pie.

"Those little cracks you hear about," Elliot continued, trying to make his voice sound like it was off on an unexpected path, one that was surprising Elliot himself. "Do they ever grow any bigger?"

"How could they?" Mr. Garenstein took a bite, and spoke through it. "The WSU close them up soon as they hear about them."

"But in the olden days, before they did that — well, did cracks grow?"

Mr. Garenstein shook his head. "As you'd know if you'd ever paid the slightest attention in my classes, Elliot Baranski, cracks don't change. They come in a particular size and stay that way. They're not potted plants."

He was taking a flight of stairs now, and Elliot shrugged and turned to go. But halfway up the stairs, Mr. Garenstein paused: "You know," he said, "there *did* used to be talk of people constructing artificial cracks. You won't find that in the syllabus, of course — the WSU banned any mention of it. I shouldn't even be talking about it, I suppose." He swiveled. "Not that I *could* talk about it — it's quantum physics." He pointed at the window behind Elliot's head. "Her field of expertise, not mine."

Elliot looked through the glass, and there was the Physics teacher, Ms. Tamborlaine, heading through the school gates.

Mr. Garenstein carried on up the stairs, and Elliot stayed at the window.

Isabella Tamborlaine. He didn't take Physics but he knew she'd come across from Jagged Edge about a year ago, replacing Mischka Tegan, the teacher who'd disappeared the same night as his father.

Isabella had taken up with Jimmy, the Deputy Sheriff, and the two of them were nuts about each other. They didn't hide it, like you might expect: They walked around town, swinging hands together like a couple in a barn dance.

She was standing at the gate now, as if she was waiting for something. Maybe Jimmy was coming to meet her — the Sheriff's station was right across the road.

Elliot thought about running over, and asking about quantum physics.

Ah, he should go right home and start packing for tomorrow's trip. He'd ask when he got back.

5.

Later that night, Elliot had packed and was thinking about a shower to cool down, when he remembered Madeleine's letter.

He sat out on the porch under the starlight to read it.

Dear Elliot,

Do you ever feel like you're running alongside a spinning carousel while the horse you want is moving just ahead of you?

I sort of feel like the Kingdom of Cello is a horse on a carousel. Taking the curve ahead of me, always just out of my reach.

No offence.

I'm sure you guys are more than just a fibreglass horse.

It's just, in all the fantasy books I've read, the character gets into an alternate dimension, and that's it. There they are.

So they never question it. Maybe they wonder if it's a dream, but everyone knows what's a dream, so they don't waste time on that. They never seem to think too much about the fact that the universe has just turned upside down.

Anyhow, I've been trying to think about what the universe is made of, so I can tell if there's room in it for Cello.

Seems to me the world is made of buildings, trees, people, bikes, telegraph poles, taxi cabs, and ice-cream cones. But I guess all *that* is made out of something.

The ancient Greeks seem quite nice. They were the first smart people in history, I think, and they decided the universe was made of fire, earth, air, water, and one other thing called *the ether.* It was outside, holding everything in place.

Then the next smart people, the scientists, figured out that actually the world is made of tiny atoms, and atoms have tinier protons and neutrons, and inside these are teenier quarks and gluons, and drifting around, like dust around the furniture in Denny's apartment, are teeny electrons —

My point is, the pieces get smaller and weirder, and we *still* don't know what things are made from. Scientists keep finding new elementary particles, and they can't even see half of them. So they just sort of imagine them.

So, Elliot, is your Kingdom smaller than a particle of light?

If so, how did I see it that time that I came through?

That was when my mum was in the hospital. I remember running through the rain, hoping you'd sent me healing beads, and terrified my mum would be dead before I got back. You could've just been a hallucination brought on by the adrenaline and shock.

But if it *did* happen, well, I think it was cause I wanted so badly to believe that you were real. Cause that would make your healing beads real, and they'd cure my mother. (Which they did. Thanks again.)

I am about to be as wise as an old Greek guy. You ready?

The world is made of more than particles. It's made of things you can't hold in your hand, like fear, love, loss, hope, truth. Or plural, truths, and you can take these by the shoulders and turn them around to face you. Or tilt them so you can see them in the light.

And maybe truths are like horses on a carousel. You could keep running around, trying to catch one, or you could just stand still and believe, and wait for it to come around to you.

When I *believed* in your Kingdom, it came to me.

How about we meet at midnight tomorrow night and try this: I close my eyes, believe in you, and there you'll be.

See ya then.

Madeleine

She was wildly strange, she talked too much, but something about Madeleine's letter felt like quiet.

He sat on the porch and it seemed like these last crowded, noisy days were folding themselves up, breaking into their constituent parts, dissolving into tinier pieces, floating away. The last two weeks were a hill he'd just climbed — that hill out past Sugarloaf, say, where he and his buddies went camping sometimes. There'd be bramble-bush stamping, dog barking, joke calling, bark crunching, rock clambering, backpack clinking, strap adjusting — there'd be pulling twigs out of boots, holding branches back so they wouldn't fling into faces — tramping, tramping, tramping, and then there you'd be. Top of the hill. Everything different, suddenly quiet — the pieces of their climb fading into stillness, fields and farms laid out before them, sky and clouds around them.

Elliot looked at the pieces of days behind and days ahead; at the particles of light in the night sky.

It was past eleven. He had to be up at five tomorrow to make his flight.

Ah, he could talk to her one more time.

Couldn't get any more tired than he already was.

6.

"Thank you very much. Cheers."

That's what the world was made from. Words. Sentence fragments. Madeleine walked through the world and watched its pieces. The wheel of a pram running over a torn phone bill. Machinery throbbing somewhere. A group of Spanish students standing at a shop window. Chairs scraping. Throats clearing. Phrases handed back and forth. *Thank you!* and *I'm in Hampstead now. A little three-bedder.*

Herself. Her bare legs and sandals moving over rain-dampened roads. Herself turning back as she passed a man holding up a camera, trying to figure out what picture he was framing.

This morning she had said to Denny: "Do you think there could be a universe next door?"

He'd had his asthma inhaler in one hand, Sulky-Anne entangled in his ankles. He'd been trying out cables on a computer he was repairing, plugging and unplugging. Belle and Jack had been sitting at the other bench arguing about something.

"Another universe?" Denny had said.

"Like magic."

"Well, now." Denny had looked up. "When people talk about magic, what I think about is this. I think that these computers here would've seemed like magic, back when Charles Babbage was working on his arithmetic machines. Magnets and electricity were once magic too. And your guy — your Isaac Newton — when he first started talking about gravity stretching as far as the moon, well, people made fun of him. 'If the moon is sending messages across all that space,' they said, 'then it ought to have a mouth and eyes and nose.' It didn't help that Newton didn't know exactly *what* gravity was. He just knew it was."

Denny had stopped and thought a moment.

"So, sure," he'd said, "if there's a universe next door, then there is."

Now Madeleine's day was moving towards twilight. She saw a tiny boat glinting in the river, looked again, and realised it was just a crushed tin can.

She saw a genie's bottle in the grass, but it was only a half-full plastic bottle of juice. She heard someone singing, *Hello there!* and thought it was a talking cat. It wasn't. It was a woman.

That's what *my* days are made from, she thought. Seeing magic in nothing cause I'm yearning for something. Before she and her mother had run away, her days had cycled and spun, taking everything with them: shadows, windows, trains, dance steps, all of it careening along.

But they'd stepped out of that life and here they were, motionless.

"Did I see a sign about the Duchess of Malfi?" said a passing voice. *"Or did I just dream it?"*

The response drifted back: *"Strange thing to dream."*

When Madeleine had asked Denny about magic that morning, Belle and Jack had turned to her with matching, meaningful eyebrows.

They still asked questions about Cello, but in a respectful way, as if the Kingdom belonged to her. Just the other day Jack had asked if there were monsters there, and she'd explained that, in Cello, colours had material form.

"Give us an example," Jack said.

"Well, Elliot told me about this rare one called Clay Brown," she said. "It rises out of the ground beneath your feet, like a patch of mud, and keeps rising until you're encased in it. Then it hardens around you and crushes your bones."

"Can't you just climb out of it?"

"No. I asked that too. It keeps pulling you back in."

"So colours come to life there?" Belle had said. "That is *awesome*."

Madeleine had felt that strange pride again. Ever since she'd come to Cambridge, she'd wanted Belle to like her. Or anyway to *see* her properly. She daydreamed that someone from her past life would show up and put her in context. Or maybe send Belle a reference letter: *This is to confirm that Madeleine Tully is actually supercool. She dances down corridors, and everyone dances after her. She skips school to play pool in the pub down the road. She does really well in exams without ever studying.*

(She never used to be obsessed by Isaac Newton and science — that's an aberration. Don't let it fool you.) She changes her hair colour constantly: She's a free spirit. People are drawn *to her. You've probably missed all this since she's sort of lost her step since she got there, but trust me, she's brilliant.*

She could hardly say all this to Belle herself. It wouldn't sound objective.

Her day carried its pieces on into the night. Her mother stayed up late watching TV, and Madeleine watched the clock, put on her own pajamas, yawning repeatedly to try to make her mother catch some sleepiness.

Finally, her mother was in bed, and then there was the suspense of waiting while Holly finished tossing and turning, adding more to the pieces of the day, telling long stories about a debate in an online forum in one of her design courses; and then finally, finally, nearly midnight, there was the quiet of sleep in the flat.

Madeleine dressed again in the darkness, slipped on one of her shoes, felt around on the floor for the other — her mother sighed in her sleep, and Madeleine caught the oven clock in the moonlight. It was two minutes to twelve.

She gave up on the other shoe.

She slipped out into the street, ran through Cambridge with one bare foot, and reached the parking meter.

She scrabbled for her pen and paper.

Hey, Elliot. You there?

His reply came almost immediately.

Yep.

She wrote:

Okay, so here's what we're going to do. I'm going to totally believe in you and your Kingdom. I'm going to close my eyes and take a step forward into your Kingdom, and you do the exact same thing, and come into my World. You get it?

There were a few beats of quiet.

Won't we bump into each other?

Ha-ha. But shut up. I'm going to do it now. Get ready. Counting down from five – starting now –

Five, four — and she thought about the pieces of her day, the pieces of the World, about the ether, the *quintessence* — the impossible thing outside it all, the inexplicable other that holds everything.

Three, two — *there's no such thing; it's a magic show; it's an optical illusion; a glimpsed hallucination; it's a camera trick* —

No, it's not, it's Elliot Baranski.

One.

She closed her eyes and took a step forward.

7.

Their fingertips were touching.

Their fingers were tangling, his thumb was pressing hard against her palm.

There was the extraordinary rush of it, the warmth and buzz of each other's hands. It was like standing in the path of closing elevator doors and stepping aside just in time: the breeze of the doors still cold against your cheeks; the quiet power of an ordinary thing like a door or the touch of a hand.

Their hands curled together, sensations on sensations.

They opened their eyes.

Elliot was standing alone by the sculpture in the schoolyard.

Madeleine was standing alone in the street beside the parking meter.

It was cold — her one bare foot was chilled through — but she didn't zip up her jacket, or turn and run towards home. She stood, staring at her empty palms. Then she put her hands into her pockets, for the warmth.

PART 5

1.

After three days of travel by husky-drawn sleigh, they arrived at a notice.

LAKE OF SPELLS

None who has celebrated more than sixteen birthdays
may pass beyond this point.

"What if you celebrate your birthdays more than once?" Samuel demanded.

The travelers stood about quietly. Some studied the notice, which was nailed to a tree. Some peered beyond the tree to where the path curved and disappeared into denser, darker forest.

There was no sign of any lake.

Some looked back toward the scattered sleighs, where drivers were seeing to the dogs, servants were unloading packs, and guards were training guns at the shadows.

"What if, say, you had tea with dear friends on the *eve* of a particular birthday," Samuel persisted, "and then, upon the day of that same birthday, *held a banquet*?"

Princess Ko zipped up her jacket so it touched her chin. Keira chewed on her knuckles. Elliot arched his back and stretched his arms high. He'd been cramped against the side of the sleigh the last half hour, while the Princess slept, her head bumping up against his shoulder.

Sergio, being a stable boy, was helping the servants.

Much of their three days of travel to this point had taken them through bright white snowfields. It was true that the province seemed to murmur with danger: There had been glimpses of wild creatures, and the threat of Wandering Hostiles had been constant — in fact, there'd been two or three scuffles. But they had started out amidst festivities and photo shoots. They had passed their nights in the castles of nobility — feasting and dancing until dawn — and mostly their days had rushed and bumped along while they dozed amidst blankets, ate foil-wrapped chocolates, now and then skirting frozen lakes, streams, or wells that gleamed under the sunshine, and misted with provincial magic.

So, the mood had been mostly upbeat.

For the last several hours, however, the sleighs had been climbing into the dark woods of the foothills. The farther they had traveled into darkness, the louder the murmur of danger had sounded, and the more subdued the party had become.

So, now most of the travelers were quiet.

Princess Ko shook her head quickly, to shake away her sleepiness. Her braid flailed about, then settled into a long straight line down her back. Her sunglasses reflected the shapes of trees and a passing husky dog.

Sergio dumped a pack in the snow by Keira's feet, and she flinched.

Elliot turned to watch the Princess's security agents.

Since disembarking, the agents had been standing by the notice, talking in low, urgent voices. Now Agent Ramsay shrugged and lit a cigarette, and Agent Nettles stepped across to speak to Princess Ko.

"That can't apply to us," Agent Nettles said, waving her thumb at the notice. "The sixteen birthday thing. I think there's a Gatehouse up ahead where they check people into the Lake. I'll go get clearance or whatever. Meantime" — she raised her voice to a shout at the servants — "unload *our* packs as well, would you?"

Then she strode past the sign, took three steps along the path, flung her arms in the air, and threw herself down into the snow.

That's how it looked, anyhow.

There was a faint clanging like the distant echo of metal trash-can lids.

"Oh, come *on*." Agent Nettles spoke from the ground through a mouthful of snow. She scrambled to her feet and walked forward again. This time, it was as if someone had shoved her hard in the stomach. *"Oof!"* she cried, arching forward, stumbling, and falling back to the snow. The clanging sounded again.

A servant paused, holding a pack. "They've got a protective shield around the Lake of Spells," he called. "It's new. To keep out dragons and vampires. And adults."

Agent Ramsay laughed. "All in the same category." He slid along the path, held his cigarette aside, and offered his hand to Agent Nettles.

She stood shivering so that pieces of snow slipped from her clothing. "There must be a way around."

Agent Ramsay stepped off the path, moved forward tentatively, and clanged with a thud into the snow.

"There's no way around," called Keira.

She was pointing, moving her hand slowly through the air, staring hard as she did so. Then she raised her arm higher, and pointed again.

"It goes up and over," she said. "Like a dome."

"You can see it?" cried Samuel, looking around wildly. "I can't see a thing!"

"She's a Night-Dweller," Princess Ko reminded him. "A *Jagged-Edgian* Night-Dweller. They have that vision thing."

"And how is it like, this dome?" Sergio gazed at Keira, his eyes even brighter than usual. "It is beautiful?"

Keira shrugged. "Depends on your taste, I guess."

The agents looked at each other.

"We can't let you go in there alone." Agent Ramsay tapped the end of his cigarette. A little tumble of fire and ash spilled to the snow, sparked and disappeared. "That was never the plan."

"It was *my* plan!" Princess Ko's leg twitched as if she was about to stamp it. She calmed her voice. "Look, if the shield stops dangerous things getting in, then it'll stop weapons too! We'll be perfectly safe! Nobody will recognize me!"

"Plenty of ways to kill a person without a weapon," Agent Ramsay murmured.

"*I* will protect her," Sergio declared. "Nobody must harm Princess Ko while I am the living!"

The agents ignored him.

"Why aren't adults allowed in anyhow?" Agent Nettles asked, still brushing snow away.

"It's because adults taint the magic with their cynicism," Keira explained, her own voice so loaded with cynicism that everybody paused, reflecting.

"As to a peppertree in monkeygrip," murmured Samuel.

"Come on, then." The Princess picked up her pack, sliding her arms through the straps. The others hesitated, but she waved at them impatiently, so they did the same.

"We'll meet you here at noon four days from now. Take the party back to the Teasel Castle and rest up until then."

Then, as the agents faltered and the guards and servants watched, Princess Ko led the members of the Royal Youth Alliance past the notice, down the path, and around the curve into darkness.

2.

At the Lake of Spells, it was summer.

They were walking to their campsite in single file, half dragging their jackets off as they walked, spilling their gloves, pulling off their hats, the straps of their backpacks slipping, iceboxes thumping against their hips, eyes wide, confused, self-conscious, and all of them getting that gathering sense.

That billowing sense. That drumbeat sense, blaring-trumpet sense — that this place was one giant party.

It was late afternoon.

They had walked an hour to reach the Gatehouse and paid their entrance fees to a skinny kid, baseball cap shadowing his eyes. He had allocated them a campsite, handed over their official iceboxes, along with keys to the washroom facilities. He'd pointed out the convenience counter where you could purchase basic provisions like milk, juice, and toothpaste; and the cubicle where the Compendium of Spells was kept. He'd explained the Compendium's classification system, and the time limits on its use.

And he'd told them the Rules of the Lake.

1. *You may leave the Lake with no more than THREE spells apiece.*

The iceboxes had three separate compartments, one for each spell. Five mini-spells counted as one ordinary spell, but most people thought the mini-spells were just about useless, so, you know, that was up to them.

2. *While staying at the Lake, you can catch, use, and trade whatever spells you like — but NOT the monster spells.*

Those were the shark-size and bigger shadows they'd maybe get glimpses of, deep in the center of the Lake. Not that they'd even come *close* to catching one, but it was dangerous, even to try, for anyone but experienced spellfishers. In fact, it was a monster spell that had made the protective shield around the Lake.

3. *It is not permitted to interfere with wildlife in the Lake.*

That especially applied to the beaver dam. It was lined with spells. As tempting as it might be to grab one, they should stay well clear of that beaver dam.

4. *No flash photography.*

It disturbs the spells.

They had walked out of the Gatehouse, their foreheads lined with the boy's ominous tone — and the complicated warnings he'd layered on top of the rules as he chewed his pinkie nail — Princess Ko angry about the limitation on the number of spells that could leave the Lake, Samuel fretting about what might happen if you inad*vertently* trapped a monster spell, Sergio trying to force good cheer by springing along like a small deer, Keira swearing that if Sergio kept up the springy deer thing she was going to take him down with her bare hands, and adding that the kid in the Gatehouse was a Farms boy like Elliot, only with an even stronger Farms accent, if that was possible, Elliot trying to figure out what Keira's point was —

But now, as they walked along the shore of the Lake into the summer, the rules and worries seemed to break into pieces: falling away with their hats and scarves, while everything turned to amazement.

This place was not just a party, it was a *dazzle* of a party. The sun was still strong on the water, a jetty shot out into the sparkles, kids were dive bombing or floating in circles, gliding by in canoes, racing one another in kayaks. Here and there were gatherings of quieter rowboats, the sun catching pieces of fishing line. On the shore, tables were set out for fishing-gear rental, and boat rental, and spell trading, all amidst an urgency of tents, music, and laughter. Kids, mostly around fourteen or fifteen, it seemed, were kicking back in deckchairs, strumming guitars, dancing, running toward or away from one another, high-fiving, grabbing one another by the upper arm to point out one thing or another, talking fast, making plans, waving their hands around, talking with their mouths full, tipping drink bottles so high the liquid spilled down their chins.

There were kids holding hands, or making out, and they passed two kids spinning in a circle, hands on each other's elbows, faster and faster, their spin losing control so that they crashed into the Lake with a double shriek of laughter.

The more they saw the faster and lighter they walked, all of them overcome with a sudden urgency to dump their packs, set themselves up, change out of these winter clothes, and disappear into this frenzy.

They got the tents erected fast, working together as if there had never been a moment of tension, irritability, or outright hostility between them. They changed into summer clothes, emerged, and glanced at one another. Princess Ko, in shorts, tank top, and sunglasses, looked like any other pretty blonde. Kids walked by, glanced at the new group, and carried on. If they noticed anything it was Samuel, not the Princess of the Kingdom. Samuel wore his knickerbockers, vest, and sailor's hat.

"You really have to wear that?" Keira asked, pointing at the hat, and Samuel's face registered confusion and mild despair.

"As to a sticky dove in —"

"Forget about it." Keira turned away. "You look fine."

Just along the Lake, a crowd was forming: Kids seemed to be doing some kind of gymnastics.

"It's the firelight spells," Elliot realized. He'd read a lot about the Lake of Spells, back when he'd planned his own trip here. "There's supposed to be a stand of cedars where they grow, so I'm guessing that's it. The idea is, you catch a bunch of them before it gets dark so you can light your campfire."

"Why not just use matches?" Samuel asked.

The others were already heading to the cedars, and Elliot called back over his shoulder, "I don't think matches are allowed."

They watched the other kids awhile, trying to figure out the trick. The firelight spells grew in clusters among the overhanging branches, and it turned out that climbing the trees was not an option. Elliot remembered that the spells burrowed deep into the bark if anybody straddled a branch.

A group of kids nearby explained: "What you have to do is, you have to run up this slope here, leap into the air, swiveling as you do, reach out, grasp, twist, pluck, and land." They mimed each move as they talked, arguing among themselves over how the swivel should look. Then one kid said, "Wait. We'll demonstrate," and pelted up the slope toward the trees. His friends joined him.

They watched, and it was more or less as the kids had described. Everyone was doing this run-leap-grab thing. Now and then someone would catch a spell, although mostly they seemed to land empty-handed.

Abruptly Sergio ran, leapt into the air, half swiveled, and crashed face-first onto the ground. He hadn't come close to touching a branch. He raised his head, looked back down at the others, his grin glowing white in his dirt-blackened face, and shouted: "These spells, they are the beautiful impossible!"

Soon all of them were running. They jumped, twisted, reached, grabbed, swore, and tried it again. They paused and checked out what other kids were doing, imitated them, gave up, and returned to their own methods. They tried springing from standing positions. Elliot was the most proficient, but Samuel was the first to actually catch one, and his elation verged on insanity. The others laughed but grew fierce with competitiveness. They ran harder, jumped higher, grabbed more ferociously, only stopping to reconsider strategies, or study which trees seemed angled best.

Over and over they crash-landed, until they were smeared with dirt, and sweating so much that the dirt turned to streaks of mud.

They took turns wading out into the Lake to cool down. The water was fresh and cold, touched with ice on the surface but shot through with warm currents. The first time Elliot swam, he caught sight of schools of darting spells skimming across the surface. Who knew what they *did*, these spells, but they'd be dead easy to catch. You could just hold out your palms as they passed. You couldn't *avoid* getting a few.

Which, it turned out, was not true. They slipped between his fingers no matter what he did or how he held his palms, or pressed his fingers, or angled his body, until he realized that they were, as Sergio might say: the beautiful impossible.

Two hours later they were heading back to the campsite, wet, bedraggled, exhausted, jubilant. Sergio was limping a little from a sprained ankle, Keira was walking at a tilt on account of a pulled muscle in her side, and all of them were cupping their hands to hold their stashes of firelight spells. The light was dimming now, the Lake awash with shadows, and the firelight spells glowed faintly in their casings.

Elliot, it turned out, had gathered the most. The others praised him for this but then Ko remembered that he was a deftball champion back home, so that gave him an unfair advantage. They immediately withdrew their congratulations and asked why he hadn't got more. He took this with good grace. They talked and laughed all at once, their stories crossing paths in the air, and turned out they'd *all* had Elliot's secret experience of noticing those schools of darting spells, and imagining they'd catch them by the handful.

Back at the campsite, Princess Ko turned regal, instructing Sergio and Keira to go to the trading tables, to see if they could trade some of their firelight spells for various other supplies, including those sweet mallow treats that you wrapped in the leaves of the maplewood and roasted on the fire. She assigned herself and Samuel the task of collecting firewood and getting the fire lit and the evening meal under way. She had something in mind for Elliot too but he interrupted to ask if he could head back to the Gatehouse first, to consult the Compendium of Spells.

"And I'll get some measurements done too," he said, reaching into his pack and drawing out measuring tape and compass.

The others stared at him.

"It's for the book," he explained. "*Spell Fishing: Tips and Techniques for Netting the Spell You Desire*? The one that tells us how we catch the Locator Spell."

He paused, and watched as the memory of why they were here rippled right across the others' faces.

"Right," said Ko abruptly, and she turned to Sergio and Keira. "While you're at the trading tables, see if you can get us some kind of a privacy spell. You can cut back on the supplies I wanted. Who needs an insect repellant spell? We can *buy* that in a *can* from the store."

She looked at her wristwatch, squinting hard in the fading light.

"After we eat," she said, "a meeting. I want to hear reports on your achievements." She stamped her foot hard on the spot then looked up, startled. "And obviously," she murmured, "while you're at the trading tables, *check* that they don't have any Locator Spells."

3.

Samuel was the first to report.

They were in Princess Ko's tent, which was the largest, but still small enough to feel overcrowded once five of them had formed a circle among the pillows, rugs, and sleeping bags. The moonlight shone golden through the canvas, but the Seclusion Spell shut out the party noise of the Lake, so it was eerily quiet. Sergio had traded ten firelight spells for this: It offered one hour of total privacy.

"Here in my trembling hands," began Samuel, "as to a scuttling clawfish in a sack of tomatoes, I hold a collection of index cards, much as the turtle takes its —"

"Stick to the facts," Princess Ko commanded.

Samuel's trembling hands now shook so violently that his collection of index cards fanned and spilled.

"Oh, say it how you want," sighed the Princess.

"I will endeavor," Samuel quavered, "to reduce my Olde-Quaintian embellishments as to a — yes. These are index cards I have compiled, based on the accounts told by travelers — both Cellians and Worldians — as to a . . . Sorry. Accounts of their journeys betwixt hither and thither. Call yourselves an example here, in the tale of Patrick Kelleher, cobbler, of County —"

"Go back a step," the Princess interrupted. "What journeys? *When* were these journeys? *Why* were there journeys betwixt or whatever?"

Samuel's cheeks wobbled. He took a breath and began again.

"The brief history of World-Cello interaction," he declared, "is as follows: Our earliest records date from the Age of Interspersing. At that time there was much movement to and fro between Cello and the World, particularly from a place in the World known as *Ancient Greece.* At the time it was not thus known. Indeed, what land would call itself ancient when still fresh? But, forgive me. At that time, the ebb and flow was constant. Seamless. People knew the precise geometric locations of the cracks and used the secret technique to open them and pass through. Cellians went to the World. They enjoyed theater, hunted, feasted, played knucklebones, and consulted with wise and philosophical men with such names as Democrates, Plato, and

Socrates. In turn, Worldians visited Cello, seeking out the Cello Wind, marveling at our Cat Walk, at the technology of Jagged Edge, the baking of the Farms, and consulting with *our* wise folk: Ella of Ye Gawyn, Bartholomew the Great, Penelope . . ." Samuel's eyes turned dreamy.

"And this carried on until the World gave us the plague?" Elliot prompted.

"No. It was stopped long before that. The World closed the cracks. Some kind of religious fervor took hold. Cello became associated with heresy and witchcraft. Contact with our Kingdom met with severe punishment. I understand the World then entered a period called the Dark Ages. Much later, in the sixteen hundreds, certain cracks were rediscovered in parts of the World, especially Italy and England, and *those* were used in secret by certain Worldians, especially a group of English scientists known as the Royal Society. Here in Cello, the Illustrious Institute for Harmonious and Mutually Beneficial Relations between Cello and the World (or the Harmony Institute) was established, and Worldian visitors were welcomed. Friendships were forged, ideas and experiments shared, and accounts of journeys between our worlds were recorded.

"This ended, abruptly, with the plague: It slipped through the cracks from the World into Cello. Our Winds blew it away before much life was lost, but it spread across many Kingdoms and Empires — including, famously, Aldhibah, precipitating the 200 Year War and being indirectly responsible for the hostilities that have flared between our kingdoms ever since, the loss of millions of Cellian and Aldhian lives, and recent border skirmishes and tensions. Cello had no choice but to seal off the cracks. The Harmony Institute was shut down, the WSU established, and two more contrasting organizations could not be imagined."

Samuel bowed slightly, to signal that his recitation had concluded.

"But here," he remembered, "are my index cards, detailing the recorded accounts of journeys from the archives of the Harmony Institute."

"Give them to Elliot," Princess Ko instructed. "They might help him figure out how to open up the crack. Okay, thank you, Samuel. That was informative. But I assume you know nothing about how to *see* the cracks, or about what the 'secret technique' is for getting through them?"

"Call yourself the truth of your assumption," Samuel agreed. "I know naught. But do you know of the Stumblers?"

"The Stumblers?"

"Very rarely, people in both Cello and the World have been known to *stumble* through a crack into the other place. Obviously they do this without using any kind of secret techniques. But there have been no reports of stumbling for several centuries."

"Interesting. But not particularly helpful."

"No," Samuel agreed.

The Princess turned to Keira, who was sitting beside Samuel. "Keira?"

Keira blinked.

"I went through six boxes of code," she said. "Cellian weather statistics. I took notes. Should I read them?"

Princess Ko shook her head. "Sergio?" She turned to Sergio, while the others looked from Ko to Keira and back again, and Keira herself narrowed her eyes, then smiled in a tight, complicated way.

Sergio launched into a flamboyant account of his new job as junior administrative clerk at the World Severance Unit.

It turned out he was in human resources, mostly filing documents, which were beautiful in their fascination. Not always. Sometimes they killed him with their desperate absence of reason for him to be the living. Figures, percentages, rules. These were things Sergio had never found beautiful. "But! The application by Raymond Kiriaki for funding for a two-day conference in Nature Strip on workplace presentations! Interesting! Because Raymond spent five percent of his worktime *doing* presentations. So where was his justification?! Although, there had been disagreement. Helena was of the thinking that it was more likely seven percent, and Jakobski put it closer to four point five —"

"Who are Helena and Jakobski?" asked Princess Ko, frowning.

"Helena is my immediate supervisor," Sergio explained. "She has the photos of her dogs on the corkboard of the cubicle. Did you know of these boards of cork? Beautiful! You have the photos, you have the reminders, you have the small jokes, and the beautiful pictures of the rivers with the trees reflecting to give the inspiring. Beautiful. And Jakobski, he is regional manager, HR — so he is the boss of Helena's boss — and he came to work with the white cotton wool in one of his nostrils the one day! Beautiful! In the hilarious sense. There was the speculating about —"

"Sergio." Princess Ko's frown was deepening. "Is this relevant?"

Sergio looked surprised.

"Strange, no?" He scratched his forehead, his voice turning philosophical. "I am working at the WSU but I am hearing *nothing* of the World."

"Maybe you should listen harder," Keira pointed out.

"But . . ." Sergio's tone remained thoughtful. "I have seen the files of the Enforcement team, and they are, how do you say? Trained. Former military mostly, and former police, former intelligence. They have the training in the hand-to-hand combat, in the sharp shooting, in the assassination. Everything. So much training that their files are as fat as Samuel's cheeks."

He said this with such a fond smile at Samuel that Samuel blushed proudly.

"Well, we knew that." Princess Ko fluttered her fingers, the way she did when Sergio grew too theatrical. "When you go back, focus less on Raymond Kiriaki's conferences, and more on getting a crack detector. Or on anything vaguely related to the World. Speaking of the World . . . Elliot?"

Elliot was caught in Sergio's gaze. He had to shift to get out from it.

"Okay." He turned to the Princess. "It might not sound like much, but Madeleine and I had a breakthrough. The night before I left for this trip."

They all waited, interested.

"It was — well."

He stopped. He didn't know how to say this. Words couldn't match up with the event. *It might not sound like much*, he'd said, but he needed to convey that it was, in fact, much.

"Okay, what you have to understand —"

He stopped again. Now he had this unexpected feeling that it was *private.* He didn't *want* to tell them. It was between him and Madeleine, wasn't it?

That made no sense.

"I touched her hand," he admitted. "We believed in each other for a moment, and then suddenly our hands were intertwined."

"And then?" said Princess Ko.

"Then she was gone. It was only for a moment. My eyes were closed."

"You closed your *eyes*?"

"Well, it just . . ."

"You did this by *believing*?" Keira spoke in a voice that could wither the Ancient and Enduring Forests of Nature Strip.

"You touched *hands* with a girl in the World!" exclaimed Samuel. "You reached *through* a letter-size crack and touched her *hand*?! But it's impossible!"

Elliot looked at Samuel and felt, for the first time, mild affection. The kid was the only one reacting appropriately.

"Imagine what Enforcement at the WSU would do if they knew this," Sergio reflected. "It would not be beautiful."

"Ah, you already made that point." Elliot was getting impatient.

"And what am I supposed to do when we find my family?" Princess Ko's tone echoed Keira's. "Touch my sister's *hand*? Tremendously helpful, I'm sure. I'll tell the King of Aldhibah that my father cannot actually *attend* the namesaking ceremony of his first and only son, but 'Here!' I'll say, "Why not hold his *fingertips a moment*?!' Truly a sparklespin of whirlshine, Elliot."

"But, I think —" began Samuel, then stopped in tremendous confusion. Supporting Elliot would mean disagreeing with the Princess. What to do?

"Oh, never mind." Princess Ko sighed. "Continue working, Elliot. You will, I trust, take greater strides over the coming days."

Elliot smiled. "Sure," he shrugged. "Oh, yeah, and Madeleine sent me those maps of the world you wanted."

He offered a pile of papers, but the Princess nodded toward Samuel.

"Give them to him," she commanded. "Samuel was to determine where my family emerged in the world, according to the location of their disappearance. He can update his findings using these modern maps. Samuel?"

There was a stillness from Samuel: the sort that draws attention. They turned to him and his face had assumed its familiar anguished dismay.

"Honestly," said the Princess, "between you and Sergio we could open a dramatic society. What *is* the matter, Samuel?"

"Did I not mention?" Samuel murmured. "A rather important omission, I suppose. As to a fig leaf wrapped in wire. I'm afraid I was not *able* to determine where your family would have emerged."

"Why not?" snapped the Princess. "What's *wrong* with you?"

"It's a wrongness of geography, although my own flaws are certainly manifold, as to —" Samuel stopped himself. "There is no *pattern*, you see, to the links between Cello and the World. Consider this. Elliot has found a crack in Bonfire, the Farms, which leads to a city called Cambridge, England. Am I correct, Elliot?"

Elliot nodded.

"Call yourselves my apologies, dear friends," he continued, "but another crack, one town away from Bonfire, say, could lead to a city on the *entire* other side of the World. There is a *randomness*, you see, to how cracks connect here to there. The only way to tell where your family arrived in the World would be if any of the accounts I collected happened to match the exact royal crossover points."

They all looked at Samuel's index cards.

"As to which," he added, "they do not."

"A rather important omission," Keira murmured.

4.

"Nonsense!"

Princess Ko clapped her hands three times. "This is of no consequence! It *might* have been useful to know where they had emerged in the World, but what of it? Did they go through to the World and then sit patiently by the crack? Are they still there a year and a half later? Hardly! All that matters is where they are *now*!"

"It might become an issue," Keira pointed out, "if we find an address for them in the World. We'd want a crack here in Cello that matches the point in the World where they are, so we could bring them back through directly, but —"

Princess Ko spoke over her.

"We are here to find a Locator Spell," she said. "By my calculations we have twenty minutes before our Seclusion Spell expires. Accordingly, we need to refresh ourselves with a mallow treat and hot chocolate while Elliot explains this *Spell Fishing* book of his."

She handed around cups, poured chocolate from a thermos flask, and placed the basket of roasted mallow treats in the center of their circle.

"Right!" said Princess Ko. "Elliot?"

Elliot had brought the book into the tent with him. He picked it up now, felt the cool softness of the cover, and studied the title page.

Here it was. The book he'd found months before in the Bonfire Library. That exquisite surge of hope he'd felt when he first leafed through its pages. Everyone he knew had shaken their heads, dismissive, contemptuous, sympathetic: *It can't be done; the book's a crock; the book's a cheat; that book's a load of —*

He'd ignored them all, studied this book late into the night. He'd believed in it — until he hadn't.

It had been part of his own desperation. It had turned itself into itself right before his eyes — a self-delusion, a load of trash.

Yet here they were at the Lake of Spells, and this book had brought them here. He had no choice. He'd have to see this through.

They waited, watching him, slurping their chocolate.

He explained the book.

Its central premise, he said, had to do with the symbols that appeared on the casings of spells. Symbols, as they knew, were unique, although they fell into certain categories.

The book recommended a procedure. First, you found the symbol of the spell you wanted. Next, you took certain measurements and ratios from the symbols, and applied those to the layout of the Lake itself.

"I don't understand," said Samuel.

"It's coordinate geometry," Elliot explained. "I can show you the charts in the book — it's simple. Well, once you've read it thirty, forty times, it's simple enough. Anyhow, I've done that part. I've found what the book calls the Precise Spot."

"The Precise Spot?" Princess Ko repeated.

The Precise Spot was the place where the spell was most likely to be caught. You fished from that spot. You didn't move from it. You could tag-team if you wanted — the book suggested teams fish in shifts, day and night.

Each member of the team should study the symbol of the desired spell until it was imprinted on his or her mind. Each should transfix him or herself with the symbol. Believe in it with his or her whole being. The symbol should be marked on the forehead of each team member. Each should allow the symbol to affect his or her mood, carriage, posture, hair —

"Hair?"

That was Keira. As Elliot had been speaking, he'd found himself avoiding her eyes. He'd looked at the others, seen them nod occasionally, maybe slight frowns of confusion, but mostly attentive and concentrating, carried along by his words.

Except for Keira. Even without looking at her, he'd sensed something growing, something gathering in her.

Now she unleashed it.

"Are you insane?" she said. "You don't honestly think this is real, do you? This is a *self-help* book! The *worst* kind of self-help book! *Believe* in the symbol? *Transfix* yourself with the symbol? Allow the symbol to affect your *hair*?"

Everyone began to speak at once. They shifted to be heard, their voices rising higher, and somebody knocked over the basket of mallows. These began to slip into the folds of the sleeping bags.

"I see your point," Elliot began, "but . . ."

"Take no notice of Keira," Princess Ko commanded. "Continue!"

"The others hereabouts will certain jeer at us," Samuel fretted. "If we mark ourselves — our foreheads — with a symbol."

"It's not just abstract ideas," Elliot said. "It's got the mathematical part. . . ."

"Of course it does," Keira blazed. "That's what self-help books *do*. They build illusions on foundations of pseudoscience. *Mathematics*. Give me a break! I guarantee I could take that *mathematics* to pieces before Samuel takes another one of those quivering breaths of his. My *dog* could take it to pieces. I bet it cites authorities in footnotes, right?"

Elliot scratched his head. On the one hand, he actually agreed with Keira. On the other hand, as he'd been explaining the book, he'd been taken right back to the time when it had held his heart: when it had seemed like the chain link that would lead him to his father. Now he had this crazy sense that he should defend the book out of loyalty to his former self.

Out of loyalty, even more weirdly, to his father.

"Well, footnotes, yeah —" he began.

"I thought so. Have you actually *followed up* on any of these references? Of course not. If you did, you'd find they were a crock. I've gotta say, I thought self-help books was *one* failing the Farms didn't have, but nope, they've got that too."

"It was sounding perfectly sensible to me," the Princess cried. "Keira, you will desist from this outrage."

"Well, it *would*!" Keira spat. "It *would* sound sensible to you."

At this point, Sergio's voice seemed to pour out, low and thoughtful, from somewhere just beneath the frenzy.

"How can we be knowing," he mused, "until we try? We will start. *I* will draw the symbols on the foreheads. Elliot, you will show me the symbol. You will show me the — how did you call it? — *Precise Spot* on the shore. I will have the symbol *imprinted* on my heart and on my mind, and then I will take the shift at this spot. We will all take the shifts."

Princess Ko straightened; at the same time, Keira slumped.

"Oh, suit yourselves," Keira said. "Whatever."

"Well." Elliot tried to figure out how to say this. "The book says we should start at four A.M."

"No matter," declared Sergio. "I will *take* the shift."

Keira's voice was flat.

"I'll take it," she said. "I'm a Night-Dweller, remember?" She gazed at the others, her contempt so palpable that it almost seemed that it was this that snapped open the silence a moment later, when the chaos of the Lake rushed back into the tent.

The Seclusion Spell had expired. The meeting was done.

5.

Tricky to stay fierce or moody at the Lake of Spells.

Everyone else was there to catch spells and have fun, and these shiny goals overlapped and interwove. There were no adults. Kids from across the Kingdom had saved for months or years to get here. Now they were sharing secrets, playing music, eating junk food, watching stars, and hooking up. They were tying ropes to trees so they could swing out over the Lake and land themselves a splash spell. They were panning, drumming, chanting, meditating, and fly-fishing for spells. A group of kids from Golden Coast had heard that an effective technique was to disguise themselves as giant spiders and crawl around the edges of the Lake. Another group, from Jagged Edge, had rigged up a hologrammatic net. (The spells were slipping right through it.) A youth band from Olde Quainte waded fully-clothed into the Lake up to their necks, held their instruments high, and played a rousing jig for the spells.

Local kids who came here every other weekend laughed until they wept, after which they stopped and scooped up armloads of spells.

The members of the Royal Youth Alliance lightened up.

They drew the symbol of the Locator Spell on their foreheads and they fit right in with the madness. They took turns fishing from the Precise Spot — a quiet corner of the Lake, not far from the beaver dam — and they also took shifts monitoring the trading tables. You never knew. A Locator Spell might turn up there. A couple of locals told them this was unlikely — those Locator Spells were rare, they said, and anyone who caught one would likely take it with them. If not, they'd need a *truckload* of spells to trade for it. So they fished, climbed, dove, and dug for spells — for *any* spells — for *truckloads* of spells — ready to trade if they had to. And because it was fun.

Three days passed.

They had each become adept at catching firelight spells. Each had filled their icebox with spells. Keira had a punctuality spell, a spell to ease a sore throat, and one to help you dance tango.

Samuel had gathered spells to find lost magnets and to entertain fractious children, along with an impressively large spell that would heat a small wooden cabin.

Sergio had had the most luck with the Household Spells: His would stop sliced apples from turning brown, get fingerprints off glass, and unclog a pepper grinder.

Princess Ko was considering trading in her spells: She had one to increase her typing speed (she was already superfast), to shine shoes (people did that for her), and to curl hair (she liked hers straight). She'd been hopeful at first that this last one might be one of the rare metaphoric spells — so she could use it in the sense of frightening people rather than *literally* curling hair — but no, it just curled hair.

Elliot, meanwhile, had caught a spell to conjure the scent of vanilla, a clear-away spell (which he thought he'd give to Corrie-Lynn, since her least favorite part of woodwork was clearing up), and a spell to take up the hem of a short tartan skirt. ("While a hot girl is wearing it?" Elliot asked, and Keira said, "Ha ha, Farms boy.")

They had learned to tell the difference between strong spells with casings as hard as oyster shells, and fragile spells which died quickly once caught. They knew that the mini-spells — the ones you could scrape from the underside of rocks or leaves — were more trouble than they were worth. Sure, those spells might scratch an itch, untangle a simple knot, give you a boiled sweet, but they kept getting caught under your fingernails. May as well scratch the itch yourself.

They'd learned to shake spells out of their shoes at night, and to brush them from their sleeping bags. They'd all given up on trying for the darting schools of spells, but none could quite give up on the impossibly pretty star-shaped spells that clustered around the twigs and blooms of the willows, birch, and crab apples.

On the third day, around seven P.M., the weather changed.

It had been summer since they arrived, but now Elliot felt chill and damp touching his sunburned skin. He grabbed his jacket and his icebox. It was his turn to fish for the Locator Spell.

Activity never really stopped at the Lake — some kids swore that night fishing got the best results, although this was controversial — but the mood did soften at twilight. Elliot passed circles of conversations around campfires, accents transforming as he walked, from the fluting lyricism of Magical North to the chains-dragging-through-gravel of those from Nature Strip. Mostly people were arguing over bait (water baits, spinner baits, minnows, dragon scales), location (lily pads, logs, rocks, weed beds), technique ("Choose a spot and stay," someone declared; "If you don't get any bites after three or four casts, move on!" his friend replied), and equipment ("I like a float made of porcupine quills," said a girl of maybe eight).

At the Precise Spot, he found Samuel swaying slightly in a doze. The rod was propped in his lap. An empty basket, a tin cup, and an icebox sat by his side.

"Call yourself a good evening from me!" Samuel exclaimed, waking abruptly when Elliot touched his shoulder. "See here what Princess Ko provided for me? This cup of ice chips, to wet my thirst in the afternoon sun. Although," he shivered, and scanned the graying sky, "winter comes apace. Your night will be chill."

Elliot sat beside Samuel, took ahold of the rod, and they effected the smooth transition one from the other.

Samuel remained where he was, gazing about him.

"It is our last night," he said, eventually, "and I fear . . ."

"I fear it too," Elliot agreed. "And I fear the guilt's doing me in. Should never have brought us all here. Been fun, though," he added.

"It has indeed." Samuel grew solemn with the weight of this revelation. "The greatest fun I have had perhaps in *years*. The magic *here* is so pure, so delightful!"

Elliot looked at him sideways.

"Magic in Olde Quainte's a whole other story?"

Samuel stirred himself, and nodded once.

"As you no doubt know, the magic in my province is naught but curses and wishes," he said, "and the wishes so tightly bound they will slice open your flesh." He stood, but remained where he was, just behind Elliot, swinging his icebox slightly. He touched Elliot's own icebox with his foot.

"We have each caught our quota of three spells," he said. "Where will we put the Locator Spell if we catch it?"

Seemed no point answering that. The line twitched, and Elliot jerked the rod, and reeled it in. Nothing. Samuel let out his breath, and watched as Elliot rebaited and cast out again.

"There are those who believe they have learned to control it," Samuel said, and Elliot tried to figure out what he meant. "But it turns on them. Always it turns on them, and they find themselves enchained — malformed — their limbs torn asunder."

Ah, he was back on the magic of Olde Quainte. Elliot glanced up at the boy. A dark shape against the dimming sky.

"The blackflies are biting," Samuel added, more cheerfully. "They have drawn blood!" He reached around to the back of his neck, and held out his fingertip to show Elliot. Couldn't see much in this light, but Elliot made a sympathetic noise anyway.

"Have to get that cleared up before we leave tomorrow," Elliot said. "You don't want to be bleeding when we're heading through vampire territory."

"At least this wintry air will quiet the insects," Samuel said. "At what hour does your shift conclude, my friend?"

"Midnight."

"Who replaces you?"

"The Princess, I think."

"Ah, Princess Ko," Samuel sighed, sitting down again. "She has done her best, has she not? As to a teacup in a quagmire. Her enthusiasm has not waned in the face of utter, abject failure. Which some may call a fine thing, others idiocy. I have seen her study the symbol until it must be imprinted on her eyeballs." He touched his own forehead, where the marks were smudged. "I have seen her sketch it in the dust with sticks; draw it on the surface of the water with her fingtertip."

Elliot was silent. In the three days they'd been here there'd hardly been a nibble. He looked over the darkness of the water.

"That Keira on the other hand," Samuel added. "*She* has scarcely noted the symbol. She is so caught up in her own fierceness! As to a tigress in the presence of a threat to her cubs!"

"Ah, Keira's all right," Elliot shrugged. "You can't blame her for finding this whole thing a waste of time. I kind of do myself." He reflected a moment. "Samuel," he said, "that might be the first time one of your similes has actually worked."

Samuel ignored this. "She does mock and taunt *your* province, Elliot," he frowned. "Does it not irk you?"

Elliot shrugged again. "Don't suppose the Farms needs Keira's approval."

"Call yourself this. Have you any clue as to *why* Keira so despises the Princess? The strangest tension zings back and forth between them, does it not?"

"It does. And no clue at all."

"They are both strong-willed, beautiful girls whose names begin with *K*," Samuel noted wryly. "Perhaps that is all there is to it."

Elliot laughed, surprised. "And that might be the first time I've heard you make a joke," he said.

Samuel was silent, gazing over the water. Maybe it hadn't been a joke.

But abruptly he chuckled and stood. He rested a hand on Elliot's shoulder as he did so.

"When we leave empty-handed on the morrow," he said, "I only hope the Princess can bear it."

Elliot nodded. That thought had occurred to him too.

"Stay warm," Samuel said, and then: "I have caught many extra spells today — I will trade them for blankets for you anon, and bring these back. What say you?"

"That'd be much appreciated," Elliot said.

He watched as Samuel turned and paused briefly. Then the boy straightened his shoulders, and marched away among the campfires. He seemed, Elliot thought, both very young and very old.

6.

Someone woke Elliot with a sharp double hit on his leg, and he'd already felt for his jacket and boots, dragged them on, and pushed his way out of the tent into the night, before he'd even thought to wonder what was happening.

Keira and Samuel were out there already, underneath the ice-cold moonlight. They were huddled into themselves, coats over pajamas. Turned out it was Sergio who'd woken them. His face had a sidelong panic to it, and he was jumping foot to foot. "She thinks she's got it," he was saying, hoarse and urgent, "Come! She thinks she's got it!"

They followed him at an awkward jog through the deep dark and quiet, stumbling over roots and tent pegs. Elliot was keeping pace but found himself slowing as his thoughts began to wake: *If she's caught it, great! But let's talk in the morning.*

They reached Princess Ko. She was crouched on the bank, a lantern lighting up the strands of hair that had fallen from her braid. They couldn't figure out what she was doing. There was a frantic sort of fierceness to the hunch of her shoulders, and her hands were clutching at something, but it was too dark to make out what.

"It's down there," she said as they reached her. She didn't look up at them but tilted her chin toward the black water surface. "It's tangled in the pondweed."

They gathered around her, trying to peer into the water themselves, but she snapped, "Get ahold of this, everyone, and help me pull it out!"

They shifted closer to her and now they saw the length of pondweed roping from the water and into Ko's hands. It was thick as a sapling trunk.

"Get ahold of it," she repeated, and her words became a groan as she gave a great yank, and more of the pondweed slithered from the lake. She stumbled back.

They lined up behind her, each reaching for the weed. It was matted with old leaves and algae, ice-cold, moist with slime. Samuel touched it, squealed, and leapt back. He murmured an apology which included the words *shame* and *mortification*, then reached for it again.

"Just hang on," the Princess said, breathless. "Now and then it loosens up a bit, and then we pull — when I say *go* we all — okay, *go*."

They tugged hard, and the weed resisted a moment, then slid slowly from the water, up over the bank with a slick, thick, glugging sound.

"Too fast!"

They slowed.

"Like this," she said, and they leaned around one another's shoulders to watch how the Princess placed hand over hand, steady and slow, as if climbing up a rope.

They copied her. Lined up behind the Princess, they fell into a rhythm. Sergio, at the end of their line, let the pondweed coil onto the ground beside him.

After a moment, it snagged.

"Now stop," said the Princess.

Keira lifted her hands away

"But don't let go! Wait. Wait. Now start again."

So they did.

They pulled and pulled and the coil of pondweed grew steadily higher behind them. Every few moments it stopped abruptly and they paused and then began again. They worked silently. It began raining, ice-cold darts hitting their foreheads, cheeks, and necks.

"How *long* is this thing?" Keira asked once. Nobody replied.

The Lake itself was quiet. The trading tables were covered, fishing-gear kiosk closed. Across the way a small group of people stood about at the boat rental, talking in low murmurs. Somebody kicked the side of a kayak and it rocked slightly, then settled again. There were four or five rowboats out on the water. You could see kids rugged up out there, some leaning down with nets, or holding fishing lines, and fragments of quiet conversations drifted over.

The pondweed continued to slide out of the Lake. Now and then they'd see a spell caught up in the weed, but this would spill back into the water, or wriggle its way into the fiber of the weed itself.

An hour passed. There was a palpable shift in the weather, as if somebody had cranked it up a notch. The rain hardened abruptly, turning to splinters of ice. Their hands were chafing, aching on the cold of the weed. The mud was growing slick, so it was harder to grip. Elliot looked down at his skidding boots and realized that Samuel, behind him, had bare feet.

"What are we doing?" Elliot said suddenly.

Princess Ko ignored him. "Wait," she said. "Stop again. Stop. Okay, start." The coils of pondweed had formed a shoulder high pile and was beginning to slip sideways. Sergio tried to straighten it with one hand.

They were half asleep with night and cold; it was as if they had forgotten how to think.

"What are we doing?" Elliot repeated. "Listen to me. What are we *doing*?"

"It's down there," Princess Ko said. "The Locator Spell. I saw it."

"When?"

"Back. I saw it — wait, stop — now start again." She wrenched hard, then got into hand-over-hand rhythm again. "I don't know. A few hours ago."

"A few hours ago," Elliot repeated. "You got a glimpse of the Locator Spell, somewhere down in the water, a few hours ago?"

Behind him, he sensed the others hesitating.

"It's still there." Princess Ko leaned forward. "I know it. I fell asleep for a moment I guess, and when I woke up the rod had got tangled in the weed and fallen into the water. I was trying to get it back when I saw the spell. It was way down. Way down in the water and kind of clinging to this weed — we just need to get the weed out and . . ."

Keira let go. She shook her hands hard in the air, and stepped aside.

"Samuel has no shoes," she said. "He'll get frostbite or whatever. I'm going to bed."

Elliot was still holding on, but he'd stopped pulling. "Princess," he said. "You were maybe just dreaming when you saw it. And if not, well, it'll be long gone now."

He released the pondweed, straightened up, and stood by Keira.

Now it was just the Princess, Samuel, and Sergio crouched in the mud, holding the pondweed, staring straight ahead.

"If you don't —" began the Princess, in little, bitten words. "Elliot and Keira, I swear, if you don't —"

Then the weed in her hand jerked hard, buckled, and flew back toward the water. The Princess screamed. Sergio swore. Samuel's hands leapt into the air. The pondweed was zipping and careening away from them and into the Lake, the pile of coils bucking and unraveling, while the Princess grabbed and grabbed at it.

Abruptly, the rushing stopped. The Princess was panting, holding the end of the pondweed tight: The rest had vanished back into the water.

"Okay, that's it," Keira said. "Go to bed."

But the Princess was leaning over the Lake.

"The pondweed's caught," she said. "It's snared in something down there. I just need —"

And then in a single rush of motion, she had thrust the end of the pondweed into Sergio's hands, wrenched off her boots, and jumped.

There was a small splash. A mighty intake of breath from all of them.

Faces in boats turned their way.

The water was perfectly still.

They scrabbled to the edge, got on their knees, leaned down. Elliot touched the water and it was the kind of cold that burns.

There was a long, dark stillness.

She was not coming up.

She was not coming up.

She was not —

Elliot looked sideways at their faces in the lantern light, and they all had that odd calm frown. The strangeness of a pause inside a panic. The almost-smile of it, the absurdity.

There was a girl under the water, and she wasn't coming up.

It was as if that fact itself was underwater; easier to leave it there, let things stay quiet, smooth, this gentle nighttime lapping, the moonlight, the shadowed tents.

The last remaining member of the Cello royal family just drowned.

That sentence shouted loud inside Elliot's head, and he sensed the others were hearing it too, all of them suddenly scrambling at that thought.

Sergio handed the weed to Samuel, and was pulling off his boots, positioning himself to dive.

"Wait," said Keira, and the water broke open.

The Princess gasped and crashed to the edge, clambering up the side. Her face was streaked with mud, her hair, like strands of pondweed itself, crisscrossed her face. Water rushed from her clothes.

"It's loose now." She was blinking against rivulets of water. She grabbed the end of pondweed from Samuel's hands, resumed her position, and began to haul it in.

"Get behind me!" she snapped.

The others remained standing, watching her, glancing at one another.

"Ko," Sergio said gently. "You *cannot* now stay out in those wet clothes. You will *die* from it. Now is the —"

"You're kidding me." Keira was leaning over the lake. She swiveled, grabbed Samuel by his ears, studied the symbol that was smudged on his forehead. Her eyes widened. She turned back to the Lake, crouched, and peered into the darkness. "It's there! The Princess is right!" Her voice kept heading into little crests, a pitch they'd never heard from Keira before. "It's *down* there. Way down. It *is* caught up in this freakin' pondweed."

Then she was behind the Princess, her hands on the weed again.

The boys paused, watching these two girls, one drenched and shivering, the other vibrant with excitement, both of them hauling, hand over hand.

"Ah, for crying out loud," murmured Elliot, and he joined them. Samuel did too, but Sergio disappeared, returning a few moments later with towels which he wrapped around Ko's shoulders. Then he joined in too.

It was different now. Rather than movement, then pauses, there was a constant sliding back and forth. They'd drag out piles of the pondweed, then it would fight back, slither-rushing into the water again. Like a tug-of-war.

"What *is* it?" Sergio said eventually. "What are we fighting?"

It was still deep night, but more people were moving around between the tents. Two kids passed by, deep in conversation, then stopped and watched them a moment. Their shapes moved close to the edge. They both made sounds like "huh."

"You're trying for a monster spell?" said one.

"No," said Princess Ko, drawing in more of the pondweed. "It just thinks we are. We want a *regular* spell that's snared down there."

The strangers were quiet, watching them.

"Don't let any officials catch you," one said eventually, and they passed on, resuming their conversation.

They carried on, nobody speaking.

They'd draw in the pondweed; it'd slip away; they'd pull it in again. The cold had them all in its clamp. The ice-rain stopped and something soft and wet touched the skin of Elliot's wrist, his neck. Snow. Ice was spangling the edges of the water, frost on the tips of grass.

Eventually, Sergio spoke.

"*That* is what we fight?" he said. "A *monster* spell?"

"All it has to do is let go," murmured the Princess. "It's not supposed to be here anyway. Right at the edge of the Lake like this."

There was an odd whimper from Samuel.

"As to a — I'm not sure the fact that it's vacationing makes any difference. . . ."

Nobody responded, so Samuel kept working.

Keira stood again, leaning forward, squinting at the water.

"I can still see the Locator Spell," she said. "We're getting there. Pull harder."

She moved to resume her position, then paused, still gazing into the Lake.

"Freakin' hell," she whispered. "I can see the monster spell too. It's like the size of a — *it's the size of a train carriage.*"

Something yanked hard at the pondweed, and they were all flung forward. Keira shouted: "The Locator Spell! It's right *there*! This time we have to *really* —"

She grabbed at the pondweed again, and now they were all ferocious in their efforts, Keira chanting at them, over and over, like someone on a sports field. "This time we *really* — this time we *really*," her voice setting the pace.

Their chests ached, their arms hurt, their hands smarted, their thighs burned. They leaned and pulled, leaned and pulled. The pondweed slithered away from them, and they wrenched it back. Over and over. Harder and harder. The coils building up and unraveling again. Until Keira's voice was stepping up an octave a word.

"It's right *there*! It's right *there*!"

The lantern got knocked over. Its firelight spell rolled away and disappeared. Sergio pulled a muscle in his neck and let loose a low stream of Maneeshian swearwords. Samuel's elbow jabbed Elliot's eye. Elliot thought his shoulder blades would split right out of his back. The snow fell and fell.

And there it was.

The Locator Spell.

It slid up over the edge of the bank, and they all caught a glimpse of its casings glinting in the moonlight. It was the size of a whistle.

Then, in that fraction of a moment while they looked at it, the pondweed was rushing away again, the spell slipping over the Lake edge.

Now they were all shouting, pulling back on the weed so hard they were falling into one another.

"Where's the icebox?" Princess Ko was shouting. "Someone get the icebox ready!"

The spell was back again, up over the edge and in the air.

Ko let go with one hand, grabbed for the spell, and grabbed again.

"Where's the *icebox*?" she repeated.

Elliot leaned over, used one hand to drag the icebox closer to them. It was lying on its side.

"Open it!" Princess Ko shouted, falling sideways into the mud, and scrambling to her feet again. The spell was right in front of her. "Tip out one of my spells to make room!"

"Which one?"

"Who cares?"

She was gouging at the side of the pondweed, and the Locator Spell was shifting sideways, wriggling away. "Oh, no, you don't —" and the weed was rushing back toward the water again, out of her grasp.

Elliot tipped a spell out of the icebox, and it rolled across the mud and vanished.

They wrenched one more time, and this time the pondweed flew out, the spell passing Ko and stopping right there in front of Samuel's hands.

"GET IT!" they all shouted at once.

Samuel fumbled, grabbed, seemed he had it — and dropped it.

Elliot let the icebox crash. He threw himself onto the mud, flung out a hand, and the spell fell into his palm. He wrapped his fingers tight around it.

"I'm sorry! I'm sorry!" Samuel was wailing.

"Get the *icebox*!"

Keira grabbed it and held it out to Elliot, who pushed the spell inside. Keira slammed the lid; Elliot reached over and snapped the clasps.

They all collapsed into the mud, breathing hard and loud. Snow fell thick and fast. The tangles of pondweed slithered and slid into the Lake and disappeared. The shadow of the monster spell drifted like a cloud crossing the moon.

7.

Each spell at the Lake has a standard identification symbol, along with additional markings that serve as an instructional code.

When Elliot woke the next morning, the Princess had already been to the Gatehouse to consult the Compendium and decode the additional markings on the Locator Spell. She had returned with breakfast for everyone, set up a new Seclusion Spell over her own tent, and called an immediate meeting.

Outside it was bright with snow. The Lake had frozen and kids were already skating and ice-fishing for spells. The RYA stood rubbing their eyes, and blinking in the snow-light, but the Princess, exasperated, rushed them across to her tent.

Her face was white.

"It is not ideal," she said, and her thoughts seemed to dart back and forth behind her eyes. She handed out coffees and pastries as she spoke. "This particular Locator Spell has precise instructions. The good news is, it can work for up to *five* missing people. After that it will fail — possibly even before that; it depends how strong and fresh it is. So it would be best to use it today if we can. But five! That's marvelous, isn't it? There being five missing members of my family?"

Sergio passed a coffee to Elliot, watching Elliot's face curiously as he did. Elliot sipped from the coffee, waiting.

"However," the Princess continued, and she straightened, raised a pastry to her mouth, then lowered it again and spoke rapidly, "to apply the spell, two steps must be taken. First, we must enter a single word — of no more than eight letters — that accurately describes the missing person, along with his or her age. Second, the spell should be placed on a map that shows the city where the missing person is located. That is to say, placed on the marker for that city. The spell will then provide an address." She took a bite from her pastry.

"Not ideal?" exclaimed Samuel. "Call yourself an impossible! As to a pine tree in a little tub of lip balm! How can we ever *use* such a spell? It has all been for naught! We grappled with a monster spell for naught! We don't *know* what cities they are in!"

The glint in the Princess's eye sharpened. She lifted her chin slightly. "It presents a *challenge*," she said defiantly. "It is not perhaps the *best* Locator Spell we could have caught. And it *might* have been helpful if we'd known the cities where my family *arrived* in the World. Of course, they might not still *be* in that city, but at least we could — at least then — but at least . . ."

The defiance collapsed and the Princess began to cry.

Sergio climbed right over Samuel, giving the younger boy an exasperated look. Samuel's face fell.

"I thought it would be all right now," the Princess sobbed, burying her face in Sergio's shoulder. "I thought, '*Now* we'll find them!' I was awake *all night* waiting for the Gatehouse to open! I was so excited! I was so, so — but what's the *point* in a Locator Spell that can't *locate*? Why did we fight and fight and fight for this *stupid — useless — spell*?" She raised her face from Sergio's shoulder and glared ferociously at the icebox.

Keira stood, grabbed a pastry, and pushed her way out of the tent.

"And *she* thinks I'm a *total* loser now." The Princess watched the tent flaps fall closed again, speaking through tears. "Which I *am*. And we're supposed to be *leaving* today, and I'm thinking, can we stay longer? Can we try for a *better* Locator Spell? But what were the *chances* we'd even get that one? And what about the Kingdom I'm supposed to be running?" This last she added in a forlorn little voice, like someone remembering they also had to do the dishes.

"Well." Elliot scratched his eyebrow. "At least we could figure out step one in this spell. Maybe that'd be something. We'll get it ready for when we — when we know more about what city they're in."

"But the spell won't stay fresh," murmured Samuel. "We need it *very* fresh to work for five different missing people. Didn't you hear the Princess say that? And how *will* we ever find out what city they're in? Given the randomness of connections?"

"You're not all that helpful, Samuel," Elliot remarked. "Iceboxes keep spells pretty fresh. That's the point of them. Okay, tell us again, Princess Ko — we've got to think of a word to describe each person in your family?"

The Princess wiped her eyes, and shook her head until a frown fell into place.

"A word for each of them. Yes."

"Okay. So. What's a word for your dad, then? One word to describe King Cetus?"

The Princess's eyes began to dart again, then they slowed. A small smile appeared.

"He is lively," she said. "He is *animated.* He can be angry — his temper can be ferocious. But mostly he is just a whirlshine of fun and charisma." Her smile grew. "He's the best."

"Well," said Elliot.

"Your description of your father is beautiful," Sergio said, "in the sense of, it is accurate." His arm was still around the Princess's shoulder, and he squeezed it. "I am thinking though . . . if we put the spell on a city — and we say, 'lively' — will the spell give us the location of *all* the lively people in that city?"

"Sergio has a point," said Elliot.

"But there's the age too," Samuel said. "We have to put in the King's age."

"So we get all the lively fifty-two-year-olds in that city." The Princess clamped her teeth on the edge of her to-go coffee cup. "We need a word that is *unique* to each member of my family." She clamped again, biting off a piece of Styrofoam. She spat it out.

"Their names?" suggested Sergio.

"King Cetus. That's more than seven letters. And if we just said Cetus, there might be others of that name."

"Madeleine said something about a whale named King Cetus," Elliot remembered. "We might end up with a whale."

"The World," said Sergio, bemused, "it is as strange as a chinning horse."

"Great scarlet!" cried Samuel, and they all looked at him hopefully, but he shook his head. "No. An idea of foolishness as that you would call me a dingbat."

"We might," agreed the Princess. "But so what. Toughen up, Samuel. You can take it. What's your idea?"

"Foolish," he said. "But I thought of the word *Cello. That* surely would distinguish the family from all others in the World!"

The others stared at him.

"Samuel," said Sergio, "this is an idea that is beautiful!"

The Princess raised a hand. "Wait," she said. "Wait. Do they have the *cello* — the *instrument* — in the World?"

Samuel's face crumpled.

"They do," he said. "I believe they do. As to a — ah, such a foolish idea."

"We enter the word *cello*, we get every cellist in the city," the Princess said.

"Call me a dingbat," Samuel offered.

"Cellian!" Sergio's eyes were suddenly wide and bright. "Cello players are *cellists*, yes? But people from Cello are *Cellians*!"

Slow smiles lit their faces.

"You're not a dingbat, Samuel. You're a genius!" the Princess cried.

"It is Sergio who has truly formed the idea."

"But I *spring*boarded from you, Samuel," Sergio said.

"Was this *brainstorming*?"

"It was," the Princess agreed, and Samuel glowed, but then immediately frowned: "Of course, we *still* don't know the city they are in, so —"

The tent opened again.

Keira walked in, sat down, and held out a piece of paper. They looked at her and she shook the paper impatiently, so they leaned in closer, and read:

KING CETUS	*Montreal, Canada*
QUEEN LYRA	*Taipei, Taiwan*
PRINCE CHYBA	*Boise, USA*

PRINCESS JUPITER *Berlin, Germany*
PRINCE TIPPETT *Avoca Beach, Australia*

"These are the places," Keira said, "where they went through."

8.

There were a strange few moments when it seemed that every person in the tent, other than Keira, was diving.

Not synchronized diving, though, so there were bumped elbows, crushed thighs, and spilled coffee. At the same time, words swooped like dives, also colliding and crashing.

The Princess was trying to unfold maps, spreading them out across sleeping bags and feet, and getting them wet in the spilled coffee. Keira was explaining that it was simple: She'd just scanned in the details from Samuel's index cards, along with maps of Cello and the World. Sergio was reaching for the icebox and people were shouting at him to be careful. The Princess was demanding to know how you *entered* words and numbers into a spell? Elliot remembered reading that you wrote them on a slip of paper and fed it to the spell. Sergio and Samuel were disputing this, at the same time as demanding more information from Keira.

"What do you mean *scanned* in?"

"Into my computing machine. Then I wrote a program to find the pattern. I entered the crossover points so now I've got the exact street address where they came through. But you only need the cities now, right?"

"I don't understand. A program to find the pattern? There *is* no pattern."

"Sure there is. It's a sort of series of crumpled spirals between here and the World. It's like you have to roll up both maps and twist them, like this —" Keira demonstrated, twisting imaginary paper in the air.

"But it's impossible!" Samuel cried. "The links are —"

"Trust me," said Keira. "There's no such thing as random."

The Princess was holding the Locator Spell on the palm of her hand. Its head was emerging, sluglike, from its casing. Sergio, his hand shaking, offered it a small scrap of paper on which he had written: *Cellian, 52.*

The paper disappeared almost at once.

"Now where's the map! Get me the map!"

Elliot slid the map her way, checked Keira's list, then pointed out the large black dot alongside MONTREAL in Canada, the World.

The Princess placed the spell on the map and nudged it a little until it was positioned directly on the dot.

"On the dot or on the word?" she cried suddenly.

"Wait," said Sergio. "Your father, he *is* fifty-two? Have I got that right?"

But something struck the air in the center of the tent like a punch of red light. They all reeled back.

The red light formed itself into numbers and letters.

Apartment 3, 181 Place d'Youville.

The letters hovered in the air.

The Princess's whole body shook.

"Is that *it*? Is that where he *is*?"

And then as the red began to unravel and fade, she cried, "Write it down! Somebody write it down!"

Sergio did.

They went through the same process for each member of the royal family, with the same pitch of urgency.

The Princess and Sergio did most of the work, accompanied by Samuel's cries of disbelief and encouragement.

Elliot turned to Keira, and spoke behind the frenzy.

"Is everyone in Jagged Edge as good at technology as you are?" he said.

Keira tilted her head, then hesitated. It seemed as if she'd been about to say, *of course*, in her usual tone, but instead she shrugged.

"Some."

"That's Prince Chyba done!" Samuel hooted. "That's Prince Chyba!" He swung around to face Elliot and thrust out his hand.

"Great!" Elliot said, trying to figure out why the hand. Then he understood, and obliged Samuel by shaking it in the OQ celebratory style.

Keira also obliged when Samuel turned to her. She looked better like this, Elliot was thinking. Less makeup. There were a couple of flare-ups of acne on her chin, but who cared, mostly her face was sunburned, windburned, real. Her short hair looked better tousled too, instead of slicked back under a net. She still had her pj's on — a shirt with thin straps, trackpants, a big coat over it all with a soft, furred collar.

Keira was watching the others work with the spell, but she spoke to Elliot. "Turns out you were right about how to catch the Locator Spell," she said softly. She wrapped her arms around her legs. "I mean, your book worked."

"Ah." Elliot shrugged. "Who knows if it was the book or just luck?"

"That's Princess Jupiter!" Samuel extracted additional handshakes.

"You know," Elliot said, low-voiced. "I kinda agreed with you about the book. I wouldn't usually believe in that sort of thing. Only, I'm thinking, maybe the usual doesn't apply here? 'Cause it's — you know — *magic*."

Keira shivered a little, suddenly cold, and pushed her chin down so she could rub her face along the fur of her coat collar. That was sweet. Like a cat warming itself. She looked up again, and her eyes went straight into Elliot's.

"That's exactly what I was thinking," she said.

"I can't read it! I can't see it!"

They turned and saw that the others were leaning, squinting, pressing their faces at pale, pale lines in the air.

"Shift over so I can see," commanded Keira. Then she narrowed her eyes, leaned back, and read aloud: "52 Avoca Drive, Avoca Beach."

The pattern in the air vanished.

"How did you *read* that?"

"It's her vision again."

"Why was it so faded that time? The others had been . . ."

"It's the spell. It's almost all used up."

They looked at Princess Ko's hand. The sluglike spell, which had completely emerged from its casings now, was paling. Its dark gray was fading to a pale pinkish-white. It was wriggling about a little, and then, as they watched, its movements slowed and slowed, until it was perfectly still.

"It's dead."

The Princess gazed at the dead spell on her hand for a moment, then she tossed it aside, and reached for the papers on which Sergio had written the addresses.

“We know *exactly* where they are!” she said, and she shone her delight around the tent so brightly it was almost weird. It seemed like she was not a person anymore but a collection of sparks.

“Now we have to *get* them!” She directed her sparks at Elliot. “Tell your contact — what’s her name? Madeleine! Tell her to *fly* to these addresses *now* and *bring* my family back to her city!”

Elliot frowned a little. “Well,” he said. “I’m not sure that’ll work. I guess Madeleine would need money for that, and I think she hasn’t got much.”

The Princess patted her own mouth rapidly. “Well, for all we know they may be *imprisoned* at these places, so my idea was ridiculous anyway! What Madeleine must do is, she must contact the *authorities* in each of these cities, and tell them that innocent people are being *held* at these addresses! Only . . .” she faltered. “Should we not contact World authorities in case they are working with the Hostiles here? Can we *trust* World authorities to do it right? But still! Still!”

She turned around, her eyes like flashlights. “We know where they *are*! We know where my family *is*! And now we *have* to get them back! We need to figure out how to open cracks! *Samuel*, you must go back home and *throw* yourself into the archives! There *must* be something there! *Sergio*, go back to the WSU, and *get a detector*! Get one! Where are they? *Find* them! And Elliot! Elliot! Pay attention!”

Elliot was lost in his own thoughts. His gaze was fixed on something.

Sergio bent his head, followed the direction of Elliot’s gaze, and there was the dead spell, shriveled now, even flaking a little, on the edge of a sleeping bag.

“Your father, he is missing?” Sergio said. “Elliot?”

Elliot roused himself, then nodded.

"Might have been good," he said, "if the spell could've lasted just one more. . . ."

"But do you know what city your father is in?"

"The agents think he might be at a Hostile compound in Trent, Jagged Edge. Only, they don't know exactly *where* it is." His eyes remained on the dead spell.

"Ah," the Princess frowned slightly. "But there *are* agents working on the issue, yes? And they are confident they will retrieve him?"

Elliot straightened. "They seem like good guys," he nodded. "Just, it . . ."

"It might have helped," Sergio agreed.

"Ah." Elliot shrugged.

"Well." The Princess seemed to shove her words through the awkwardness with the force of her own excitement. "Well, Elliot, the moment you get back home, you must work your heart out with Madeleine to figure out that crack. Draw up a *table*, perhaps, some kind of *chart* — about — at any rate, you *must* solve it!"

"What do you want me to do?" Keira said.

"Oh, there are more of those boxes of code for you. Read them."

Keira flinched. In fact, the whole tent seemed to flinch.

"Isn't she sort of wasted on that?" Elliot ventured.

But the Princess was looking at him fiercely.

"We know where they are!" she cried. "I *need* to contact them! The *moment* you get home you must have Madeleine contact them!"

"Well," Elliot said, and he breathed in deeply. "I'm thinking I might stay another few days. Try to get another Locator Spell. If the book worked for you —"

"Nonsense! You *must* go home! I *command* it!" The Princess was trembling violently. "Think of my family! They must be frantic! They must be *desperate* for news of me, for news of Cello! *Think* of —"

Elliot was shaking his head, slow and firm, but there was an odd sound from Samuel. A sort of yelp.

"As to a tree snake in a teapot," he declared. "As to that — well, no —" And then more firmly: "No, they would *not* necessarily be frantic. Nor is there much chance they'd be desperate for news about Cello."

The others stared.

"Have I not mentioned this yet? No, I fear I have not. Ah, my report, it was so filled with holes, as to a . . . ! Have I not told you this?"

"Told us *what*, Samuel?"

"Your family would no longer know themselves, Princess Ko. No, neither would they know you. As for the Kingdom of Cello? Not the faintest clue!"

Keira actually slapped his arm. *"Would you explain yourself?"*

"Within twenty-four to forty-eight hours of crossing over to the World," Samuel said, "sometimes a little longer, sometimes sooner — a Cellian ceases to be Cellian."

9.

There was a baffled silence.

"In their own minds, I mean," Samuel hastened to add. "They are still Cellians in fact. But memory is stronger here than it is in the World. There, time is unstable: Did you know they have different time zones?"

"Beautiful," murmured Sergio. "In the impossible sense of the word."

"No," said Samuel. "Quite possible. Time drifts in the World. It is fleeting. And thus memory is weak. Cellians, suffering a severe and rapid form of culture shock, subconsciously translate themselves into Worldians. Their memories are reassembled until they make sense in a Worldian context. Real people from their past are given different names and slightly different roles — real events are converted, relocated, and reshaped. It's fascinating. And it's why earlier visitors to the World were always careful not to stay more than a day or two."

There was a long pause.

"Samuel," Sergio reflected. "I am thinking. This is maybe another one of your *rather important omissions*, no?"

There was another surge of conversation, as the implications of Samuel's words filled the tent.

"If they don't know who they are, how can we ever get them back?"

"They won't even try to get *themselves* back, if they've forgotten Cello!"

"It's brilliant," Keira said. "It's like amnesia as prison."

"They're probably *not* under any kind of guard, then. I mean, if they think they belong there, why would they need to be?"

They talked in such a clamor that it took a moment to realize that the Seclusion Spell had expired, and the noise of the Lake was back amidst them.

Almost immediately there was a shout from outside: "Get out here now!"

It was the boy who'd registered them when they first arrived. He was standing, arms folded, waiting for them. His face was grim.

"You kids out of your darn minds?" he demanded, and they all stared down at him. What was he, ten years old? He straightened up, even lifted on his toes a little. "You are hereby ordered to get out of the Lake right away and never come back."

"Why?" demanded the Princess. "And on whose authority?"

The others looked toward the Princess uneasily. Was she affronted enough to reveal her identity?

"Word is, you tried to catch a monster spell." The boy shook his head. "You realize how lucky you are to be standing here right now? With your dumb heads still attached to your dumb bodies? And your arms and legs? And still breathing? You realize what a sweet darn *miracle* that is?"

For a brief moment the air was filled with equal parts discomfort and defiance.

"We didn't try to catch a monster spell," Princess Ko declared. "It just happened to be *there* — it was in the *way* of the spell that we wanted!"

"You think that sort of technicality makes a difference?" The kid was skinny but the bones in his face were standing up in fury. "You're all banned from the Lake for life, and my authority's this here badge. You've got fifteen minutes to be gone."

"And if we don't?" Keira said acerbically.

"Go ahead and try me if you like," he replied, smiling now. "Just maybe keep in mind that I *have* got authority to catch monster spells, and I *have* caught them before, and heck, maybe I've even stored a couple at the Gatehouse ready to use on folks who don't do as I say."

Princess Ko actually flounced. "We were planning to leave anyway!" she declared. "Come on, guys!" Which was sort of schoolgirlish and embarrassing.

The others turned away, glancing back at the official as they did. He had folded his arms, and was glowering.

Seemed he planned to watch them pack.

"I guess you won't be staying after all," the Princess murmured to Elliot.

"I guess not."

"Can you ask Madeleine to post letters to my family?" she said cautiously, not quite looking at him. She paused. "I'm sorry, Elliot," she said. "About your father."

He was pulling up tent pegs, and didn't look at her.

"It's just," she said, a little louder, "I can't believe they can *really* have forgotten themselves — and Cello — and me."

Nearby, Samuel took a quick intake of breath through clenched teeth. "I think you will find that they *have*, Princess," he said.

She ignored him.

"I just want," she said to Elliot, "to reach out and touch my sister's hand."

They were escorted from the Lake, tramping through sludge and ice. The official's stride tried to make this a parade of shame, but what they felt, as they looked up at the cold blue, and around at the bright white, was a rising sense of jubilation.

They'd done what they'd come here to do. They'd decided on a spell and they'd caught it — and everybody knew you couldn't do that. On top of which, they'd taken on a monster spell and lived.

Sure, they hadn't paid much attention to that part, or what it meant, but there it was. They'd done it.

The kids they passed stopped and stared. Word had gotten around about the monster. Some even whistled, or clapped.

The official's shoulders stiffened at this, then lifted in a sigh that was almost resignation.

PART 6

Maximillian Reisman sits at a table in Olive et Gourmando, a bakery-café on Rue St-Paul in Montreal.

Opposite him is a potential new client. The guy's name is Harry. He makes nail scissors out in Winnipeg, and he's hoping to break into the Quebec market.

"Nobody," Harry jokes, "can make nail scissors sexy." He says it like he makes that joke a lot.

"Try us." Maximillian winks, and they both laugh.

The meeting has gone well. Harry is standing now, wiping his mouth with a napkin.

"What's your story anyhow, Max?" he asks. "Heard you were a rock star?"

"That's too strong a word." Maximillian smiles. "But I fronted a band. It did okay."

"Yeah? What kind of music? Would I know the name?"

"Big in Europe, never cracked America. It was new wave crossed with punk/blues/metal."

Harry laughs. "That's quite a combination." He takes his jacket from the back of the chair, slips his arms into the sleeves. "It end the usual way? Bass player run off with the drummer's wife? Trumpeter arrested with a suitcase of cocaine?"

"Something like that. Plus, you get to our age, you can't keep up the pace." He shrugged. "Have to know when to cut and run before you end up dead in a hotel room."

"I hear you." Harry nods sagely, as if behind the blue eyes, plump cheeks, bow tie, nail-scissor factory owner, there's a wild and shady past. This seems doubtful.

"It was stolen wristwatches," Maximillian adds.

Harry looks startled.

"In the trumpeter's suitcase. Not cocaine. Stolen wristwatches."

Now Harry laughs, relieved that it's a joke, and reaches out to shake Maximillian's hand.

Maximillian says he might stay awhile, get himself a *pain au chocolat.* He watches as Harry pushes out into the morning, strides off in the wrong direction, hesitates, and turns, waving and clowning through the glass as he heads the other way.

That's not a *potential* new client anymore, Maximillian thinks.

It is Friday, 11:00 A.M., September 23.

Maximillian orders another espresso. Leans back in his chair. Feels something crumple in his pocket.

It's the letter he found in his mailbox that morning.

He takes it out, opens it, and reads:

To the Man Living at This Address
Who is 52 years old
and believes his identity — indeed, his entire life so far —
to be something Entirely Other than
What, in fact, it Is

Dear Incorrect Name/Dad,

Apparently, you have forgotten this.

Hence, I am hereby reminding you that:

1) You are the King of Cello.
2) King Cetus is your name.
3) You and the rest of your family (except me) were sent to the World by a branch of Hostiles (we think).

I understand that you have probably given yourself a new identity and past.

However, surely the above has woken the truth! Memories are crashing back? You are shaking violently, looking around you wildly, etc., etc.?

Stay calm.

Do not be too troubled that you have been living a translated life. I hear it is common: Indeed, that it happens to ALL who go to the World from Cello.

Give yourself time to reflect, and ponder.

But don't give yourself long.

The Kingdom needs you urgently! Obviously it does. You are King.

We've been pretending you and the others are here, just out of sight, but we cannot keep this up for much longer.

I must stress that. We cannot.

Furthermore, the King of Aldhibah has invited you to be Candlemaker at the Namesaking Ceremony of his first and only son. This is to take place in exactly two months. There are tensions in both our Kingdoms about this invitation — the Aldhian military are particularly disgruntled and skeptical, and they have increased their presence along the border tenfold; our military have done likewise (they are tricky to control; how do you do it?) — your failure to attend the ceremony would be like a match struck in a Nature Strip hay-mountain.

So. You know. Hurry.

We have found a small crack through to the World and we have a contact there in Cambridge, England. She is going to add her name and address, along with something called an "email address" to the envelope. Please write to her IMMEDIATELY, confirming receipt of this letter, and answering the following, to the extent that you can:

What do you know about the people who took you, and why?

What do you know about the crack that you went through, and cracks generally?

Any ideas on how we can get you back?

Thank you.

We are working around the clock to find a way to bring you home. Be ready to leap through a crack the moment we've found one/figured out how to open it, etc.

Looking forward to seeing you again soon.

Your daughter,

Princess Ko

P.S. If, however, you continue to believe in your current hallucination about who you are/what you are, etc. (which Samuel tells me is quite likely — he thinks simply reminding you won't be enough), well, STOP IT. I must insist that you set aside these false ideas at once! Trust me. You're embarrassing yourself. I cringe just to think of you walking around thinking you are somebody else.

P.P.S. Any tips on how to run Cello much appreciated.

Maximillian chuckles.

What he can't figure out is what they're trying to sell. He turns the paper over, looking for a tiny footer, a watermark. The subliminal message.

It must be one of those brand-saturation campaigns. Kingdom of Cello will turn out to be a new nightclub or fashion label or bowling alley. He's not keen on that sort of strategy — the risk is you irritate people. People don't like to feel confused.

He puts his elbows on the table, closes his eyes, and presses his face into his hands for a moment. He likes to think that way, palms warm against his forehead and eyelids, wrists against his cheeks.

He becomes aware that he must look like someone lost in private anguish. He straightens. The woman at the next table is watching him curiously.

He asks her if she'd like to have a drink with him. Crumples the junk mail in one hand, while he reaches for his phone with the other so he can enter her number.

"I was married to a gang leader," Sasha Wilczek says, "back in New Zealand."

She's at a job interview. Her income from the dance classes is not enough. She's hoping to supplement it by teaching English.

The interviewer, a slight man with a lisp, allows his mouth to fall open.

"A gang leader?"

"I want to be honest with you," Sasha explains. "I met the gang leader when I was very young. Realised too late what I'd got myself into. For years, my work was buying groceries for the gang's safe houses. I've got rheumatoid arthritis in all my joints now — I guess it might not be related, but those groceries were pretty damn heavy. Anyhow, when I broke up with him, he said I'd have to leave the country. I knew too much, see?"

"So you came to Taipei?"

"I have references here," Sasha reaches for her handbag. "I don't want to tell you that the only reason I'm here in Taipei was that I was running away to the least likely place —"

She looks down and sees the letter she picked up that morning.

To the Woman Living at This Address
Who is 49 years old
and believes her identity — indeed, her entire life so far —
to be something Entirely Other than
What, in fact, it Is

She pushes that envelope away.

"But like I said" — she hands over the correct envelope and smiles brightly — "I want to be honest."

"Yeah, I never want to get back into modelling," Monty Rickard tells his friends. "I know I made a lot from it, but it's better here in Idaho."

"No offence," says Gianni. "But would you say your appearance has changed since your modelling days?"

The others examine Monty's face.

"He's got an *interesting* face."

"Maybe they used him as a sort of reference point — to highlight the gorgeousness of the other models."

Everyone laughs, including Monty.

Monty's roommate stands to go get popcorn. She stops in the front hall for a moment, then calls: "There's a letter here for you, hot stuff. At least it must be for you." She comes to the door of the room and reads it out: "'To the boy who lives at this address, Who is eighteen years old and believes his identity — indeed, his entire life so far — to be something Entirely Other than What, in fact, it Is.'" Then she looks up: "Does anyone else here besides Monty have delusions of a former life in modelling?"

Ariel Peters sits in the empty bar, clipping her toenails. The eczema on her ankles has crept down to her feet, almost to her toes. She's looking for patterns in it. Now and then she flicks a toenail to the floor, and turns back to the letter that is open on the bar.

She thinks about her childhood. Foster homes. Detention Centres. Pole dancing. Nightclubs.

And now here she is in Berlin.

"Bist du immer noch da?" a voice calls, angry.

She ignores it. Imagine, she thinks, if my entire life so far had been something Entirely Other than what it In Fact was. She sets down the toenail clippers. Makes herself a Long Island Iced Tea.

Finn Mackenzie sticks the letter on the fridge with the dolphin magnets.

Then he goes upstairs, climbs onto the main bed so he can reach up into the wardrobe there, and takes down an old beach towel.

He sits on the bed, rolls up the towel, presses it under his arm, takes a corner, and rubs it between his thumb and forefinger.

It's no good. He wipes his nose on the beach towel instead, then tosses it onto the floor.

He has tried all the sheets, quilts, bath towels in the house. He even tried a piece of seaweed once.

There was a blanket. Soft, edged in satin, knotted, unravelling, dirty-yellow. He remembers almost nothing at all, but of the blanket he is sure.

PART 7

1.

Madeleine woke to find her mother lifting up the television.

It was dark though, so what she actually woke to was a monster with a rectangular prism for a head. Little knobs along the monster's chin as facial features. She screamed and gasped at the same time, which meant she sucked the scream back into her throat and choked on it. The noise was enough to trip her mother forward. The TV went *donk* against Madeleine's head, then *thud* onto the floor, and her mother landed sprawled on top of Madeleine.

"GO BACK TO SLEEP," Holly shout-whispered, scrambling from the couch to the floor, where she groped around for the TV. "PRETEND THIS IS JUST A DREAM."

Madeleine sat up, blinking hard to adjust to the moonlight. The blinking hurt her forehead where the TV had just hit.

"What are you doing?"

"Go back to sleep." This time Holly crooned the words, as if in gentle lullaby, although the *sleep* was strained as she wrenched the TV back into her arms. "That's my darling little girl, sleep now, my darling, go to sle-e-e-e-ep, this is *just* a *dreeeam*."

"Mum," said Madeleine. "You just thunked me in the head with a TV."

"Shhh," agreed Holly.

Madeleine sat up and watched as the shadow of her mother stumbled about the room. The linen closet was wrenched opened with a shadow hand, the TV shoved inside, sheets and towels spilled out, the cupboard was rammed closed.

Holly turned and squinted across at Madeleine.

"I just put the TV into the closet," she whispered.

"I noticed." A pause. "Why?"

"Radioactive waves."

"But it's switched off. We don't even leave it plugged in anymore."

Holly started to move towards the bed, feeling her way around the couch where Madeleine slept.

"There's the licence issue too," she said. "Night after night I lie awake worrying about the licence police."

She climbed back into her bed and spoke into the darkness: "Do you want me to sing you a lullaby?"

"No, Mum," Madeleine said. "Thanks, though."

After a moment, Holly sat up again. "Sorry about your head," she said.

"Go back to sleep."

"TV should be free," Holly added. "Then I wouldn't have to worry."

"Well, it's for the BBC," Madeleine explained. "If they didn't have the licence fee, there wouldn't be such high-quality TV on the BBC."

There was another long quiet, then Holly said: "I don't know why I just said TV should be free. Why should it? It's not like there's some fundamental right to free-to-air TV. Or is there?"

"Go to sleep, Mum."

Eventually, her mother stopped twitching, turning, and making abrupt pronouncements about the European Convention on Human Rights, and the definition of sadness, and whether it embraced the sadness you feel when a TV series goes off the air — those characters weren't *actually* your friends, but it *felt* like they were, so is that true sadness or an *illusion* thereof — and so on. Her breathing slowed and found its way to sleep.

Madeleine looked at her watch.

It was just before one A.M.

She looked over at her mother's bed again, watched the still form rise and fall awhile, then she got up, dressed, and slipped out of the flat.

Hey, Elliot, you there?

Yep.

Madeleine wrote fast.

Sorry I'm late. I fell asleep. Plus my mother's in another crazy phase. She keeps coming up with some weird new twist on how the universe might plan to bring her tumour back. I don't get it. The doctors are happy, the scans are clear, she seems fine. She's even signed up for a fashion design course by correspondence and she's been telling Belle, Jack, and me to wander around in clothes shops, talking loudly about Holly Tully Design so she can get brand recognition going before she even has a brand. But tonight she put the TV in the closet, and the other night I found her crying by the window. Turned out she'd thrown her wedding ring out onto the street. She said she'd had a dream that it was emitting negative cancer-causing vibrations, so she'd got up and thrown it away, but then right away she'd realised it had actually been protecting her from cancer. So she's crying cause she doesn't know how to get it back. I went downstairs with a torch, and found the ring in the gutter. "This is how," I said, and she put it on her finger and we both went back to sleep.

Madeleine posted her note into the parking meter, and stood in the Cambridge night, an odd swirl of hopefulness gathering inside her, a strange lightening of her mood. She hadn't told anybody about that wedding ring incident, and writing about it now had formed tears in her eyes. Except that the last part — about herself finding the ring — had turned into a smile. Something about sharing this with Elliot seemed to lift her right up, so she was in the air, free and glad, way above the solid, crowded darkness of the memory.

After a moment, his reply appeared:

It's tangled up in your mother's head, maybe — the fear about getting sick again, and the hope that your dad will sort out his own issues and come and find you guys? So the wedding ring turns into something bigger? I don't know. But I do know she's lucky she's got you for a daughter.

Madeleine felt herself shining. She touched the note and it was as if she was touching darts of Elliot's kindness and calm.

She decided to change the subject fast so there'd be no chance of his saying more, and accidentally veering in the wrong direction. Jack and Belle sometimes suggested that Madeleine's dad would probably *never* come back — that if he hadn't figured out his drug and alcohol issues by now, he never would.

If Elliot started saying that too, she'd have to detonate the parking meter.

Anyhow, I posted those letters to the members of the Cello royal family like you asked. I'll let you know if there's any reply. Do you want to try the "BELIEVING" thing again now, and see if we can get through/make contact, whatever?

Yeah, only this time we have to step it up a notch so we do more than touch each other's hands.

Madeleine blinked hard.

Since Elliot had returned from the Lake of Spells the other day, they'd only spoken about his trip, and arranged for her to forward the letters. Neither of them had mentioned their moment of connection. She'd felt reckless and brave bringing it up just now.

And he wanted to "step it up a notch"?

Holding Elliot's hand was plenty.

It was everything, she thought.

But she wrote:

How do we do that?

I guess maybe we have to believe in more than just the other person's hands. Specifically, we have to believe that our hands are attached to arms, and that our arms are attached to bodies, and that our bodies are hanging loose in other worlds.

This was crazy. He was making jokes and her heartbeat was skittering. Talk about *arms* and *bodies* was too much. She needed to get scientific.

I've been thinking we need to look at the issue from some different perspectives. We could try "believing" again, but the thing is, I sort of DO believe now. I think if I did that ferocious "I BELIEVE" thing, I'd be faking it, cause I just – I mean, of course I believe. Okay. Great. Whatever. If you see what I mean? So we need to think of a different angle: philosophy, geology, cosmology, chemistry, astrology, paleontology, holography. Take your pick.

There was a long pause, during which Madeleine wondered if she'd sounded like a total twit.

A young couple turned into the laneway, their hands swinging. The girl's heels tapped quickly, keeping up with the guy's steady stride. They stared at Madeleine as they passed, and she folded her arms and stared back.

Elliot's reply was short.

Let's just try the believing thing again. Countdown from five starting now.

Cold hit her in the chest, and spread up and across her cheeks.

I'm not ready, she panicked.

That couple were still in the laneway. Their shapes were slowing in the distance. The boy was swivelling the girl around to kiss her. Madeleine looked away. She looked back. The boy was murmuring something into the girl's ear. Her giggle tossed and turned its way down the laneway toward Madeleine, and got itself tangled in the fear in Madeleine's chest. The couple started walking again, more slowly now, leaning into each other. Another pause while the girl wrenched her heel out of a crack between the cobblestones. Then they turned the corner and were gone.

Madeleine looked back at the parking meter.

5, 4, 3, 2, 1, she thought in a rush, closed her eyes, held out her hands and thought:

Elliot Baranski.

A slam of a moment. A boy's wrist: narrow, brown. Dirt in a fingernail. The frayed edge of a jacket.

She was back again, breathless.

She shook back and forth a moment, trying to settle her thoughts.

What just happened?

Maybe nothing.

Then a note appeared:

Did you feel that?

I think so. I saw a wrist, a fingernail, and a dark blue jacket. Do you have dirty fingernails?

I'm a farm boy. What do you expect? You got more than me. All I saw was a sort of blur of dark hair, like you were running past me. Do you have dark hair? Were you running?

Why would I be running? It felt more like falling. And it was over in, like, a crumb of a second.

For me too. Like falling, I mean. And over fast.

Maybe falling is what we need to do? Maybe the idea of believing is more in the double negative – like not disbelieving. Like letting go of doubt – and if you let go, you fall.

And fall through the crack. Nice. Want to try that now?

What? Try falling. That makes no sense. I think we need to think more. Like haven't you found any more about the history or science of cracks? I can't look anything up here since your Kingdom does not exist.

I went to the library today, but there's nothing in the catalogs and I can't ask the librarians. I'd get arrested.

Madeleine read this and frowned.

Wait. You only looked this up in the library TODAY? Why not earlier?

Well, no offense but the whole thing has seemed like a waste of time. I didn't really believe the royals were in the World until the Locator Spell gave us those addresses. And I didn't believe we'd ever crack this crack until we held hands before I went to the Lake. Anyhow, quit it with the attitude. I'm a busy guy. I still think we should try FALLING through the crack. It's got a nice, relaxing sound to it.

Ha-ha. Okay, listen, the idea of "falling" makes me think of gravity, which I'm into, cause I'm into Isaac Newton. Do you even have gravity in Cello? Or are all the people and animals there just, sort of like, flying around in the sky?

We've got gravity. We've also got these little creatures called "birds," and they do just, sort of like, fly around in the sky. I think they just, sort of like, work <u>around</u> gravity.

We've got birds too. Or are you making fun of me?

A little. I knew you had birds.

While Madeleine was still blushing, another note from Elliot appeared.

Actually, we also have flying machines — fixed wings and choppers. Do you have those? And we've got Occasional Pilots — people who get exemption from gravity now and again, but they're rare. I can't figure out how a discussion about gravity's going to help anything, Madeleine. Let's just fall into each other's worlds.

You go ahead and fall. I'll wait.

There was a brief pause then Elliot wrote again.

Okay, that hurt. You win. Talk about gravity.

Well, gravity is a mystery. Nobody knows how it works – some people think there are teeny things called "gravitons" – but they've never been found. All they know is that every single thing is drawn to every other thing. The reason gravity makes us fall is that we're drawn to the planet Earth. But Earth is drawn to us too.

My dad demonstrated that for me once. We were walking along and he stopped in the middle of the pavement and jumped on the spot. He said, "See this? The earth is pulling on me, and I'm pulling on the earth. Only," he added, "the earth's a little bigger, so it wins." Then his phone rang and while he answered he held up his hand at me, meaning I should wait, cause he had more to say on the issue. I remember thinking: His work's a little bigger, so it wins. Am I getting off topic?

Kind of. But you're allowed. I guess you miss your dad, just like your mother does. Sometimes I think I've got used to not having my dad around 'cause so much time has gone by, and then it's like the opposite—it's like all these hours and days of NOT having him have been quietly piling up, one on top of the other, and now I have to walk around with a huge tower of missing on my head. It does my shoulders in. I woke up last night and couldn't stop thinking about the Locator Spell we caught at the Lake—how it had enough power to find five people, and there are five members of the royal family. Why'd there have to be five? Why not just four. Or why couldn't the spell have had room for six missing people?

Madeleine felt her heart hurting for him. She wanted him to see she understood. She wrote:

I hear you.

You hear me?

No. I mean—I don't HEAR you. I just get what you're saying.

Okay.

There was a long quiet. Then Elliot wrote again:

Gotta go. It's late. Night.

Sweet dreams.

2.

Elliot was sitting at a table outside the Bakery Café.

He had a coffee, a blueberry pastry, and a pile of Samuel's index cards. Also, his Algebra textbook.

It was an idle Sunday afternoon, and there was a wandering to everybody's footfall. There'd be plenty of time to hide the cards under the textbook if somebody stopped by to say hello.

Clover Mackie, the town seamstress, had already waved at him twice from the porch of her house. She was the only one in town who knew the truth about the missing royal family, and the real reason he was in the Royal Youth Alliance. There was some comfort in that, the invisible line from him here at this table, to her up on her porch, with her needle, thread, and patterns, and her jug of lemonade.

Actually, now that he thought about it, *she* was the real reason he'd been selected to the RYA. She'd sewn dresses for the Princess Sisters since they were little, and become close to them, and they communicated by sewing messages, in secret code, into seams. When she'd discovered Elliot had a contact in the World, she'd risked his life by telling the Princess about it.

He looked back at Clover. She seemed set to wave at him a *third* time, but she must have caught that recollection on his face. She dropped the wave, and began to whistle quietly, a range of expressions — sheepish, defensive, defiant, thoughtful, remorseful — crossing her face. Then she got over it and picked up the whistling, turning it into a friendly tune that carried all the way across the square.

Ah, you couldn't stay mad at Clover Mackie.

These index cards, though. You could be plenty mad at them. He'd read over twenty already, and hadn't learned a single useful thing. They were all from the seventeenth century when the Harmony Institute was active. Some were by people from the World, some by Cellians, but none said a word about the journey from one place to the other.

Elliot picked up the next card in the stack. It was about a Worldian who called himself *Sir James Gwynn.* As usual, it started with a date (*May 6, 1663*). Then there was the place of departure (*Chatham, England)* and arrival (*Beeks Vara, Nature Strip*).

No mention of the crack Sir James had come through, or how he'd found it, or whether he'd clambered over it, sidled under it, shoved it aside, or shot it to pieces with a rifle.

Here he was, though, being warmly greeted by a young Cellian man in Beeks Vara. The young man clasped Sir James's *left* hand with *both* his hands, which hands, Sir James observed, were "*somewhat rough and calloused*," and next, Sir James observed, the young man began to "*apply some measure of pressure*," to Sir James's left hand, by means of those *two* "*somewhat rough and calloused*" hands, the second and third fingers of which were, inexplicably, "*intertwined*." Sir James experienced some "*discomfort*," as a result of this "*pressure*," and even became somewhat "*affrighted*," wondering if the young man intended him harm, yet recalled, almost at once, the warmth of the young man's greeting moments earlier. Sir James, accordingly, found himself "*confused beyond all measure*."

It all ended happily. Sir James was "*greatly relieved*" when the young man, after what, upon reflection, had been only a "*comparatively brief period of time, measuring, perhaps, upwards of two minutes*," released his hand.

For crying out loud.

That was how they said "hey" in Nature Strip! They grabbed your hand, crossed their fingers for luck, and gave you a good, solid squeeze!

Four index cards, front and back, to tell us that?

And of course the guy's hand was calloused! What did Sir James think, you could live in Nature Strip without working as a Color Bender? You could Color bend without getting yourself a little scratched and battered?

It was more or less how they all went, the index cards — not that they all described a basic handshake as if it were the plot of a horror film, but they meandered off into the same breathtaking pointlessness.

Sometimes they'd start off seeming kind of fun — these guys from hundreds of years ago, describing Cello customs or fashion, vegetation or politics — with their fresh and baffled eyes. But within a few lines the fun would get trampled by the details. He might as well be reading his Algebra textbook. There was never a good, solid survey of how a town looked, say, or what people were drinking at the bar, or what *sport* might have been on everybody's mind. No. It was comparing the toes on an *Olde-Quaintian Liama* with the claws of the World's *Mauritian broad-billed parrot*. It was the *angle of reflection* on the surface of a mudpond made by a *Golden Coast ostling tree*. Measurements taken and recorded around the clock.

The Cellian accounts of visits to the World were just as useless. Here they'd be in Cello — there they'd be in the World. *"Neither have I now any great Curiosities to impart with respect to my Journey,"* one card asserted. What a surprise, Elliot thought, feeling snarky.

He supposed it must have been so obvious to them there was no point in describing it. As if a group of factory workers were asked to describe what happened on the production line, and they all took the

7:25 A.M. express to get to work. Why would they bother mentioning the 7:25 A.M. express? It just was.

The Cellian accounts went on about botany, insects, and "*wondrous contrivances*" of the World. Like magnets. Now and then there was talk of political issues. In a 1648 account, there was mention of a King Charles I being in captivity at Newport on the Isle of Wight. A couple of cards later, there we were in 1660, Charles had been strung up, but here was another Charles stepping up to the throne. *Why not?* thought Elliot. *Live dangerously.* There were hints that there'd been some kerfuffle in the intervening years. "Rump Parliament," Elliot read. And: "Oliver Cromwell."

Something rushed over him. There was a thin outer layer to this rush, which he recognized as the memory of studying for exams: stress shot through with boredom. He must have had to study this Oliver Cromwell for World Studies.

But under the crackling was something else: another, better memory.

His mother, leaning against the wall in the hallway, talking. His father, with a paintbrush, listening. Himself, Elliot, a kid on the floor, playing with one of those pull-back-and-go toy cars. His mother had loved World Studies in high school and liked to talk in long paragraphs about it. He'd never paid much attention, except to notice that her voice always got a happy, pleased-with-itself note, the one that people get when they talked about something they liked, and felt clever about. His dad used to get the same voice when he listed the components of a circuit board.

It was just a short memory. The toy car bumping up against the paint sheets on the floor. His dad dipping the brush into a tin. The wall shining up under its new coat of pale yellow. *Oliver Cromwell. Interregnum.* "There was a newspaper called the *Moderate Intelligencer*,"

Elliot's mother had said, and he remembered his father's smile and glance back at her. "Only *moderately* intelligent," he'd joked, and she'd laughed too. The pleasure of the drag of the toy car's wheels before it shot itself forward.

Now Elliot looked up from the index cards. Nothing new in the square. People buying groceries, eating pastries, chatting by the fountain — everything moving so much slower than his heart. There was no reason for the quickening. It was just one of those nothing memories that took his breath away. They'd come out of nowhere and grab him like a Nature Strip handshake.

They'd been coming a lot the last few days, actually, these commonplace memories of his dad. Must be the hope that the agents had ignited in him as they inched their way toward bringing Dad home.

Might also be, he realized, on account of all the stories he'd told Madeleine these last few days. They'd been talking a lot, exchanging stories about their missing fathers, but also about everything and nothing.

They'd talked about relationships — she'd been seeing her friend Jack for a while, she told him, and he'd been seeing *his* friend Kala, until she'd moved away to boarding school. Kala had a new boyfriend there. (She'd mailed him a photo of the guy, which he hadn't especially needed.)

Question after question about each other's world they'd asked, slipping into ever stranger topics: leaves, musical instruments, water shadows on buildings. He'd got into the habit of bringing a deftball along, and he'd toss it while he waited in the schoolyard for her replies. Half thinking this could be his cover if anyone stumbled on him there: couldn't sleep so came out for some deftball practice.

Now and then he and Madeleine would experiment by sending tiny objects across to each other. Or by *believing* or *falling into* each other's world. Mostly, nothing happened. Once or twice there'd been a spark, a flare, a glimmer. It was tricky to know what to call it. Like the kind of electric shock you got when you touched the shelf in the local library, only more pleasant than that.

He'd caught a scent of something like strawberry once, and she'd told him that could be her lip balm. Another time, his palm had felt her elbow through the soft cotton of her jacket sleeve.

There was always a jolt of astonishment and then it would be over. In less than a second. And he'd never seen her face, or got an image of the street or buildings around her. Never seen the pieces fit together.

Like the stories on these index cards. Nothing but glimpses. Close-ups of irrelevant details. Nobody ever stood back and gave the full picture.

Even Samuel's handwriting was too caught up in the details, actually.

He took a card now and studied the flourishes of calligraphy. Why all the loops and curls? It was like the kid thought he had to decorate every second letter. Same with Olde-Quaintian language, Elliot realized. Words and phrases were never left alone to be themselves; those Olde-Quaintians kept getting in and messing with them.

An image came to Elliot of Samuel himself: short, plump, twelve years old, sitting at a table in some library basement, frowning over the original manuscripts, dipping his quill in a pot of ink, turning to the index cards, pondering how he might decorate the letter *I*. They didn't have copy machines in Olde Quainte; that's why he'd written out the index cards.

For the first time it occurred to Elliot that Samuel had a life. When he wasn't researching in a library for the Princess, what did his days look like? His hometown, Twy Eam Peak, was as Hostile as a chained-up rooster, but Samuel was a member of the Royal Youth Alliance. If he wasn't an outcast already — and Elliot suspected that the kid was one of those earnest, confused types who got taunted constantly — well, they'd have tossed him overboard by now. They must despise him. Probably not just kids either, but adults too. He could even be in danger.

Ah, Samuel was annoying, but you had to respect that. He should cut the kid a break.

He stretched his arms above his head, and as he did, he caught sight of Jimmy and Isabella. They were across the square at the grocery store, and they saw him and smiled. He switched his stretch to a wave.

They had stopped at a tray of eggplants, he saw. Isabella picked one up, and went to put it in her basket, but right away Jimmy leaned over and took it back. He replaced it on the tray, chose another, and placed that in her basket instead. Shaking his head.

You could almost hear his murmur of mock-disapproval — *these Jagged-Edgians*, he'd be saying, *haven't got a sweet darn clue about how to choose a vegetable.* Isabella's laughing protest drifted across the square.

She was tall, that Isabella, and she held her back straight, not afraid of her own height. Her eyes, narrow and green, had a brightness to them, and her smile was always thoughtful, and slow.

He ought to ask her about the quantum physics of cracks.

Should have done so by now, but he kept finding excuses. There was how to phrase the question, for one thing: the reason he'd give her for his interest.

And he wasn't all that sure what quantum physics *was.*

So that was another issue: He probably wouldn't understand her answer.

Ah, if he was truthful, he was scared. It was that Sergio, always going on about the World Severance Unit, and how they'd pickle his eyeballs or whatever. It had finally got under Elliot's skin: He'd used up his stockpile of indifference.

The fact was, he didn't *want* to be arrested and executed.

To be fair, who did.

It didn't help that Isabella was always walking side by side with *the law* — that was how Elliot's mother liked to refer to the Sheriff and his Deputy. She was joking: Both Hector and Jimmy were good friends. But still. They *were* the law. Who could tell what happened when friendship crossed paths with a felony?

Now he could see that Jimmy and Isabella were passing sentences back and forth at the cash register. They appeared to be arranging something, pointing at their watches and the clock tower, tilting their heads to indicate direction and plans.

Next thing Jimmy had the paper bags of groceries under his arms. He was leaning over to kiss Isabella good-bye, and striding out across the square. He passed the Bakery, and looked over at Elliot.

"See you at training later," Jimmy called. He was the deftball coach. "I've got a strategy in mind for Saturday's big game."

"Those Rangos are in for a beating," Elliot agreed.

They grinned at each other, then Jimmy headed out of the square.

Elliot turned back and watched Isabella. She always wore that green pendant around her neck. It was the size and shape of a chicken's egg. Her walking pace was fast, practically a jog, so the pendant would bounce up and down. It must hurt, banging against her chest like that.

He felt like suggesting she slow down.

Well, she was a physics teacher. He guessed she knew how these things worked.

She was not far away now.

He could call out to her.

He could say, "Hey, Ms. Tamborlaine, can I ask you a question?"

She'd come over to his table, ready to answer.

She was friendly, easygoing. It'd be fine.

"Hey, Ms. Tamborlaine," he called.

"Hi there, Elliot."

She smiled. He smiled. She kept walking.

She was heading for the cheese shop, he saw. She pushed open the glass door and walked inside.

Ah, he'd get around to asking her another time.

3.

"Do you ever want to, like, take someone's face and twist it? The edges of it, I mean. And it'd go *clack-clack-clack* as you twisted, a bit like a lens cap?"

Belle was lying on the couch, feet on Jack's lap.

They were in Belle's living room. It was small and overcrowded: mismatched couches, dining chairs, dressers, side tables, a birdcage (empty), an art nouveau standing lamp, a stack of paperbacks, a cushion embroidered in butterflies, a doll's rocking horse —

Madeleine stopped cataloguing. There was nowhere you could look in this room without your eyes going into a panic.

She'd been at Belle's place often before, because Belle's mother, Olivia, home schooled them in French and Citizenship. But that was always daytime, and always in the kitchen. This was Madeleine's first nighttime social visit.

She'd arrived as Belle's parents were leaving, dressed up, both laughing.

"The oven mitt!" Olivia had trilled. "Why not the oven mitt? The use of it, it escapes her?"

"Ha-ha," Madeleine had agreed politely.

Inside, she'd found Belle at the kitchen sink with the cold tap running on her fingers. It turned out she'd taken a tray of spring rolls out of the oven with her bare hands. Forgetting they'd be hot.

Ha-ha, Madeleine thought, but she couldn't see what was so funny.

Now, here they were in the living room listening to music. They'd eaten the spring rolls, and they were sharing pretzels and vodka.

"You want to twist his face off," Jack said thoughtfully. "Isn't that, I don't know, psychotic?"

"Ah, it's not like I'd *do* it." Belle lifted her feet from Jack's lap and sat up. "Faces don't work like that. His face," she added profoundly, "is not a lens cap."

She lay back down and thudded her feet onto Jack's lap.

"Is it," she added for emphasis.

"Oof," he said.

Madeleine did not know what they were talking about. Since she'd arrived, Belle and Jack had been talking like parallel streams. Now and then the streams converged, forming a larger, louder stream, before setting off again on separate paths.

She felt like she was running back and forth between them in her bathing suit, trying to figure out how to get in.

At the start, she'd said, "Who's that?" and "Wait, how do you know him?" and "So that's his sister, right?" and they'd veer in her direction to answer, but they usually got excited by her question, the streams getting tangled, turning into rapids.

Eventually, Madeleine had given up.

She decided to stop thinking of them as streams, and to see them as a stage show instead. She'd arrived at the show after intermission, so that's why she was baffled. She sat quietly, waiting for the plot to make sense.

The conversation seemed to be about the boys that Belle was seeing. Three at once, Madeleine thought at first, but then it turned out to be four.

There was a tyre fitter with an aura like an old tea bag; a baker whose aura was droopy and bloodshot (because he had to get up early to turn on the ovens and make the little sugar mice); a student whose aura was like a mediocre episode of *How I Met Your Mother*; and a machine operator with an aura like seedless watermelon (and whose face Belle wanted to twist off).

"None of them sound all that sexy," Madeleine observed.

"Oh, they are," Belle assured her. "Dead sexy. As long as you don't look at their auras."

It was morally complex, Belle explained, seeing four boys at once. She had rules for keeping things technically casual, mainly to do with how many texts she sent, and how many *x*'s she added to the texts. She always called it off if their auras turned all moony, meaning they liked her too much. And she never accepted gifts.

"I'd only *ever* accept a gift," she said, "even something tiny, like, say, a wheel nut from the tyre fitter, if I had decided that he was the *one*."

"What if he wanted to give you a free wheel alignment?" Jack suggested. "Say you had a car."

Belle thought about that and decided it would be all right because you could see a wheel alignment as a sort of extended kiss.

The conversation turned to girls that Jack had hooked up with in the past. It sounded like he'd hooked up all over the place, like he was a coat rack or something.

"Sophie," Jack recalled sadly. "Never worked out with her. She just wasn't into me."

Belle gave him a sharp look. "Yeah, I don't buy into that whole *just not into me* thing," she said. "If a guy's not into me, what the eff is wrong with him?" She swung her legs around so she was leaning forward again. This was a recurring pattern for Belle, like an exercise routine. Lie down, put legs on Jack's lap, swing legs to sit up, lie down, put legs on Jack's lap. It didn't seem to bother Jack.

"Sophie's just not *into* you?" Belle continued. "What's *wrong* with her? Seriously. Stupid cow."

Jack reached for the vodka, and handed it to Belle, who said, "What happened to that girl, Katya, you were seeing last year? Why'd you call it off with her?"

"Just wasn't into her."

"Yeah." Belle drank from the bottle. "What can you do?"

They paused, then both laughed hard. Their laughter was like flat hands pounding on a wall.

Madeleine watched Jack with a vague, increasing sense of awe.

The thing was, it wasn't that long ago that she and Jack had been together. Back then, she'd thought she had him all figured out. She'd thought there were three components to him: He talked a lot; he liked astrology; and he was crazy about her.

That was it. Jack.

Now it turned out he had a trail of secrets, jokes, stories, broken hearts, and broken-hearted girls behind him. The more Belle and Jack talked, the more complex and remote Jack became. At the same time, he seemed to be growing taller and stronger. He was opening bottles with a twist of his wrist. He was standing to go to the bathroom and he seemed more in control of his body than she remembered — she'd always thought of him as sort of goofy.

He was pretty hot, actually.

There's a whole world just behind everybody's eyes, she thought. Not just behind eyes either: parking meters too.

Maybe not *all* parking meters.

Belle and Jack were back onto twisting people's faces. Turned out they used to get into fights all the time, and they were reminiscing about ribs they'd broken and bruises they'd inflicted.

"What were you two, bullies?" Madeleine asked.

"We only beat up people who deserved it," Belle explained.

"Like dweebs and that," Jack said. "People who wore glasses. Anyone with a stutter. A good beating can only help that kind of person."

That sort of humour. She'd never seen it in Jack before. His jokes used to be sort of obvious and cheerful. Now he had this dry, ironic thing, with an edge. She kept believing him for a moment, then feeling a bit stupid.

"It was more we had to defend ourselves." Belle closed her eyes. "People were always pissed at us. For one thing and another."

"It was our aura and astrology readings," Jack explained. "Belle was always telling people their auras showed they were up themselves. Or that they had multiple STDs."

There was a quiet while the three of them listened to the opening chords of the next track. It was a suspenseful opening. The kind where you can't figure out where things are going, then the drums come in, and the song settles down and finds itself.

"Hey," Belle pounded a fist into the couch in time with the music.

"What's up with the Kingdom of Cello? You found your way through yet?"

Madeleine felt confused for a moment. She'd got used to watching the Jack-and-Belle show. Now it was as if they'd invited her onto the stage, and were waiting, half smiling, like performers standing back to catch their breath, spotlight swinging from their face powder to the startled audience member.

"We've been sending things to each other," she said eventually.

"Like what things?"

"Well, whatever you can fit in an envelope and the envelope's still flat."

"So you don't have to pay extra postage," Jack agreed. "I get you."

"I've sent grass seeds, tea leaves, sugar crystals, and one of those flat chocolate circles with orange in it. Orange thins. And I've sprayed my letters with different sorts of perfumes too. To see if he can smell it."

"Can he?"

"Yeah. So. There's that."

"Grass seeds," mused Jack. "Are there quarantine restrictions on the cracks?"

"You'll disrupt the entire delicate ecosystem of the Kingdom of Cello," Belle said comfortably. "Nice. What's he been sending you?"

Madeleine looked around the room. An electric heater stood in the corner, its cord straggling across the floor until it ran into the legs of a small, plush sheep, which leaned towards an old laser printer.

Your eyes could climb this room forever, Madeleine thought.

"Madeleine?" Belle leaned forward.

"Oh, sorry, forgot what we were talking about."

She hadn't forgotten. She just didn't want to tell them that Elliot had sent her: a handful of shredded coconut, a Cellian leaf, half a cinnamon cookie that he'd baked himself, and a paper cone filled with gem dust from a Purple cavern in Nature Strip.

Or that she and Elliot had talked until almost five A.M. the night before, about their parents, their pasts, but mainly about the rules of a Cellian sport called deftball.

She still didn't get the game. She'd been eating the cinnamon cookie while he wrote to her about it.

Send me more of these cookies, she'd written.

I thought you wanted to know how deftball works.

Now, in Belle's living room, she closed her eyes and tried to sort out the rules.

There were fifteen players in each team.

The field was huge.

It had some kind of ditches in it, the field, with raised sides. These ditches could trip you up. You had to sprint, trying to catch a falling ball while you jumped over the ditches.

Furrows, he'd called them. Not ditches.

Other players tried to intercept the ball, or tackle you.

You could fall into a furrow and break a bone. In the last two years, Elliot knew of three players across Cello who'd fallen and snapped their spines.

That's stupid, she wrote. *Sports where you can get paralysed are stupid.*

He didn't know what to say to that.

Also she'd written: *What, are you saying you throw a ball FORWARD in the air and then run forward and catch it yourself?*

Right.

That doesn't make any sense.

I'm not sure how else to explain it.

No, seriously, it's not physically possible to run as fast as you can throw a ball. That's like a rule of physics or something.

Okay, I should have said — a deftball has a kind of ring around it, that slows down its path through the air.

A deftball has a ring around it. They'd exchanged notes about this ring. Trying to figure out what he meant. She was imagining the rings of Saturn.

The ring was soft. It felt spongy. No, it would not cut the palm of anybody's hand.

If you were good enough, you could get more than one deftball flying at the same time: catch one, throw it, catch another, throw that. Calculate where each was going to fall.

Like a juggler? she wrote. *Like a clown juggling?*

Nothing like a clown.

How do you get to be a hero in deftball? she wrote. *Is there one player who's always, like, a hero?*

He'd started to explain the zones between the furrows.

At this point, she'd lost interest. He'd written a long note about the scoring system, which she'd skimmed, her eyes blurring, then she'd asked him again for another cinnamon cookie.

He said he had no more with him. She told him to go home and get some. Bake some. Bring them back. They redefined delicious.

He'd ignored that and written some more about the scoring system.

She wasn't sure if it was that her mind always faded when people explained the rules of sports, or if it was because it was four thirty A.M.

Are you good at it? she wrote.

I do okay.

Ah, he was probably rubbish. Knowing all the rules like that. He was always on the sideline, waiting for his chance to play.

When he first started writing to her a few months ago, Madeleine had thought of him as a local Cambridge nerd who'd invented a fantasy world. Now she knew that he and his Kingdom were real, but she also sensed she'd got his character right. Not a fantasy nerd, a farmer nerd. His hands had felt fine and warm when she touched them. His wrist seemed narrow. He must have skinny arms. Could he lift bales of hay with those skinny arms? Probably a concave chest. His ears probably stuck out. He probably cried easily, but turned his face away from you, buried it in his arms even, when he did so. His nose was probably snotty.

She liked him anyway. He was sweet and he could bake.

"Is it working?" Jack asked. "Sending things across? Is it stretching the crack?"

Madeleine opened her eyes. "I don't see how it can be. The parking meter's a parking meter. There's a crack in it, and it's a crack. If you see what I mean."

Belle and Jack considered this. They looked at each other.

"You have to *explore* the idea of the crack," Belle said.

"Write an essay on it," Jack suggested.

"Cause I'm thinking," Belle continued, "the crack can't just be *direct* from parking meter to TV. There must be something *between* those things."

"Right," agreed Jack. "So, sort of like, what *is* a crack?"

Jack and Belle were back onstage, looking intently into each other's eyes. The music had picked up, and they were rocking in time to it. Their words stopped and started with the beat.

"If you *crack* a nut," Belle said, "you crack it open — with a nutcracker — so — you need a *giant nutcracker*. To open — the crack."

"It means you *solve* it," Jack pointed out while he cranked up the music. He had to shout over it now. "Like — you say — *let's crack this nut* — you mean, solve — this — nut. So — Madeleine — you have got to — crack — the crack."

"Okay," shouted Madeleine.

"But the crack's *already* there," Belle yelled. "So how did it get there? — It's like — how *do* cracks — get places?" She narrowed her eyes, trying to concentrate. "When I get cracked lips — it's cause of the wind."

"IF YOU WANT TO MAKE THE CRACK BIGGER," Jack bellowed. "YOU NEED A HAIR DRYER!"

He looked at Belle. They both nodded. The problem was solved.

Jack held the button down on the remote.

"Let us know what happens next!" he shouted, but they only saw the movement of his lips.

Then both he and Belle were jumping from the couch, and it was like the floor was a trampoline, that's how they danced.

This, she could do. Madeleine was on her feet and dancing too. Belle danced with her palms facing out and there was a strange white glow to her fingertips. Burn blisters, Madeleine remembered. She lost herself in dance, and Jack and Belle turned to each other, impressed — the girl could dance — and then all three were leaping over clutter, knocking over clutter, blowing around the room.

4.

Elliot was flying.

The silence up here, the break in his own footfall.

There'd been the *thud-thud-thud* and the frenzy of windrush, then this: up here, his body flying, the air holding still, the air holding him, sailing him, under him, around him. His hand outstretched, fingers stretched ahead, his body holding its own shape. The spin on the deftball just above, just ahead, a perfect curve, exactly right.

He'd almost cleared the furrow. He'd catch the ball, his feet would hit the ground, and he'd be running. Now though, right now, in this moment, up here, there was the quiet, the kindness of the sky — then a front-end loader hit him from the left.

Hard not to take it personally.

Not so much the illegal tackle, the head butt in the eye, the clawing at his hand. Not even the fact that they could have just about killed him, or at least cracked some bones, hitting him right over the furrow like that. It was more the interruption of his flight. There was something so big and peaceful, so solitary about that flight. Whereas, a couple of Rangos players slamming him from out of nowhere — that felt crowded. And noisy.

He was standing on the sideline now, an ice pack to his face, and somebody was strapping up his ankle. The game had been stopped, and the whole place was letting loose with outrage. Whistles were blowing, fists pounding the air, angry shouts intersecting.

"No *way* that was an illegal tackle," the Rangos coach was bellowing, while Jimmy, the Bonfire Antelopes coach, took a breath, ready to attack.

Of course it was an illegal tackle.

"*Now* it's a deftball match," said a nearby voice, grim with satisfaction.

It was a big crowd today. The locals were out, and the Rangos had brought along a busload of supporters. So there was plenty of volume to the outrage. But something, Elliot realized, was askew about the shouting. Between the words, below the words, unease.

He glanced up at the sky, shifting the icepack. It was a low, gray, scowling sky, full of cold and rain. To the west was a fresh batch of storm cloud, and now he saw the reason for the tension. Those clouds had the kind of twist and lean that made you think of third-level Grays. Somebody walked by with a string bag full of bottles, and heads turned swiftly at the jangle. Sounded a little like warning bells.

Corrie-Lynn emerged from the crowd, and walked right up to him.

She watched as he peeled the ice pack away, flinching a little, and looked at the pieces of blood and skin.

"It's swelling up nicely," she informed him. "Gonna be a beautiful shiner."

He pressed the pack against his face again.

"There was another article in the paper about you guys today," Corrie-Lynn added.

"About the Antelopes?"

She shook her head.

"The Royal Youth Alliance. A photo of you all just before you went to the Lake of Spells."

Elliot nodded.

The guy strapping his ankle sat back on his haunches.

"Can it take your weight?" he said.

Elliot tested it. His ankle protested like an angry coach, then the shouting settled down to an irritable mutter.

"I can play."

The guy twisted his lips into a skeptical grimace, then shrugged.

Corrie-Lynn was still standing by his side.

"You really went to the Lake of Spells," she said, "and talked about educational issues across the Kingdom?" Her blue eyes studied his face. "You sat there on the edge of that lake and you said, *hm, is there too much homework*?"

"We caught spells too."

Elliot glanced up at the scoreboard, calculating what they had to do to win.

He looked back at Corrie-Lynn. Smart kid.

"You use that clear-away spell I gave you yet?" he asked.

"Saving it for special. For a real big mess."

The shouting had picked up in some places, quieted down in others. The cold was distracting some people. They were buttoning their coats, clapping gloved hands together. Grown-ups were chasing kids around, to warm themselves up, and the kids were in fits of excitement at the attention. Then kids were slipping in the mud and scrambling back up, shrieking outrage at the adults: "You *made* me *fall*!"

"That girl from Jagged Edge," Corrie-Lynn was saying.

Elliot was looking at his hands. They were turning a violent purple from the cold, and the welts from that scratch were rising up.

He turned back to his cousin. "Keira?" he said.

"Yeah, that's her name. She's super pretty."

"I guess." Elliot shrugged.

"You're going to the next Alliance thing tomorrow, right? In Jagged Edge?"

"Yep."

"So you'll get to see her there. She's got those gray-green eyes I like."

"She has?"

"The picture in the paper was color this time. And it said she's a Night-Dweller! What's a Night-Dweller like? Had you met any before her? Before Keira?"

Elliot held the ice pack away from his face again. His sweat was turning to ice drops. The cold of the ice pack was getting right into his spine. He dropped it to the grass, tested out his ankle again, this time with some stretches.

"Yep," he said. "And so have you. Plenty of Night-Dwellers in town."

"No way."

"Sure. Yolander who does the dawn shift at your Inn? She's a Night-Dweller. And Cam Monterino who collects the trash?"

Corrie-Lynn's face shone with surprised pleasure. "Oh, *yeah.* I *have* met Night-Dwellers! I guess I knew that, but I kind of forgot. I'm usually asleep when they're around, so . . ."

"But you see some in the day too," Elliot told her. "There are Night-Dwellers with day jobs. They switch their sleeping patterns."

"No way," Corrie-Lynn said again. "They must be so cranky, whoever they are, sleeping at their not normal time. Like who? Give me an example."

"Well," Elliot said, "like the high-school physics teacher. Jimmy's girlfriend. Isabella Tamborlaine." He touched Corrie-Lynn's shoulder, and pointed, and she followed the line of his hand.

Isabella was usually quiet and elegant, but now she was standing with her legs apart, her hands on her hips, and she was talking in a fast, strident, angry voice that carried right over to them. She was alongside Jimmy, lecturing one of the referees, and both Jimmy and the ref were gazing at her. Elliot could see some of his friends over that way, grins in their eyes, watching too.

Not that long ago she hadn't even known the basics of the game, Elliot remembered — she was from Jagged Edge, where it wasn't played so much — but now the rules were flying out of her mouth, turning beautiful technical circles. She was citing rules and measurements, and the referee's face was paling with respect, while Jimmy watched with a grin made out of pride.

"And what's more," Isabella explained, "I *heard* the Rangos players earlier — I *heard* them saying, *'Get number twelve!'* I heard it clearly: *'Take down number twelve!'* That's Elliot. *He's* number twelve! They were planning it!"

"Uh," said Jimmy, and "Well," said the referee, and they both rearranged their facial expressions, exchanging a brief glance.

"Well, *that's* okay," Jimmy said to Isabella. "That's sort of part of the game — you always want to take down the best player. The hero is fair game. It's not —"

"That's ridiculous!" Isabella cried, and she began to throw strident rules at them again, but now she'd lost their respect. They turned to talk to each other.

Corrie-Lynn and Elliot laughed.

"It's true, though," Corrie-Lynn said. "You *are* the hero of this game. When you jump over the furrows like that, it's like you're flying."

Elliot was stretching his hamstrings.

"That's why I think you're an Occasional Pilot," Corrie-Lynn continued. "You should read the description from the Guidebook." She opened her hand, revealing a folded paper. "I copied it out for you, 'cause I'm not allowed to keep carrying the book around anymore. *'It belongs in the front room! It's for the guests of the Watermelon Inn!'* "

The last part she spoke in a perfect imitation of her mother's voice. Elliot could even see Auntie Alanna's expressions on her little face.

"You've got to at least read it," Corrie-Lynn urged, still holding out the paper.

A whistle was blowing again. A decision had been made. It *had* been an illegal tackle. There was a lift in the shouting, cheers from the locals, boos from the visitors, and then a settling down.

"Okay, kid," Elliot said, touching his swollen eye, and squinting around to see where his backpack was. He saw it, and pointed. "Can you put it with my stuff?"

He jogged across to take the penalty.

5.

Madeleine was walking the Cambridge night again.

There was something in the moonlight tonight. It was stroking the stonework and spires, leaning into cracks between the cobblestones, caressing the stained-glass windows. She felt her heart lift with magic.

A young man, shaved head, walked by, shouting into a mobile phone. "You are *fookin* kidding me!" He paused, and she could see the intensity of his listening face, furious intensity, tightening his cheekbones. "You are fookin *kidding* me!" he shouted again.

Her footsteps slowed a little, subdued, then the moonlight picked back up again. Windows, arches, signs jutting from buildings. Streets that curled and turned, window frames in primary colours.

She passed bicycles chained to fences, and a pair of drooping, empty chains.

She reached the parking meter. The alleyway was quiet.

Hey, Elliot. You there?

She waited.

Yep.

There was a strange unfolding, a slide of relief. Last night with Belle and Jack had left her feeling displaced. Here, with Elliot, she belonged.

You had a big deftball game today, right? Against the Rangers? Did you win?

Rangos. But close enough. I'm impressed. And yeah, we won.

She changed the subject fast, before he could start on a play-by-play account of the game. Boys did that. She'd already given enough of her life to deftball.

Listen, we keep saying we need to figure out the "cracks," but never getting into it. So I'm thinking, when does something crack? There's wind and heat. But don't tell me to bring a hair dryer. I am not going to stand here in the middle of the night blowing this parking meter dry.

Take it easy, don't even know what you're talking about. Okay, cracks. Well, there's erosion. Wear and tear. Vibrations over time. If you drop something like a glass jar, it can get a crack in it. Is that the kind of thing you mean?

If you crash into something it can get cracked.

Hurts anyway. Someone crashing into you.

So, what do you think caused the cracks between our world and Cello? A giant collision? Like a meteor hitting? And is it WRONG that they're there?

The WSU think it's wrong.

Are they right? I mean, a crack means something's broken, right? Like things are misaligned. Like broken families. Like the crack down the middle of our families — running down the space between our mothers and our fathers. Between <u>us</u> and our lost fathers.

You're on fire tonight. Sorry if I'm not keeping up, I'm half dead on my feet after the game. Got a bit injured. Keep going, though. I want to see where you're headed.

Madeleine smiled at that, *Half dead on my feet after the game.* She thought again of Elliot, his skinny arms. They must have let him play today. He wasn't used to it, tripped over his feet. He was probably proud of his injury. She should have let him give his detailed account.

Not right now, though. She wrote again:

It's like something has gone wrong. "Cracked" means crazy or high or insane. It means broken. It's like flying, then falling, then you hit or crash and break.

So you mean Cello fell? Or the World? Or both. Or what. Sorry, what?

You're missing the point. I'm thinking of gravity again. Flying, falling, crashing, cracking. We need to make a crack – make a bigger crack – so we need to fly and fall.

Tried that. Remember? It hurt. Turns out cracks hurt.

Madeleine held her pen over the paper. Elliot's handwriting was fading into scrawl. She had the sense he was slipping away, slipping into sleep. She also had the sense that she was on the edge, on the verge.

She wrote:

There's a formula for gravity. It's to do with centres of things and how far apart they are, and their masses. Mass is not exactly what you weigh, more what you're made of. So, those are the questions. How far apart are we? What's inside you? What's inside me?

You're losing me again. I have no idea how far apart we are. We could be standing side by side, or forever apart. Either way, my eyes are closing.

This was like a race — she had to reach her point before she lost him. But what *was* her point? She was losing that too. She wrote:

Here's a line I read today: The force exerted on you by something far, far away may be vanishingly small, but it's still there.

She posted that, and something rose inside her. That was the point. She had caught the point in that note. She felt she had reached across the crack, and touched him. His reply would sing its way into her heart.

Yeah, okay. Seriously, I can't see the paper or hold the pen anymore. It's like I'm already dreaming. Gotta go, sorry. Talk tomorrow night?

Or maybe it wouldn't.

She tapped her fingers fast against her forehead. She felt in the strangest trancelike state herself. Before she could write again, another note appeared.

Forgot — I've got the next RYA conference tomorrow, so I can't talk then. It's just for one night, though, and it's in Tek, Jagged Edge, which is only a few hours by express, so see you here Monday night? I'm sure there's sense in what you're saying but you're sounding like a total lunatic. Night, Madeleine. Sleep sweet.

Wait, she thought. *Wait*.

She whispered: *the misaligned centre of you, the misaligned centre of me*, and there was a mighty drag sideways and there he was.

Just there.

Right there.

6.

Elliot walked away from the sculpture.

He stopped in the school gate, trying to remember where he was.

You could be asleep and awake at the same time, turned out.

Or maybe he was purely asleep.

He scratched his head, and it came to him. The truck was parked just up the street. He teetered a little, felt a presence behind him, and turned.

7.

Night in a cold schoolyard, and there he was, Elliot, walking away from her.

The shape of him, the width of his shoulders in a big coat with a hood. He was wearing old boots and his stride was fast. He was at the school gates. She tried to call, but she had no voice. She wasn't there, but she was there. He had stopped and was scratching his head in an artless way — using his whole hand, like a child, thinking about something else. He took another step through the gate, and there was that lack of consciousness about his body again. It was in the way he swung his arms, in his head's movement from side to side.

Then he turned right around.

He was facing her.

And there he was.

It was as if someone had shoved her hard from the side. The shock of it.

That he'd have *that* kind of face.

Even with his right eye swollen shut and bruised, even with his distracted look, even in the half-light, you could see what it was.

It was the kind of face that makes everything that's tight or tense inside you fade away. The kind that makes you smile a slow, slow smile. The kind that makes passersby turn to look, then turn again. The kind you want to press closer to. To see all its expressions. You want to see it in the light and in shade.

She ran her eyes over his nose, his forehead, his cheekbones, his hair. Ah, that kind of hair. The kind that has a messiness to it, that he probably didn't notice except to wash it, or to run his hands through it when he recalled he was supposed to look neat. The kind that gets all kinds of sunlight in it.

Her eyes returned to his face. The kind of face you want to pause, then let it free, then pause again —

There was another pull sideways.

She was back in Cambridge.

8.

There was nothing behind him. Empty schoolyard.

He turned back again, and walked through the school gate. Under a streetlight, into the dark, under a streetlight, into the dark.

He shook himself. Ah, this was ridiculous. He shouldn't have stayed talking to her for so long, but he wasn't *this* tired.

You have to be awake to drive, he reminded himself. Maybe he ought to just fall asleep in the truck? Just for half an hour maybe, then drive home?

He found the keys in his pocket, and a hand fell on his shoulder.

The clash of keys on concrete juddered through him.

He swung around, and there were two of them.

Shapes with grins, one big shape, one small. Agent Tovey, Agent Kim.

"What are you doing out this late?" Agent Tovey said.

He started to answer. "Just," he said. He couldn't remember the reason he had planned. Up his sleeve. Something about deftball.

"Heard you were a hero in the big game today," Tovey said. "Have to watch you play sometime."

"Looks like you took a hammering," Agent Kim added.

They were both grinning at him. Their eyes were all on fire.

He fumbled for thoughts again. *What? What* was he doing out? The sideways tilt of it.

"It's great," Agent Tovey said. "It's great you're up and about."

Why is it great? he thought, reeling. They *like* arresting people?

Well, he guessed they would. It was their job. Catching the bad guys.

Elliot stared at them. Or tried to. They were fading in and out.

"Thought we'd have to wait until morning," Kim added. He was jerking his thumb toward the Sheriff's station across the road. "We've been in there on conference call all night. We've got news, Elliot."

"Good news," Tovey added.

Something shifted again in Elliot. They were swaying with their smiles. They were rolling on their feet. Or maybe his eyes were swaying and rolling them for him. Did they mind? That he was making them sway?

"That recipe book that you found," Tovey said, and Kim's smile widened. "You were right. There was a code in it. Our guys cracked it," he said. "So we know what your dad and Uncle Jon were up to. Where they hid their samples."

They were watching his face, smiling at his eyes.

"It's a huge step," Kim added.

"It's good news, Elliot," Tovey said. "It just about tells us where he is. Setting aside the implications of the invention. Smart guy, your dad. Impressive guy."

"Swing by the Watermelon in the morning," Kim said. "We'll explain."

"We'll *show* you one of the samples." Tovey smiled. "Know how to have a good time, don't you, kid? You look half dead. Not too drunk to drive, are you?"

Elliot shook his head.

They walked on, grinning back at him.

"It's great news," Tovey called again.

Something snapped awake in Elliot. *It's great news*, he thought.

He opened the truck door. His hand trembled. *It's great news.* The tremble took ahold of his heart. He climbed inside and allowed himself to smile.

PART 8

1.

"There is no button."

Elliot had been in an elevator before. Not one with a waterfall for a door, sure, and not one set in a corridor lined with green apples and glass chutes. But there was a bank of elevators in the new shopping complex in Sugarloaf, and he knew that you had to push a button.

"There's no button," Keira repeated. "It's got a sensor. It'll come."

"But how does it know if you want to go up or down?"

"Senses that too."

Elliot shot her a look to see if she had her glint, but she was watching the waterfall. Dancing a little too. She kept doing this sideways thing with her shoulders, and now, as he watched, she added a quick swivel with her hips. It just about killed him, that swivel. She was dressed in the Jagged Edge style: the short tunic with huge pockets, where all the Edgians kept their fold-away computing machines, a capelbeast wool cape, tied loosely at the throat, and black tights. The only thing he didn't like was the netting over her hair.

He looked away and noticed he was tapping his own foot. It was that music they had going all over this place. Its rhythm got right inside your body but it also felt like a manifestation of Elliot's own excitement. There was a high-speed drumbeat, and it was running alongside his own heartbeat, like it wanted to keep it company. Like the beat and his heart were jogging companions.

Something kept rising out of the drumbeat too. He didn't know much about this sort of music, but he guessed it was electronic? And that rising part was the melody? Nope. It was too weird to be melody. It was more a twanging, supernatural thing, which might have been underwater bagpipes played with steak knives. Now and then, surprisingly, there was something sweet about it.

Anyhow, whatever it was that kept rising then folding itself back into the beat, *that* matched up with the hope that kept surging inside Elliot.

The agents knew where his dad was. The agents were about to rescue him.

But here, now, he was at the Cardamom Palace in the city of Tek, Jagged Edge.

This was a night-dwelling city and Princess Ko had decided that, as a gesture of respect, the Royal Youth Alliance should immediately adjust to the time zone. So they'd all arrived at eight P.M., in time for hair and makeup — the makeup guy was looking lost and bored until he saw Elliot's black eye, lit up, and performed some kind of magic with a tube and brush so it completely disappeared — followed by welcome reception and photo shoot.

Sunshine cocktails, papaya squares, and pecan clusters had drifted into their hands, apparently riding on drafts. They'd been invited to partake of light washes and chilled by mini-tornadoes.

He got the sunshine cocktails and light washes — Night-Dwellers had to compensate for deficiencies brought on by their hours — but the mini-tornadoes? What were they all about? Apart from messing up your clothes and your hair. "They're a facet of the Ethos," Keira explained, which was helpful.

The photo shoot too was bewildering. JE photographers seemed to work without cameras and without actually looking at their subjects. Who knew where to turn or when to smile? Or which person actually *was* the photographer.

Next they'd been shown to their rooms to relax for a moment. But how could you relax with hologrammatic image consultants dressing you up, restyling your hair and then holding up mirrors: *"Do you like?"*

"Well, sure," Elliot had said at one point, just to be polite.

The voices had faded instantly then, as if they'd lost interest, and he'd found himself back in his own jeans, shirt, and scuffed boots. Right away, though, white light had shot across the air and a new voice had spoken: *"Time for a sunshine massage before your meeting. Would you like?"*

"Thanks, but no," Elliot had said, and he'd headed out into the corridor.

He'd run into Keira at the elevator.

He couldn't help it. The excitement was like a puppy that keeps jumping at you.

"They think they've found my dad," he said, and Keira turned, and he'd never seen her smile like that before. It was a beam. It heightened her cheekbones, and gave her one disconcertingly cute dimple.

"Turns out he and my Uncle Jon invented a listening device," Elliot continued, and he reached into his pocket. "The agency decoded his recipe book, see, so that told them his secret hiding place — an air vent behind the corkboard in his shop — and there were a bunch of samples there. This is one."

He held out his hand. The listening device sat on his palm, looking exactly like a paper clip.

A door opened somewhere down the corridor, and Samuel emerged backward, calling to his room: "Call yourselves a good evening from me! As you suggest, I will turn my mind to your sartorial suggestions, but I *cannot* promise any *fondness* for your fashion choices, for . . . oh." The door had closed itself, firmly. "I did not mean offense," Samuel muttered, then he turned and saw Elliot and Keira, standing at the elevator.

"They wish to dress me!" he shouted to them. "The voices in my room don't like my clothing!" This last he added with a jocular downturn of his mouth, as if they would share his astonishment.

Elliot and Keira regarded the approaching ruffles, frills, and jodhpurs, and tried to muster some echoing surprise. Tricky.

"Just ignore the voices," Keira advised.

She took the paper clip from Elliot's hand, and studied it.

"Looks good," she said, "but I don't get why the Hostiles would care. There are plenty of smaller, slicker listening devices than this. I made some myself at school when I was ten." She glanced up. "No offense to your dad."

Samuel looked at the waterfall-elevator.

"Picturesque," he said. "Shall we locate the stairs? We are convening in a Conference Room labeled with the letter *Q*, which is on Level 3, I believe, and that needs must be *up*."

But Elliot's attention was on Keira. "This one's different," he said. "It's super-nano technology. It works with particles smaller than light." He paused. "Finer than particles of magic."

"Does magic consist of particles or waves?" Samuel murmured, half to himself, as he drew out his pocket watch. "Should we not locate the stairs?"

"The agents were raving about it," Elliot said.

"This thing transcends *magic*?"

"Right."

"It can *bypass* magic?"

Elliot nodded.

"So you're saying it will work in Olde Quainte and the Magical North?"

"Exactly."

"But that changes everything! It gives the Loyalists an unbelievable edge!"

Elliot was grinning.

Samuel, meanwhile, was studying the waterfall again. "Oh," he said. "Like to a cobblestone in brill cream, this must be one of those people-moving machines. Thus, we have no need of stairs?" He turned to the others, and followed their gaze to the paper clip, now on Keira's palm.

"There were also a couple of transponders in the hiding space," Elliot said. "And it turns out the woman who was working with my dad — Mischka Tegan — she used one of those to communicate with her people — which was dumb, and might be how Dad and Uncle Jon figured out who she was — which was when everything went to hell. But it also means —"

Keira's eyes widened: "It means they've got the frequency she used. They can figure out the location of her unit."

"Right."

"You are talking of your father, Elliot? You have good news of your father?" Samuel reached out and shook Elliot's hand vigorously. "Call yourself my congratulations!"

"They narrowed it down to two possibilities, and they're pretty sure which it is. They're going to start negotiations to get him back."

Down the corridor, two further doors opened. The Princess and her stable boy stepped out of facing rooms, caught each other's eye, and right away began a synchronized dance, in time with the pervasive drumbeat, toward the others.

Both were dressed in the Edgian style, and they danced as if they were locals. Just as they slid to a stop, there was a rippling of chimes. The waterfall slid open like curtains.

"Lucky timing," enthused Samuel.

"Slow." Elliot countered. He and Keira had been standing there almost ten minutes.

"Neither," Keira said. "It was waiting until we all got here."

They stepped through the gap into a diamond-shaped space, Elliot looking sideways at Keira. The elevator paused for a fraction, then flew upward.

* * *

By the time they reached the doorway to Conference Room 3Q, they all knew about Elliot's father, and his magic-circumventing listening device, and they all wanted to try it.

Although, as Keira pointed out, there was no loose magic in Jagged Edge, so there was nothing for it to circumvent.

"So you don't want to try it?" Elliot asked.

"That's not what I said."

The conference room had a vaguely circular shape, but its walls were composed of protruding spikes. The effect was like a child's enthusiastic drawing of the sun.

The security agents had placed themselves inside one of the smaller spikes. They were somewhat squashed in there, and off center from the room, but their expressions, as they gazed toward the opposite side of the spike, were as solemn as ever. Each member of the Royal Youth Alliance — apart from Princess Ko, who strode directly to the conference table — paused to stare at the agents, and reflect on notions of dignity.

After a beat, though, each carried on into the room, all talking at once about the listening device, and how to test it.

One of the larger protruding spikes turned out to be a kitchen nook ("a refreshment point," Keira corrected), so they placed the paper clip on the sink in there, then took turns murmuring beside it while the others ran up and down the corridors of the Palace wearing the ear phone.

Eventually, when they had all agreed that the sound quality was superb, and Sergio was offering to take the paper clip into an Edgian fixed wing, place it on the cockpit floor, then *lean out the window and whisper* — for who could tell when one's enemy might be galloping across the plains? And what use was a listening device unless it could operate above the sounds of rushing wind and pounding hooves?

Such sounds could be duplicated by the rushing wind outside the fixed wing!

At this point, Agent Nettles stepped out from the small spike.

"Princess!" She gave a slight bow, which might have been a gesture of respect or an assertion of authority. "Apologies for the interruption, but could I remind you that this meeting is scheduled to conclude in exactly one hour? And that we need another list of royal activities from you as a matter of urgency? Certainly by the morning."

The Princess paused. A sigh seemed to wash across her face.

"Of course," she said. "Thank you."

Agent Nettles stepped back.

"A list of royal activities?" Samuel queried.

"Remind me to have a brainstorming session before you all leave," Princess Ko said. "I need to invent things that my family are doing — regular, unremarkable things like opening hospital wings or attending charitable galas — so we can feed them to the press." She stepped toward the table. "It gets tiresome."

She waited until Elliot had retrieved his paper clip from the refreshment point, and taken his seat.

"As delighted as we are that Elliot's father is on the verge of being recovered," she said, "we need to pursue the recovery of *my* family now. I wish *never* to have to make another list of royal activities. I need reports from all of you. Keira, you have already informed me that your documents contain soil analyses from the dusky regions of Nature Strip. In other words: useless. We will say no more about that. Samuel, I understand you have compiled another set of accounts of journeys between Cello and the World. Hand these to Elliot, in case they are of use. Sergio, you will begin our meeting by informing us of your news from the WSU. And Elliot." She turned to Elliot and spoke in a strange monotone, not quite meeting his eye. "I am saving for last. I assume you now have responses from my family. I assume you have opened the crack. In you, Elliot, I place all my hope."

2.

Princess Ko's mood had flattened, but so had the chairs.

In fact, they would not stay still. Immediately after the Princess's speech, the chairs folded upward so that their occupants were forced into standing positions. A moment later, they flattened themselves into almost-beds.

"What the —" Elliot swung to his feet.

Samuel's chair began to move again and he toppled to the floor.

Sergio laughed aloud.

"It's to stimulate creativity," Keira explained, riding along with her chair's movements calmly. "All conference-room chairs do this. You think best when you're upright, but you're most imaginative lying prostrate. So they rotate positions."

"I'm not sitting on that thing," Elliot said. Samuel murmured his agreement.

"Sit on the chairs," commanded Princes Ko.

Samuel obeyed. His chair swiveled, and he thumped back onto the floor.

Sergio laughed again. Elliot put a knee on his seat to hold it still, then went to sit. The chair moved and he swore and stood up again.

Sergio's laughter rippled. A smile was forming on Keira's face. Samuel whimpered from the carpet.

"Oh, very well!" The Princess pressed a button, and the chairs adjusted themselves into regular chair position and stayed that way.

Elliot sat down. The table was clear except for several tall glasses of celery sticks. Now that the room had grown still, things felt strangely close and intimate.

"All right, Sergio," said Princess Ko. "Any news on the detector?"

Sergio launched into a long description of the improvements he had made to the internal communications system at the WSU. He realized that some might think his improvements were "the trivial," even "the unnecessary." To him, however, the changes had the beauty of the whinny of a Southern Clime Highlander compared to, say, the bray of a Spotted Saddle Horse.

There were murmurs of congratulations around the table, and a long, slow sigh from Princess Ko.

"Please," she said.

Sergio handed out a chart showing the "beautiful complications" in the structure of the WSU.

They studied the chart.

"As you will see," Sergio said, "there are the *many* departments and many twists and turns. This reports to that, and then your eyes go *sideways* and, ho! It is the Classification department! The Policy, the Detection, the Censorship, and see the big and beautiful rectangle? The Enforcement!"

"How is this helpful?" Princess Ko asked.

"It is not," said Sergio. "But interesting, no?"

"Well, Sergio, I assume you're no closer to getting the detector."

"Ah." Sergio breathed in deeply. "If I were only allowed the access!

But, alas, I am not." He paused, then spoke carefully: "I am thinking I should say this, that I have now seen myself some people from Enforcement. In the coffee room."

"And what, they're all superheroes?" Keira interrupted. "They extend their limbs around corners and spit ice cubes from their toes into their espressos?"

Sergio regarded her. "For what would they want ice in their coffee?"

Keira spoke impatiently: "We *know* they're tough guys with degrees in sharpshooting who can kill twenty men by blowing their noses. You keep giving them this supernatural aura, but how is that helpful to Elliot?"

Elliot smiled. Her support was surprising and sweet, but no longer necessary. The WSU had stopped scaring him. He was back to indifference — contempt even.

He played with the paper clip, tossing it on the palm of his hand, spinning it between his fingertips. His father had made this. His father was a genius. His father was coming home.

Therefore — and a part of him knew this didn't make sense, but here it was anyway, a beautiful truth — therefore, he was indestructible. No way was the WSU coming for him. If they did? He could take them. Compared to the huge and wondrous news about his dad, the WSU were dust mites.

"It is more than their superpowers," Sergio addressed Keira, glancing toward Elliot as he did. "There is a look in their eyes. I have seen horses with such eyes."

"Of course you have," Keira said mildly.

"A piece of these people, it is lost. In the stead, there is a passion, and the passion, it has hooves. I see two types of passion. One is about disorder. These people, they hate the mess or the untidy or the things that are broken. A crack, to them, is something broken. So. It *must* be fixed."

The others were silent, considering this.

"And the other type?"

"The other is this word, *xenophobic*. They fear what the cracks might let in."

"You have seen horses with xenophobic eyes?" marveled Samuel.

Sergio ignored him. "I am not just meaning that the cracks might let in the plague again — and so lead to war with other Kingdoms, especially Aldhibah — no. These people have a bigger fear — it is the fear of anything strange or different or *outside*."

"Ah," said Elliot recklessly — and irrelevantly — "we're always fighting with Aldhibah over one thing or another."

"Which is why," snapped the Princess, "we need to get my father back before the Namesaking Ceremony. It's a month away!"

She tapped her fingernails on the table, then fixed her eyes on Sergio.

"You're in human resources. Couldn't you use *blackmail*, or let's say, *bribery* to get a detector? Threaten to fire people. Offer them holidays — sick leave, pay leave — *I* don't know the terminology . . . or am I wrong? Isn't this what human resources is about?"

Sergio smiled. "It is, yes! More or less. Beautiful strategy, Princess! But impossible. I am thinking that my clearance level is not quite . . . that high."

The Princess's face fell into a scowl of frustration. She took a deep breath and turned to Elliot.

"I need better news from you," she said. "News of my family. Now."

3.

Elliot couldn't see a way around this.

It would have to be the truth: Madeleine had not heard back from a single member of the family.

The Princess blinked rapidly.

"None?"

"None."

"Do you trust her?"

Elliot considered this a moment. Then he nodded. "Got no reason not to.

"The postal system might be slow," he said next, "but I'm thinking — if Samuel is right about the amnesia thing — well, no offense but they probably just think you're a crackpot."

Princess Ko stared.

"As to a coffee bean in sneakers," Samuel murmured, "I'm afraid that I *am* right about the amnesia thing."

The Princess shook her head, pursing her lips. "Then we need to *trigger* their memories. Quick!" She snapped her fingers. "What brings back memories?"

"Smells," said Sergio at once. "No matter where I am if I smell the leather, the jasmine, and the bacon, I am thinking of saddling Kafka, a purebred Highlander stallion. He was stabled alongside a jasmine bush. And he loved the breakfast."

"How often do you smell that combination, Sergio?"

"Shush," said Princess Ko. "No jokes, Keira. Tell me a memory trigger."

"Wasn't joking. But okay. Music."

The Princess nodded.

"If I *re*read a novel," Samuel offered, "it sometimes takes me back to the place where I was when I *first* read it, as to a —"

The Princess gave a half nod and turned to Elliot, who thought a moment.

"Little things that my dad used to use," he said, "bring back whole memories of him. Like we've got this pepper grinder in the shape of a panda bear — you turn the bear's head and pepper comes out. Every time I see it, I remember Dad sitting at the kitchen table arguing with my mother about some school meeting they were supposed to go to, while he ground pepper onto slices of tomato."

"Very well. I will prepare further letters for my family — in these letters I will include techniques to *make* them remember. You will have your Madeleine mail them, Elliot."

"Make sure they're small enough to fit through the crack," Elliot reminded her.

"So you have not yet opened the crack?"

Elliot held her gaze.

"We're trying," he said. "We keep getting glimpses of each other, but we can't work out a pattern."

"Were the accounts of historic crossovers not useful?"

"Well." Elliot looked across at Samuel. "See, the thing is — no. There's not a single word in them about cracks, or about *how* those people got across."

Samuel frowned. "Of course not," he said. "Did you expect such a thing?"

There was a confused shuffling.

"Uh?" said Keira eventually.

"*Those* parts of the accounts have been removed! Call yourselves my apologies if you did not know this! I bethought me everyone knew! Surely you know that the WSU is *rigorous* in ensuring that nothing about the mechanics of cracks is available to the public? Long ago they took to the accounts with heavy black markers! The archives of the Harmony Institute — why, they are a veritable *cheese.* I mean, by this, that they are filled with holes."

"This makes sense," Sergio nodded. "I wondered what the Censorship Department did with their hours, besides the arguing about deftball scores. Their department is coming first in the Deftball Sweepstakes." He smiled suddenly. "At picnic day, Censorship provided the cheese platter!" He glanced at their confusion. "I am thinking of Samuel's cheese reference — it is the bad joke — of course."

"Of course," echoed Princess Ko, crestfallen. "I should have known this."

"Do not blame your royal self!" Samuel cried. "It has been so for centuries, and thus I suppose none bothers mentioning it afresh. Only those with particular interest in World Studies — such as classroom teachers of the subject — would know. There are regulations upon the syllabus, a single authorized textbook, so they must know — and me, of course — I know." Samuel reached for a celery stick. "Even with all the censorship, it is impossible even to gain access to the World-Cello archives. They're kept behind a locked gate at Brellidge University Library. Only those certified by the WSU may enter."

The Princess leaned forward.

"Samuel," she said, studying him. "How do *you* gain access?"

Samuel crunched his celery stick. The room grew still around the crunching.

He swallowed, and wiped his mouth.

"As to a swan in an icebox," he began, and then stopped and started again. "Each Saturday morning, I arise at dawn and take the mail cart on the two-hour journey to Brellidge. It is comfortable enough — I am given blankets on wintry days, and the ricketting and shaking only bothers me when I have a headache.

"I am known to the librarians as a member of the Royal Youth Alliance, and have betold them that my task, for the Alliance, is to complete a thorough history of the royal family. Hence, the assistant head librarian — a bright-eyed elderly woman, with mischief in her smile and rigor to the shoulders of her smartly tailored suits — usually, these suits are ash gray or midnight blue, as to a sausage in a — yes, Princess. You are right. Forgive me. At any rate, when I arrive, she leads me down, down, down into the dungeons — do not alarm yourselves, friends! 'Dungeon' is merely the nickname given to the underground floors of the library. At any rate, she unlocks the Royal Archives for me, ensures I am wearing the white gloves that all who handle antique manuscripts must wear, and checks that I have naught with me but pencil and paper."

Samuel looked sideways, aware that the security agents had turned their heads, and were watching him, listening. He blushed, self-conscious.

"Once she has left me to myself, I slip across to the locked World-Cello archives, which are in the next wing along, and I unlock the gate myself. I have acquired me a secret key, as to which you must not concern yourselves. At any rate, I slip in there, take what I can from the archives, and bring it back to my original desk. I work until late Saturday night, at which point I simply sleep on the library floor. The librarians have come to accept this — in fact, the junior assistant librarian once kindly slipped me a hand-stitched cushion for my head. By the midnight clock, I return the archives I've been copying — and the next day, I call myself a farewell to the librarians, and take the milk wagon home."

There was another silence.

Eventually, Keira spoke. "How do your parents feel about you spending your weekends sleeping in the Brellidge University Library?" she said.

Samuel reached for another celery stick, then looked around fretfully. "Why only celery?" he demanded. "I could not fathom the strange foods in the welcome reception, and now my hunger is as to a steam train in a chimney."

"It's usually just celery or carrots at meetings," Keira explained. "In Jagged Edge, we believe in crunch foods — that's why all the apples in the corridors — they're the foods that vigorate and reflexate."

Elliot swung around to look at her. "What language are you speaking?" he said. "Crunch foods? Vigorate? Reflexate?"

Keira narrowed her eyes at him. "It's just Jagged Edge slang, there's nothing —" but then seeing the spark in Elliot's eyes, she said, "Quit making fun of me. You know what I mean," her dimple returning.

Samuel spoke again. "My parents have passed on," he said. "An accident. I live alone above the kitchens at the Cat and Fiddle Inn."

Keira's dimple faded.

"When did you lose your parents?"

"At the age of eleven."

"But how old are you now?"

"Twelve."

Again, there was a rustle through the room.

Everyone looked at Samuel. His face was smooth and plump, but there was something worn about the edges of his eyes, gaunt in the lines around his mouth.

"The index cards you gave me are all written in fountain pen," Elliot remembered. "Didn't you say you were only allowed to use pencil?"

"I am," agreed Samuel. "I write them out again when I get home.

Late into Sunday night I work on them." He shrugged. "My pencil scrawlings are pale and nigh illegible! I would not wish them upon you!"

The Princess leaned her elbows onto the table, her chin on her hands. "Samuel," she said, "do you think you could get us the originals? I know the important bits are all blocked out and whatever, but maybe — I don't know, with the right kind of magnifying glass — maybe we could get something useful?"

Samuel looked at her, aghast. A tremor ran across his face. "You wish me to *steal* from the archives? To sneak the originals out of the library?"

The Princess shrugged. "Yes."

Samuel looked at the celery in his hand.

"If I could get some *real* food —" he began.

"Chocolate!" exclaimed Sergio.

He flung back his chair. "Come!" he said. "We are needing the break, and we are needing the hot chocolate! *My* chocolate, in especially!"

The others turned to Princess Ko. Her shoulders rose and fell.

"But will they have what you need in their kitchen thing?" she asked.

"Refreshment point," Keira corrected automatically.

"Let us see!" cried Sergio, and he danced into that room, the others following.

He stopped at the sink, and opened the cupboard, gazing at the rows of containers and canisters.

"It is well stocked," he said. "See this? The Jagged Edge dark chocolate is the best in the Kingdom, yes, but the *secret* ingredient —"

"That Samuel's a surprise," said a voice, clear, deep, thoughtful — and Sergio stopped, confused.

"Impressive." That was a woman's voice. "How's he breaking into the archives anyway? What's he mean about getting himself a key?"

In the small kitchen space, they frowned at one another. Then Elliot drew the earpiece from his pocket, and placed it on the sink.

The paper clip was still on the table in the conference room. It was transmitting the voices of the security agents.

"But *Sergio*," said a male voice — Agent Ramsay — "seriously, *what* is the Princess thinking?"

Princess Ko reached for the earpiece, but Sergio stopped her hand.

"It wouldn't be so bad," said the voice of Agent Nettles, "if he didn't have to *dance* everywhere. Honestly. The leaping, prancing, and twirling! Does he have to be *that* effervescent?"

"And that effeminate," agreed Agent Ramsay. "He's so ridiculously slight."

"Well he's from Maneesh. They're a little people. But I know what you mean — people that skinny give me the heebie-jeebies. Can't he eat more? Or work out or something? I think he's even got one of those concave chests."

"And the *horse* analogies!" said Agent Ramsay.

Agent Nettles laughed, then her voice grew quieter.

"The Princess is blinded by her friendship," she said. "I mean, the boy is —"

Princess Ko grabbed the earpiece and switched it to the Off position.

There was silence.

"They're security agents," Keira said eventually. "You'd think they'd have noticed the listening device still on the table."

The Princess returned the earpiece to Elliot. The silence continued. It was occurring to each of them that the agents *did* know. They just didn't care.

"Cayenne pepper!" said Sergio. "And cloves," and his hands moved along the shelf, reached for containers, pulled them out, the faintest color crossing his cheeks and fading away almost at once.

4.

It was eleven P.M. and the warning bells were ringing.

According to the schedule, they were *at their leisure on the Palace Entertainment Terrace.*

In fact, they were in an alleyway outside the Palace Kitchen.

Princess Ko had knocked back Sergio's hot chocolate in one gulp, closed the meeting, dismissed the security agents, then told the others to meet her out here.

As they'd arrived, she'd handed out armbands: "to get around the city."

"We are seeing the city?"

"It's a sparkleshine," the Princess had said. "We have to see it. I've been here often, but it's Keira's hometown so maybe she'll give us a tour?"

Keira had blinked, then turned to study Elliot in his faded jeans, and Samuel in his ruffles and sailor's hat.

"Take off your hat, Samuel."

"My hat! As to a curling iron in lip balm! But my hat is the height of my identity! It is my declaration of fashionable aptitude!"

"You want me to show you my city, lose the hat."

So Samuel had removed it, and at that moment the warning bells had chimed.

He replaced his hat at once. (Keira swiped it off. "Your *hat* didn't make that happen.")

They all hesitated, deciphering the bells.

"That's twinned Colors."

"Blue and — what? Aquamarine?"

"No, Blue and Green."

"Level-four Blue?"

"Better: 5(a)."

"Then it must be Green 6(b). They travel together."

Sergio spun on his heel. "Then it is Turquoise Rain! It is what I have wanted to know ever since I am coming to your Kingdom!"

The Princess and Keira were both grinning. They caught each other's eyes.

"You've been in Turquoise Rain before too?"

Keira nodded.

Nobody else had.

"Anyone who wants to go inside, go now," the Princess said, swinging her elbow back toward the kitchen door. "But I'm staying out."

"What's it like?" Elliot asked.

They were speaking over the warning bells, which continued to chime. Nearby, doors were slamming, shutters clattering, footsteps running. Something made of glass hit the ground, spiraled, then stilled. The laneway was empty.

"It's like possibility," Keira said, her eyes searching the night sky.

"You feel wild," the Princess explained. "Like you could dance on the wildness — catch ahold of it, straddle it, and fly it."

"I have read," said Sergio, "that it makes the world sing with hidden doors. That the effect is so beautiful you wring it from your clothes for days to come."

Samuel took a step backward, eyes alarmed.

"Turquoise Rain!" He crouched to find where his hat had fallen, hands trembling. "It is dangerous! It has been known to quicken the heart so that some fall dead!"

"Not many," the Princess countered. "And they've usually got a preexisting condition or something." A thought occurred to her. The volume of the bells was increasing, so she shouted to be heard: "Some people get addicted. They do it once and then basically ruin their lives chasing it around the Kingdom."

The bells stopped.

"So if you're an addictive personality" — the Princess looked from Sergio to Elliot — "it's maybe a mistake."

"And if this is your first time in a night-dwelling city," Keira added, twisting on her heel, "it'll be sensory overload already."

She regarded Elliot.

"Especially you, Elliot, since you're pumping about your dad."

He shrugged. "I'll risk it." He was trying to see how the armband hooked up. Keira reached out and wrapped it around his forearm, clicking the ends together. Her fingernails, he noticed, were no longer chewed. Now they were long and cut into arrow points.

Sergio danced down the laneway. "When will it start?"

"I will see you all on the morrow!" Samuel pressed up against the kitchen door. "Please to be alive at that point." He reached for the handle — and a drop hit his hand.

The Turquoise Rain fell for only a few minutes.

Elliot felt it touch his scalp through his hair. He felt pieces hit his neck, run down the open collar of his shirt. Each drop was like a gentle twang that seemed to fold itself into his skin. Like the folding of the melody back into the drumbeat of the music. The folding sank, sank again, and then fanned out. There was something faintly familiar about that fanning, but his thoughts were running like rain. He was stepping into the center of the laneway, turning his face to the sky.

The Colors fell like splinters of city lights. The blue was electric, the green emerald, and now and then they mingled to form flares of deep, bright turquoise. Sergio was singing something loud in Maneeshian, his palms out. Samuel had leapt out from the doorway, and pieces of Rain were sliding down his cheeks, shoulders, arms. He held out his sailor's hat, filled it, and tipped this over his head. Puddles had formed almost at once and the Princess and Keira were jumping between these, fragments splashing out around their ankles.

It was soaking through Elliot's shirt, sparking, folding, fanning; sparking, folding, fanning. He pushed his shirtsleeves up to feel it hit his skin direct. The hits to the back of his neck sent rushes down his spine that fanned across his back, then wrapped around his chest and abdomen. He pushed down his collar, and arched his back to feel more. He watched the girls stamping in puddles, and tried that too, and the sparks rose and foamed against his ankles, shins, and knees.

It was better than the moment of flight in deftball; better than hitting the ribbon in a sprint; better than the surge you feel when your favorite band plays the opening chords of your favorite song and you're right there by the stage in a stadium. It was better than a sky full of falling stars — and then it stopped.

Elliot looked at the others, and their eyes caught his and caught one another's eyes. They were all breathing hard and fast, their chests heaving, and then their breathlessness turned into laughter. He hadn't known that laughter could form an orchestra, but turned out you could play it like instruments. They were playing one another's laughter, spinning it against walls, catching it, and throwing it back. And then they were running, chasing the laughter, trailing it behind them.

For the next several hours, they ran through the crowded streets of Tek, Jagged Edge.

At first they searched out gutters or drainpipes that still streamed with Turquoise Rain. When they found one they jumped in it, or crouched and splashed one another, or trailed their fingers back and forth through it, or fell on their knees in it. Princess Ko and Sergio ran side by side, sometimes joining hands and breaking into sprints. Elliot, keeping pace with Keira, looked at her swinging hand and thought he might hold it and sprint with her too, but he skidded on a slick of Rain, saved himself, and ran on alone. Samuel pounded behind them all.

After a while, their bodies were running with Rain, veins lit with it, so alive with Rain they no longer needed to search for it. Then Keira took over, and led them on a tour of Tek, her body curving like ribbons, her hands pointing out where they had to swipe their armbands, her voice calling phrases over her shoulder. They ran behind her, running on the music that rose out of the grates in every street.

"See that?" Keira called, pointing up to windows of skyscrapers where the shapes of men and women moved behind blinds. "They're running Cello up there."

"You mean Tek," the Princess called. "You mean they're running the city of Tek."

Keira ran on.

The city wove through moonlit lanes, lamplit tunnels, torchlit passageways, and unexpected doors. Now and then Keira would fling open a door, and they'd be met by the shock of a square.

Each square was a fanfare of traffic, arcades, billboards, screens, Coffee Rings, and surges of people who moved frenetically, glinting and beaming with Rain. Stripes of laser light crisscrossed the air like giant chopsticks. Taxis slid past and slid past, like the Turquoise Rain that slid around their bodies, constantly folding and fanning. They kept turning to one another, bright with amazement, to check that the others felt it too.

"That's a Dance Arcade. It's hologrammatically linked to other Dance Arcades across the province."

"We will go into it!" Sergio commanded.

So they changed course, swiped their armbands, and joined the strange intermingle of dancers, some real, some images from elsewhere. You could smile at faraway strangers, step up to them, dance with them, step through them. You could insinuate and blend with your partner.

Sergio went wild, dancing the Maneeshian punk-rock style, his body like a dart, then he grabbed the Princess and led her in a low, slow tango.

Samuel swayed from side to side, his eyes closed, his fingers fluttering.

Keira danced with Elliot. She leaned close and spoke in his ear — "The Rain has washed your makeup away," she said. "Your black eye's back." — then she touched the welts on his hand, raised an eyebrow, smiled, and started dancing again. They alternated between JE style and Farms style for a while, and she studied the movement of his hips, then looked into his eyes.

"It's easier to fall in love at night," she said.

They watched couples pressing close on either side of them.

"Into love and out of love," she amended.

"Come on, let's go somewhere else," the Princess shouted suddenly, and they were running through the streets and squares again.

They were falling against one another as they ran, linking arms, unlinking arms, and all the time the Turquoise Rain seemed to braid and blend them.

There were fountains of light. Sudden cheers rose and fell from every direction, and now and then a sharp scream or clamor of shrieks. Each time that happened, Elliot would feel an adrenaline surge, and he'd look around wildly. Once he saw Sergio trip in surprise at a scream, and Samuel often stopped altogether.

But Keira always ran on, her face shining and calm.

"Is it always like this in Tek on a Sunday night?" Elliot asked. "Or is this the Turquoise Rain?"

"Both."

"You guys know how to party," Sergio shouted.

"It's the Ethos," Keira called back.

"The what?"

But she had slipped ahead, and was touching her armband to a door.

Sometimes, when the crowd in a square got too solid, they had to pause, then Keira would talk faster, her hands pointing, phrases accumulating, twisting like her body.

"That's a Coffee Ring. The snacks are all turmeric, chili pepper, lime. That's the Ethos too.

"That tower's an Observatory. Night-dwelling cities have the best mathematicians and astronomers in the Kingdom.

"Those giant chess pieces? That's a semi-virtual game."

Outside one square, Keira counted a row of green doors — one, two, three, and stopped at the fourth.

"I'll show you something."

Down a flight of steps into a tunnel and out into another square.

"This is a Sky Square," she said, and they looked up to see airspace crowded with streaks of light and fixed wings. A series of drawbridges were strung between the skyscrapers, and flying machines darted amongst these.

"Night makes people want the sky," Keira explained.

They looked up, and directly above them, a thin girl balanced on a tightrope.

They ran out of the Sky Square.

"We like to get *air*," Keira called. "To get *up* in the air. We like danger."

"She's a motocross champion," Princess Ko confirmed.

They saw Keira's shoulders shrug as she ran. "It's the Ethos."

There was another scream.

"That's a stadium," Keira called. "Motocross, skate park, bike spinner, or skydiver. People crash and fall all the time. That's why the screams."

They turned into an alleyway where colored cubes were suspended, passed a series of Graffiti Walls, then crossed a grassy area. A snake slithered across their path.

"We let wolves, snakes, bears wander the streets," Keira said. "For the danger."

"Don't people *die* here all the time?" Elliot asked.

"Of course they die here all the time," Keira's voice sang back.

People and objects appeared and faded on street corners: a shower of pebbles, the prow of a ship, a woman crouching to button a child's pajama top.

"Those are holographic effects," Keira called.

They crossed another square, swiped their bands, walked through another tunnel.

Keira pointed to a doorway.

"Never go through a green door," she called. "They lead to the Shadow Quarters. Dangerous."

"We went through one earlier!" Samuel cried from behind.

"Fourth green doors are okay. Be careful how you count."

"I thought you liked danger," Elliot pointed out.

"I like that we *have* Shadow Quarters. They keep us alert. Crime is part of the Ethos. But you've got to be alive to be alert."

Samuel's voice sailed forward again: "Keira, *what* is the *Ethos*?"

Keira slowed. She was pointing up.

"See the architecture?" she said. "Impossibly narrow, impossibly tall? Edges and angles? That's the Ethos. Ruthless and extreme. It's our ideology."

She threw open the door to another square, and colored lights spilled over them. In the center of this square, people were passing around buckets of the Rain, pouring it over one another. Music pumped. Three men sped past them on wheeled boards, followed by children in wheeled shoes.

A fox ran by, its eyes glowing red. Light fell down a tunnel.

Keira jogged more slowly. "It's about extending ourselves. Our minds, bodies, the *spaces* of us." She spun in a circle on the spot, then ran on. "Cut yourself down to your essence. Party hard. Stretch. Sharpen."

She picked up the pace again. "*Break* yourself!" she shouted.

"But why?" Elliot shouted back.

Her voice jangled and flung at him. "To go as far as possibility, break *that* into pieces, and reach the impossible!"

"But why would you want to do that?"

"That's a stupid question. . . . That's a *ridiculous* question. . . . I can't believe you'd even *ask* that question!"

There was music and rhythm to her speech. She ran with the rhythm and he saw that her body was angles and bones, that the buildings they passed were angles and bones, and then —

"Here," Keira said, and stopped.

She swiped her armband at a turnstile, led them down an alleyway, and opened another door.

5.

The mood, which had been flying, abruptly took a seat and put its feet up.

This was a smaller, cobblestoned square.

It was almost empty. Two or three people wandered past, speaking softly. One wore a necklace that dripped with Turquoise Rain. A jazz trio stood silent in the corner, the double bass leaning up against the piano.

They were breathing hard as they stepped in, then their breathing slowed and quieted.

The Turquoise Rain was gentling. It still fanned out but had a whisper quality, a warmth.

"This is the Art Quarter," Keira said. "And see that caramel colored door? That leads to a Conversation Corner. You want to go?"

They followed her across the square. Above them empty birdcages were strung along a crisscross of wires.

They swiped their armbands and entered an empty courtyard. A fountain played in shadows, and they could make out a few plants and trees, shaping darkly in pots, and a scattering of couches at odd angles. The electronic music played, but its pace was slower, volume lower.

"Sit anywhere," Keira said. "You can get coffee, chocolate, and bananas from that wall over there. Swipe your armband and touch the image you want. Then sit."

"Coffee, chocolate, and bananas?"

"They're conversation stimulants."

The others hesitated.

"Night is for conversation," Keira explained patiently. "See how dim it is in here? We can hear each other's voices, and see the light in each other's eyes, but that's it."

There was another silence.

"When there's only words, and the spark behind words," she elaborated, "that's when conversation finds its voice. Everyone, sit down and *talk*."

Elliot and Keira sat cross-legged on opposite ends of a couch. From across the courtyard they could hear the rise and fall of voices from the Princess, Sergio, and Samuel.

"It's the silence," Keira said to Elliot. "Just night-distant winds, water, owls. You hear the shifts in nothing. It softens things."

"Wait," said Elliot. "I thought the point was edges."

"Exactly."

They both laughed, and Elliot felt the couch tremble.

"It's both," Keira said, a horizontal slide to her voice. "*That's* the essence of night. Duality. Sharp and soft. Dark and light. By day, all you get is light."

"We get shadows in the daytime too."

"Shadows are just darker light. Listen to me."

"I am."

"You'd better be."

There was another silence. They were looking at each other, seeing nothing but shapes and glints. The music was doing something sweet, rising up to an exquisite point and holding, and Elliot felt it holding him suspended. Then it fell back down into the low, fast drumbeat, and he exhaled.

Keira spoke again. "All that glare and light of day," she said. "You need darkness for beauty."

"Not much point in beauty you can't see."

Keira leaned closer to him. "See that?" She pointed to a pale gold paper lantern that was standing in an alcove. "It's the glow from inside that makes it beautiful. You don't get that by day." Now she waved across the courtyard to where the others were leaning together. "We can't see the scar on Sergio's forehead, or the puffiness of Samuel's cheeks, or the tension in Princess Ko's neck. All we see are pieces of them. The light in their eyes. The glow. That's their true beauty."

Elliot was quiet, watching the shadows of the others, hearing their murmurs.

"Of course," Keira added, "*you're* beautiful by day as well, Elliot Baranski."

Elliot laughed again.

"Pieces make me crazy," he said. "I need the whole picture."

The couch trembled again with the force of Keira's head shaking.

"That's wrong," she said.

"Is that a fact?" said Elliot, mocking.

"It is. Details clog your mind and trap your eyes. But darkness" — she reached out and rested her sharpened nails on the surface of his skin — "and a single strand of light? That's when you see the single detail that counts."

"If the strand of light happens to land in the right place," Elliot pointed out, but he was trying to study Keira, to find the detail that counted.

All he could see was her outline and the movement of her mouth. How it kept shaping words and sentences, how it tried to be heard, the Keira behind the words.

Maybe that was the detail that counted. Her wanting to be heard.

Out of nowhere he remembered Corrie-Lynn's voice discussing Night-Dwellers: *They must be cranky, whoever they are, sleeping at the wrong time like that.*

Was that all it was that gave Keira her edges? She was a Night-Dweller living in the day?

"Daytime is too flat for you?" he said.

"Exactly!" Her voice seemed to sing its relief through him. "Night has a depth, see? You never hear people talk about the deep of the day. But you can lose things in the depth of night. You can throw a piece of jewelry into a snowbank and never see it again."

"Huh," said Elliot. He thought awhile. "There's a piece of jewelry in a snowbank somewhere?"

"Right."

"And that's — a good thing?"

"Right."

He waited, but she sighed deeply and said, "You can lose your*self* in night."

"And that's good how?"

Her voice sighed away into the darkness. "Trust me. It's good. Endings are good."

"Wait," said Elliot. He was remembering standing by a window with Keira, watching the snow. "Weren't you being sort of romantic about thaws that time? And aren't they special because they're a new beginning?"

"Nope. I like thaws 'cause it means the snow is done. You Day-Dwellers are so obsessed with beginnings." She scraped his arm gently with her nails. "When what really counts is *the end*."

Across the courtyard came the sound of Sergio's voice raised slightly, then a low chuckle from Samuel, and a giggle from the Princess. Their voices faded again.

There was a long quiet. Drops of water drifted from the fountain in the breeze.

"Elliot," Keira said, pitching her voice lower, somehow matching the odd urgency of the music. "Remember at the Lake of Spells when you had that book, and I was so angry about self-help books?"

"Yes."

"My mother . . ." she began, then stopped and started again. "Self-help books aren't usually big here in Jagged Edge, but now and then one of them takes off. So a while back there was this one that told you how to find the love of your life. My mother read it — she'd been single all my life — and it told her she had to *make room* for her soul-mate. Like, if she had a double parking space, she shouldn't park in the second spot. Always leave it clear for *his* car. This imaginary guy's car. And clear space in her wardrobe and in the bathroom cabinet, ready for his things."

She sat back, so she was a little separate from Elliot.

"My mother followed the book so carefully. All those empty spaces on the shelves. I remember seeing how carefully she'd lie on just one side of the bed, her body like a straight line of chalk."

Elliot waited.

"Did it work?" he asked.

"You bet. She met a *cracking* guy." The edge to Keira's voice was sharper than razors.

"Not so cracking, then," Elliot suggested.

Keira was silent.

"What happened?"

"Ah," she sighed. "I don't want to talk about it." Her silence poured into the courtyard.

Elliot thought a moment. "Has this got something to do with the jewelry in the snowbank?"

"You're sort of amazing, Elliot."

He waited again.

"It was a necklace he gave her," she said. "I threw it into the snowbank, and it didn't change anything — it was too late by then — but that moment of throwing it . . ."

She sighed blissfully, and shifted again so she was closer to him.

"It's what everyone should do. Open your hands and let things fall. Endings are what count," she said again. "Give up. Let go. Night lets you fall into the darkness —" and her own voice seemed to fall into Elliot's hands, so he held them out to catch it, and as he did he found that he himself was falling — falling toward her — and there she was, falling too, the smooth of her and the edges, the exquisite of her, the gauntness of her bones.

They were holding each other, pressing together, entangling, closing their eyes. He was peeling that stupid net from her hair, and pressing his hands into the softness underneath. Those nails of hers through his shirt and under his shirt.

Their skin ran still with raindrops of color, and now the raindrops ran together, and they were lit up by the colors, lit up by each other, by each other's hands and mouths, and falling.

6.

Rooms look different by day.

The final meeting was at seven A.M., Monday, back in Conference Room 3Q. Early sun glared through the windows, paling, graying, fraying.

The security agents seemed taller, crisper, sterner, but the members of the Royal Youth Alliance sat silent and curling at the table. Elliot felt as if a frown was riding slowly around their circle: a carousel of frowning.

"This will be a brief meeting." Princess Ko's shoulders were rounded as if she was cold. "You will then depart on your trains home. Our next meeting will take place in a fortnight. The details are in your folders. For now, I only want to clarify your assignments, and to brainstorm —"

There was a crunch as Samuel bit into an apple.

The Princess swung toward him, her eyes flaring.

"Call yourself my apologies," Samuel muttered through a wet mouthful. "But I must needs eat, and I must needs request an extension to my stay." A piece of apple slipped from his mouth. He pushed it back in, chewed fast, and swallowed. "Indeed, and I am somewhat drawn to this city and see no harm in another day of wandering its pavements."

The Princess blinked hard, staring and breathing through her mouth.

"I do not have the faintest idea," she began.

"It is the Turquoise Rain," Sergio said suddenly. "He wants more."

They all regarded Samuel, who cried, "No!" his cheeks flaming.

"It'll all be gone now, won't it?" said Elliot.

"He's thinking there must be puddles left," Keira said. "But there won't, Samuel. It disappears."

"Indeed, and you mistake me!" Samuel blustered. "I am longing merely to gather more memories of this fine city, this —"

"Yeah, you don't really strike me as a city boy." Keira leaned forward, took an apple from the bowl, and tossed it from one hand to the other. "You need a long, cold shower and a glass of kale juice. It cleanses Turquoise Rain." She turned to the security agents. "Can someone get kale juice in for Samuel? And fast."

Elliot was watching Keira. Pieces of the night before kept coming back at him, hitting sharp points in his memory. Her fingernails. Music that had seemed to wind through his body.

Now the same music seemed stale and self-important. Last night it was a sleek black cat: Today the cat had picked up a frying pan in its paws, and was slapping the side of his head with it repeatedly. He felt like he needed a long, cold shower himself. He felt ugly.

He couldn't figure it out, this mood, then it came to him: He felt as if he'd cheated. That thing with Keira — fantastic, intense, sexy as hell — but it seemed like a betrayal. Which made no sense. He didn't *have* a girlfriend right now.

Samuel looked ready to protest again, then he buried his face into his arms, and began a muffled sobbing. "I, of all people," they heard, and "Addictive! But I?" and "As to a heather-swan in turmoil!"

Agent Nettles, meanwhile, was speaking fast into her earpiece, and then, to their surprise, was stepping to the table.

"Princess," she said, "before you go on, I need your permission to speak."

The Princess's face seemed made out of a scowl. She sighed. "Go ahead."

Agent Nettles tugged at her own ear, brushing against the pearl earring.

"I will say nothing," she began, "about the fact that you all blatantly disregarded the schedule and set out onto the streets: alone, unaccompanied, without security, with utter disregard for your own safety and for the interests of the Kingdom, and, what is more, into the heart of a storm of Turquoise Rain."

That's not exactly nothing, Elliot thought.

"Nevertheless, *while* you were all out gallivanting with such breathtaking foolishness" — another shot of nothing — "during that time, we received a further communication from the King of Aldhibah, intended for your father. It explained the dress code for the Namesaking Ceremony, and queried your father's dietary requirements."

The Princess contributed another deep sigh, her scowl changing shape.

"Well, may you sigh," Agent Nettles continued. "This, of course, we can deal with, but it reminds us that the return of your family is a matter of utmost urgency. We need your father back, Princess Ko, in less than four weeks from today."

"This is not remotely helpful," said Princess Ko.

Agent Nettles straightened her thin shoulders.

"Which brings me to my point. As you know" — she gazed around at the sleepy, worn faces — "we agents doubted the theory that the royal family was in the World. We have now reconsidered. All *our* theories have dried up — paths to dead ends. It seems that — and what are the chances? — you've had more luck. You've caught a Locator Spell. Nice going. You've used it to confirm that they *are* in the World. Again, wow. Okay, you win. We accept your theory. They're in the World."

The Princess raised her eyebrows. "Thank you."

"But now . . ." Agent Nettles drew her lips together. "*Now* it's time for this game to wrap up. Have your showers. Drink your kale juice. Run through city streets. Whatever. But it is critical that we take over. We need the stable boy out of the WSU, and one of our guys in his place. We need to bring the family home."

The Princess's scowl was slipping. It was falling into her cheeks. She looked across at Samuel, still sobbing quietly into his arms.

"You need a break, Princess," Agent Nettles said gently, touching Ko's shoulder. "You need to lie in a hammock and read a book. You need to go for a ride on your favorite horse. You need a bubble bath. A massage. I don't know, a vitamin supplement, no doubt! You've worked so hard, but now you need to let these kids get back to their lives, and let *us* get on with the real work."

The Princess seemed to be curling up. Everything about her was falling.

"We'll extend the circle of knowledge," Agent Nettles added. "We've all agreed to this point that it should be very limited. But we can't work under those conditions. We need more resources. We've weighed the risks and we think a slight extension is essential."

You could see thoughts flying behind the Princess's eyes. You could even see her neck muscles tensing, ready with a nod.

"We already have five or six agents in mind. We'll brief them on the situation, and get this mess under control."

Now the Princess did nod. A whimper came from Samuel.

"Give me your list of agents," the Princess murmured.

"Of course. I can tell you now that it includes the two agents working on the recovery of Abel Baranski." She jutted her thumb toward Elliot. "They happen to be two of the best in the Kingdom," she said. "You've been lucky to have them on your dad's case to this point, Elliot, but it's time to bring them in."

Elliot's hands were on the edge of the table. He actually raised it a little.

"No," he said.

The Princess turned vague eyes on him.

"I'm sure some other agents," she began, "will be perfectly —"

"No," Elliot repeated. "You must —" Then, "There is not a chance in —" In a moment he'd get his words together, but now they were zipping back and forth in his head, and all he could do was watch them scramble, all of them shouting to be said.

"Your *family*, Princess —" He rose so fast his chair toppled, and then he stopped and tried to speak again, and now at last his voice had gathered a soaring flame of words: *"Agents Tovey and Kim are staying right where they are until they get my father back."*

He stopped. The room vibrated with his shout. He was trembling all over.

The Princess was staring, but a faint mocking smile played on Agent Nettles's face.

Elliot took a step, ready to kill Agent Nettles.

Keira spoke. "What I don't understand," she said, and she clicked her sharp-edged fingernails together. "What I don't *get*, Princess Ko, is why the recovery of Elliot's father has taken this long at all. He was working with the Loyalists, right? So why did you people not *know* what he was working on? *He was on your side.* He was working on something ingenious. Revolutionary. How did you not *know* this until the agents tracked it down? Okay. There's that. But now they know where he is? Why is he not back? They want to *negotiate* with the Hostiles? What's *that* all about? Why are they not storming the compound? Arresting the people who took him?"

Princess Ko closed her eyes tightly and shifted her shoulders.

"It doesn't work like that," she began. "It's more complex — more sensitive — there are branches of Loyalists that don't know each other — there are . . ."

"Sounds like a mess to me." Keira looked at Elliot. "Your dad's listening device. Can I borrow it until the next meeting? I'd like to look at it more closely."

Elliot was still trembling but Keira's contempt had reshaped and settled his fury. It was as if she'd manifested his anger for him. He felt calm again.

"Sure," he said, drawing the paper clip from his pocket.

"No," said Princess Ko.

There was a knock on the door.

A waiter entered carrying a jug of kale juice. He set this on the table and retreated.

When they turned back to Princess Ko, she had straightened in her chair, and gathered her face again.

"Take the paper clip back, Elliot," she instructed him. "Keep it, please. I have other work for Keira. Several more boxes of code."

Keira laughed.

Elliot looked at the paper clip, lying in the palm of his hand.

"As for you, Elliot," Princess Ko said. "I have prepared letters for my family, each containing a memory trigger. I need you to go home and have Madeleine forward these. I also need you to work harder, faster, and better at opening the crack between the worlds."

Elliot closed his hand on the paper clip. A headache flared across his scalp, and tightened around his forehead.

"You, Samuel," Princess Ko said, and Samuel glanced over the rim of his kale juice.

"As discussed, you will steal the original accounts from the archives."

Samuel nodded forlornly, and poured himself another glass of juice.

"Sergio, you will go back to the WSU and get us the detector. And if you can't, get something else. I don't know. Equipment. Bring us some equipment. They use machines to seal up cracks. Get us one of those. We'll reverse engineer it or whatever, and use it to *unseal* the crack. I have no idea what I'm saying. Just. Do your job. And, Agent Nettles," she glanced up at the woman, still standing at her shoulder. "My team and I have come this far. We will continue. We will retrieve my family. Should a point come when I decide that we require help from you — or that we need to widen the circle of agents, and to requisition Agents Tovey and Kim from Bonfire — I will not hesitate to take that step."

That facial tic passed over Agent Nettles's face. Her mouth stretched suddenly, her eyes widened, then her face relaxed. She returned to her usual position.

"What else did we have to do at this meeting?" the Princess demanded, almost fretfully. "There was something else."

"You wanted us to do the brainstorm," Sergio said. "Ideas for what your family might be doing."

The Princess sighed and began to speak but Keira interrupted.

"I wrote a program for you," she said. "Last night, when we got back. It compiles media reports of royal activities for the last several hundred years. Hit the Activity button and it'll give you a random example. Like the Queen opening a dog show, or the Princess has a cold. Whatever."

"Good," said Princess Ko. She blinked. "Thank you," she remembered.

"I could do more work on the tech side of things if you like," Keira added. "I know you've got an agent creating artificial fan pages, and airbrushing royals into current events, and that." Keira paused. "No offense, but whoever your tech person is, they suck. I could do better."

The Princess stared, then roused herself. "My tech person is fine. Just read the documents, Keira. Now everybody: Go."

She closed her eyes, and as she did, Elliot slipped the paper clip into Keira's hand.

Elliot took the train home to Bonfire.

He went straight from the station to the Watermelon Inn, and asked to see Agents Kim and Tovey. It was noon, Monday. They weren't there, Auntie Alanna told him. They'd stepped out to the Sheriff's station to borrow some equipment.

Elliot walked from the Inn to the Sheriff's station.

He stood on the street and watched the profiles of Tovey and Kim through the windows.

At four P.M., they were still there. He walked into the schoolyard, empty now, and sent the Princess's memory letters through to Madeleine, with a note asking her to forward these.

Then he went home.

For the next week, he got up an hour early every day. He worked in the greenhouse, then rode his bike to the Watermelon Inn. He sat on the couch in the front room, while guests breakfasted around him.

Eventually, the agents would come downstairs.

They'd smile at him across the room, and shake their heads meaning, "No news yet," then they'd choose from the buffet. Usually they had the waffles with maple syrup, but now and then Agent Tovey chose granola, fruit, and yogurt instead. They poured themselves coffee and glasses of grapefruit juice, sat at a table, and ate.

As soon as he saw them wipe their mouths and push back their chairs, Elliot would go to school.

After school he did his homework, helped his mother, went to bed.

He did nothing about the crack.

He avoided the sculpture in the schoolyard. He had no idea if Madeleine was sending notes or not.

His head ached constantly.

After a week and a half of this, Agents Tovey and Kim wiped their mouths one morning, and then, instead of heading out, walked over to him.

They sat down, one on either side.

Agent Kim opened his sketchbook, and flipped through the pages.

He stopped at a page, and passed it over to Elliot. It was a portrait of Elliot himself, sitting on this couch.

"Turn the page," Kim said.

He turned, and there was a second portrait, almost identical to the first.

"Keep going," said Kim.

Elliot turned page after page. There were twenty-five portraits altogether. He must have been drawing two or three a day.

"I sketch people's faces because they tell me people's thoughts," Kim said. He touched a small shadow on a portrait. "But this is spilled maple syrup, and not one of your thoughts."

Elliot smiled a little.

Agent Kim raised an eyebrow across at Tovey.

"You think we're planning to give up on this," Tovey said. "Your thoughts are shouting so loud I don't need Kim's sketches to read them. I don't know where you've got it from, Elliot, but you think we plan to ditch you."

Kim took his notebook back, and closed it.

"We *are* heading out," Tovey continued. "Tonight, actually. To Jagged Edge. To the Hostile compound where your dad is being held. It's time for the next step."

Now Tovey scratched his chin, frowning hard. He sniffed.

"Elliot," he said, "there's not much I can guarantee in this life, but this I'm going to swear. Not a thing in all the Kingdoms and Empires would make me abandon this case. Not an order from the highest authority. Not if my wife went into labor with triplets. Well, I haven't got a wife and if I did she wouldn't be pregnant with triplets if I could help it, but you see my point. Are you listening to me? I aim to bring your father home and *no one's* going to stop me."

Tovey stood. "Do you believe me?"

There was a long pause.

Then Elliot nodded. His headache slipped away like a scarf.

PART 9

In Montreal, Canada, the weather is subsiding into greyness.

Maximillian Reisman sits on the open window ledge. In one hand he holds a letter; in the other an audiocassette. *Listen to this*, the letter instructs him. He laughs. The "kingdom-of-cello" campaign has a few cracks in it. Where would anybody find a cassette player these days?

> *It is the voice of the Queen — my mother, your wife — and you will surely remember her — yourself — your Kingdom — everything — if only you hear her sing.*

The laughter snaps back into his face.

He drops both letter and cassette to the floor, and kicks them away.

In Taipei, Taiwan, Sasha Wilczek holds the paper to her nose and breathes deeply. The scent seems at first like honeydew melon, then it sweetens into freesia before swooping unexpectedly towards something spicy, like cloves.

> *This letter has been sprayed with Essence of Kia. Kindly smell it. It's your perfume! It will surely return you to yourself, my darling mother, for you wear it every day.*

Or wore it. I suppose it may not be available in the World. Or, if it is, I suppose you have forgotten that you wear it. But you do! Speaking of wearing, what about your wedding ring? Is it not on your finger? Surely if you look at THAT you will remember your husband — my father — and then, onward, from him to yourself and your children (such as me, for example) and your Kingdom. Stare at the ring now! Keep staring! (Do you know that your husband is living in Montreal in Canada at the moment? I'm afraid he has forgotten you too.)

I hope your ring is not lost along with your memory.

Sasha looks at her bare fingers, bare hands. She looks down at her bare knees, the cracks in her knees, and she holds that word, *lost*, until it's lost amidst her tears. She sold her wedding ring to pay her first month's rent here. She doesn't *know* what's lost, but something is and it's more than a ring, more even than Sasha herself.

In Boise, Idaho, USA, Monty Rickard grabs the envelope, grinning. He recognises the crest from the last letter. He figures it's connected to a new computer game that his friends are designing, and they're playing it out through these messages to him. He's perfectly okay with that.

He can be Prince Chyba of the Kingdom of Cello anytime they like.

This time a small square, wrapped in cellophane, slips into his hand.

You love the chocolate of the Southern Climes, Chyba — you seem to have inherited that passion from our mother, the Queen. Close your eyes as you taste this and let the memories come crashing back.

Ha. Chocolate! This game gets better all the time.

* * *

In Berlin, Germany, Ariel Peters is reading a letter:

Hello there, Jupiter,

It is four A.M. and I am in the Penthouse Suite of the Cardamom Palace in Tek, Jagged Edge. I can't find anything special of yours here — it must all be at home in the White Palace. So I'll just say this. Do you remember when you and I were staying here, and we were about six and five, and we both had colds, and our noses snuffled, and there was snow outside, and you wanted to go out, but this was forbidden, and you opened the window, saying, "Let's climb out," and at that moment — for just the faintest moment — for the first time ever — we heard the Cello wind?

You must remember.

Just remember. Please.

At Avoca Beach, New South Wales, Australia, Finn Mackenzie is also reading. The writing is small, though, and the words stumble along. He keeps looking around for somebody to read it to him, but the house, of course, is empty.

Dear Tippett,

I am sending you this little piece. To remind you of who you really are.

You must be missing it so much. I suppose you've learned to fall asleep without it. Or you've stayed awake for over a year!

That does not seem likely.

I suppose there are grown-ups taking care of you. I hope they are kind. Maybe they have found you a new one?

Of course, some things cannot be replaced.

And of course, we all used to tell you that you were too old for one of these, but secretly, we loved to see you hug it. When we hugged you, it was like YOU were a blanket just for us. So why did we try to make you give it up?

Nobody was going to make us give YOU up.

Except that now they have.

Anyway, here is a little square of it from the corner. I tried to get some of the satin lining that you like to rub.

I carry it with me, in the front zipper part of my suitcase, wherever I travel. It makes me feel like I've got YOU in my suitcase. Only you'd be squashed. So I'd get you straight out.

Write back and tell me you're okay?

Love,
your sister,
Ko

Finn turns back to the envelope, tips it up, shakes it, and it falls into his hand —

And here it is.

Here it is on his palm, a piece no bigger than a postcard, but the texture, the weave, the colour: He closes his eyes and imagines he is winding it around his arm, snaking it up to his face. He lifts the piece and presses it against his cheek. Here it is, at last, his blanket. A piece of his blanket so small that he doesn't want to get it wet with tears.

PART 10

1.

On Monday night, Madeleine returned to the parking meter.

She'd swung by earlier that day, just to check, and she'd picked up the letters he wanted her to forward to the royal family. She'd gone straight to the post office and sent them.

Now she wrote:

Hey, Elliot. You there?

Then she waited.

She looked at her watch. She was wearing a new scarf, lime green with a white dragonfly print, which she'd found at Oxfam for 50 p. Her black headband held her hair back. There was the smell of rain and drainpipes, car tyres, spray paint, roller doors, and cat. A chill touched the air, autumn curling in on them.

She was full of the brightness of an orange. She was trembling with things she had to tell him. She imagined she was tipping towards the parking meter, pouring in her thoughts. What would she tell him first?

That she'd seen him, of course. On Saturday night, crossing his schoolyard. His bruised eye, limp, overcoat. She'd say — she hesitated — she'd say he looked different from how she had expected.

She'd tell him how it had happened. *The misaligned centre of me, the misaligned centre of you.* Gravity and matching displacement. Did the cracks in their lives draw them to each other? If you focused on cracks, were you drawn across the crack?

How she'd been thinking about displacement, and its power.

She'd tell him about the class they'd had with Jack's grandfather, Federico. He taught them History in the office above the porter's lodge at Trinity College. A few months back, he'd made them choose from a hat full of famous names — people who'd been there at Trinity — for an assignment.

Belle had chosen Charles Babbage, the almost-inventor of computers, but had switched to his friend, Ada Lovelace, the almost-inventor of programming.

Jack had chosen Lord Byron, the poet.

She herself had chosen Isaac Newton.

Anyway, in the office above the porter's lodge, Federico had instructed her to say more about Isaac Newton.

"What do you want me to say about him?"

"What? How shall I know this? It was your assignment! Just say it!"

Then he closed his eyes.

So she told them how, when he was sixteen, Isaac's mother had taken him out of school so he could run the family farm. His sheep had trampled the neighbours' barley while he built waterwheels in the stream. He'd been fined in the manor court for allowing his pigs to trespass in the cornfields. He'd lost the horse. His fences had fallen apart. Eventually, his mother gave up and sent him back to school.

"No wonder so much went wrong," Madeleine concluded. "Isaac Newton as a farmer was a total displacement. The universe was misaligned."

"It was nothing to do with the universe," Belle said. "Newton was just crap at farming."

"It's cause he was a genius," Jack reasoned. "So his mind was on higher callings than sheep. I get like that when I'm thinking about Byron's poetry. I just find that things like doing the laundry don't matter."

"Yet they do," said his grandfather, caustically.

"*I* know what it was," Belle interrupted. "He did it *on purpose* so his mum would stop making him be a farmer. It's what my dad does with the washing up."

"It's what?"

"My dad. When he washes up he does a rubbish job, like he leaves bits of mashed potato in the saucepan, so when you get it out the next day you want to kill yourself. So eventually Mum'll go, Oh là là, *get away from here!* And he'll go, *Yeah, all right, I'll watch the telly, then, will I?* And she does the washing up instead."

"How do you know it's on purpose?"

"His aura goes crusty when he does it, exactly like dried-up, left-over beef stew. That's how I know. Seriously, Madeleine, that's what your Isaac was up to when he lost the sheep or whatever. His aura probably turned to sheep dung."

"*Basta!* Enough!"

They all swung around to look at Federico. Or at least at the top of his head. His chin was pressed against his chest.

"This Isaac Newton. Madeleine?" Federico's voice was muffled.

"Yes."

"You remember, on the day you chose him — you remember you took *two* papers from the hat? And I said, no! I said, *choose one* — open only one?"

"Oh, yeah. I remember that."

There was a long silence. Federico's chin remained pressed against his chest. They glanced at one another.

"Has he gone to sleep?" Belle asked.

"No, he has not!" Federico looked up, blinking fast. He held out his hand, his fingers curled. "Madeleine. Come. Take this."

His fingers uncurled. A tiny strip of paper lay flat on his palm.

"It is the other," he said. "I have been thinking. You are supposed to do *both*!"

"How can that be fair?" Belle asked, surprised. "She already did the first famous person ages ago. Now she's got to do another one?"

"Ah." Federico shrugged. "She will live."

The name on the paper was James Clerk Maxwell.

"Oh, well, not famous," Belle said promptly. "Never heard of him."

"He's probably famous in his own way," Jack suggested. "Like in his circle of friends. Maybe he does magic tricks when they get together down the pub? Or could be there was this famous incident at a party once, when someone dropped their keys in a pond, right? And he fished them out using his mum's prosthetic leg. People still talk about it years later."

Madeleine said she'd look him up.

But she was lying. She'd chosen Isaac Newton and he'd explained the world. There wasn't room for anybody else.

So there was that.

She'd tell Elliot that story.

The bit about Isaac Newton being a useless farmer, he'd be interested in that, seeing as he was a farm boy himself.

Although, actually, he might not like it. The point of the story was that it was a *misalignment* for a genius to be a farmer.

Which might be insulting to a farmer.

For all she knew, Elliot *was* a genius. He'd never provided her with copies of his academic records.

She thought of the strength she'd seen in his shoulders.

She looked at the parking meter. Still nothing.

Maybe her note had not got through.

She wrote it again:

Hey, Elliot. You there?

Well, then, instead of the Isaac Newton story, she'd tell him about the science lesson she'd had with Darshana Charan.

Darshana was a bedder (which is what they call a cleaner at Cambridge) who taught them Science and Mathematics in exchange for free babysitting of her two daughters. She often incorporated the daughters into her classes, and she'd made them spin around the house being electrons. They had spilled from the couch, fallen off tables, and crashed into walls, and Jack had wondered aloud if this might be child abuse. Darshana had belted him over the head with a cushion.

Electrons come from the stars, Madeleine would tell Elliot. They come from the Big Bang. They're what started everything. They make reality.

She looked at the parking meter again.

Hey, Elliot. What's the story?

The parking meter looked back, unimpressed.

She sat down on the footpath.

It was all right. He was running late. He'd been away, right? So maybe he had homework to catch up on or something.

She'd treat him the same as always.

She wouldn't be afraid.

She wouldn't tell him he looked like a freakin' movie star, the kind everyone loves in a secretly convinced way that he belongs to them, because he's weirdly normal-looking at the same time as hot, and his eyes, if they glanced your way, would see you.

He had eyes that see the truth, that see what's funny or ironic and what's not, that see what's strong, what's weak, what's wrong, and always get it right.

But she wouldn't tell him that.

Nor just how wrong she'd got him. Like she'd got Jack wrong, actually.

The trouble was, she started off thinking everyone was a nerd.

Be careful who you call a nerd: That was the lesson, she supposed.

And here she was, planning to give Elliot a History class, or a Science lesson on electrons. Speaking of nerds.

She wouldn't say any of it.

Hey, Elliot. WHERE ARE YOU???

She'd talk about other things. Nothing scientific. Her words would spark and spin like spilling electrons. They'd catch his words and spin them back her way. Force fields spinning back and forth between them.

The parking meter gazed at her blankly.

She went home.

The next night she tried again.

The night after that it was raining, so she took her umbrella.

The following three nights she waited for half an hour.

After that she stayed in bed.

She stopped going to the parking meter altogether, day or night.

But then, the next Wednesday, she received this email.

Hi Madeleine,

I got your email address from this mad letter that came to me from someone who calls herself Princess Ko. (Cool name. Ko.) And she calls me Princess Jupiter. HA-HA. LOL. Anyhow, so she says I'm actually from a Kingdom called Cello and I just don't remember it. Like, I've "created" my own memories or whatever. ROFLMAO. (But not sure why.)

The actual truth is, I don't remember much about me. That sounds mad, right? But it's true. Who am I? I'm just, like, pieces. Like, here I am in Berlin, right, and WTF??? I don't even speak German!!! Existential crisis coming out of my NOSTRILS!!

I've sorta alwayz thought this situation of mine was cos of all the drugs I've done, and that's why my memories are like rice pouring into a shopping trolley. (So, like, they're all in little tiny pieces — like rice-size pieces — and they keep falling through the gaps in the trolley? That's my memories all over.)

So, you wanna tell me more of the story?

Ariel Peters

Madeleine wrote a short reply, saying that she'd pass on the message to Princess Ko and get back to her.

She printed out the email, got some notepaper, and thought for a while.

Then she wrote:

Elliot. This came. M.

She sealed her note and the email into an envelope, and rode her bike to the parking meter.

There was nobody around.

She got the envelope out of her backpack, ready to press it into the crack.

Then she stopped.

There was a thin line of white in the crack.

She pulled it out.

Just got all your notes. Sorry. Can we talk tonight (Wednesday)?

2.

The headache had been strapping him down.

It had been like something buried underground that reached up and dragged on his ankles every time he took a step. At the same time, it had wound itself around his face and blurred his vision.

Once the agents cleared the headache away, Elliot could walk again without resistance. His vision cleared, and right in front of him was the next meeting of the Royal Youth Alliance. Here it came, hurtling toward him just three days away and he hadn't done a sweet-darn thing about it.

From the Watermelon Inn that morning, he ran to school. Most kids were heading into their classes, so he took a risk and went right to the sculpture. Five short notes from Madeleine came sliding out, one at a time, but she must have sent them a while back. They had that faded, crackling feel. Seemed she'd been waiting there for him one night. He couldn't remember arranging a meeting but life was confusing and sleepy these days. He must have screwed up somehow. Ah, well.

He looked around quickly. A couple of kids and a teacher were standing by the water fountain, but they were arguing — both kids' arms were folded — so he wrote, *Just got all your notes. Sorry. Can we talk tonight (Wednesday)?*, delivered the message, and ran to class.

At recess that day, he knocked on the staff-room door and asked to speak to Ms. Tamborlaine. He still hadn't figured out how he'd put the question but there was no time for any more figuring.

Isabella appeared in the doorway wiping chocolate frosting from the corner of her mouth, a leftover smile in her eyes. The smile turned to mild surprise.

"Elliot Baranski!" Her voice was just above him, tall and slender as she was.

"Could I ask you about something?"

Right away, Isabella called over her shoulder to someone in the staff room, "Nobody take my cake — I'll be back in a moment," and there were jokes and laughter from in there that he couldn't catch.

"Mr. Vacarello's birthday," Isabella explained, stepping out of the staff room. She paused, thought a moment, then turned right. "Let's talk in here."

It was impressive how smooth and brisk she was — with other teachers there'd have been blinking and puzzled frowns and "Ask me about what?" or maybe long, slow sighs as they checked their watch, and "Can you come back in ten minutes?" or even a dumb joke, "*Now* you're thinking about taking Physics? Little late, isn't it?"

Anything! But no, here they were in an empty classroom, Isabella sitting up on the edge of a desk, her eyes on him, expectant.

He'd sort of hoped for a little more lead time.

"You know how I'm in that Royal Youth Alliance?" he began, winging it.

"I do."

"Well, we've been talking about the relations between provinces in Cello, and how we might, you know, improve them."

"Okay."

He had no idea where that had come from or where it was going.

"So, anyway, we have to do a presentation this weekend. Give a new perspective on the issue. And I was thinking maybe I'd compare it with the historic situation of Cello's relations with the World."

That's where he'd been going.

Huh. Weird. But not bad.

"Okay," Isabella said again. Her narrow green eyes almost closed in thought. "So why speak to me? Mr. Garenstein's the World Studies teacher."

"He is," Elliot agreed. "I did talk to him, and we got onto the subject of where we all came from originally." He was impressed by his own powers of invention. "I mean, whether we were always part of two separate realities, then the cracks opened up between, or did we all start in one place and get dispersed across realities? If so, where did we come from originally? From the ether or what?"

Isabella had been watching Elliot, smiling faintly as he talked, but when he said that word, *ether*, a fine line ran between her eyes, like confusion.

Ether. That was a Madeleine word.

He spoke faster, getting back on track: "And where did the cracks come from? Were they always there, or was it decay or erosion or something? Or did scientists *create* them in another dimension maybe? Mr. Garenstein said he'd heard about scientists who tried to construct artificial cracks, but he said it was quantum physics and I should ask you about that. What the idea was behind it."

Now her face changed again, and her eyebrows lifted.

"I don't know much about *that*," she said, and she gazed at the ceiling, thinking. "Okay. Here's what I do know. You remember from your World Studies classes that when people used to come and go between Cello and the World, there'd always be a displacement? Some sort of tremble in reality, like a photo in a frame would switch directions so it was facing inward? Or a cup of tea would turn itself to coffee?"

"Sort of."

"I think there was a point when a bunch of scientists got the idea that maybe if you *started* with the displacement, you'd induce a crack."

Elliot nodded. "Switch the direction of the photo in the frame yourself?"

"Not exactly. If you did it yourself, that's not a displacement of reality, that's you picking up a photo and switching its direction. It follows the everyday laws of physics. What you want to do is jostle things a little. So, tell me one overriding law of physics that governs your everyday reality."

He hadn't meant this to turn into a Physics lesson.

He looked at her.

"If I pick up this pen and let it go, what happens next?" she said patiently.

"Oh, right. It falls. So. Gravity."

"Exactly. Our everyday reality is drenched in it. So these people thought about the things that displace gravity — like magnets or electricity — and they thought, maybe play with those a bit and see if that might construct a crack."

Elliot frowned.

"But we use electricity everywhere. If that made sense, there'd be a crack at every streetlight and along every telephone wire."

"We don't just *use* electricity everywhere." Isabella nodded. "It *is* everywhere. It's just as fundamental as gravity, and quite similar actually. They're both forces between objects: The difference is that gravity *always* pulls the objects together, but electricity sometimes pulls and sometimes pushes apart. Electricity binds reality together at the subatomic level. It's making your brain work — it's making you give me that half skeptical, half when-is-she-going-to-get-to-the-point look that's on your face right now." Isabella smiled. "It's okay, I'm not offended. And I'm skeptical too — I'm just setting out a theory for you. It goes like this. When we grab ahold of electricity and use it to make a tractor engine work, that's not a displacement of reality, that's *part* of the reality of life on a farm. People invent new things all the time, and reality adjusts almost instantly — or you could say that new realities are forming constantly. It's only sometimes, in that tiny, tiny fraction of time when reality first gets displaced by the new — the first time someone plays with an electrical current, say; the first time a compass needle gets magnetized — *that's* when a tiny crack might form."

"Wouldn't that still mean a lot more cracks around than there are?"

"Just because we don't hear about them doesn't mean they're not there. Think about it. Cracks are invisible. You can't touch them. They're almost always tiny, so they only let small things come through. It's only if something is somehow marked with something of the World. Or if the crack happens to get caught by a material object and starts catching things that come through. *Then* we know it's there."

"So there could be a lot more cracks around than we know about."

Isabella shrugged. "It's just a theory, like I said."

"And the people who tried to experiment with jostling reality to make their own cracks — did that ever work? Did they ever try to make a small crack bigger?"

"No idea. Not the kind of thing that anyone could put in a book if they wanted to stay out of prison."

Elliot thought about how to ask the next question. Ah, he'd come this far. Just jump in.

"How exactly *did* they jostle reality?"

Isabella laughed. "That's where it gets complicated. Gravity and electromagnetism are just two of the four fundamental forces in our reality. There's also the strong force — that holds the protons and neutrons together inside the nucleus of an atom — and the weak force, which causes radioactive decay. If you really want to jostle reality, you have to get down to the quantum level. Smash protons together, mess with the gluons, separate — I think I've lost you."

"No," he said. "Well, yeah, but thanks. I'm not sure how any of this'll help with a presentation on interprovince relations, but like I said, thanks."

Isabella laughed.

"Well," she said, taking a step toward the door, "we're not supposed to talk about cracks, so you should probably leave this entire conversation out of your presentation. You know that, right?"

He nodded.

"I guess," she continued, "you're not planning to *use* the information to construct your *own* artificial crack? So I should hold off on reporting you for now?"

They both laughed. Their laughter carried them right out of the empty classroom and into the corridor, where they faced each other, still smiling, friends.

* * *

Later that night, Elliot headed to the crack to talk to Madeleine. He arrived right on time, and waited for her usual opener.

It didn't come, so he wrote his own note:

Hey, Madeleine, you there?

He was sure she'd reply *yep*, but there was a long silence, and then:

I am.

He told her what Isabella had said and suggested they try it over the next couple of nights, before the RYA meeting on the weekend.

She said she didn't have the technology to *jostle reality*, and he said maybe they could just jostle the *crack*. Since it was already there. He didn't understand the subatomic level, but let's say they tried magnets on Thursday, and electricity on Friday? She said it all sounded preposterous, but whatever.

The tone didn't sound like Madeleine. Elliot was looking at the notes trying to figure out what was up — were her friends writing to him, pretending to be her? But this was Madeleine's handwriting — when a new message arrived, along with a printed paper.

This email came from "Ariel Peters" today. Princess Jupiter. Whatever. The girl in Berlin.

This was followed immediately by:

Going home now.

That was another surprise. A message from a missing royal was huge! They could analyze this for hours. Or Madeleine could, and he could throw his deftball in the empty school grounds waiting for her long, long notes. But she was going home?

He'd been thinking she'd have more to say about quantum physics too, seeing as she liked science. And about the linguistic and cultural crossovers between Cello and the World. She'd wondered about those before, but they made sense if tiny cracks were everywhere. Papers and objects blowing back and forth would seep into the subconsciousness of both of their realities.

Plus, he'd wanted to tell her other stuff. Once they got the technical talk over, he wanted to tell her about his night in Tek, Jagged Edge. The Turquoise Rain, and maybe the Keira thing — try to figure out, with Madeleine's help, what that was all about, and also because it felt weirdly like a lie *not* to tell her.

He'd wanted to tell how Princess Ko had threatened to take away Agents Tovey and Kim, and how it had seemed like the world caving in — plastered a headache over his existence for the last week and a half — because he had this crazy conviction that the *only* people in all the Kingdom who could get his dad back were those two agents.

And a lot more. He had a lot more to tell her about.

But they said good night, and went home.

3.

Hey, Madeleine, you there?

Yeah I am, and I've got a whole bunch of fridge magnets that Belle loaned me plus a big horseshoe magnet that I sorta borrowed from Denny's when he wasn't looking, plus paper clips and needles and stuff. I guess I'll mess around with these in the vicinity of the parking meter, and I guess you'll do the same over there, and we will be looking like a pair of complete tossers to anybody who happens to be up above our realities looking down on us. They will be laughing their heads off at us. Because the idea that tricks with magnets might split open the universe and let us into each other's world, is about as likely as an African Grey-Necked Rock Fowl (rare bird mentioned on a TV nature show today) strolling out the front door of that house over there and asking me to go for a cocktail. Cause if it were true, we'd have lost half the world's schoolkids. They'd be tipping through holes into Cello all over the place, in the middle of their science classes. You guys wouldn't be able to take a step without being hit by a falling science kid.

Not to mention all the falling fridges.

There was a long pause. Madeleine folded her hands under her armpits, and rocked up and down on her heels. The night was dark and chill.

She watched the parking meter.

Nothing happened.

She sighed and gave the parking meter the sort of rueful, disapproving, resigned, I-am-a-complete-idiot-and-I-have-no-idea-why-I-am-doing-this-but-here-I-am-about-to-do-it look that her mother used to give when she gave in to six-year-old Madeleine's begging for extra chocolate-toffee ice cream right at bedtime.

Then she pulled open her plastic bag and started taking out the magnets. She waved one or two in the direction of the parking meter (and felt a tug, since the parking meter was metal — "This is *ridiculous*," she said aloud), and stuck a few owl magnets and Paris magnets and Call Your Local Plumber magnets on the meter itself.

Then she drew out the horseshoe magnet and aimed it at the crack where their notes came and went, swinging it around a bit listlessly. She directed a magnet into the plastic bag and let it collect a frenzy of paper clips. She fished out the sewing needles and rubbed them against a magnet for a while until they were themselves magnetised.

She took a short break to widen her eyes at the stupidity of it all, then continued playing. She shuffled magnets around, built towers of magnets, forced magnets together when they didn't want to go. She almost forgot Elliot; she disappeared into her own head.

Facts flew at her, like the paper clips flying at the horseshoe magnet, and gathered there, darkening her mind. The earliest ships used lumps of natural lodestone to navigate. The finest kind was a rich deep blue from Ethiopia. In Isaac Newton's time, the Royal Society used to measure a magnet's power by the number of keys it could pick up.

Compasses and keys.

She brushed the paper clips from the magnet — or maybe she pressed another magnet to the parking meter — afterwards, she couldn't remember what she had been doing, but whatever it was, the next moment she was not.

She was clamped in a blackness of noise. Extraordinary noise. A clamour of roaring, clanking, and pounding. As if she'd been shut into the engine of a jet aeroplane, or trapped in a steelworks factory, or tied to the drum kit while a thrash band played while it was caught up in machine-gun crossfire. The sounds closed in around her face. She clenched her eyes, hunched her shoulders, the noise in her cheeks, grinding at her teeth.

It was noise so powerful, it was lifting her into the air. Her body curled tighter, but the noise carried her higher and higher, and the more she rose, the louder it grew. Now it was blending with the rush of height itself, the blaze of wind, and her body, instead of being clamped, was tossed, pitched, and flung.

The air pressure sealed her eyes closed, and she dragged her arms against the wind, forcing them through the pounding, until her hands were at her face. She felt for her forehead, found her eyelids, peeled them open, and looked.

She was in a rush of grey, held by the force of the roar, and far below — impossibly far, impossibly small — she could make out a landscape. There was a pattern to the landscape — her eyes squinted in the wind, but she squinted them more, to make herself see — it was a pattern of squares, rectangles, fields. Her vision flared and flashed, then sharpened suddenly, and farms formed, farmhouses, barns, sheds. The streets of a town. A square. A clock tower. A schoolyard, a tiny, tiny figure — and she knew where she was. Bonfire, the Farms, Kingdom of Cello —

And she was back.

Standing by the parking meter, breathing fast and hard, her face wet with tears, heartbeat tumbling.

Her breathing slowed. She wiped her face.

She looked at the bag of magnets, still hung over her arm. Her body swayed.

The parking meter gazed at her, implacable.

A car started somewhere. A door slammed. Cambridge hummed.

She put the bag of magnets down on the path, and took her pen and notepad. Her hand was trembling.

The only thing she could think to say was:

Huh.

Exactly.

I think I just saw your town from the sky – and maybe a tiny, tiny you.

Are you okay?

Not really. I want to go home.

Tomorrow?

Madeleine stared. She held her pen over the notepaper. Ah, there was only one thing to say:

Okay. Night.

Night.

The following night, Madeleine regarded the parking meter.

It regarded her right back. She raised her eyebrows at it.

All day, she had felt an aching in her muscles, as if she had the flu, or as if she had spent the previous week climbing drainpipes.

A message came through from Elliot.

You ready?

She thought of possible answers: *Jack said my horoscope for today told me not to mess with kingdoms in parking meters, and Belle said my aura looked like it had been hit by a train, so no.* (Actually, Jack had said her horoscope warned her to beware of clothes pegs, but it was true about Belle and the train-wreck aura.) Or: *Let's talk about the deftball scoring system instead.* Or just: *No.*

Yep.

She unzipped her backpack.

Then she wrote again:

Before we start electrocuting ourselves/each other, this came for me today.

She looked once more time at the envelope that had arrived in that morning's mail. There was a row of Australian stamps, an Express postmark, and in large print on the back: *DO NOT OPEN. SEND TO PRINCESS KO RIGHT NOW.*

She sent it through to Elliot.

There was a pause, and then Elliot's reply.

It must be from Prince Tippett. That's huge. Now I've got two letters to bring to her tomorrow. Good

if I can also tell her we got through the crack.
You got anything electrical there?

Madeleine looked into her backpack again.

That afternoon, she'd run downstairs to Denny's flat and asked him what games you could play with electricity.

He had stared.

"You repair computers, right?" she'd said. "So isn't that, like, electrical?"

"Electricity doesn't come in to computer repair much. And I don't do it for *fun*."

"Okay, not games. Very serious things that I could do with electricity."

Another stare, this time with wider eyes.

"Serious things that won't kill me," she remembered to add.

Denny had been sitting up at his workbench. He nodded at the opposite stool, meaning Madeleine should sit herself, and started talking about static electricity, conductors, insulators, semi-conductors —

Madeleine thought of Denny's accent. It was loose and easy, like a swinging footbridge. His words wandered across the bridge, only pausing now and then to get themselves untangled when they hit a patch of asthma.

He was in a patch now. He had stopped talking and was leaning down towards the floor, reaching for something, and she could hear him working to breathe.

"You have any thoughts about displacement?" she said.

He straightened up with a wheeze like a whistle, and looked at her.

"Displacement," she repeated.

He stood abruptly, walked around the bench until he was standing next to Madeleine, then carried on until he reached his seat again. He sat down.

"Distance is the journey." He spun his fingers in the air, to show where he'd just walked. "Displacement is the result." He pointed to his own head and looked down at himself in mock surprise. "I got nowhere! Zero displacement."

"I'm talking about a different sort of displacement," she said.

He nodded as if he'd been expecting that, and bent down again.

When he sat up, he was holding a sagging cardboard box. He placed this on the bench and drew out a coil of wire.

"You know the story of Archimedes?" he said. "The King asked him to calculate the volume of his crown — so he could tell if it was made of gold or not." Denny placed the wire on Madeleine's head, like a crown. "Archimedes is in a panic. He doesn't know *how* to measure a crown! The shape's all weird and *crowny*! So he has a bath. To calm down. And when he gets in? There's a splash, I guess, and what happens to the level of the bath water?"

"It goes up?" Madeleine guessed. "It gets displaced?" She tilted her head, and the wire slipped back onto the bench.

"Exactly. Archimedes thinks: *That's it! That's how you do it!* Put the crown in water and measure the displacement of the water! From *that*, you get the crown's volume! He was so excited, the story goes, he ran naked down the street."

"Nice story," Madeleine said. "But that's not what I meant either."

Denny took a couple of batteries and a ruler from the cardboard box, and placed these on the bench beside the wire. He picked up a fluorescent light bulb, considered it, and replaced it in the box.

Then he looked across at Madeleine. "Displacement is a concept in psychology," he suggested. "You're mad at your boss, so you shout at your wife when you get home. Displaced anger."

"I haven't got a wife," Madeleine said.

"Fair point." Denny took out a piece of PVC piping and a pair of safety goggles. "Geological displacement? The displacement in the earth caused by a crack or a fault?"

Madeleine shook her head again.

Denny moved to his kitchenette, returned, and added a roll of paper towels and a handful of rubber balloons to the bench.

"I mean," Madeleine said, "displacement of a person."

The silence stretched across the flat. It woke Sulky-Anne, who was asleep on the bed. She sat up briskly, spilled onto the floor, and walked across to form a shadow by Denny's knee.

"Sure," Denny said eventually. "Displaced persons. Wrong country, wrong friends, wrong family. Well, what are you going to do? Get your work done. Make new friends. Pat your dog." He leaned down and scratched under Sulky-Anne's chin. Then he grabbed her around the neck, and hugged so tightly that Sulky-Anne pulled back, appalled. Or pretending to be appalled. She might have had a secret smile.

Denny raised his eyebrows at Madeleine. "You can be in the right country, right family, and *still* feel displaced," he said. "Take Belle, for instance. I mean, she grew up here, still lives with her mum and dad, but sometimes . . ."

He rolled the PVC piping along the bench, reconsidered, and started again.

"Sometimes you *need* to be displaced to find yourself," he said. "Or to find a better part of yourself."

"Like Isaac Newton," Madeleine remembered suddenly. "You know he lived here in Cambridge for years and years, hidden away like a crazy professor? Then one day he moves to London. Next thing you know he's got a social life. He's President of the Royal Society and

Warden of the Mint. He's chasing down counterfeiters, and shaking the whole place up."

"Is that a fact? Well, then, great example."

"But say there's a guy and he's still sort of in the same place he's always been," Madeleine continued, "but his *family* have run out on him. Can that be the good sort of displacement too? The kind that might help him find his better self?"

There was another long silence.

"I honestly do not know," Denny said.

Sulky-Anne sniffed and returned to the bed.

Denny looked at his dog, then back at Madeleine. "Let me tell you," he said, "some games you can play with electricity."

Now Madeleine stood in the dark street.

She glanced sideways at the parking meter, as if it were a stranger standing next to her on a bus. She wanted to know what the stranger was thinking, but she didn't want to be seen staring.

She took a balloon from her backpack. It was a dark colour, maybe blue or green, hard to tell in this light. She shook it out and blew it up.

It was blue.

She wound the end around two fingers and looped it through to tie a knot.

Then she rubbed the balloon against her hair.

A man was walking down the path towards her. The streetlights caught his face as he came closer. Lined and creased, purple veins across his nose.

He was wearing a suit coat, but on his legs were striped pajama pants, and on his feet, slippers.

He stared at her. The balloon held to her head.

She stared right back. His pajama pants and slippers.

They held the stare.

The man carried on walking. He reached the corner. He paused, as if he might glance back, then changed his mind and carried on.

Madeleine rubbed the balloon against her hair again.

It felt dry and scratchy. She lifted it away.

Static electricity.

This is stupid, she thought.

But she wasn't sure if she meant that.

She thought about Benjamin Franklin flying his kite in a thunderstorm, a key tied to the string.

Keys again.

Keys to the Kingdom of Cello.

Distance is the journey. Displacement is the result.

She wondered what was keeping the Kingdom of Cello from the World, and Elliot from her. Was the distance between them an impossible journey, even though he was just fingertips away? Or was he right there beside her in the parking meter, displaced by a universe?

She reached into her bag again, and found that she was vibrating.

At first, it was a low trembling sensation, running across her body. It felt a little like how your lips feel when you play the comb with a tissue. Or how a car feels when you drive fast down a highway with one back window lowered. The faint juddering. She realised, vaguely, that she could only see darkness. The darkness sighed around her, intensifying to blackness.

The trembling sensation continued, odd but interesting, then slowly increased. Now it was a jostling. A silent jangling. It grew uncomfortable. Her muscles tightened. It started to hurt. Her body was being jerked and flung in sharp, vicious movements like a fever fit. Something angry inside her started shoving back. She spoke. She didn't know what she was saying. Phrases rushed past and she was catching at them randomly.

There was a blinding flash of light.

She was *inside* lightning, wrapped tightly inside it, as if lightning was a rope winding around her.

No, she *herself* was being spun into lightning.

There was a rush of colour towards her, a frenzy of colour, pieces of colour racing one another, or racing towards something, and the panic took her like a fist through the chest.

There was another shove and she was back in Cambridge.

She got her breath back. She leaned on the parking meter.

She thought that might be a note coming through from Elliot, but she couldn't tell because everything was blurred, and then she realised that the blurring was her tears.

I'm done with this, she thought.

4.

Elliot ran to his truck.

The moon was big in his chest. The stars hurtled through his bloodstream. His smile kept up with his heartbeat.

That had been *insane.*

He'd been doing mad things with wires, cables, clippers, big old batteries — his buddy Shelby, who liked to fly planes and blow things up, had given him a stack of electrical junk.

He'd stood apart from the TV sculpture to do this: seemed like it might be a mistake to plunge an electrical charge into the open back of a TV.

Then, out of nowhere, there'd been that wild shaking. Like being trapped in a stalling threshing machine, in the center of the darkest black —

And then her voice.

For the first time he'd heard Madeleine's voice.

Is anybody there? she'd said. And: *What's going on?* And a tiny, distant, fading: *Can somebody help me?*

Those pieces of phrases, pieces of voice, like a trail through the darkness.

He hadn't known people had voices like that. He hadn't known voices could run soft palms across your juddering soul. He'd found himself reaching for it with both hands, reaching out for her voice, like a thing you could hold, trying to force his way through that impossible — that pressure that had stretched his cheeks so his mouth could not form shapes, his throat could not form sounds, and then there'd been the shock of brightness. The rush of color. As if her voice had made itself into a fountain of light.

Ah, it was possible he'd never met anything as beautiful as that voice.

He got into his truck, turned the keys in the ignition, and the vibrations took him back there. He sat a moment, following the rope of memory back, through that jostling, the voice, the colors, the light.

This whole thing with Madeleine. He'd always liked chatting with her, sure. She seemed sort of funny and weird.

But she'd never been *real* to him before. Well, he'd never even seen her face, so you couldn't blame him for that. And more to the point, he'd been distracted.

It was like this, he decided. His mind was a field, and its primary crop, its biggest earner — the thing that needed all his attention — was his missing dad.

Say that his dad was carrots.

Meanwhile, the Royal Youth Alliance had been a storm of leafhoppers that kept swooping in to infect his carrot crop. He'd had to keep dealing with them — getting them out of his way with sticky traps and insecticides or whatever — before he could go back to the work of the carrots themselves.

Whereas Madeleine, she'd been a sort of cute apple tree stuck over in the corner of the field. Which the leafhoppers kept telling him to talk to. Which made no sense, but analogies were not really his thing. But anyway. So he'd been heading over, now and then, to prune the apple tree or train its branches — whatever you did with apple trees; he'd never grown them — and that was always pleasant. Like a little break from his real work with the carrots and the leafhoppers. But, to be honest, mostly he forgot that it was there.

Only, now the apple tree had a voice.

He put his truck in gear and remembered Turquoise Rain.

He smiled. Of course. It was that exquisite sensation — the blending in, the folding-out — that's exactly how her voice felt to him.

Actually, the Turquoise Rain had been familiar the moment he felt it, and now he knew why.

It was just like the touch of Madeleine's hand.

That first time they'd made a connection, they'd held hands, and he'd gotten that sweet sensation, that merging, folding sensation.

He'd touched the apple tree's hand.

Ah, he had to stop thinking of her as an apple tree.

She was a girl.

A girl with a killer voice.

He drove home and listened to that voice play in his mind like a new favorite song.

The next morning he woke early to the sound of the telephone ringing.

He heard his mother answering it down there in the dawn dark. He heard her silence, waiting for the voice on the other end to say its piece. He sat in bed with his fear and his heart, waiting on that silence.

Then her voice broke into a surge of laughing talk, and he was out of bed, and running down the stairs.

She looked over at him, her tired eyes, sleep-tousled hair, her smile forming as she listened more, and then, "Really? No! Really? And the tartan cover?" Then she was laughing and chatting more.

"He's here beside me. He's just come downstairs. You want to tell him yourself?" She handed Elliot the phone. "It's Agent Tovey."

Agent Tovey's voice was brimful of something. "Elliot? That you? You okay? You've got another Royal Youth Alliance thing today, haven't you? But you'll be back tomorrow?"

"That's right."

"By then," Agent Tovey said, "your dad should be back too."

Elliot's mother was watching him, waiting for his smile, and when it came, she matched it with her own. Eyes reflected smiles reflected smiles, their grins dancing back and forth between them. Then she skidded toward the kitchen, sliding on her bed socks, calling as she did that she was going to make pancakes.

They'd actually spoken to Elliot's dad, Agent Tovey said. They'd gotten through to him. For just a few moments, but he sounded fine. A little scared, a little weary, but mostly relieved. He'd asked whether Elliot won the deftball championships, and how Petra's raspberries were doing.

"He's got your voice," Agent Tovey said, and Elliot smiled again. "Older, deeper, a bit rougher, but basically he's a bigger you."

"The negotiations are just about wrapped up," Tovey continued. "They've given us his magnifying glass — that special one that your mother gave him? The one with the tartan case? As a token of good faith. Next we'll get your dad. By tomorrow at the latest, we think — well, of course, there can be glitches. You know that. But it's all lining up at the moment, and I wanted you both to know."

Elliot ran upstairs to get dressed.

His mother was calling that maybe they ought not to have pancakes until they were absolutely sure, for superstitious reasons, but he could hear the pan clanging onto the cooktop right through her voice.

Now she was calling that actually it was lucky Tovey had woken them so early because didn't Elliot have to start packing soon?

This was true. Maybe if he packed fast he'd have time to run by the schoolyard and drop off a note to Madeleine before he left. He wanted to tell her the news right away.

This RYA trip was only overnight, so he'd just take his regular backpack, not the big one. He grabbed it from the floor, and unzipped it. It didn't smell so great. Maybe he should set it at the open window while they had breakfast. He tipped out its contents: sweaty old socks, a half-empty drink bottle, crumpled papers, damp from where they'd rubbed against the drink bottle. One of the papers was a sketch Cody had done of a cat with ringworm. Should keep that: It'd be worth a fortune one day. He laughed, and tossed it in the trash.

He unfolded the other paper, and laughed again at the heading:

THE OCCASIONAL PILOT

It was the paper Corrie-Lynn had given him on the deftball field.

He was about to crumple it too, but that seemed disrespectful after Corrie-Lynn's work. All that careful handwriting. So he read it over fast.

The Occasional Pilot can, on occasion, fly. When the buzz hits, he or she can jump without landing. (Or, at least, without landing until ready to do so.) Once Occasional Pilots have taken to the air, they need only brush their hand against the hand of another to bring that person also to the air. The "passenger" in turn may touch a third person, to bring that person to flight, and so on. I have witnessed the flight of the Occasional Pilot (my friend, Jeremy), his companions trailing behind him like a string of plastic monkeys.

Elliot recalled how much he disliked this guidebook writer. Always with the namedropping. Of course he had an Occasional Pilot buddy.

Occasional Pilots are very rare. Generally, they do not know their true identity until they find themselves flying. Their hidden talent will often emerge at times of great danger, possibly triggered by a rush of adrenaline. They are invariably people of great courage and strength: explorers, soldiers, officers of the law. Sometimes they have already trained as aircraft pilots, before they know their calling — perhaps sensing the air in their wings, the blue in their hearts, the gold on their shoulders. . . .

Ah, this guy.

"You want blueberries with yours?" Elliot's mother called.

There were only a couple more lines.

The Occasional Pilot is not as useful as you might think. I must repeat, for the sake of emphasis, that he can only fly when the buzz hits him. I have heard that there are certain indications that the buzz is going to hit: He feels tired, disconsolate, agitated. He craves peanuts. His fingernails grow unnaturally fast. Of course, all of that might be plain nonsense.

Elliot grinned. *She really thinks that* I'm *an Occasional Pilot?*

But it was sweet of Corrie-Lynn to believe in him.

He tossed the paper.

His dad was coming home. There was a girl in the World with a voice like Turquoise Rain.

He jumped the last few stairs and it did feel a little like flight.

PART 11

Jimmy Hawthorn was the Deputy Sheriff of Bonfire, but he was also its deftball coach, and some days he brought his pistol along to training. He'd split the team in half, gather one group around a basket filled with deftballs, position the others adjacent to them, and fire his gun into the air.

Instantly, the half with the basket would begin throwing balls in random directions; the other half had to chase and catch. Five minutes later, he'd shoot the pistol again and they'd swap roles. They'd alternate in this way until the entire team had collapsed or Jimmy had run out of ammunition.

Jimmy referred to these training sessions as "Chase Nights," and the team had a theory that he instigated them after a bad day at work, or an argument with Isabella. And it was true that he always seemed more cheerful when he was looking down at them at the end of the night, flat on their backs, panting, and dripping with sweat.

The RYA convention in Olde Quainte felt to Elliot like one long Chase Night. From the moment the train pulled in to Chester-on-Brell, he seemed to be running.

The Royal Staff who welcomed him were half sprinting to the horse-drawn carriage while they were still curtsying, proclaiming their greetings, and pulling him from the train. The driver cracked the whip until the horses cantered, and the carriage swayed and clattered over cobblestones, slipping and tilting on corners.

At the Magenta Palace, the Royal Butler beckoned Elliot so urgently that he found himself running to the entry. He was hustled to a wood-paneled room where a frantic woman named Gretel dressed him (in breeches, stockings, slippers, a ruffled cotton shirt, a surcoat with gaping armholes, all green except for the surcoat, which was golden), snipped the ends from his hair (before he'd realized that the glint in her hand was scissors), pressed a peaked velvet cap on his head, and gave him a snappy tutorial in Olde Quainte etiquette.

It turned out that it was a "scurrilous insult," the "height of coarseness," worse, "far worse than rummaging about in one's nostrils with one's fingers" — to speak more than two sentences without a simile.

"It matters not what the simile *is*," explained Gretel, "neither must it make any sense. Indeed, the better simile bears no relation to that before or after. As to a hammer in a carpetsnake. All that matters is that it *must needs be there*."

No wonder Samuel had so much trouble speaking plainly.

Now it seemed that Gretel planned to teach him how to dance.

"Call yourselves my apologies," she said, "but to dance *with* a boy from the Farms would be beyond and beneath me. As to a shudder in a rocking horse." Then she flung open a door and called, "Send in the lass."

Elliot was still trying to figure out if he should be offended by Gretel's refusal to dance with him, when Keira walked into the room.

"Don't laugh at me," she commanded. She was wearing a floor-length gown and a pointed hat with a streamer attached to it.

"Nothing to laugh at," Elliot said. "You look beautiful."

"Come *on*."

Elliot shrugged. "Trouble is, you do."

"Oh, well then, good, I'll laugh at you 'cause you look like deep-fried zucchini."

Gretel declared that there was neither the time nor the cause for laughter, and indeed, had there been time, she herself would have laughed fit to a rain shower of fingernails when she saw how they were dressed upon their arrival, and it seemed to her that both the Farms and Jagged Edge could set sail under the wind of the laughter they triggered, for the ludicrousness of all and sundry about them, not just their clothes but *everything* (waving her hands vaguely around Elliot and Keira), but she was saving her laughter for the end of this Convention, which, needs, she looked forward to, with the alacrity of a hatpin in a tree house.

She then gave them a rapid lesson in Olde Quainte dancing.

"You both show unexpected skill," she admitted irritably. "I was hoping to gather more laughter at your ineptitude, but here and you have deprived me of this, as to a tortoise on a tea tray."

Then she surprised them by reaching her arms around their necks, hugging them roughly, and shoving them toward the door.

"Call yourselves my good wishes," she said. "And *fly* to the banquet hall! The others await you. Let the festivities begin! Fifth doorway on the left."

"What's up with all the hysteria?" Elliot murmured as they ran along a wide hallway.

"I heard the Royal PR department have co-opted this Convention," Keira said. "Apparently, we spend too much time having meetings behind closed doors. They say the people of Cello need to see us out and about, especially here in Olde Quainte where Hostility's gone a bit wild."

"But we need to have meetings behind closed doors. The Princess should tell PR to stick it."

"I know, but all we've got scheduled for this weekend is a mad list of provincial pastimes, so I'm guessing she didn't tell them anything."

Elliot turned to stare at Keira, but they'd reached the fifth doorway now, and at once were swooped into a frenzy of activity.

The activity only stopped at two A.M., when they were allowed to rest for four hours. It resumed at an even faster pace.

Frequently, platters of meat and fruit were thrust at them, but it seemed they were expected to continue with their schedule as they ate: Melon juice ran down Samuel's chin; Sergio clutched a chewed chicken bone for over an hour, trying to figure out where to put it. Eventually he tossed it in a flowerpot.

Everywhere they went they were surrounded by reporters, minstrels, troubadours, musicians, and a continually revolving group of "honored and privileged" villagers. The reporters carried tablets and fountain pens, and were accompanied by assistants with pots of ink. The minstrels sang in high, sweet voices, telling tales about the history of the Kingdoms and Empires, which might have been interesting except that they all sang at once so that their stories overlapped: Ancient battles with Aldhibah got tangled up with the curse of Olde-Quaintian magic, which itself ran smack into the legend of the giant sweet potato.

One of the troubadours took a liking to Keira and spent most of his time dancing circles around her, his fiddle pressed beneath his chin, his eyes fixed on her eyes. She didn't take this very well.

Musicians pranced, playing trumpets, whistles, horns, drums, and bells, at the volume of jackhammers.

The villagers hovered, turning to one another to exchange wry comments, and occasionally reaching to touch Elliot's cheek or rub the sleeve of Sergio's cloak.

The RYA toured villages, admiring bathhouses, tulip gardens, and pigs in pens. They pitched quoits. They jousted with lances, fought with cudgels, and strapped the shinbones of calves to their feet so they could skate on a frozen pond. They played backgammon. They bobbed for apples. Frequently, they were called upon to display the dances that Gretel had taught them, and they found themselves spinning, clapping, springing, gliding, and kicking, occasionally in the correct order.

Samuel, of course, was an expert at all these activities, and he seemed to alternate between being both more cheerful and more anxious than Elliot had seen him yet. He was cheerful when he himself was engaging in an Olde-Quaintian pursuit — especially the dances, which turned his plump cheeks pink and his blue eyes bright — but he turned pale gray with terror when the others took a turn. Either way, he also seemed more tired and edgy than usual, which was no wonder, considering all that swinging back and forth between moods.

Princess Ko undertook every task with practiced ease, interspersed with fits of her signature verbal excess. "Does a starspin make the moon shine?" she exclaimed, when somebody asked if she liked clam chowder.

Keira widened or narrowed her eyes in turn, but otherwise participated adroitly. Sergio leapt between the games with his usual effervescence, dancing so well that the villagers threw petals at him. Elliot shrugged and had a good time. He tried not to mind about the villagers stroking his face, but he drew the line when somebody tried to pry his mouth open to examine his teeth.

Eventually, with only an hour before the Convention's official conclusion, they found themselves in a barge on the River Brell, anchored just off the bank. The schedule called for them to partake of a banquet in the dining hall, which, it turned out, was a small room built in the center of the deck. There was just enough space for the five of them to encircle the table, while the security agents — who had trailed them grimly throughout their pursuits — pressed into a corner. The four walls of this room were lined with windows, so the entourage was invited to watch, play music, dance, and sing on the deck.

The door closed, and for the first time they were alone in quiet. To the extent that you can be alone and quiet while faces press against glass all around you, and shouts, songs, cheers, bells, and fiddles shrill just beyond that glass.

"Smile and talk when I tell you to," Princess Ko instructed. She laughed suddenly. "Laugh each time I touch my nose. And help yourselves to the food."

The table was set with huge silver platters, each crammed with cold meats, seafood, fruits, and cakes. There were also goblets of wine.

Elliot was seated beside the Princess. He touched the front pocket of his breeches, and there was the crackle of paper. There had not been a moment in the last two days to give her the letters from her sister and brother, and that had been making him crazy: She deserved to see these. He kept thinking how he had felt, hearing word from his own dad, and it seemed unfair that the Princess was being deprived.

"Princess?" he murmured.

Outside on the deck, a man in a tricornered cap knocked on the glass with the knuckles of both hands and grinned.

The Princess beamed back at the man.

"Wait," she told Elliot. Then she addressed the group. "We can't be seen interacting with the security agents, so I won't have Agent Nettles tell you the latest." She touched her nose. After a brief pause, Elliot and Sergio remembered to laugh. Samuel looked confused, and Keira raised her eyebrows.

"Don't look at Agent Nettles, Samuel. Look at me." The Princess smiled around her words, and sipped from the wine. "Here's the latest. They now know which Hostile groups are behind the abduction of my family. It was an alliance between five separate factions. They know that the original plan was, as we suspected, to assume control of Cello amidst the consequent disruption.

"Disagreements between the factions meant this never happened. The alliance fell apart. As we speak, however, it is reforming. It is only a matter of time, and time is moving with haste."

She paused, beamed around, and held out her goblet, as if to make a toast.

"My father's failure to attend the Namesaking Ceremony next week would not only destroy our relations with Aldhibah. It would also give the Hostiles the impetus they need to iron out the last of their differences." She grinned again, raised the glass, and drank from it.

There was a general *"Awwwww!"* from outside, and calls of "What has occurred?" and "The Princess raised her glass!" and another, louder "Awwww!"

"Now," said Princess Ko. "What has everybody learned since we last met?"

Nobody spoke.

Keira reached for a plum.

"I learned the distances between every city, town, and village in the Kingdom," she said, "by reading code the size of an ant's toenails."

She bit into the plum, watching Princess Ko. "It strained my eyes so much I had to close them for two days."

Princess Ko responded with a beautiful smile.

"Brilliant!" she said, and clapped her hands.

There was a rise in the voices outside, and the sound of somebody shouting: "The Princess just clapped!"

"Huzzah!" roared the crowd.

"Sergio?" the Princess said. "The detector?"

"My clearance level . . ." Sergio began helplessly.

A low, relaxed voice seemed to swing across the table.

"Don't look at me," said the voice. "I'm not speaking. I'm just saying, Princess, you need to put an agent in the WSU. Take Sergio out and —"

"Agent Ramsay," said the Princess. "I told you not to speak."

Outside, it had started to rain. People huddled closer to the glass, and to one another, arms and elbows above their heads. There was a brief lull in the shouting.

"They're going to break the windows," Keira observed.

"Samuel?" Princess Ko commanded.

Samuel said that, as requested, he had stolen a stack of original accounts of travel between the World and Cello.

The others regarded him curiously.

"How did you do it?"

"As to a figtree in a waternoose," he said with a modest shrug. "Neither do I see how they can help. The key passages are thoroughly blackened, and I have beheld them with candlelight and lamplight, and struggled and strained, and still? Nothing but black."

"Maybe Keira's eyesight?" Sergio suggested, but Keira was shaking her head. "Can't see *through* things," she said.

"Well, that's Elliot's problem," the Princess said. She touched her nose, and some of them managed a chuckle. "Do better with your laughter, everybody. And, Samuel, get those archives into Elliot's backpack before we leave here today."

"How?" wondered Samuel.

"You got them out from behind bars in a library." The Princess shrugged. "Getting them to Elliot should be — what was it you said? A figtree in a waternoose. Your turn, Elliot."

Elliot told them about how he and Madeleine had been messing with magnets and electricity, and how they'd jostled reality — or anyway, jostled the crack.

"We're working with a tiny crack," Elliot said, "and things are happening. I'm thinking, the same thing would set a major crack wide open."

"Huzzah!" came a roar from outside, which was disconcerting. It seemed like they were cheering Elliot's words.

But it was just that the rain had stopped. People were stepping back, shaking themselves out, peeling off wet outer layers, removing their hats, and shaking these so that sprays of rainwater splattered against the glass.

The musicians drew out their instruments and resumed playing.

"Very well, before we leave today, I need Keira to calculate the timing for a staggered reentry of each member of my family — my father, obviously, as first priority — and to get this to both Elliot and me. Before the end of this week, I need Sergio to acquire a detector. I need Elliot to *confirm* the best way to get a person through a crack, and to pass on Keira's schedule of reentry to my family. Next Saturday, we will meet at Ducale, Golden Coast, proceed to the location where my father disappeared, and bring him home. Over the following twenty-four hours, we retrieve the rest of my family. By Sunday afternoon, they will all be home, and my father will be attending the Namesaking Ceremony in Aldhibah."

All of this the Princess delivered with the tone and facial expressions of somebody sharing a lively anecdote.

That part was impressive. Her plan, however, seemed a little fragile.

"Eat and drink," the Princess commanded. "And stop looking at me with those faces full of tragedy and doubt."

"There's something else." Elliot obediently picked up a cob of corn. "I've got letters from your sister, Jupiter, and your brother Tippett."

The Princess's hand had been reaching toward the fruit platter. She paused.

"Give them to me one at a time," she said, and she allowed her hand to carry on, and pick off a bunch of grapes. Sideways to Sergio she murmured: "Can you do something distracting?"

At once Sergio stood up and began to dance on his chair, keeping time with the music that was playing on the deck.

Villagers noticed this, pointed it out to one another, and huzzahed.

Samuel frowned.

Elliot slid the email across. Ko read it fast. She grinned.

"That sounds exactly like Jupiter," she said. "Who knows what WTF means, but all those exclamation marks. They're like the jewels with which she adorns her words. The next one, Elliot? Keep it up, Sergio!" She looked up and applauded.

"The Princess is clapping again!" came a shout from outside. "The Princess likes the Olde Quainte dance!" There was enthusiastic stamping on the deck. Several villagers began to dance themselves, slapping their hands on the windows.

"This place doesn't *seem* all that Hostile," Elliot observed.

"Trust me," said the Princess, waving at the dancers. "It is." She took the envelope from Elliot, opened it in her lap, and drew out the letter.

Sergio stepped onto the table and continued his dance amongst the platters. He beckoned to Samuel to do the same. Pleased, Samuel obliged him.

The Princess lowered her eyes as if she was fixing a napkin on her lap. Elliot glanced over her shoulder.

He could see large, square handwriting.

> Dear Ko,
> I remember You. You're My sister.
> Can you please come and get me?
> Love
> Tippett
>
> P.S. You're right my name is tippett.
> I had forgotten. I was thinking It
> Was Finn. Actually Finn is better
> so please call me that every second
> day from now on. Thank you.
>
> P.P.S. Stop Cutting Pieces From MY
> Blanket. Just send the whole thing.
> or bring it when You come for me.

The Princess stilled for a moment. Her careful smile froze, trembled, and froze again. Elliot could see her jaw clenching.

She curled the letter into her palm.

"Okay," she said in a low, clear voice. "I want every single one of you to laugh. Keep dancing, Sergio and Samuel, but also laugh. Laugh like you're off your face with GC teakwater. Laugh like you're three years old and your parents are tickling you. Laugh like you can't *stand* how funny it is."

Abruptly, she shouted and the others recoiled, then realized it was supposed to be a shout of laughter. She screamed, pounding her fists on the table.

The others joined her. They started a little tentatively, but caught one another's eyes, and the absurdity — of this pretended laughter, of the Princess's list of impossible tasks — began to convert their performance into genuine mirth.

Outside, the people hesitated. Their faces lit up. They caught ahold of the laughter themselves, and joined in.

"I need to say something," Keira laughed.

"What?"

"This is ridiculous."

Everybody hooted.

"What is?"

"Trying to communicate while the entire population of Olde Quainte watches."

"I agree. But we have no choice."

The Princess burst into another storm of laughter, tears streaming.

"If we're trying to get your dad back next weekend," Keira said, "ha-ha-ha — we need — ha-ha — to be able — ha-ha — to get messages to each other this week."

The Princess chortled. Sergio fell off the table with his laughter.

"I agree! But how do you propose we do that?"

"Carrier pigeons!" said Samuel.

"Messages baked in loaves!" Elliot shouted.

"Hide secret notes in laundry hampers!" Sergio cackled.

"We need a code!" panted the Princess, heaving with laughter. "Rearrange the stars! Put messages in comets!"

"We can have holographic interface meetings!" Keira giggled.

"No, we can't! Too easily intercepted!"

"We can use encryption keys!"

"They'll just circumvent them!"

"Not these ones, they won't! I have to tell you something else! Are you ready? *Elliot gave me the paper-clip listening device!* The one his father invented!"

There was a fresh roar of laughter. Now Samuel tumbled from the table, crashing to Elliot's lap and then to the floor. He rolled under the table, howling.

The Princess caught her breath and spoke fast and low: "Are you saying that Elliot gave you the listening device I specifically instructed him *not* to give you?"

There was a movement behind them.

"Stay where you are," Princess Ko shot at the security agents, then she shrieked into another cascade of laughter.

Outside, the villagers and musicians were in hysterics. There were crashes as they fell against the windows or onto the deck, overcome.

"I've reconfigured the technology to make communication devices: one for each of us. They're embedded in rings. Nobody will be able to intercept our transmissions."

"How can you be sure?"

"You can't intercept transmissions that are smaller than particles of magic."

There was a pause. The Princess nodded.

"Give out the rings at our farewell. We'll have a virtual conference call, this Wednesday, eight A.M. Not that Sergio or Samuel have heard a word of this."

She pointed to the floor where Sergio was curled in a fit of laughter, and Samuel was clutching his stomach.

"One more thing," the Princess said to Keira. "New plan. When you calculate the timing of the transfers, I want my little brother, Tippett, to come first."

"Princess," murmured the agents from behind her. "Your father *must* be —"

But Princess Ko flung out a fresh peal of laughter.

PART 12

1.

Elliot's father was not home yet.

"There's just a glitch," his mother said, collecting him from the 11:55 P.M. train, moonlight brushing stripes along the platform.

He threw his backpack into the truck, and climbed into the passenger seat.

"Wednesday, they think," she said, and their glances skittered sideways, crossed, and returned to the road ahead.

She turned the key in the ignition, put the truck in gear. "Okay. Let me get you up-to-date. You missed an ice storm that snapped the power lines in the town square. Clock tower lost about forty-five minutes and nobody's got around to giving them back just yet. Some guy staying at the Watermelon Inn tied his bedsheets together and let himself out his window in the middle of the night. Guess he didn't want to pay his bill. Your Auntie Alanna was laughing fit to bust a gut, thinking how he could have just walked out the front door during breakfast and she'd never have noticed — but no, he went to all that trouble with the sheets. She was impressed with the way he'd knotted them. Not so pleased with how he broke the window latch but she forgave him that, for giving her a laugh. He hadn't run up much of a bill, I guess. And your buddy Gabe's had a bumper crop of beets. It's put everyone in good spirits, thinking it's a sign of change ahead. That's the local news. Not bad for one weekend. Your turn now. Tell me everything. Olde Quainte, eh? I'm thinking old and quaint?"

Elliot settled back into his seat, looked at the streetlights puddling the gutter, and told what he could about his weekend in Olde Quainte.

The next day, Monday, Agent Tovey called while they were eating breakfast.

Elliot answered.

"We're all set for Wednesday," Tovey said. "Listen, I know that the waiting's a killer for you both, but if it helps, Agent Kim and I are about to watch a dolphin show in a water park here. That's how confident we are that things are going to plan. Nothing to do but wait, so we're going to watch dolphins pick up hoops with their noses. You and your mother should do the same."

"No dolphins here in Bonfire."

"I meant do something in the same spirit."

"I know what you meant."

"I know you know."

Elliot smiled, hung up, passed this on to his mother, and the mood in the farmhouse lightened. They found themselves half grinning as they reached for the toothpaste, or buttoned up their jeans, widening their eyes now and again with the wonder, excitement nearly tripping them up.

After school, Elliot found his mother mopping the floors.

"Don't walk on the floor!" she shouted, and he pulled off his shoes, dropped them by the front door, and took big steps toward the kitchen.

The sink was gleaming, and two dish towels he'd never seen before were hanging briskly from the hooks. There were daisies in a vase on the kitchen table, which was laid with the red-and-white checked cloth that Elliot's dad liked. He used to say it reminded him of birthday picnics. Elliot remembered how his dad had tried to hide the disappointment when his mother spilled coffee on that cloth once.

The stain was almost gone now, he noticed. Maybe she'd tried some new laundry product on it.

He and his mother spent that afternoon like a pair of pendulums, swinging between ordinary activities such as homework or paperwork, and more jittery activities like suddenly washing down the deck and setting up a row of potted plants to make it look welcoming.

When they passed each other, they chatted about ordinary things. There was extra effort, extra words and phrases in their speech, Elliot thought. They kept adding layers, varnish to their speech, lilts and jigs like a pair of Olde-Quaintians.

It was as if they were clinging to this happiness with both hands. It made him think of when they folded freshly laundered sheets together, each holding an end. That moment when they decided who would walk forward, take the sheet from the other, and finish off the folding. Only now they weren't making any choices: They were standing there, holding tight to the ends, smiling at each other, waiting.

It helped that he was going to speak to Madeleine tonight. Every now and then he checked the time, and the hours kept taking their solid steps toward the chat with Madeleine tonight, and his dad returning home on Wednesday.

Maybe he'd hear her voice again, and this thought kept adding to those grins he kept catching in the mirrors as he passed them.

He'd never even *seen* Madeleine, he remembered. That stopped him a moment. Did this even make sense, his Madeleine excitement?

"People in the World look the same as people here, right?" he said to his mother while he fried burgers for their dinner.

She was tearing lettuce leaves.

She looked at him, perplexed.

"I mean, they're just ordinary people, right? They don't have three eyes or an extra hand growing out of their shoulder or anything?"

He remembered holding Madeleine's hand. Things would be different if the hand had been extending from her stomach. There was just no way around that.

"Well, when I was doing World Studies they never had extra eyes," his mother grinned. She reached for a tomato, then paused. "I'll tell you what I read once. That there was just *one* difference, as far as they could tell, between people from the World and people here."

"Which was?"

His mother squinted, remembering. "The lemon juice test. You and I squeeze a little lemon juice onto our inner elbows, we'll see a faint pattern of colors. Little specks of it. That's true of every person in Cello. You can't live here all your life, without some Colors getting underneath your skin, and they accumulate at the inner elbow."

"Is that a fact? I never knew."

"Never had cause to squeeze lemon juice on your inner elbow, I guess."

She grinned at him, and he smiled back, then Petra pulled on her lip. A tomato seed smeared onto her chin as she did.

"You're doing a *lot* of talking with your girl in the World these days," she said. "Every other night, you're at the schoolyard. I know I'm always on about this, but you're being careful, right?"

Elliot nodded, reaching out and wiping the tomato seed from her chin.

"The Sheriff's station being right across the road," she continued. "I mean, Hector or Jimmy could look out any moment, and get to wondering what you're up to. I'm glad you and Madeleine are making friends, and it's a shame you guys can never meet. But it's dangerous. It's also not clear to me when you ever sleep, Elliot. Between Madeleine and the RYA. Well, I guess, things will change when — I mean things will settle down when —"

She was smiling, but he could feel it in the room: the superstition rearing at her, hitting her in the throat, stopping the words: *when your father gets back.*

He changed the subject. Told her the story of the banquet on the boat, how they'd fallen about laughing, and the villagers had laughed, how laughter echoes laughter echoes laughter. They both smiled at that, and got on with their burgers.

He was early to his meeting with Madeleine, and there was already a letter in the back of the TV.

He felt himself light up to see her handwriting.

Then he read her words.

2.

Dear Elliot,

I know we're talking tonight, but I wanted to explain this now, without the pressure of knowing you're waiting in a schoolyard in the middle of the night in a snowstorm. Or heatwave. Or attack of Lime Green, or whatever.

First, though, I have to say how incredibly happy I was to get your note about your dad coming back. That is FANTASTIC news. I hope it all worked out okay, and that he was there waiting for you when you got back from Olde Quainte. Maybe he even collected you from the station? I hope he's well, and that you're all happy catching up.

How was your weekend with the RYA? I spent my weekend trying to do homework in one part of our flat, while Belle messed around with coloured lights, crystals, and my mother's aura, in another part. Tricky to focus on trigonometry in those circumstances.

It was cause Mum's decided she wants her aura toughened up – reinforced or double-glazed or fine-tuned or something – so it won't let her get another brain tumour. Not sure of the precise terminology for what Belle's doing, although I'm pretty sure that she'd twist my face off if she saw the disrespectful words I'm using here. (She has a thing for twisting people's faces off.)

Anyway, what I wanted to say is that I like writing notes to you, and I'm happy to keep passing messages to the royal family or whatever – but I definitely don't want to keep trying to get through the crack.

I don't want to play any more games with magnets or electricity or believing-falling-gravity, or with *anything* actually.

I THINK you'll understand why I'm saying this. The last couple of times were scary and weird and uncomfortable, and we still haven't really come close to actually being in each other's worlds. Or not for more than a second, which is no use to anybody. So maybe we could go back to the way things were? When we used to just write to each other?

The thing is, who knows what the trick is to getting through to you guys? Maybe if the whole world just engaged our imaginations, and believed in the impossible – like believing in Tinker Bell – maybe *then* we could get through to you?

It could be that thing about people only using 10 percent of their brains (I don't know if that's true, I just keep hearing it), and if we used the rest we'd know how to fly, teleport, and walk into your Kingdom?

Maybe you're right there in front of us and we just can't see you – but we would if we looked through the right kind of tears, or through a smokescreen, or 3-D glasses, or 5-D glasses, I guess – because maybe you're a whole other dimension. Another dimension of us.

Who knows what it is. All I know is, it's way beyond our comprehension, and messing around with it – without having a clue what we're doing – is just dangerous.

Talk soon,

Madeleine

3.

The night was oddly quiet.

Madeleine pulled her sleeves over her hands, and looked at the parking meter. It shone coldly back at her, like a rebuke.

She thought back over the letter she'd written to Elliot earlier that day.

It was a good letter, she argued with the parking meter. *Elliot will understand. He'll agree. It's the right thing to do.*

She breathed deeply, took out her notebook, and wrote:

Hey, Elliot. You there?

His reply came a few moments later.

Yep. Just reading your letter. My dad's not back yet — they think Wednesday. I've got mail for you to forward to the royal family. Weekend was good — crazier than ever, and I never want to eat another bowl of clam chowder again, or anyway never again while I'm trying to dance the Olde Quainte Tambourine Jig at the same time. I'd teach you the Tambourine Jig, but I see you've decided you don't want to try getting through the crack anymore. What's up with that?

Madeleine felt a flutter of confusion and mild panic. The parking meter seemed to raise its eyebrows: *I told you so.* She wrote fast:

Well, I explained in the letter. It's just the right thing to do.

There was another long pause, and then Elliot's reply.

Okay, just looked at the letter again, and as far as I can see you want to stop trying because the last couple of times it was "weird" and "uncomfortable." Not sure how you do things over there, but I don't usually quit at the "weird" and "uncomfortable" point. So. Then you go on about how our Kingdom might exist if you just used your imagination, or got the right glasses, and that we might actually be another "dimension" of you. Which if you don't mind me saying is all kinda intensely egocentric. Finally, you say that figuring out the cracks is really hard, which I agree with, but you seem to conclude from that that it must be "dangerous" to try, which makes the least sense I've ever heard in my life. Anyway, I guess you can make your own decisions but you should know that the Princess is relying on us to figure out the cracks before Saturday so we can get her family home. And I kinda thought we were on the verge of doing that, so it seems like a "weird" time to stop.

Madeleine read this note with the sense that there were elbows jostling her from either side. She made louder and louder exasperated sounds and muttered to the parking meter, "Come *on*," and "You must be *kidding*." Her pen had trouble keeping up with her trembling thoughts.

Yeah, well, with great respect to your Princess, why does she have a Kingdom that SEALS up the cracks to our World anyway? What's up with you people that you're not even allowed to TALK about how to get through? You run around locking the doors so we can't get in, like we're so repellant that you can't even KNOW we're here, then expect me to help you open them???

She watched the parking meter through narrowed eyes and tapping feet, and grabbed at the reply when it arrived.

Okay, that's a fair point, but if you're going to start laying into my Kingdom, just keep in mind that your World isn't exactly a pecan pie. I've been reading about it a bit, and turns out you guys turned actual people into SLAVES, and women weren't allowed to have the same jobs as men, and you actually had issues with same-sex relationships. Maybe you've got over all this now, but just remember that there was a time when you were all the Kingdoms and Empires' distance from perfect.

Anyway, we're getting away from the point here. I guess it's up to you if you want to quit. All you really need to do is send the letters to the royals. Can you send them priority or express or whatever, 'cause they need to get them before Saturday.

This time she actually shouted her anger, and it echoed up and down the empty laneway. Heat swarmed over her, burning her cheeks and the back of her neck, then abruptly slipped away. Now she felt cold with calm.

I'll send the letters to the royals by regular mail. I can't afford to send them express. (Do you have any idea how much international express costs?) They probably won't get there before the weekend, but that's the best I can do.

Elliot's reply sped back to her.

If you can't get the message to them before the weekend, then it's pointless. The royals need to be at certain places at certain times.

Well, people aren't always where they're meant to be.

Yeah, I get that, but that's even further off topic right now.

Madeleine shook her head slowly. Again, she wrote with cold composure:

I don't think you "get it" at all. What about the time when I came here to talk to you at the time we'd arranged and you didn't turn up? And then night after night I kept coming back into the cold and dark and nothing, nothing, nothing except silence. Then suddenly you were back, and it's just "sorry," and "here are some more jobs for you." Seems to me like I'm doing a lot of running around to post offices and trying to rescue your royal family (who mean NOTHING to me, by the way, and neither does your kingdom, which is not egotistical, it's just my reality – it's all I've got to go on) and trying to get through the crack is a lot more than "uncomfortable," it hurts like HELL, and who are you to say when things are dangerous or not – I KNOW it's dangerous what we've been doing, and not just cause I don't understand it – I just KNOW it. And meanwhile, it's not exactly clear what YOU'RE doing for me, except giving me days of silence, and making me the "quitter" and yourself the hero.

A car turned into the street and drove slowly past. A man turned and stared at Madeleine, and another wave of anger warmed her. Here was Elliot mocking her fears about the cracks. Here she was, a fourteen-year-old girl standing alone in a deserted street in the middle of the night.

She watched the car disappear around the corner, and another note appeared from Elliot.

Now I'm really confused. You mean that week when I got back from Tek in Jagged Edge? I guess I didn't come and talk to you for a while then. I was caught up here – it looked like Agents Tovey and Kim were going to be pulled off my dad's case and taken into the missing royals thing and I was trying to stop that happening. Did that seriously bother you?

Of course it bothered me. I had no idea where you were. I had no idea if I was ever going to hear from you again. We'd been talking for HOURS every night. We were, like, really good friends, or that's what I thought. I had all these stories I'd been planning to tell you, and they ended up clogged up in my throat. Who even knows where those words have gone now?

Madeleine waited. She felt like crying.

Okay, well, I'm sorry—I didn't have a clue that was an issue. And I'm kind of thinking maybe this is not about me? You're thinking about the silence from your dad really? And how you don't know if you'll ever hear from him again?

OF COURSE I'm thinking about my dad. But that doesn't mean it's not about you too. It just means it hurt me MORE when you disappeared because it was like somebody ELSE I cared about ignoring me. And of COURSE you didn't "have a clue that it was an issue." You're one of those stupidly hot guys. You're so stupidly hot I have no doubt that ALL girls like you. You probably can't even walk anywhere without tripping over a girl.

I have no idea what you're talking about.

I saw you, Elliot. I never told you that, but there was one night when I saw your face in the schoolyard. You looked right at me, but you didn't see me there. You don't hear me when I need you, you don't see me when I'm right in front of you. But, like I said, of COURSE you don't. Your life must be a party of girls. I bet you've just spent the weekend getting it on with *those girls in the Youth Alliance. I remember you said that the princess is "super pretty." And that Keira girl – you called her "beautiful." I bet you and Keira have a thing.*

This time there was a long pause. The parking meter sat silent. The pause continued.

There was a sound like a distant shout from a block away, and then the crash of a garbage-bin lid.

Madeleine grabbed her pen and wrote again.

See what I mean. You do the silence thing. You have no idea what silence feels like, the different shapes it can take.

Yeah, well, I kinda do know how silence feels. My dad's missing too, remember?

Madeleine read this, rolled her eyes, and stamped her foot.

He understood silence? Her life was *made* of silence at the moment. Just the night before, they'd been at Belle's place again, listening to music, and Belle had abruptly switched it off.

"Music is a lie," she'd said.

"What are you talking about?" they'd asked her.

"It alters your state of mind," she'd said. "Gives you false hope."

She'd refused to say another word, and they had sat in the new silence until Belle had said abruptly, "Do you miss your mother, Jack?"

"Of course not," Jack had said. "She died when I was two. I don't even remember her, and we haven't got photos. Although one thing I've noticed is that in all my memories of former lives, my mother is always the same person. So maybe that's her."

"You and your former lives," Belle had said contemptuously.

For the next few minutes Belle and Jack had looked oddly at each other, their eyes exchanging silences. Then Madeleine and Jack had walked home, silently.

Between Madeleine and her mother too, she could feel silences expanding. Holly would be kneading her forehead as they chatted, but they wouldn't mention headaches: They'd discuss Madeleine's allergies, and how her nosebleeds were back, and the taste of blood at the back of the throat, and which over-the-counter medications she should try next.

All these silences, meanwhile, were just lily pads in the dark pool of silence that was Madeleine's dad. She'd thought she was "facing the truth" when she accepted he had drug and alcohol problems. It had never occurred to her that he might not *solve* the problems. That he might be lost forever.

She and her mother never talked about her dad, which added another dimension to the silence between them. So it went on. Silences on silences.

She wrote to Elliot:

Your dad's not missing, he's coming back. Wednesday, right? It's completely different anyway. I thought we were the same — that our absent fathers meant we were like echoes or reflections or matching displacements or whatever, but we're not. My dad is gone because of drug issues, and seems like he's decided not to deal with those. YOUR dad is gone because he was stolen by Hostiles. My dad's a loser. Yours is a hero coming home. So don't tell me you understand silence.

There was a short pause, and then Elliot's handwriting, more careful than usual:

You're angry with me because my dad is coming back?

That's not what I'm saying.

Yeah, well, sounds like it is. Heading home now. Bye.

Madeleine panicked. She shook her head as she wrote.

Hang on, that's NOT what I meant. I'm GLAD your dad's coming back. WAIT.

She sent her note.

She folded her arms tightly.

She stared at the parking meter, but no more notes appeared.

The silence of the street drew itself out, stretched, undulated. It slowly took on different shapes, grew closer, colder, more and more reproving.

Eventually, she gave up and went home. The silence walked with her, hanging its head.

4.

The next morning Elliot woke at five A.M. As his feet hit the floor, his thoughts hit Madeleine.

He let that flare through his bloodstream a few moments. Then he stood, stretched, and sniffed. That'd be it now. He wouldn't think of her again. Disappointing, sure, that she hadn't matched up to her voice, but she could live her own story. He'd live his.

He'd just have to figure out the crack on his own. Keep experimenting from his end.

There were those reports that Samuel had stolen too. He hadn't seen much point in looking at them — if nobody else had figured out how to see through the blacked-out bits, how could he? — but he'd give it a try now.

The key was to keep busy, and — something startled in his chest as he recalled this — *his dad was coming home tomorrow.*

Who cared about a girl in the World. His dad was coming home. If it all went okay; if —

Actually, he wouldn't think about that either.

He reached for his backpack, found the envelope of stolen accounts, and tipped them out. They were yellow-brown, spotted with age, the creases where they'd been folded almost tearing the paper at some points.

He leafed through them.

Every second page had blocks of black. No wonder Samuel's transcriptions had been so useless. He held a couple up to the window to let the sun shine through. Turned them over. Shone his flashlight on them. Nothing.

His eyes fixed themselves on a random block of black. If he could scrape it away with his fingernails. There was something about it — how impenetrable it was, how frustrating and implacable — that made him think of Madeleine. The way she'd slammed a door between them.

Wait. He was supposed to have set her aside.

He sat on the edge of his bed. Looked like summer outside. That blue haze in the sky, the warmth on the glass.

What *was* this blackness? Was it ink? Couldn't you just pour water on ink and wash it away?

That'd be dumb though — it'd sog up the paper.

Two words came to him, precise as mathematics: *art restoration.*

Of course! There were people who did this sort of thing professionally! They took old paintings that were covered in grime or mold or whatever — paintings that had been *painted over* by smugglers or forgers — and they did something to them. Who knew what. They used chemicals or solutions, he thought, and they gently washed away the top layer. And *ta-da*! Whisked back the curtain. Revealed the truth beneath.

He was pretty sure there were no professional art restorers here in Bonfire. He'd have to go into Sugarloaf, or even as far as Forks.

He pictured himself arriving at an art restorer's office, handing over these documents, asking what they said.

Huh.

Nope. Couldn't do that.

He needed someone close to him. Someone he could trust.

An artist maybe?

Half an hour later he was riding his bike to school. The pedals seemed to revolve him through moods, from almost-cheerful to furious, to indifferent, to elated, to scared, to *set-it-all-aside.* By the time he arrived he was exhausted.

His friend Cody lit right up when Elliot asked if he could help with something "seriously illegal" and "completely confidential" and he couldn't "tell him any more than that, sorry, buddy." Turned out Cody had done a couple of classes on restoration as part of his Art course here at school.

"Leave the papers with me," Cody suggested. "I'll go to the small Art Room later today — it's always empty at lunchtime." He ran a hand through his hair thoughtfully, then lifted it away, and his wild curls sprang back. "Elliot, I've gotta tell you, I only took a *couple* of classes on this, and paper is its own specialty. You'd use infrared or UV or even X-ray, I think, to try to see through the black. But I haven't got those technologies. I could try a solvent. Might clear the black away — might also clear the words behind the black. He looked Elliot square in the eye. "And then they're gone for good. You want to take that chance?"

Elliot looked back at him. He shrugged.

"Got no other choice. You sure you don't mind risking a life sentence?"

"Ah, I hear they've got art supplies in prisons these days. See you at the end of lunch."

Elliot handed over the envelope.

By lunchtime, the spinning wheels of mood were getting too much for Elliot. Turned out none of his teachers had a single thing of interest to say. You'd have thought they might have learned techniques for entertaining students at teachers' college, but no, seemed all they'd learned was how to drag their voices along classroom floors picking amongst dust, bugs, and the spongy bits in the wood.

Students were allowed to leave the school at lunch, and Elliot ran straight to the Watermelon Inn.

"Hey," he said, skidding in the front door. Auntie Alanna looked up from behind the desk. "Heard you had someone do a runner on the weekend?" he said. "Broke a window latch on the way out? You want me to fix it for you?"

Alanna replaced the lid on the pen she'd just been using. She tilted her head.

"Already fixed that myself, Elliot," she said. "But that's a sweet offer."

"Well, then, what *can* I do for you? You must have something else?"

The door jangled, and they both turned and watched as Corrie-Lynn walked in.

"You know I don't like meat-loaf sandwiches," she said to her mother in a voice of mild, disappointed reproof. "I saw you'd packed it for my lunch and I had to throw it away and come home."

Alanna sighed. "I'm *sure* you liked meat loaf last week," she said. "But okay, go on into the kitchen and see what you can find. Today's lunch menu has chicken and leek pie. Maybe try one of those?"

"Maybe." Corrie-Lynn echoed her mother's sigh. She turned to Elliot. "Hey," she said.

Elliot laughed. "Hey, Corrie-Lynn. Any new puppets you want to show me?"

"Nope. You know what, though? That spell you got me from the Lake of Spells? It's a metaphoric spell. Did you know that?"

"Don't even know what you're talking about."

"*Yes*, you do. Those spells that work in a more airy sort of way. My room was a disaster the other day after I built a puppet theater on my bed, so there was wood shavings, nails, sawdust, everything, everywhere, and I thought: This is *just* the time to use that spell that Elliot gave me. Okay?"

"Okay," Elliot agreed.

"So I got it out. And I was about to use it when I noticed a tiny, tiny metaphor mark — it's like a little dash with a squiggle through the middle? It's so tiny I hadn't even seen it before. So don't blame yourself that you didn't."

"Well," said Elliot. "I can't say I was. But how did you even know what that mark meant?"

"I read all the extra stuff about the Lake of Spells in the Guidebook. So then I had to clean up the mess myself. 'Cause that spell won't work on regular mess. It'll be for clearing away things that are blocking the truth or whatever. Which I don't see when that will ever come up. And if it does, I'll forget to use the spell for sure. I've got to go and eat now. I'm starving. See ya, Elliot."

"Okay, well, sorry about that, Corrie-Lynn."

"That's okay. Like I said, don't blame yourself."

Elliot looked at Alanna and they both smiled. They watched Corrie-Lynn walk in her straight-backed, listless way toward the kitchen.

"If you really want to help, I've always got things to do," Alanna said. "You must be going crazy, waiting for your dad. You want distracting, right?"

Elliot looked at her. "You bet I do."

"Well, if you feel like grabbing a paintbrush, there's the cornices need touching up in twenty-three, twenty-four, and — what was the other room?"

"Wait," Elliot said, staring. "What did Corrie-Lynn just say about the spell?"

"She thinks it would clear away something else? Not a regular mess? Things blocking the truth, wasn't it? Anyhow, it was up on the third floor, so it's room thirty-seven. That's the other one, and —"

But Elliot had gone.

5.

The Watermelon kitchen was busy in a low-murmuring way. It smelled of warm bread, crushed tomato, chopped onion. Elliot nearly tripped over a trash can full of eggshells, and the assistant chef, dusting flour from her hands, rebuked him sharply: "Slow down!"

Corrie-Lynn was climbing onto a stool in the corner, while the head chef slid a plate of chicken-and-leek pie in her direction.

Elliot pulled up a stool and sat beside her. She nodded at him.

"That spell I gave you," Elliot said. "What would you think about me asking for it back. And not explaining why?"

Corrie-Lynn picked up her knife and fork.

"It'd be wrong, I know," Elliot continued.

"It sure would," Corrie-Lynn agreed, concentrating on the pie. She seemed to be deciding where to slice into it. She chose, and the pie toppled gently sideways.

After a moment of chewing, she looked up at Elliot.

"I don't know what else to say," he admitted. "I just really need it back."

Corrie-Lynn gazed at him critically. *The people she had to put up with*, her gaze said. *All of them so much taller and older than she was, and yet so much less reliable.*

"I promise I'll go back to the Lake of Spells one day, and get you another spell," Elliot added. "A better one if I can."

Then he remembered himself.

"Actually," he said. "I can't promise that. I'm banned from the Lake of Spells."

Corrie-Lynn broke off a piece of the pie crust with her hand, and shrugged.

"You'll be too old to get into the Lake soon anyway," she said. "I plan on catching *plenty* on my own."

"You're going to the Lake of Spells, Corrie-Lynn?"

She turned back to him. "I'm going everywhere," she said. "I'm seeing *all* of the Kingdoms and the Empires. Why do you think I never stop reading that Guidebook? One of these days I plan to *meet* the guidebook writer. I'll ask him if he's a tosser."

"I wouldn't do that," Elliot suggested mildly.

"Everyone knows your dad and mine were adventurers. The Baranski brothers were famous for it," Corrie-Lynn continued, her voice almost grim. "Well, guess what, I'm a Baranski too."

"So you are." He smiled, but he was thinking how it must be for her and for his Auntie Alanna: one Baranski coming home tomorrow; the other never would.

"Just wait a few years before you go," he suggested.

"Well, of *course*." She took a bite of pie.

He was watching her, trying to keep the panic from his face and eyes, but he couldn't help a glance toward the kitchen clock.

Might clear the black away, Cody had said. *Might also clear the words behind the black.*

If the words were gone for good, this spell of Corrie-Lynn's couldn't get them back either.

It was twenty minutes into the school lunch hour.

Corrie-Lynn followed his eyes to the clock. She set her knife and fork down.

"Nobody take away my pie!" she called to the kitchen generally. "I'll be back in just a minute," and to Elliot: "Come on up to my room and I'll fetch it for you."

* * *

He flew to the school, pumping the pedals, slung his bike inside the gate, and ran across the lunch-time schoolyard.

He had to dart and skid between kids who turned and looked, or ignored him completely, or blocked his way, or called things like, "Hey, you want to go up to the deftball field and practice pitches?" in ordinary voices, and they seemed surprised when he ran by without stopping to answer, just as if it wasn't blindingly obvious that he was in a hurry.

He was pounding toward the small Art Room — but which one *was* the small one? They both seemed about the same size. There should be a better way of distinguishing, he thought. This one had green drainpipes, for example, and the other red. They could be the green art room and the red art room. No confusion there.

Would Cody have already done it? Cody had the dreamy way about him, but when it came to his art, he was slapdash fast and efficient.

The one on the left must be the small Art Room. From this angle, it seemed a *tiny* bit narrower.

He tried the door, but it was locked. He knocked and waited. There was silence from inside. Had Cody finished already? Was he gone?

He moved along from the door and knocked on the window.

The blind lifted a little, and there was Cody's face at an angle, squinting at him, suspicious, then frowning. "Hey," Cody said, raising the window and leaning his elbows on the sill. "I said I'd see you at the *end* of lunch."

"Have you done it yet?"

"Still deciding on the solvent."

"Can I have them back? I've got another idea."

Cody's face fell for a moment, then brightened.

"You bet," he said. "I'm almost positive I was going to destroy them."

* * *

Elliot thought he'd skip the class after lunch, find somewhere quiet to try the spell. But seemed that the teachers at this school — who'd had no apparent pedagogical enthusiasm that morning — were suddenly full of vim.

"Elliot Baranski! You're walking in the wrong direction if you want to make it to Biology in time!"

How did Ms. Piper even know Elliot *had* Biology right now? She was a Music teacher.

He was trapped in classes by similarly dedicated teachers the rest of the day, then swooped on by friends, then his mother needed help packing boxes of quince — and so the day continued. Just hours back he'd been frantic for distraction, now all he wanted was a moment of peace.

At last, late that night, he was alone in his bedroom. Through the window, a slip of moon, and a big curve of black, starry sky. He tipped out the papers. The edges almost wilted into dust.

It suddenly seemed like the dumbest idea he'd ever had, telling Cody to pour chemical solutions on these.

Ah, well, he'd stopped him in time.

He took out the spell. Corrie-Lynn had had it stored in an icebox in her bedroom, and she'd packed it in an insulated bag for him to transport, but it already seemed warmer than it should.

This one had a shinier casing than most he'd seen — it was a deep mud color, and almost a perfect circle. He thought of this spell lying in Corrie-Lynn's hand. How she'd passed it straight across without hesitating. How thin her arms were, and her ankles, poking out of her cutoff jeans. Her fraying sandals, her black toenail growing out from when she'd dropped a hammer on her foot.

Elliot found himself standing up. He was going to take this shiny spell straight back to his cousin. It was all wrong taking it away from her. It was the opposite of what he should be.

Ah, but this might be the only way to get the royals back. There was Ko without her family. There was the Kingdom of *Cello* on the brink of collapse. The Hostiles secretly gathering. That ominous King of Aldhibah: Who knew what trouble he'd get up to with his army if King Cetus didn't turn up to the Namesaking Ceremony?

There was no choice.

He fanned the papers out on his desk, trying to decide which blacked-out block to try. Corrie-Lynn had explained how the spell worked, and it seemed he'd only get one chance.

The second-to-last page contained an account by a Cellian. She was *Jane Whitehall* of Marlow in Golden Coast, and the date was *February 28, 1662*. Elliot glanced at this, then leafed through the papers a few more times before returning to it. Something about the name *Jane Whitehall* struck him as hopeful. It seemed a sensible name. Or anyway the name of someone attentive to detail.

"I bethought me that ample time had passed since my last sojourn to the World, and finding myself willing, and most desirous, to visit once more, I bethought myself that I should do so, and so, after I had supped, I took me to the" — here the words ran up against a solid blackness, which carried on for the next four or five lines.

Okay, Jane Whitehall, Elliot took the spell into his hand again. *Let's see where you be-took yourself after you be-supped.*

He felt around the smooth surface of the casing until his fingertips touched a faint seam. Then he dug in his nails, carefully pried it open, and held the opening over the blacked-out paragraph. Nothing happened. He recalled Corrie-Lynn's suggestion that he might have to tap the bottom and shake it a little. The moment he did that, there was a faint buzz against the palm of his hand and a tiny fluttering shadow slipped from the casing and fell softly onto the paper.

Again, nothing happened. Elliot leaned forward. The shadow seemed about the size and shape of a small moth: It also seemed to be disintegrating into dust as he peered at it. Had it been out of the ice-box for too long?

But then the black ink slowly curled itself upward. It rolled along, collecting the next line of black, and the next after that, like someone rolling up strips of turf. Handwriting, clear and bold, emerged beneath the rolling ink. It was exactly like the hand which came before and after, except brighter and cleaner, as if the blacking-out had kept it crisp. Like carpet, protected under furniture for years.

"and so, after I had supped, I took me to the place, and employ'd our system of pulleys and weights to locate the precise position of the Crack. I performed the usual ritual with mirror and candlelight, and within a mere quarter of an hour I had success, and a great joy it was to me to feel myself so transported to the World, mindful though I was that, in upwards of a day and a night, I should"

There, the account carried on as it had, detailing her careful preparations for avoiding the loss of her memory, and her time in the World, and her return, all in the faded script.

I performed the usual ritual with mirror and candlelight.

Elliot dropped the casings onto the table and smiled.

6.

Madeleine and Jack were waiting at the door of Darshana's place, listening to the clamour inside — little running footsteps, a sudden howl, a sharp crash, children's television, Darshana's voice singing — when Jack, who'd been standing silent and thoughtful for a moment, turned to Madeleine and said:

"So, we'll go no more a-roving
So late into the night,
Though the heart be still as loving,
And the moon be still as bright.

For the sword outwears its sheath,
And the soul wears out the breast,
And the heart must pause to breathe,
And love itself have rest.

Though the night was made for loving,
And the day returns too soon.
Yet we'll go no more a-roving
By the light of the moon."

"Yeah," said Belle, who had arrived halfway through this recital, and waited, staring at Jack with an expression of mild distaste. "Another thing: The time has come for you to quit with the Byron obsession."

She leaned between them and knocked hard on the door, which opened at once with a gust. A small girl fell out onto the mat.

"What are you waiting for?" Darshana cried. "Come in!" while the small girl — it turned out to be Chakiki — shouted at her mother: "You knew I was leaning on the door! Why did you open it?"

Madeleine walked in with pieces of strangeness slotting themselves into her like playing cards:

So, we'll go no more a-roving
So late into the night,
Though the heart be still as loving,
And the moon be still as bright.

She had run into Jack on her way to Darshana's place just now, and she'd told him about her argument with Elliot the night before.

"So, it's over," she'd told Jack, and then raised her eyebrows, trying to convert the melodrama of those words into a sort of ironic self-parody. "Me and the Kingdom of Cello are officially finished." He had been quiet and thoughtful until he'd turned on the doorstep and offered her the Byron.

"Though the night was made for loving,
And the day returns too soon.
Yet we'll go no more a-roving
By the light of the moon."

Darshana was ushering everyone into the living room, at the same time as instructing her little girls that they were magnets, one north, the other south.

As usual, Madeleine sat on the couch with Belle beside her. Jack was on the floor, leaning up against their knees. The little girls were set to crashing together, flying apart, and picking up various metal objects. Then their mother informed them that they were no longer magnets, but electrical charges. They cried about this for a moment, but they were adaptable girls and adjusted to their new roles quickly.

Madeleine looked around the room. A cluster of stickers adorned the opposite wall, just above the skirting board: She could make out a Cinderella, a smiling Aladdin, a small blue figure with enormous eyes giving her a manic thumbs-up. LEGOs scattered the carpet. A wilting slice of tomato stained the arm of this couch.

These are the pieces of their lives, Madeleine thought, and her mind faded back onto the pieces of her own life: the life she had lived before Cambridge.

She and her mother had been electrical charges themselves then, hurtling around a superconductor world made of music, shimmer, glint, froth, jasmine; made of saxophone, berries, buckles, petals, espresso, and flames; of silver snow, chocolate meringue, glacial blue, fragrant tea; of walls of glass, skies of sparks, the pleasure of shoes, the sighing of pillows, the soft fall of dresses, the feathers of peacocks, the spinning of wheels and tops and doors and coins and girls.

"You are a positive charge," Darshana was instructing Chakiki, "and you, Rhani, are negative. So, what do you do? You do not know? You are no children of mine! Great big four-year-old and you do not know the behaviour of unlike electrical charges?! You *rush* towards each other! Good! That's it! Excellent. Ah, your knee is all right, Rhani, do not be a crybaby. Just, maybe, *shift* the knee the next time a positive charge rushes you."

There was a brief delay then when the girls were distracted by a ball of Silly Putty that Jack had found underneath the couch. Darshana threw the Silly Putty against the wall (where it stuck) and resumed the lesson.

"Now, you are both negative! So, run away from each other! You,

Rhani, into the kitchen! You, Chakiki, as far as you can down the hall! Oh, do not be a crybaby, it is not that we wish you away from us. No! Do not come back! We *do* wish you away from us! For the sake of science! Science needs you in the linen closet!"

Then Darshana summoned the girls back and explained that charges were surrounded by invisible fields of power —

"Magical powers?" Chakiki interrupted.

"With powers that extend to the boundaries of those fields," Darshana said, ignoring her, reaching out to the little girls' arms, and twisting this way and that, entangling and disentangling, to demonstrate the lines of force.

It was the right thing to do, Madeleine told herself. Calling things off with Elliot. Even if it did mean that she would *go no more a-roving by the light of the moon*. Dangerous, anyway. Teenage girl. Roving by moonlight.

She'd been entitled to say that the games were too much for her, and if he couldn't respect her wishes, he wasn't a true friend. Well, he wasn't. She knew that now. He was clearly only interested in what she could do for him, how she could help with the crack and the missing royal family. She'd been stupid to think there'd been more to it, that he'd been enjoying their conversations the way she had. It was disappointing. That was all.

Also, annoying that it had ended the way it had — with him thinking she was a quitter, and accusing her of not caring about his dad. Which made her feel guilty now, which was unfair. She hadn't *meant* it that way, but now *he* had the moral high ground. When, actually, *she* should be up there, proud.

Darshana was talking fast. "Hans Christian Orsted," she said, "was a Danish physicist. He was giving a lecture in Copenhagen and about to demonstrate a form of battery, when he noticed that the needle of a nearby compass moved every time he started or stopped the electric current. The compass, of course, was magnetic. Electricity had created magnetism."

Madeleine straightened up.

"Michael Faraday," Darshana said next, "was a poor little uneducated English bookbinder. And he thought, *If electricity creates magnetism, maybe magnetism creates electricity?*

"Do you see what I am saying?!" Darshana continued. Jack and Belle were both lost in thought. They shook themselves a little and turned politely towards Darshana, who crouched down, leaned into their faces, and spoke in a low, ominous voice: "They are *intimately* connected. Electricity and magnetism are *closely* interrelated. If Chakiki is an electrical field and Rhani is a magnetic field, then Chakiki and Rhani are *sisters*!"

"We *are* sisters," the little girls pointed out in unison.

"Exactly!" shouted their mother, standing up again, and reaching for the girls. "An electrical field moves" — she pushed Chakiki forward — "and it creates a magnetic field!" — she pushed Rhani — "which creates an electrical field . . . which creates a magnetic field . . . which creates an electrical field . . ." And she grabbed and shoved at her giggling girls, looping them around in figure eights, across the living room, down the hall, and back again.

Madeleine turned sideways. Belle's eyes had glazed again she saw, but Jack was watching all this with raised, skeptical eyebrows.

The pieces of strangeness intensified.

She and Elliot had played games with magnets one night and games with electricity the next. Who knew their games had been connected in this way, intertwined like this?

"Take a magnet and coil a wire around it," Darshana was saying. "Spin the magnet. Keep it spinning! Use coal or water or the best mother in the world to spin it!" She reached out to the girls' shoulders. "Spin! That's it! Spin! Generate electricity!"

The girls spun until they tipped sideways, fell, stood up and spun again. Rhani bumped her head and howled, but her mother told her not to be a crybaby.

"Maybe the girls should have a break?" Jack suggested.

"What?" cried Darshana, gleeful. "You are accusing me of child abuse again! Please, by all means, report me! I will say to the authorities, *You think this is bad? You know there was a scientist who placed magnets in his little boy's hand, and then electrified him? So that colourful streams of light came from the boy's hand!* I will say that to the authorities, and they will say, *Ah, then. Please. Forgive us! Get back to spinning your girls! But please do not electrify them.*"

"Yes!" cried Rhani and Chakiki. "Make colours stream from our hands!"

"*Please*, Mummy, electrify me!"

"No, me first!"

Darshana was laughing wickedly.

The sun was picking up the dust on the TV screen. Madeleine noticed an old teabag on the floor. A coil of tangled leads and a double adaptor. The girls' pajamas scattered on the floor from that morning, along with shreds of breakfast cereal, soggy with milk.

The pieces of other people's lives.

She looked at her own palms, and imagined they were holding the pieces of her life here in Cambridge. History with Federico above the porter's lodge. Science here with Darshana. French in Belle's crowded living room. English with Madeleine's own mother. The sewing machine. Beans in a pot. Her mother's mood swings. Belle and Jack, laughing or fierce. Chats with Denny wheezing downstairs. Midnight conversations with Elliot.

Now she lifted her hands. She imagined she was letting the Elliot piece fall to the carpet. In her mind she heard a loud thud.

There was no question. He was a big piece of her life.

"Nobody is going to be electrocuted!" said Darshana, suddenly stern. "Keep spinning! Spin! Faster! Faster! Whoa! Watch where you spin! You could blacken your eye doing that!" She was laughing again. "Come, get up. You eye is all right." She beckoned her three students, speaking over the high-pitched giggles and squeals of her daughters: "Come, we will have cake. Leave them to their spinning," and she walked towards the kitchen, tall and proud. "It was a good lesson, was it not? And next week we will talk about James Clerk Maxwell!"

Her voice disappeared into the kitchen, and Belle, Jack, and Madeleine wandered after her, looking back at the spinning, falling, spinning, falling girls.

"James Clerk Maxwell," said Belle. "I know that name." She frowned. "He's that famous actor, yeah? The one with the deep voice?"

"James Earl Jones," said Jack.

"Oh, right." Belle drifted a moment, then brightened abruptly. "Stupid! It's the Prime Minster!"

She sauntered down the hall.

Madeleine was distracted by a falling lamp. By throwing herself across the room, she managed to catch it before it hit the floor.

Jack watched her, and when she turned back, he said, "It's the name from the hat, isn't it? James Clerk Maxwell. Your extra name from the hat."

Madeleine nodded.

He looked at her. She shook her hair out of her eyes and looked back. Their eyes held, and she didn't understand what Jack was trying to say, but she felt fragments slide towards her: *We'll go no more a-roving*. Unexpected pieces of paper. The light of the moon.

Jack was right.

She'd given up on Elliot, on magic, on unexpected papers, on moonlight — and that was a mistake.

But then, as Jack started heading down the hall, something else came to Madeleine.

That night when she had been trapped in the juddering, shaking darkness, she had spoken.

She remembered now what she had said.

Can somebody help me? she'd said.

There'd been nothing but silence.

7.

Madeleine sat on her couch-bed, papers and books scattered around her. Her mother was at the sewing table, and there was the *flick*, *flick* of Madeleine's pages, and the *bzzzz* of the sewing machine; sofa springs, slow thoughtful breathing or quick impatient breathing, clicking tongues, and the silences between.

James Clerk Maxwell.

There were pieces of James Clerk Maxwell on the couch with her.

His name in a hat; his name in Darshana's voice.

The universe must want her to read about him. She would fill up the empty space left by Elliot with pieces of James Clerk Maxwell: his three-tiered, pointy name.

She was flicking pages randomly, taking fragments at a time.

James Clerk Maxwell grew up in a manor house. He liked hot-air balloons. His mother died of cancer when he was eight.

That stopped her.

She'd only just met him, he was still only eight, and already his mother was dead.

At the sewing table, Madeleine's own mother was clearing her throat — once, twice, three times — each time more vigorously than the last, and Madeleine said, sharply: "Drink some water."

She felt as if a person was standing in her path, elbows spread, casting the shadow of an unspoken everything: *Your mother almost died from a brain tumour, you know.*

Well, I *know,* she thought back. *Don't you think I* know *that?*

If she almost died once, the shadow persisted, *it could happen again. Listen to her clearing her throat. What is it this time? Lung cancer?*

Now Holly was threading a needle for hand sewing: She was holding the needle in the air, aiming the thread, and Madeleine thought how fine the thread was, how fine the needle, how fine the space between her mother's life and death.

If Elliot had not sent the healing beads from Cello. If Madeleine had not run from the hospital to the parking meter to get them. If she hadn't got back in —

James Clerk Maxwell.

He had a broad accent and a stutter.

He showed how colours merged on a spinning top. He took the first ever colour photograph: a picture of a tartan ribbon.

Madeleine looked up from the notes again. She was thinking of the Colours of Cello, and realising that she no longer had even a fine thread of doubt about the Kingdom. She believed in it completely.

Only, she thought next, she no longer believed in Elliot.

Or not his essence anyway. He was empty, a phantasm. The qualities she'd ascribed to him had all come from her imagination.

It was the same with her father, actually. She'd believed in him all her life, but now he was nothing but a puppet made of cloth. You put the strings down and it folds itself up, face down. A strong wind and the puppet blows away.

She looked across the room at her mother, who was concentrating, leaning forward. Her mother was stronger than a cloth puppet, but there are always winds that are bigger than people; always the chance of a hurricane.

She thought of herself blown around in that darkness — the splintering light — *Can somebody help me* —

James Clerk Maxwell.

When he was eighteen, he wrote a paper *On the Theory of Rolling Curves*. He analysed the rings around Saturn.

Madeleine yawned.

"Why don't you go to sleep?" said her mother, without looking up.

"You should go to sleep yourself."

Neither of them moved, then Holly smiled at Madeleine — and it hit her.

All this time she'd been focusing on her mother's state of mind, pretending that her *own* terror didn't count. But there it was. A giant shadow blocking her path. A haze of electrons. The shape of the darkness in the space between worlds.

Fears *do* come true. Tumours return. She looked at Holly again and imagined her mother not there, an empty chair —

James Clerk Maxwell.

Ah. Here he was studying the interplay between electrical fields and magnetic fields. This must be why Darshana had mentioned him.

Only, James Clerk Maxwell was saying something more. Electricity and magnetism were not just closely related, he was saying. They were the same thing. Two sides of the same thing. Spinning together at the speed of —

They were *light*.

James Clerk Maxwell had put two pieces of a puzzle together and come up with light: Electrical waves and magnetic waves make light.

Why had she never heard of this guy before? He'd seen light, translated it, gathered it, and turned it into messages on paper.

Across the room, Madeleine's mother was packing up, scraping her chair back, yawning noisily.

"I'm going to have a cocoa. Want one?"

She was moving around the flat, opening cupboards, closing drawers, changing into her pajamas, disappearing into the bathroom. The water was running. She was humming in there as she brushed her teeth.

Madeleine felt sleepy herself. She picked up a random piece of paper. *Incandescence*, she read. *Luminescence.* She closed her eyes. When she opened them, her mother was standing in the open bathroom door, drying her face with a towel. *Incandescent. Luminous.*

Madeleine picked up a book, scanned a few paragraphs, then sat back, thinking.

Maybe she was half asleep, but it seemed to her that the story of light took three giant steps — from Isaac Newton to James Clerk Maxwell to Albert Einstein.

Holly was pouring milk into a saucepan and setting it onto the stove. She was taking mugs and cocoa from the cupboard. She was yawning again.

"Stop yawning," Madeleine said. "You're making me sleepy."

“It’s nighttime,” Holly replied. “The ideal time for sleepiness. Put your work away.”

Madeleine picked up another set of papers.

Newton thought that light was made of tiny pieces. James Clerk Maxwell said: No, it’s waves, and it rides the ether. But people used mirrors and lights to prove that the ether did not exist. Someone else found a piece of light. Einstein flew the universe with it.

“So which is it?” Madeleine said. “A particle or wave?”

“What? Which is what?” said her mother, handing her a mug of cocoa.

Light, she read, *has a dual nature, as both particles and waves.*

“So it’s both,” she said, and her mother repeated promptly: “What?”

“Nothing,” murmured Madeleine, stirring the cocoa, but: *Everything*, she thought.

It’s all dualities. She closed her eyes again. She thought of Darshana’s two girls spinning. North and south. Positive and negative. Electricity and magnetism. Belle and Jack.

Herself and her mother.

There was a creak as her mother climbed into the bed, and a click as she turned off the bedside lamp.

She thought of her mother standing by the window, staring at nothing, twisting the ring around her finger. Her mother asking Denny if she could borrow his computer to sign up for online dating. Her mother arguing with strangers in her sleep.

She and her mother were a broken pair, a mismatched pair, but a pair.

The World and the Kingdom of Cello, she thought next.

She took a sip of cocoa.

“Listen,” said her mother, from the darkness of the bed. “There’s a hell of a good universe next door; let’s go.”

The room cracked like a power cut.

Madeleine stared.

"What did you just say?"

Her mother shifted in the bed, turned the pillow, stilled again.

"It's a line from a poem. It's e. e. cummings. I'll get it for you — just a moment — nope. Can't. Too tired. I'm amazed my mouth is forming words. A hell of a — well, my mouth won't finish — but just let me — Nice. Night. Gnight — Swee. Dre — You —"

Madeleine continued to stare into the shadows where her mother now quietly snored.

There'd been a moment, and inside that moment, her mother had known Cello. *A hell of a good universe next door.* Also in that moment, her mother had known how to *get* to Cello: *let's go.*

A door inside Madeleine had revolved, opening onto a new place — where Cello was accessible — and onto an old, where her mother was in charge.

But the door had spun again and here she was.

In this attic flat and uncertainty. Frightened mother. Absent father. Lost friends, lost life. New friends fading into mystery — like Belle and Jack — or into flimsiness — like Elliot.

But for just one moment —

She set the cocoa on the floor, and closed her eyes against the shock and disappointment.

Behind her eyes, at once, she saw Elliot.

She saw his face turning towards her in the dark schoolyard, towards her, then away again, lost. Now she saw herself walking beside Elliot, scuffing through autumn leaves. She saw her boots, his boots. *So we'll go no more a-roving.* But they'd never *roved* anywhere. She'd never scuffed through leaves with him, but here were the details of a memory: fine threads of cracks in his worn boots; damp-edged, wood-smoked leaves.

False memories from an invented past, or an imagined future?

Night after night, she had leaned against a parking meter in a dark Cambridge street while Elliot tossed a deftball in the darkness of a schoolyard. Opposite each other, alone but together, waiting on each other's thoughts.

The silence while she waited for his replies: wondering how he'd reflect her words, rotate them, smooth their edges. Or fling them back, turn to his own stories — that silence while she waited for his words. It was a silence, she thought now, that had both purity and sharpness. It was the colour of a candle. The flavour of pecans, or mango, or nutmeg. It had spin and dimension, particles and waves.

She saw herself with Elliot again. Both of them placing their hands on the hood of a car and flinching at the heat.

She felt Elliot pressing his thumb onto her shoulder blade: "Is this where it hurts?"

Herself calling to him on a crowded street, "If you don't get a move on, we'll miss the start," while he smiled, distracted by the display behind a plate-glass window.

These imagined glimpses — they were neither invented past, nor imagined future, she saw that now.

They were translations of the silences. The space between their words; the space between their worlds.

Elliot was not an empty cloth puppet. He was himself. He could be silent and lost; she could call for his help and he might be busy or he might need help himself. They didn't have to fit or meld or blend to be a pair: They could be mismatched, broken, displaced; a pair that had to shift and twist to see each other, a pair that could be separate, together and apart.

He was a face turning towards her, a hand reaching —

She was slipping towards sleep. Papers rustled, a book spilled to the floor with a thud.

She sat up, confused. Who was she, where was she, what was she?

Ah, it was night and she was Madeleine.

She should change into pajamas, make up her bed, wash out the cocoa mug, switch off the lights —

She leaned down to pick up the fallen books and fanned papers.

James Clerk Maxwell on her floorboards.

Phrases caught her eyes.

Here he was inviting a friend to come and stay: *If you are particular about your lantern*, he wrote, *bring it yourself like Guy Fawkes or the Man in the Moon.*

Here he was using mirror-writing: *Why have you forgotten to send Alice. We remain in Wonderland until she appears.*

Again, having a bad day: *I am desolated*, he wrote, . . . *a mere man in a mirror.*

Madeleine liked him.

She reached to close a book and saw that it was open at a quote from Edith Wharton:

There are two ways of spreading light: to be the candle or the mirror that reflects it.

Lights, she thought, and mirrors.

Now she picked up the teaspoon from the floor beside the mug. Her own sleepy face looked back at her: elongated, mournful, her forehead rising up like a hill.

She thought of Isaac Newton's reflecting telescope: mirrors catching light.

Lights. Mirrors.

Mirrors. Lights.

Elliot's face again.

I believe in you. You believe in me.

You play with magnets there. I'll play with magnets here.

The misaligned centre of you. The misaligned centre of me.

In a rush, she was standing, slipping on papers as if on autumn leaves, wide awake, breathing hard, looking for her jacket and shoes.

8.

11:55 P.M., Elliot arrived in the Bonfire High schoolyard.

11:57 P.M., Madeleine turned onto a narrow Cambridge street.

He approached the sculpture. She ran toward the parking meter. They both hesitated, then scribbled notes. Their notes crossed.

I know you don't want to try anymore, Madeleine, but it's something to do with a mirror and candlelight.

Hey, Elliot, it's mirrors and lights.

They saw each other's notes and wrote again:

Are you there NOW?

Did you just say the same THING as me?

Elliot started to write another note, then, "Ah, for crying out loud," he said, and he dug through his backpack, sliding out the mirror he'd unhooked from the wall on his way out.

It was heavy, the size of a painting. It occurred to him that there might have been a smaller, more efficient mirror somewhere in his house, but he shrugged and leaned this one against the base of the sculpture.

Next he took out his flashlight.

He'd also brought along a couple of candlesticks from the dining room dresser, but he figured he'd try the flashlight first. It might be just a question of *light*: He'd move on to candles if it had to be literal.

Madeleine, in Cambridge, was scribbling fast. She'd covered a page, flipped it over, and was trying to draw little sketches of electrical and magnetic fields. The sketches looked wrong.

She stopped. What was she *doing*? Why did Elliot need to know how electrical and magnetic fields worked? She wasn't even sure she understood it herself, to be honest.

She dropped the notepad to the path and took out the matches and teaspoon instead. The teaspoon still had a streak of cocoa on it.

Should have brought a real mirror, she guessed, but she'd been in a rush.

Who knew what to do?

In Bonfire, Elliot shone the flashlight at the back of the TV. He hoisted up the mirror, awkwardly under the other arm, and tried to tilt it in the same direction.

In Cambridge, Madeleine lit a match. She held it up carefully, sheltering it from the breeze. It flickered faintly. She kept one eye on the match, and in the other hand twisted the teaspoon, aiming it at the parking meter. She spun it around, and spun it back —

The mirror crashed; the flashlight rolled. The match touched the footpath, flame vanishing; teaspoon clattered.

There was shove and clutter, blaze of darkness, clatter of light. There was the deafening blast and bellow of wind, their bodies were yanked, stretched, tossed.

They were folded into darkness. They were rolled into layers and layers of darkness. Their hands reached out and found each other's hands.

They gripped so hard that their nails cut flesh and the tension seized them right up to their shoulder blades.

The roaring slowed. The blasting settled. There was the sense of a ferocious mood abruptly slipping — shrugging and moving on. Maybe throwing a warning shout behind its shoulder as it left.

They were suspended, hands clutched, in perfect blackness.

Their grip relaxed a little but not much. They could hear each other breathing, feel the breathing rise and fall in the shifts of the other's hands.

Elliot spoke.

"Are you okay?" he said, and there, for the first time, was his voice.

She'd never heard it before, its tone, the song and warmth of it, and he squeezed her hands a little as he spoke, as if to say he knew that she was *not* okay. Or maybe that her answer mattered.

That voice in the stillness after all the noise and bluster. The gentle squeeze of his hands — Madeleine found herself shuddering into tears.

"I'm so stupid," she sobbed, "— what I said about your dad — and that you don't know silence — of course, you do — your dad's been missing all this — and you didn't even know where — or why — or if he'd ever — I was just scared — and you called me a quitter — and I was scared of the dark — of getting lost — in the space in between —

and scared that my mum will get sick again — and I don't think my dad's *ever* coming — and it's like now I know he's a loser — but I'm *glad* that your dad's a hero — and I'm *glad* that your dad's coming back — and I —"

Elliot was pulling her closer as she cried, and now her face was against something soft — his cotton T-shirt — and hard, his chest behind the shirt, and there was the warmth and the bones of his arms tightening around her.

She grew quiet as she realized this: his arms and his body. She felt his body close to hers, his face close to her hair, then he spoke.

"One thing," he said, speaking into her hair. "One thing you should know is that my dad — it's not as simple as him being a hero. Nobody's talking about the woman much — Mischka Tegan, the teacher who tricked him and my uncle. It could be he *was* in love with her — could be there *was* an affair. So yeah, he's my dad and he's a hero — but he's also kinda flawed. And you don't have to give up on your dad yet. He might be more a hero than you think."

Madeleine was silent.

"You just said you're scared of the dark?" Elliot said.

"Yeah."

She felt him shift a little, turning his head this way and that, felt him trying to penetrate the darkness. "Perfect place for you, then," he said, deadpan and bemused.

"Where *are* we?" Madeleine said, and they broke their close hold a little, but kept their hands grasped.

"Don't let go," Elliot said.

"I wasn't planning to."

The darkness seemed complete, and then, in some remote distance, there was a faint drizzle of light.

They both saw it and breathed in sharply, but then it was gone.

"I guess we're in the space between our worlds," Elliot said. "I guess the mirrors and the lights got us here?"

He told her what he'd found in the account, and she tried to explain about electromagnetism and light.

"It sort of made sense to me for a moment," she said, "while I was falling towards sleep. Something to do with how your world and our world are the same — like we're reflections of each other — and if we shine a light on that reflection then we're drawn together. So, before, when we focused on the links between us — our misaligned centers or whatever — when we focused on the ways that we reflected one another — that sort of worked too."

She was quiet, thinking.

"Or maybe it's not that our worlds are the same," she said. "Maybe it's more *us*. Like people are the same. Maybe the idea is that we're drawn to each other, drawn to reflections of each other — the light of each other. I don't know."

Elliot withdrew a hand briefly, to scratch his eyebrow, then found his way back to her hand.

"Well," he said, "my mother says we're the same. I mean, she says people in Cello and the World are identical, except that *we* have a little sprinkle of color in our inner elbows that you guys don't."

"That doesn't seem fair. I wouldn't mind a sprinkle of color in my inner elbow."

"You can only see it if you squeeze lemon juice on your skin."

"Are you serious?"

"Well, I'm not *serious* about it, I'm fairly lighthearted. But I think it's true."

They both turned as another streak of light flared in the distance.

"This is making me crazy," Elliot said. "I can't *see* you. I keep feeling like my eyes just need to adjust, and your outline will appear — or

I'll start to catch the light in your eyes — but even when that distant lightning strikes, it's still total blackness."

"Do you think that's lightning?"

"I haven't got a clue."

They were quiet again, pressing each other's hands.

"What's holding us up here?" Elliot said. "It's like we're suspended in nothing."

"And I get the feeling it's not going to last much longer. I think we'll fall back to our own worlds any moment. We should talk fast here."

"You already do talk fast. You talk like your notes. Like you're rocket-propelled."

"Ah, cut it out, farm boy."

"It's not a criticism. Your rocket-propelled, lightning-fast voice is beautiful. It's just, I honestly don't see how you could talk any faster than you already do."

"I don't mean we should *literally* talk faster, I just meant we should get to the point. Like, figure out what all this means. The mirrors and light thing must have *kind* of worked, cause here we are — wherever we are — and for longer than we ever have been. But we're not exactly walking around each other's streets, so . . ."

There was a sound somewhere, like chimes fading.

"Did you hear that?"

"Yes."

They waited. But the silence returned, draping itself into the darkness.

"Well," Elliot said. "I'm thinking the problem all along has been that this crack is too small. It's not meant for people. We'll only ever get pieces of ourselves through, and this is as good as it gets. I think you were right when you said it's dangerous to try."

"I don't know if it's really dangerous," Madeleine admitted. "I was just scared of being trapped — in this space — with all the darkness. I never used to be scared of the dark — I used to like it even — it's only since Mum . . ."

Elliot was quiet. It was like she could feel him listening — his listening seemed as slow and thoughtful as his speech. She could feel his thoughts moving around in the subtle shifts in his hands.

"Makes sense," he said eventually, "for the dark to scare you now. It's like, if there's no light, there isn't any hope."

"Exactly. And it's not just about my mother getting sick, it's also about my dad. Like I don't want to give up on him. And maybe about *me* too — I don't want to be this self-obsessed person, I want there to be light inside me too."

"There's plenty of light in you," Elliot said easily, and this time he spoke without pausing first. "And actually, me going on about your fear of dark representing your fears about your mother, that could be plain bollocks. As you would say. The fact is, it makes perfect sense to be afraid of this place. You'd be a damn fool if you weren't afraid." He stopped and they both felt it, the darkness and silence rolling and pressing around them. "If you weren't here with me right now," Elliot continued, "I might just lose my mind. But I think I'm more afraid of something else — it came to me in the night a couple weeks back. I woke up and I was running through ideas about how to get through the crack, and I was thinking back to the jackhammer idea — like tear up the sculpture and see if the crack opens underneath it. I was half asleep, I guess, and I was half serious, thinking I might get my buddy Shelby to come and blow the sculpture up, and I was sort of laughing to myself thinking how pissed Cody would be, cause it's his artwork — and then halfway through the laugh I felt something streak right through me like ice. It hit me out of nowhere: If I blew up the sculpture, you might be gone forever. Your world might be gone."

He twisted around a little, brushed his thumb against her palm, readjusted his grip. There was a different sort of glimmer, a little closer, and something like a faint breeze brushed against them and was gone.

Madeleine waited. Elliot spoke again.

"What if our two worlds are *hinged* at this crack?" he said. "I mean, that's what I thought in the night. I know you have time zones that change all over the World — but I also know that here, at this crack, our times match up. So what if this crack is not just a way through, but a connection — a link — and what if I killed it off somehow, by taking a wrong step? So you and your world just blew away. Gone forever. Utterly unreachable. It hit me like a boulder."

There was another crack of light, and they tightened their grip against Elliot's words: the terrible possibility of a loss like that, the strangeness and density of the idea, bigger than death. It was like picking at the edges of the concept of despair.

"I know," said Madeleine. "I've only just caught you — I mean, I've only just started to understand that your Kingdom really exists. It's like with all the science I've been reading — about what the universe is made of — I keep realizing it's mostly just theories. Like ideas — metaphors even — to describe things. Ways of looking sideways to see what can't be seen. And it's like your royal family are escaping electrons, and it's left you with a charge — with — I don't know where I'm going with that — I'm just trying to say . . ."

Madeleine paused and Elliot looked at her words, because that's all he could see in the darkness. The notes in her voice, the strange corners it turned, the way she laughed unexpectedly in the middle of a phrase, then picked up the phrase and carried on, pieces of the laughter strewn behind her.

"So, the scientists make up stories," she said now, "to imagine how things work, then they do experiments — to see if the truth matches up with their imaginings — and I was reading about this cat. This imaginary cat in a box, and you don't know, until you open the box, if the cat exists or not. And I just now read that light is both wave and particle, but so is *everything*. But it *can't* be: They're opposites. And you don't know if something's a wave or particle until you measure it — but measuring makes it one thing or the other — you measure it into existence — so I'm thinking, did I just measure you and Cello into existence? Imagine you into existence, I mean? If I open up the parking meter, will Cello be there? Is Cello a cat? And is there any *point*, if the box can't be opened? I mean, there's a cat or there isn't, but what's the point if the box stays closed? And if I stop imagining, if the box stays closed, if I get on with my life and leave you here — it's like, you're an effort of imagination, and so —"

Elliot wove his fingers through hers.

"Okay," he said, "you're doing the egocentric thing again. These particles or whatever — if the scientists stop thinking about them, they're still there, right?"

"I guess."

"Cello too. Me too. I'm not blowing away. I'm not a cat or a wave, I'm me."

They were both quiet, holding hands, and his words seemed to blow away in the darkness. Elliot could be here or he could not. They could be holding hands, right now, or empty-handed.

"My father's afraid of the dark," Elliot remembered suddenly. He chuckled to himself, and it was an unexpectedly deep, wicked chuckle.

It made his hands tremble in Madeleine's hands, and she felt something swift inside her chest.

"There was this day we went to the Sugarloaf Fair," Elliot said. "I was ten years old, and — well, my parents are both tall people — I mean, literally, and also in themselves. The sort of people with big strides and long reaches. They look people in the eye and get things done. If you see what I mean. But this day at the Sugarloaf Fair, I saw the cracks in both of them." He stopped and lifted one of her hands along with his, so he could brush something away, some itch from his arm, then their hands fell down between them again, still intertwined.

"Both in one day," he reflected. "How about that. Anyhow, the first thing that happened was we all went up in the Big Wheel. As soon as it got to its halfway point, my mother was down on the floor. Right on the floor of the carriage. By my feet." He pushed their hands down a little, pointing into the darkness below. "She's crouching down there like she's examining the floor, and I was going, 'What are you LOOKING at?'" Elliot laughed aloud now. "And she's going, 'Just checking how they've nailed this thing together here, it's real interesting, see' — and I look across at Dad, and he's laughing in his silent way, rocking back and forth, his eyes kind of squinting with his laughter, at the same time as he's reaching out and stroking her back, like he loved her even more than usual. He looked over at me and said, 'Your mother's afraid of heights — didn't you know?' and I grinned back at him, and laughed too, but I remember it was a sort of jolt. I'd never known my mother to be afraid of anything. She's still down there on the floor going, 'No, no, just checking how they put this thing together' — and my dad's shaking his head at me, still laughing.

"Anyhow, same day, my dad and I went in the ghost ride they had. That's when I knew he was afraid of the dark. He didn't say a thing. He didn't do a thing. It was just, the train turned a corner into blackness — and I suddenly knew. There was a moment and I felt him change. He felt different beside me. A year or so later he actually told me he was scared of the dark. He didn't say it like he was ashamed, more like it was a really dumb fact about himself, but just a fact. But I knew it already — I'd known it from that day, and I felt the same jolt about my dad, only this time it was a quieter jolt, cause the thing with my mother meant I was sort of prepared.

"I remember the three of us taking the train home from Sugarloaf, and eating our sugar candy and pecan pies with all our showbags and prizes piled on the seat, and I remember feeling kind of sad, but also kind of proud. Like I was tall myself now. Like I had a sense that now I had a job — that it was my job, if my mother was ever stuck on the edge of a cliff, say — or my dad was somewhere in the dark — well, that's when *my* job would come into play, and it'd be my job to bring them both —"

Out of nowhere his voice, which had been perfectly ordinary, cracked.

It broke into pieces, and then there were the strange sounds of Elliot trying not to cry, grabbing on to his sobs, and then the sound of the sobs getting the better of him.

Madeleine could feel that his shoulders were heaving, and she could hear the strange, dry rasping, and she slid her hands along his arms so she could reach around his back and hold him close.

Eventually, some broken phrases scratched their way between his sobs: "And I'm *not* doing my job — he was afraid of the dark — and he was taken in the dark — so the things that you're afraid of do come true — and what if it goes wrong? — he's coming back tomorrow, but what if it goes wrong? — he could come back — or he might not come back — it could go wrong — it could go wrong, it could go —"

There was a dash of light, and far away a fountain of color.

Elliot stopped weeping abruptly.

"Pretty," he said in a clogged-up but ordinary voice.

"Yeah."

They laughed, still holding each other, pieces of his tears still in their laughter.

"What if something goes wrong?" Elliot said again, voice small but direct.

"It won't go wrong," Madeleine said, and she spoke with such conviction that she felt his body easing in her arms.

"Sorry about that," Elliot said now, but he didn't sound embarrassed, more surprised. "It's just. I don't know. I keep thinking about what Keira said."

"She's the one on the Royal Youth Alliance, right? From Jagged Edge?"

"Right. And she's a Night-Dweller so she's, like, a darkness junkie. Darkness is part of her ideology — she sort of embraces it, and believes in endings and letting go and that. It's like she's trying to tell me all the time that things will end — things will go wrong — like she wants me to recognize that. Let go of hope. It's like she's trying to say that giving up is good."

"Keira's an idiot."

"Well." Elliot smiled in the dark. "I don't know if she's an *idiot.* I might be misrepresenting her. It's more that she believes in facing reality, I guess, and reality is sometimes dark."

He could feel a strength in Madeleine, a resolution he hadn't felt before, and he shifted his hold on her in the darkness, adjusting to that change.

"She's an idiot," Madeleine repeated. "And your dad is coming back."

There was a tilt to the way they were standing. A softening, or loosening, in the nothing that was holding them.

"Is something —?"

"Yeah," Elliot said. "I can feel it too."

"Now I'm scared that once we're back I'll never see you again."

"We're not seeing each other right now," Elliot pointed out.

"But you're here."

"I know. I'm just making a dumb joke. We shouldn't have had that whole conversation about losing each other's worlds. Now we've gone and scared ourselves."

There was another tilt.

"Okay, talk fast, Elliot. As fast as a farm boy can, anyway. What do you need me to do?"

"Can you get the letters to the royal family before the weekend?"

"If I send them by courier, I could. I'll borrow money from Jack or Belle. They're cashed up from their aura and horoscope readings."

"Thanks. I appreciate it. The Kingdom of Cello appreciates it."

"Yeah, you're just trying to make up for treating me like your World slave before. You can do that another time. When are you seeing your royal people again?"

"I've got some conference call with them tomorrow morning, so I guess I'll tell them about mirrors and lights. Do you think it needs to happen at both ends like we just did? Or will it work if someone on one side does it — like the woman in the archive report — it seemed like she didn't have anyone on the other side matching up with her. She just used a mirror and light."

Madeleine found herself swaying slowly. She tried to grip Elliot's hands more firmly, but his grasp was swaying too.

"I guess that makes sense." She spoke fast. "Hold a light towards our world, eventually it will catch a mirror here and be reflected. Or face a mirror our way and you'll catch some light." She tried to straighten up against the swaying. "Maybe," she said, "we're trapped in between right now because we both did the light-mirror thing at the same time — maybe if just one of us did it, we'd have crossed over by now?"

"Yeah, I don't think so," Elliot smiled. "I think the crack is too small — I'd try again when I get back, but I might just end up here alone."

"I think," began Madeleine — but her voice was being tugged away from her. She fought against the pull. "I think I'm going back now."

"Me too," said Elliot, his voice fading, but he fought his way forward one more time, pressed himself toward her, and spoke into her ear in a low murmur: "Nice to meet you, Madeleine Tully —"

Elliot was back in the Kingdom of Cello; Madeleine was back in the World.

9.

Madeleine woke early on Wednesday morning to the sound of sighing.

The sighs kept repeating at quick, regular intervals, like gusts of warm wind from a rotating fan.

As if a fan had been placed right by her head, which made no sense — who would have —

She opened her eyes, and swore.

Her mother was crouching on the floor, staring at her from less than a hand width away.

"Oh," said Holly. "Did I wake you?"

"What's wrong with you?" Madeleine said. "Why are you breathing at my face?"

"Nothing's wrong," Holly said, and sighed. "Just, the milk's off, so I'll need to go and buy more but, as you know, it's important to me to eat breakfast in my pajamas. It's a priority of mine."

Madeleine sat up. Something wonderful was happening inside her chest. Fragments of light zigging and zagging. She smiled.

"You have a beautiful smile," Holly said, and then sighed as if this was also something to be mourned.

Madeleine's smile grew.

She had found her way through to Elliot. They had talked. They had cried in each other's arms. They'd shared secrets. He'd held her hands.

Holding hands. The fragments of light swerved and careened inside her, running up and down her arms and legs.

Of course, they'd been holding hands to stop each other blowing away into a mysterious abyss of darkness. But still.

At least he hadn't *wanted* her to fly off into an abyss of darkness.

And he could have gone back to Cello at any point! Couldn't he?

Well, maybe not.

But still. He *hadn't.* He'd stayed and talked to her. That was the point.

Madeleine focused on her mother, still sighing, still crouched awkwardly by the couch. "You could get dressed, go buy milk, come home, and change *back* into your pajamas," she suggested.

Holly gazed into a wistful distance. "I could," she agreed, "but it wouldn't be the same," and another sigh, so long and slow, that Madeleine burst out laughing.

She looked at her mother and her laughter faltered a little. This close she could see how much Holly's face had changed. Lines slunk around her eyes, her cheeks seemed high and swollen, more lines and wrinkles above her mouth, a sort of bruising under her eyes. Things were being added to her mother's face. It reminded Madeleine of sketches Holly did sometimes — how she'd draw the outline of a simple dress and then she'd start adding to it. Swoops, curves, puffs, frills, zips, sashes, shading, lines — *Stop*, Madeleine would think, *it was perfect as it was!*

"*I'll* go and buy your milk," Madeleine said. "You just sit at the table with your pajamas on and the cereal in the bowl and your spoon ready in your hand."

Her mother spent the next ten minutes detailing the scope of her gratitude — the measurements for which were just dizzying — you'd need calculus, really, she said, to properly demonstrate — while Madeleine herself got dressed and thought about Elliot.

Just making a dumb joke, he'd said at one point. He must have been nervous! Boys like Elliot didn't make dumb jokes unless they were. Now that she thought about it, his speech patterns had been faintly edged with nerves. He must *like* her.

Of course, he might have been nervous because of the abyss and potential oblivion, etcetera. But *still.*

At the shop, Madeleine pulled a milk carton from the fridge, cold against her hand, and recalled how Elliot had leaned in close, and murmured in her ear, *Nice to meet you, Madeleine Tully.*

He hadn't been nervous at that point.

He'd been the boy he could be, the boy who looked like Elliot Baranski, the boy who knew exactly how to make a girl feel like some kind of carbonated sugar drink was running through her veins.

Or maybe he was just pleased to meet her, like he said. After all their efforts and letters and so on. And her being a girl in the World.

Still, she let the soft, warm murmur replay in her mind as she walked home.

After breakfast, Madeleine ran downstairs to Denny's flat to use one of his computers.

She found the email address for the girl who thought her name was Ariel Peters.

Ha. That seemed funny. Well, today, everything seemed funny. Also, moving. It was deeply moving that Ariel Peters had been living in Berlin all this time, totally clueless that she was Princess Jupiter of Cello.

Not moving, funny. She laughed aloud and Denny glanced up from his workbench.

"It's nothing," she said.

Madeleine took out the letter Princess Ko had written to her sister. It set out the precise time and location for her "transfer" back to Cello this weekend.

She typed it into an email. The flat was quiet except for faint wheezing and clinking from Denny, the occasional swish of Sulky-Anne's tail against the quilt cover where she was dreaming, and Madeleine's own giggles as she typed.

"Whatever you're writing there," Denny said eventually, "read it to me when you're done?" He paused, reached for his Ventolin, inhaled, coughed, wiped his eyes. "It sounds like a hoot."

Madeleine looked up.

"Not really," she said, her eyes filling with tears. "It's pretty sad." She looked back at what she'd just typed and laughed hard. "Nah, it's funny. But I can't read it to you, sorry; it's someone else's letter."

The mouse swerved across the screen.

Something occurred to her.

She added a quick P.S. to the email, and hit Send.

As she left, Denny was talking — something about borrowing change for the laundromat — but she was only half listening. Her mind was thinking: *Elliot Baranski.*

She couldn't imagine a better name. Elliot alone, with its gentle opening *El* sound, how it climbed up over the double *l*, and slid into a playful, yet strong-willed *iot*, that was brilliant.

Why would a mother name a baby boy anything *other* than Elliot?

But combined with Baranski! The symmetry of syllables! The sprawl and crunch of the Baranski! It was ingenious!

Ten minutes later, she was knocking on Jack's door, while *Elliot Baranski* still flew across her mind, the letters and syllables like circus performers.

Jack seemed distracted.

He was eating toast and he nodded right away when she asked if she could borrow money, but he didn't quote Byron, and he didn't tell her what the stars had planned for today.

"See you at Belle's place in a bit," Jack called as Madeleine ran down the steps.

"Yep." She turned to wave at him one more time, but those fragments of light inside her seemed to blur his face.

Light, she remembered, had taken her through to Elliot Baranski.

Which was funny because she'd read so much about Isaac Newton and colours in the last few months, and colours were just *pieces* of light.

All the colours of a prism, Newton wrote, *being made to converge again, and mixed, reproduce light, entirely and perfectly white.*

She dodged around two elderly men, both in academic gowns, who were walking slowly, their heads close together. "The committee has decided," one said to the other, "*not* to accept your application."

"Ah," the man responded, and was silent.

Madeleine left the silence behind her, swerving through a crowd of chatting students. It was a windy morning, and it seemed as if the students were being blown against one another as they walked.

She pushed open the door to Staples — it was a stationery store, but they also did DHL couriers, she thought — and sorted through Princess Ko's letters.

To King Cetus in Montreal, Canada; to Queen Lyra in Taipei, Taiwan; to Prince Chyba in Boise, Idaho; to Prince Tippett in Avoca Beach, Australia.

The woman behind the counter had dirty Band-Aids around three of her fingers. Madeleine stared at these while she listened to the rates for overnight express delivery.

At the last moment, she grabbed the letters back and scribbled in the P.S. that she'd added to Princess Jupiter's email.

Now she had ten minutes to get to Belle's place.

The wind had grown stronger, but the sky seemed blue enough to take it. She smiled, picking up her pace. She'd spent her morning buying milk for her mother and sending messages to the royal family of Cello and thinking about how light had taken her through to Elliot.

Not just light, she remembered. Mirrors too.

She remembered once writing to Elliot that the pair of them were like reflections. Like two grey cats. Like a cat and the shadow of a cat.

Everything comes in pairs, she thought now, running faster.

Newton's third law of motion: *All forces occur in pairs, and these two forces are equal in magnitude and opposite in direction.*

Two hands, two legs, two eyes.

The World and Cello. Madeleine and Elliot.

Even light itself came in pairs: electricity and magnetism.

It was all part of a giant balancing act, she decided. Light balanced dark. Inside atoms, strong forces held things together, weak forces tore them apart. Out in the universe, particle motion pushed galaxies apart; gravity drew them together.

The balance was fragile.

Too much particle motion and you got a Big Bang; too much gravity, a black hole.

Light had to move at precisely the right speed or that fine balance of electricity and magnetism would be lost — and so would light.

Too much light could blind or burn you; too much darkness meant death.

Madeleine turned into Belle's street and slowed.

You never knew whether the balance would hold — on which side it might fall. It was always uncertain. Light itself was uncertain — both wave and particle — and could never be pinned down.

From here she could see that Jack had already arrived. He was standing on the front step, his back to her. The door was open, and Belle's mother, Olivia, was leaning against the frame, talking.

Madeleine slowed even more. The wind blew her hair across her face, and instantly her morning changed shape.

It wasn't milk and royals and light.

It was the shadows on her mother's face. Denny's wheezing, his bloodshot eyes. It was Jack's expression skittering. Old men in academic gowns, crestfallen by news; women with injured fingers.

She stopped. She'd read something about blindness just the other day. It seemed important, but what was it?

She pushed open Belle's front gate, and Olivia and Jack both turned.

"Come see," called Olivia, laughter in her voice. "It seems we have lost Belle!"

Jack was staring at Madeleine.

He held up the paper in his hand. "It's a suicide note," he said.

Madeleine stared back, bewildered.

She remembered now what she'd read. If you are born blind, and years later, a doctor repairs your vision, that doesn't mean you'll be able to see. You never will. Your mind will not comprehend images: It won't understand what it's supposed to do with light. Too much darkness will have killed off all the light.

10.

The Baranski farmhouse had a ticktock feel to it.

Elliot came downstairs around seven, and the rooms seemed wide-eyed, the air quiet with noisy hope. It had rained in the night, but now the sun shone on wet windows, which added to the sense of fresh suspense.

He imagined telling Madeleine this — that the house had a tick-tock feel, only without ticking or tocking — and he remembered the movement of her hands in his, and how he'd held her close when she cried, and how tricky it had been to sort out the reason for her tears, and to speak, with her chest pressed up against his and her breath coming warm through his T-shirt.

His mother stood in the living room, her back to him, arranging flowers. Yellow gerberas. His father's favorite.

She turned and smiled. She was wearing lipstick, and her hair fell loose around her shoulders. Usually she tied it back first thing, but now it was brushed straight, mostly hooked behind her ears, but she must have pulled a strand of two forward, to frame her face. Something else seemed a little odd about her, but he couldn't figure out what that was.

"Hey," he said. "Not at the greenhouse yet?"

His mother turned back to the flowers.

"Agent Tovey called again yesterday. He said it might be anytime today. Thought I'd better stay here just in case."

The casual to her voice was the finest layer of ice over an ocean-deep of terror and excitement.

Elliot went into the kitchen. He made himself toast, poured juice, ate breakfast. He looked around while he ate. The red-and-white cloth was on the table again: It looked like it had been ironed, and this time he couldn't find the coffee stain at all. There were gerberas in a vase here too. The kitchen sink gleamed so silver it almost hurt his eyes. Also, those lime green canisters — the ones labeled "flour," "sugar," and so on, that were usually scattered around the kitchen with their lids missing and half full of old nails or stale almonds — were now in a neat line on the counter. Elliot stared at these awhile. Then he stood, and lifted their lids. Flour in the Flour, sugar in the Sugar, salt in the Salt.

That seemed to be taking things too far. His whole life they'd never used those tins properly. He felt a little uneasy about this, as if it tipped him into a strange new dimension.

He cleared his breakfast away, washed his hands at the sink, and was just shaking them when his mother came into the room. She was wearing the same bright, calm smile, but the smile twisted itself sideways and fell to the floor, as her eyes caught Elliot's shaking hands — the water droplets hitting the linoleum.

"Just —" she said, and she breathed in hard, trying to catch ahold of her smile again. "Just watch the floor, all right? I've already washed it."

She stepped past Elliot, reached for a paper towel, and got down on her hands and knees, wiping up the water droplets.

Elliot said, "I'll do that."

But his mother, still on the floor, had caught sight of the toast crumbs under the table, and was lunging for the dustpan and broom.

It was almost eight o'clock.

Elliot left her there, ran upstairs, and closed his bedroom door.

The ring was still in his sock drawer. It was a simple ring, gold. He slid it onto his finger and looked at it doubtfully. This was somehow going to enable him to communicate with the members of the Royal Youth Alliance? Now he glanced around his small bedroom. Holographic images were about to appear in here? That seemed even less likely.

He waited, uncertain, in the middle of the room. Then it occurred to him that if he was going to see the others, they'd be able to see *him* too. Maybe even see his room?

He looked down at himself. He was wearing the old T-shirt he always wore to bed, and trackpants.

Ah, well. They'd live.

Might as well straighten up his room a bit, though.

He grabbed the dirty clothes from his floor and tossed them in the closet, rammed a pile of schoolbooks back into his backpack. There was a pen leaking ink all over the carpet. He wasn't sure what to do about that, so he turned to the bed and was pulling the cover over it when the ring tightened around his finger.

It was quite a squeeze, sort of hurt a bit. He touched the side of it, the way Keira had explained, more to stop the pressure than to answer.

Next thing, the outline of Princess Ko appeared, standing in his wastepaper basket. She was scratchy in parts, but slowly filling in. He shifted the wastepaper basket — it seemed disrespectful to leave her standing in it — and said, "Hey," but Princess Ko was gazing hard over his head. He looked up. Nothing there.

Within a few minutes, Keira, Samuel, and Sergio had also appeared in a sort of cluster. They each seemed to be suspended and filmy — just their faces and shoulders, no background. So he guessed they couldn't see his bedroom after all. Straightening up had been a waste.

The images were hazy but were quickly filling in, and each flickered now and then, so they all had an agitated look.

"Can everybody hear me?" Princess Ko said. She wore a close, concentrating frown.

There was a confusion of responses. It seemed pretty remarkable that here they all were, clustered around Elliot's wastepaper bin, talking at once. The images were pale, colors odd, but their voices were clear, with just the faintest static. Elliot thought of his mother downstairs. She'd hear this. She'd come upstairs, baffled, and throw open the door.

"This!" enthused Samuel, his image flickering alarmingly. "This is beyond all imaginings of possibility! As to a —"

"I have exactly three minutes," Princess Ko interrupted, her image leaning forward a little. "Only speak when I address you. Elliot?"

"Yep?"

"Have you figured out how to get through a crack?"

Elliot looked back at the wavering shape of the Princess.

"Well," he said. "I think I have."

The Princess nodded. The others exclaimed.

"Hush," said the Princess. "Did I address any of you?"

"I found the answer in one of the accounts that Samuel stole," Elliot explained. "Turned out Madeleine had figured it out at the same time, which —"

"You read beneath the block-out?" Samuel cried, his image flickering again, his eyes huge. "But how?! As to a petal in a paper clip, so did I *struggle* and *lament* and *weary* and *sweat* and *ache* to achieve such an end! Whereas you . . ."

"Used a spell from the Lake," Elliot said.

"Magic!" cried Samuel. "Oh, but I cannot foretell how my heart does anguish, Princess, for long, I swear, *long* did I —"

"All right, Samuel," the Princess's eyes remained focused above Elliot's head. "Take it easy. Magic was probably the only solution. The only magic *you* have access to is Olde-Quaintian, and you would be a bigger fool than you appear if you tried to grapple with that. Kindly desist from beating yourself up. It is unseemly. Elliot, congratulations. Tell us the details when you get here. In the meantime, have my family been informed of the schedule for their transfers?"

Elliot hesitated. He'd been framing the words — an explanation of mirrors and lights, how you used them, why he thought they'd work on major cracks; he even wanted to explain the sound of Madeleine's voice in the darkness — but now he was supposed to explain the details when he *got there*?

Got where anyway? She expected him back at her dumb palace?

The Princess was waiting.

"Uh, yeah," he said. "Madeleine says she'll get the letters to your family."

"Very well." The Princess turned her head. Her face, wavering in Elliot's room, still held the intensity and frown. "Keira. Anything of note in the new boxes of documents?"

There was a long pause during which Keira's head tilted slowly.

"We have no time for pauses and tilts! Kindly answer!"

Now Keira raised her eyebrows.

"You really think I'm going to find something useful in those boxes?"

This time the Princess paused.

"Maybe," she said after a beat.

"Well, then." Keira smiled faintly.

"Did you?"

"No. Just a whole bunch of racing statistics."

"Keep reading." The Princess's image swiveled. "Samuel, have you found anything further in the archives?"

Samuel offered a respectful bow.

"My dear and worthy highness," he began. "As to a bellyache in —"

"Have you?"

"No."

The Princess turned smoothly.

"Sergio. Have you acquired a detector?"

Sergio, whose eyes had been bright and lively throughout the conversation, now faded a little. "Well," he began. "Not *exactly*. There is the *beautiful* difficulty —"

"But you will," said the Princess. Her voice rose. Elliot looked at his bedroom door, but at that moment the vacuum cleaner started up downstairs. Surely his mother had nothing left to vacuum?

He turned back to the Princess, who was still talking. She was leaning forward, her image crackling and breaking up as if collapsing under the intensity in her voice. "My security agents are in the room with me right now." She waved a hand behind her. Elliot looked and saw his own bedroom window, fields stretching out to distant trees. "They are listening to this conversation. You will recall what they once said about you behind your back, Sergio. Do you know what you will do? You will get that detector, Sergio, and *prove them wrong*."

This was the first time anyone had mentioned that overheard conversation. There was a deep silence, then a stir of static, everyone glancing sidelong at Sergio.

Sergio's face seemed oddly twisted. He was trying to gather his usual smile. He managed it, and beamed at the Princess. "I will," he promised. "I will get it!"

"I know you will." The Princess swiveled, trying to see each of them. "I have set up an official tour of the Kingdom for the Royal Youth Alliance. This will be our cover as we move between the cross-over points. We commence at the White Palace, where we will collect Prince Tippett."

She explained the itinerary of press conferences and provincial activities to take place between the gathering of family members.

The vacuum cleaner droned and clunked downstairs. Elliot listened vaguely. He was thinking there was not much chance that this tour would go as smoothly as the Princess's voice seemed to suggest. He wasn't even sure if his mirror-and-light trick would work, but anyhow, before they could try it, they'd have to *find* the cracks — and unseal the cracks — and they could only do that with Sergio.

Sergio was a good guy. He could dance, he made great chocolate. He was loyal, passionate, and he meant well.

But seemed unlikely he'd ever track down a detector.

The Princess was still talking.

Downstairs, there was an abrupt silence, a dragging sound, and the vacuum started again.

More to the point, Elliot thought, there was not a chance in hell that he himself was going on this tour.

If his father got home today — he remembered Madeleine's certainty, and changed that: *when* his father got home today — well, once that happened, he, Elliot was only going to leave his side when his dad brushed his teeth. (He was too enthusiastic a brusher — blizzards of toothpaste foam. Elliot had never enjoyed that about his dad.)

He'd get word to the Princess about the mirror-and-light trick, and then he'd respectfully withdraw from the RYA.

He was done with it.

"Is this all clear?" Princess Ko demanded.

Elliot saw the others nodding in their various ways, and he added his own nod.

There was a crackle and then the Princess was addressing Elliot again: "Any news on your dad?" she said, her voice a little different.

"We're expecting him back today," Elliot said.

"Wonderful," the Princess said, both warm and distracted, then: "Time's up. Over and out," and her image faded.

The others glanced around uncertainly, and then, one by one, each faded too.

Elliot touched the other side of the ring to cut his own transmission.

He looked around the empty bedroom.

He listened to his mother, switching off the vacuum cleaner again. This time she seemed to be done. There was the rustle of the cord being wound back up, and the hallway closet opening and shutting. Her footsteps down the hall. The laundry door. Water running. Her footsteps again, slower this time, and a faint, low, sloshing sound.

Seemed she was walking with a bucketful of water. Must be planning to clean something else.

He opened his bedroom door, then paused, imagining his father standing in this doorway.

Today.

His dad would be standing here sometime today, looking around, asking what Elliot had been up to —

Sometimes an idea is so sweet it aches.

Sunlight was picking up the dust on Elliot's bookshelf; his posters were peeling from the wall. The windows were smudged and smeared.

He thought again of his father in the doorway, then he ran downstairs to the laundry himself, got his own bucket of water.

Half an hour later he'd done the window, and he was taking books from his shelf so he could give it a good dust.

He was late for school, but his mother hadn't said a word. They were both working silently, her downstairs, him here. He kept glancing back at the sparkle of the window. Should do that more often, he thought. Clean glass. Makes the sky a brighter blue, fills the room with brighter sun.

It seemed shameful now, the idea that he'd almost let his dad see a dusty window.

Something was biting his finger. He shook his hand a couple of times as he worked. Kept on biting. That was *hurting* —

He looked down and saw he was still wearing the ring. It was calling him again. Ah, the Princess wanted to know the details after all. Must have got impatient. Good. He touched the side of it, and an image unfurled in his bedroom. Right beside his desk.

Looked like a cutout girl for a moment, then as he watched it seemed to color itself in. It flickered a little. It was not the Princess.

"Keira," he said.

"Elliot."

There was a pause. Keira had her messy, ruffled look, the one he preferred. New patches of acne on her cheeks.

"Have you got a minute?"

"Sure." He kicked his bedroom door closed, and turned back to her.

"You really figured out how to get through a crack?" she said, with half a smile.

"Just hold up a mirror and a light," said Elliot. "And wait. I think that's how it works anyhow."

"You think?"

"Well, the crack here's too small so I can't be sure, but . . ." He shrugged, looked sideways at the streaks on his door handle. Now he'd got started with this cleaning thing, he didn't want to stop.

"I have to tell you something," Keira said, her voice steady and careful, as if it were walking on a wire, and if it stopped it would lose its balance.

"Okay."

"About why I got chosen for the Royal Youth Alliance."

Now he turned from the dusters and buckets and faced her directly.

"My mother," she began, "you remember I mentioned my mother?"

"Sure do."

"She's a Hostile. She has been all my life."

Elliot chuckled. "Come on," he said. "You wouldn't be on the Royal Youth Alliance if . . ." Then he stopped. "Wait. Are you saying they don't know about this? You're a Hostile yourself? You're under-*cover* on the Alliance?"

"They know," said Keira. "It's not that. Here's how it went. About six months ago, my mother got arrested. Remember I told you she met a man? Using her stupid self-help book? Well, turned out *he* was undercover for the Loyalists. He made her fall in love with him, gave her jewelry with a — with a listening device embedded in it — and trapped her that way."

Elliot was shaking his head slowly.

"The necklace," he said. "The one you threw into the snowbank."

"Too late," she said. "My mother was in prison by then — awaiting execution. The only reason she's still alive now — is a deal that the Princess made with me."

"Join the Royal Youth Alliance and your mother stays alive?"

"Right."

"But why would the Princess do that?"

"Oh," Keira shrugged. "I guess she thinks I'm dangerous. She *knows* I'm dangerous — I'm actually better at the tech stuff than most people. I grew up making listening devices for my mother — for the Hostiles. That's why it's ironic — that my mother got caught out with —"

Keira's voice was crackling, the image was flickering and blurring. She seemed to drag herself together.

"The Princess thought it would be smarter to have me working for her — *owning* me — than let me loose. They didn't have any proof against me, see? They just knew my reputation. Only, she can't seem to bring herself to give me anything useful to do. Just all that tiny, tiny printed paper, so I've got a constant headache."

"She wants to punish you," Elliot guessed. "She takes your background too personally."

"Our Princess has some limitations," Keira said.

Elliot was still staring.

"No wonder she didn't want you to take my dad's listening device home with you," he remembered. "She thought you'd take it to the Hostiles."

Keira smiled faintly. "There's something else," she said.

There was a crackling, a pause, more crackling.

Keira's image straightened. She angled herself so she was facing the spot just to Elliot's left.

"Mischka Tegan," she said.

He flinched. Normally he cleared a space around that name before he used it, or heard it. Prepared his defenses. Having it spoken so clear out of the blue, felt like a sucker punch.

He breathed through it, then spoke carefully.

"That's the woman who betrayed my dad," he said. "What about her?"

Keira's face changed — became disheveled — then she cleared it again, and spoke clearly.

"It's the name my mother used," she said.

The room had taken on a slow, lethargic spin.

Elliot tried to smile. "What are you saying?"

"When she went undercover in Bonfire, the Farms," Keira said, "my mother called herself Mischka Tegan. She met Jon and Abel Baranski, and worked with them until the night they realized who she was. It all fell apart then — as you know. She called in her people — they dealt with the situation. She came home, started work on a different project — and that's when she was betrayed herself. Another irony, I guess — and arrested." Keira's mouth was twisting oddly. "The Princess doesn't know that part — I mean, she doesn't know about my mother's connection to your father — they don't know that she was Mischka Tegan — she used an effective disguise then. I'm sorry," she said. "Everything that's happened to you — to your family — to your dad . . . it was all my mother's fault. I'm so sorry."

Elliot was stepping back from her image. He kept backing up until he thudded against the door. That spin to his room was getting faster and more reckless.

"Don't be sorry," he found himself saying, some remote instinct for manners kicking in. "It's not your fault. You're not your mother. But listen, can we not talk right now? I just need — my dad's coming back today, so I need to clean. Talk later, okay?" His hand was on the side of the ring, ready to cut her off.

"Elliot." Keira's voice rose clear again, urgent now. "I'm telling you this for a reason. I *had* to tell you now. I couldn't stand seeing you — so happy — hearing you say your dad is coming home."

Anger came at him like an iceberg.

"Well," he said. "I'm sorry if my happiness offends you. Bye, Keira."

"No!" Keira's image lunged toward him. A mad rush of tears was careening down her cheeks, which he found both bizarre and infuriating.

"What *is* it?"

"He won't come home today," she said. "Your dad is not coming back today. They'll delay again. The agents will call and say they need more time. A few more days, they'll say. Then they'll say that again."

"What are you talking about?"

"Elliot." Keira was crying properly now. "Your dad is never coming home. He died the same night your uncle died. My mother saw him die."

Now Elliot felt a surge of clarity. The anger vanished.

"Well, that makes no sense," he said, clear and precise. "We found my Uncle Jon but there were no traces of my dad. Which is why we know the Hostiles took him. Which is why the agents have been negotiating with the Hostiles. Which is why they're bringing him home today."

That felt good. Irrefutable.

But Keira was still shaking her head.

"They wanted it to look like your dad and Mischka ran away together," she said. "And that your uncle was taken by a Purple. So there'd be no suspicions. So other Hostiles could come in undercover and find where your dad had hidden the technologies they were working on. But then Central Intelligence figured out that Hostiles were involved — that Mischka Tegan had been a Hostile operative — so the Hostiles changed the story. They led them to believe they were holding your dad prisoner."

Elliot maintained his calm. "I trust the agents," he said. "They've heard my dad's voice. They wouldn't lie to me."

"The agents are not lying," Keira said. "They don't *know* the truth. They *believe* they're speaking to your father, and that his release is all lined up. They're being played. The Hostiles will find some other excuse — make one more demand, get one more Hostile prisoner released in exchange for your dad's release. It'll keep being postponed until your agents figure out the truth. But I can't stand you believing in this lie anymore."

At the edge of his mind, Elliot heard a car in the driveway.

An engine cutting.

"It's not true," he said, firmly. "Tovey and Kim are smart. If what you're saying was true, they'd have figured it out by now. My dad is coming home today. See ya."

He pressed the side of the ring.

Keira's image faded.

Outside, the car doors opened and slammed.

He pulled off his ring, and dropped it onto the floor.

He opened his bedroom door.

He ran down the stairs.

There were footsteps on the gravel. He stopped.

His mother was in the hallway. She glanced up at him, their eyes caught.

They both waited, formal. Elliot, on the stairs, held the bannister and angled himself so he could see the door.

Footsteps on the porch.

A firm knock.

His mother paused. She reached for the handle. She opened the door.

Agents Tovey and Kim: two shapes, one big, one small.

Elliot looked beyond their shoulders, looking for a third man, his father, then looked back.

He saw it in their faces.

No light. No light at all.

His mother caught this. Elliot saw her face reflecting it at once: that total absence of light.

Then a sound came from her, a form of scream, and it came to Elliot, simple and precise: *That's how you crack open a world.*

The agents reached out their arms to her.

PART 13

Princess Ko was in the upper-level boardroom of the White Palace.

Her spine was straight, but she kept dipping and raising her head like a swan searching for pondweed.

The Social Secretary drew his hands out of his pockets.

"Have you an issue with your neck, Highness?"

Princess Ko paused, and looked at him. His shirt was bright mint green.

"That's a moot point," she said.

The Social Secretary twinkled. "You don't know what that expression means, do you?"

She twinkled back. "That, *too*, is a moot point!"

Then she lowered her head again, pressing her fingers into the back of her neck.

"Tension in the muscles!" pounced the Social Secretary. "I knew it! I will alert the Royal Masseuse at once. You, my dear Highness, have concerns that your father will not be back from the Narraburra in time for the Namesaking Ceremony this weekend! Admit it!"

The Princess straightened again and beamed at him.

"Does a starspin whirl in sunshine?" she exclaimed. "No! It does not! Because I'm totally non*plussed* about that issue. My dad will be *rocking* Aldhibah this weekend, and the whole event will be a total *minefield* of perfection!"

The Social Secretary returned his hands to his pockets.

"Look, I don't blame you for worrying. Between you and me, the entire Palace is buzzing with how fine he's cutting it. What if a storm comes up before they make port? Issues with the mainsail or the hoist or the jib or whatever they call the various bits that go on sailing ships? Not to mention delays with the Royal Jet once he does let the anchor down, or come into the dockyards, or whatever it is that ships do once they've completed their — sailing."

"*That*," said the Princess, nodding wisely, "is a *deal breaker*."

The Social Secretary drew his hands out and drummed them lightly, one on top of the other. "You don't know what *that* expression means either, do you?"

The Princess smiled faintly, but she was twisting the ring on her finger, a frown falling into her smile.

"Are we done here?" she said. "I mean, my eyes are alight with the fire of everything you've said about upcoming events and banquets and so forth, so maybe we could call this meeting quits, and I'll fan the flames in my eyeballs until I'm ready to extinguish them and get on with my life?"

"Of course! Until next time."

"Stay total!"

"Hope so!"

The Social Secretary jived toward the door, turning once to wink at her.

"And can you ask the Commissioner for Education to give me ten minutes?" she called. "I know she's waiting out there."

The Social Secretary winked again and closed the door behind him.

Princess Ko glanced back at her security agents. They blinked at her, silent.

She touched the side of the ring.

A haze formed just above the boardroom table, crackling faintly, and then resolved itself into a shadowy head and shoulders. It was Sergio. A miniature circular tower of gold seemed to be growing from his shoulder.

"Sergio," Princess Ko said. "I'm in meetings."

There was a faint buzz and crackle from the static that was Sergio.

"I can't hear you."

"I know." Sergio's voice hissed into the room, just above a whisper. "I'm in the stationery cupboard. I'm trying to speak softly."

"Very well," said Princess Ko. "What are you doing in the stationery cupboard? Is there a crack detector in there? If so, grab it and get out."

She was distracted by the miniature tower.

"It's not about that," whispered Sergio. "I cannot get through to Elliot. I have been trying but he does not answer his ring."

"Why do you need Elliot?"

There was a pause, the image blurring further.

"Apologies," Sergio said. "I heard footsteps at the door — but . . ."

Another pause, and then Sergio's whisper changed to a low, urgent murmur.

"Ko," he said. "There's a WSU unit on its way to Bonfire. Someone has reported Elliot. They know he's been communicating with the World. He's been classified as a Flagrant Offender."

The Princess's hands shook. She steadied them.

"But who would have reported him?"

Sergio shrugged. "Did you hear me? They're on their way now, and he's a Flagrant Offender."

"What does that mean?"

"It means," Sergio whispered, "the orders are to Identify and Dispatch."

"And what does *that* mean?" the Princess almost shouted.

"Hush," whispered Sergio, his head swinging around in the darkness. "It means they shoot to kill. Execute on sight."

The Princess touched her mouth.

"What else do you know?" she said.

"Only that they're flying there now."

There was a slight pause.

"Sergio," said the Princess. "What is growing out of your shoulder?"

Sergio moved. The tower separated.

"It is tape," he said. "It is a pile of tape. I am in the stationery closet. Remember?"

The Princess nodded.

"Get out of the closet," she murmured. "Get the detector. Get out of that place, and take the next plane here to the Palace. I'll take care of Elliot."

Sergio's face relaxed.

"Thank you," he whispered, and his image paled and vanished.

The Princess looked across the boardroom at the open fireplace. Logs crackling. She looked through the window. A wolf crossing the snow.

"Princess," said a voice behind her, and she turned.

It was Agent Ramsay. His eyes were narrowed slightly, questioningly.

"You know," he said, "that there's nothing you can do for Elliot?"

"I know," she agreed.

"We warned him about this," Agent Nettles put in, leaning forward, intense.

"I know," she repeated, her voice threaded with irritation. She looked at the pile of files on the table before her, the Royal Stamp beside it, glinting in the snow-glare.

"You have to cut him loose," Agent Ramsay said with his most soulful, sorrowful expression.

Across the room, an ornate telephone sat on the sideboard.

"Does that telephone work?" the Princess asked.

The agents exchanged glances and cleared throats.

"To the extent that any telephones work in this province," Agent Ramsay said, and shrugged. "Which means, sometimes yes, mostly no. But there's nobody to call, Princess. You have no authority over the WSU."

"Not planning on calling the WSU," she said, still gazing at the phone.

"Well, whatever you're planning, don't," Agent Nettles said briskly. "The call could be intercepted. If a member of the royal family was exposed interfering with the WSU? It would bring down the monarchy. You understand that, of course."

"Bring me the phone," said Princess Ko.

The agents stood motionless.

"Bring it to the table," she repeated.

"Let him go," Agent Nettles said. "He knew the risks."

"I doubt the cord on that phone would reach this far," Agent Ramsay mused, "even if we *were* to bring it over."

"Very well," the Princess said. "I'll get it myself." She pushed back her chair.

PART 14

1.

At the Bonfire Sheriff's Station, Hector Samuels, County Sheriff, was smoothing out his Road Safety posters. His annual visit to the Bonfire Grade School was scheduled for this afternoon: Next, he'd check his collection of antique firearms, and he'd bake a batch of cookies for the kids.

Jimmy was standing on a chair, hanging photographs. The station made a good gallery space for Jimmy's exhibitions, and he'd taken a series of shots of the mulberry trees around town. Some depicted just a single tree, sun behind the leaves; others showed rows of trees swarming with kids and townsfolk.

This one he liked in particular: It was Clover Mackie, town seamstress. You just about never saw Clover anywhere but sitting on her porch in the square, but here she was, high in a tree, waving a berry-stained hand.

Which is why it startled Jimmy so much when the door jangled open, and there she was, Clover Mackie herself. Walking into the station. He looked back and forth between the photo and the person for some seconds before he stepped down.

Hector let go of the poster he was smoothing. It curled itself back up.

"Clover Mackie!" he exclaimed. "Well, if it isn't a pleasure to —"

"No time for chitchat, boys." Clover stood in the middle of the room. "I've just had a call, and I'll thank you not to ask who the caller was, but to trust me when I say that the source was reliable, and I have news."

Hector and Jimmy waited, impressed.

"The news is urgent," Clover said. "First up, Elliot Baranski has been communicating with the World."

"Well, now —" Hector began, and, "That can't be —" Jimmy shook his head, but Clover was waving a brisk hand at them.

"*That* part I *know* to be true. He *has* got a contact in the World. Writes letters to her. The next part of the news is what counts. Seems Elliot's been reported. The WSU are on their way here now."

Hector gave her a look. "Come on, now," he said. "You're having us on."

"Well, no. Like I said, my source is reliable. Of course, she was talking fast, and in secret code, and the line kept cutting out. Still, I'm pretty sure that's what she said. Naturally enough, I am *not* informing the local Sheriff that the WSU are on their way, and the local Sheriff is *not* going to get word to Elliot, and get him the heck out of town and into hiding. I'm not even *here*." She looked up at Jimmy on his chair, and at the wall beyond his shoulder. "Well, except in that photo. There I am."

Hector and Jimmy stared from the photo to Clover and back, as if that coincidence were the real issue.

"So," Clover continued. "I'm just here to discuss taking up Jimmy's trousers for him, but how about that, they look to be exactly the right length!" Hector and Jimmy glanced at Jimmy's trouser cuffs, and felt faint surprise that in fact they *were* the right length. "And now I'll head on home. Nice to see you, boys."

She pressed both hands against the station door, then turned, and spoke again.

"Seems they've classified him as a Flagrant Offender," she said. "So whatever you don't do, you'd better not do it fast." She paused. "Might have got my negatives in a tangle just then," she said, and grinned. The grin turned fierce as they watched. "You take care of Elliot," she said, and there was another jangle.

Hector and Jimmy watched the door close behind her, then faced each other.

"It can't be right," Hector said.

"But Clover Mackie," Jimmy pointed out.

Hector nodded. He was thinking.

"Let's say Elliot *did* find a crack through to the World," he mused, speaking slowly. "You think he'd *use* it? You think he'd be more keen on the adventure of the World, than worried about getting himself arrested?"

As he spoke, something shifted in them both.

This was Elliot Baranski.

Jimmy lunged for the phone.

"Dumb kid," Hector said, grabbing his jacket. "Who you calling? He'd be over at school right now. Let's head —"

Jimmy held up a hand.

"Hey there, Patty," he said. "Jimmy here. Wondering if you might track down Isabella for me?"

Ah. The Sheriff nodded. Patty was the school secretary. Jimmy must be planning to have Isabella get Elliot out of class in some innocent-seeming way. That was smarter than storming over there themselves.

"She didn't?" Jimmy said. "Well, now, that's surprising. I guess she's not feeling so good. Can I trouble you to call Elliot Baranski out of class for me, then? I want to have a quick word with him about the deftball — I know, I know, we take it way too seriously — and yes, that's the truth, his education *must* come — but it's just the — oh, now. He's not either? I guess there might be some bug going around. Thanks for your help, Patty, see you soon."

He hung up.

"Isabella didn't show at school today," he said. "I guess she's sick. And Elliot's not there either."

Hector took the car keys from the hook.

"We should have thought of that," he said. "His dad's due back sometime today — he probably stayed home to wait for him."

Jimmy nodded, and they tried to saunter to the car, but ran the last few steps.

"How long do you reckon it'll take the WSU to get here?" Jimmy asked as they turned onto Broad Street.

Hector changed gear, and braked a little. The streets were still wet from last night's rain. He waved at Norma Lisle, town vet, who was washing her shop-front window. A couple of kids who probably should have been at school ducked behind a trash can.

"Who can tell?" Hector said eventually. "Fact is, if they catch us helping Elliot, we'll both end up behind bars. You okay with the risk? I won't blame you if not. You can hop on out right now — we're only a block from Isabella's now, you could run down there and check on her."

Jimmy was silent. He seemed to notice the seat belt, pulled it across his waist, and clicked it in.

"The fact that you could even *ask* me that," he began, "that you could even —"

"All right, all right." Hector turned onto Acres Road. They were heading away from downtown now, houses were getting farther apart, giving way to meadows, fields, barns. "It's okay for me, I'm on my own, but I doubt your Isabella would *ever* forgive me if I got you locked up."

Jimmy smiled. "Well, that's true enough," he said.

Hector gave the car some more gas.

"The sculpture," Jimmy said abruptly.

Hector glanced sideways. The car swerved a little as he did, and he turned back, clutching the wheel with both hands, but not slowing down.

"The sculpture in the schoolyard," Jimmy repeated. "The one Elliot's always hanging around late at night. You think *that* could be . . ."

Hector was shaking his head slowly. The car bumped twice, skidded a little, and settled down again. He pressed his foot harder on the accelerator.

"It'd explain why he's there so much," Hector said. "Always thought he just needed some alone time — wanted to be close to the old TV that his dad once worked on — and he was writing a journal or something — but a crack, now that would be a much more likely explanation."

"Elliot Baranski." Jimmy was shaking his head now. "Sitting out there plain as day, writing messages to the World. You've gotta admire him."

"I want to throttle him."

"That too," Jimmy agreed.

They were almost at the Baranski farm now.

A new thought occurred to Hector. "We've got to get that sculpture out of the schoolyard," he said. "If it *is* where the crack is, might be something there could implicate Elliot. The only hope is to get him into hiding now, before they get here, then clear his name somehow."

Jimmy put his hand onto the dashboard, to steady himself. The car was racing, mud splattering up against the fenders. "I'll ask Isabella to get rid of it. She's surely not too sick to make that happen — matter of fact, I've mentioned Elliot's regular visits with the sculpture to her, and I remember now she said she thought that thing was dangerous. Exposed wires in the middle of a schoolyard. I'll tell her to make its removal an urgent safety issue."

Hector nodded.

They were bumping up the driveway now, and he was slowing a little.

There was a car parked out front.

"That's Tovey and Kim's car," Jimmy said.

Hector switched off the ignition, and took out the keys.

"You think they've already got Abel?" he said. "You think they might be here, bringing him home?"

They both sat in the car a minute, the quiet seeping in at them.

"There," said Jimmy, pointing.

Elliot Baranski was across the field by a fence, a hammer held high. As they watched, he brought it down fast. The thud echoed out toward them.

Jimmy and Hector opened their car doors.

They watched Elliot. They saw him look up, see them, then turn back to his hammering.

They took a couple of steps.

The quiet was full, but something was edging its way in sideways. A distant, shuffling, mechanical sound. Tiny but relentless.

Hector cupped his hands to his mouth, and shouted Elliot's name.

Again, Elliot looked back, and again he returned to his hammering.

"Elliot!" they both shouted, and both waved their arms.

Now Elliot shaded his eyes a moment, then they saw him lower the hammer to his side, and begin to cross the field toward them.

"Never saw him move like that," Jimmy said.

Elliot was wearing his usual jeans, boots, and T-shirt, but everything looked too big for him. His body seemed small. Too small to carry his head, which was set at an angle like it hadn't been properly affixed, might topple to the ground any moment.

Hector and Jimmy glanced at each other.

They looked back to the farmhouse. Through the window, they could see Tovey and Kim seated side by side, Petra Baranski opposite them. Nobody in there seemed to be speaking.

"None of this looks good," Hector said.

Jimmy scratched his eyebrow. "Whatever's happened," he said. "We can't let the agents know the reason we're here. They'd be compelled to arrest Elliot."

"Agreed. Hey there, Elliot! You okay?"

Elliot was getting closer, swinging that hammer as he walked. There was something defiant in his expression. It looked like he was trying for a smile.

He opened the gate, stopped a little short of them.

"Hey," he said. "Tovey and Kim are inside. You hear the latest? Seems my dad's been dead all along. The Hostiles have been playing them. Used some old recording they had of Dad's voice. Showed them his magnifying glass. Kept them negotiating over nothing all this time."

"Oh, now, Elliot," said Hector, and both he and Jimmy moved toward Elliot, but Elliot let the hammer fall with a thump to the grass so he could hold his palms up in the air to stop them.

"Don't even worry about it," he said. "This is just another way of Dad being gone. How's it any different really? It's been over a year now; we're used to it."

He raised his voice a little for this final phrase: that distant, mechanical noise was getting more persistent.

The three of them looked up. It was high, just a speck, and it was far, but it seemed to be heading this way: a black chopper.

Behind them, the door to the farmhouse opened.

The two agents stepped out, and more slowly, Elliot's mother. Their movements seemed cautious. You could see their heads swinging from the Sheriff's car to Hector, Jimmy, and Elliot by the fence. Then to the chopper up in the sky.

"This is crazy timing," Hector said, speaking low and fast, "but see that chopper? I'd say that's coming for you. We hear you found a crack through to the World and never got around to reporting it the way you should have?"

Elliot gazed at Hector.

"I'll take it that's not a denial," Hector said. "Well, seems someone's found you out and reported you. You've got about two minutes to get inside, throw together a few things, and get the heck as far from here as you can."

"Go into the woods," Jimmy advised. "See if you can make your way through to Sugarloaf, and hitch a train from there. Disappear awhile, and we'll see if we can sort things out for you."

Elliot was turning a stone over with his boot. He looked at Hector and shrugged.

"They want me," he said. "They can come and get me." Then he smiled that new, freakish smile again.

The chopper was growing in the sky, its noise building. Not enough to drown their voices but getting close to that.

Hector looked back at the porch. Petra and the agents were lined up now, each staring up at the sky.

Petra was wearing a dress. Hector had only a handful of memories of ever seeing her in anything but trousers. She had dark pink lipstick on too, he could see from here, and her hair soft and pretty, so her face looked younger than usual. Something else too — her eyebrows were different. They were thinner and higher.

She must have had them shaped in a beauty parlor.

This was all, he realized suddenly, because she'd been expecting her husband home today.

She was about to see her only son shot dead.

A noise sounded, without his meaning it to, in the back of Hector's throat.

"Elliot," he said, speaking slow, stopping to clear away that noise. "Elliot, you're the bravest boy I know. You've spent the last year doing things would terrify people twice your age in the hopes of rescuing your dad. Not that surprising, I guess, since your mother's the toughest woman I ever met. And today you'll be feeling like you're broken into pieces."

"Nope," Elliot said, shaking his head firmly. "I told you. I'm fine. It's just —"

"All right, as you like. I won't argue, I'll just give you an order. As Sheriff of Bonfire, I am now ordering you, Elliot, to find one more piece of courage — just a little scrap more. See your mother over there? She's standing on a ledge. She's on the very edge. She's lost her husband today." Elliot swung around irritably. "Don't let her lose you too."

Elliot was wiping his hand, back and forth across his mouth, like a kid who's been drinking milk.

By now the helicopter was a roar, a big dark shape. It had a sharp lean to it, like something skidding.

"You don't have time to pack a bag," Jimmy yelled. He pulled a handful of cash from his pocket. "Take this —" Next, he drew a crushed paper bag from his other pocket and shrugged. "And half a cherry pastry. All I've got."

Agent Tovey was suddenly behind them.

"That's a WSU chopper," he shouted. "You know what that's about?"

Hector looked at him, considering.

Tovey took all this in: Hector's gaze, Jimmy turning away, Elliot tapping a foot.

"It's coming for you?" he said to Elliot.

Elliot ignored him, but Hector made a decision.

"It is," he said. "Flagrant Offender."

Tovey startled, then at once grew still.

"Get out of here," he said to Elliot. "I'll stall them. But you've gotta go right now."

Elliot turned back, saw his mother on the porch.

Tovey spoke urgently to Hector and Jimmy: "You two, get back to the Sheriff's station, and see what you can do. I'll tell them you were here about Elliot's dad. I'll do what I can for Elliot."

Elliot glanced toward Tovey.

"You're in shock," Tovey said. "Use the adrenaline now —" And as he spoke, he took Elliot by the shoulders, swung him around, and shoved.

Abruptly, Elliot was running.

They saw his mother's confused stare as Elliot, still running, ducked around the side of the house and disappeared.

Then they all stood watching the sky.

2.

"It is not a suicide note!" Olivia cried. "It is merely a — how do you call it? — a *cry for help*!"

"How can you tell the difference?" Jack demanded.

"Can I see it?"

They both looked at Madeleine.

Jack handed over the letter.

She read it standing by the rose bush in Belle's front yard.

To Mum and Dad,

Hiya. Look, people always start these things off by saying, "Don't blame yourselves," and all that, but I'm thinking, why would I say that? You go ahead and blame yourselves if you want. LOL.

Seriously. You can. It's totally up to you.

Anyhow, the fact is, I've Fallen in Love with this Man, and it turns out he sees things the way I do. I mean, he sees that life is a useless crock, and what are we all doing living it? Until something random such as illness or an accident or whatever calls it off? That's just balmy, going along with that. Is what he thinks, and I agree.

So, anyhow, you'll be all right without me. Tell Jack he'll be all right too. He might be sad for a bit but his aura is the strongest I've ever seen. Tell Madeleine hey and I hope she keeps up with her Kingdom of Cello cause if she does she'll be okay too.

Tell Holly that I haven't done that essay about symbolism in Chaucer yet, which I know I told her I was just checking the footnotes, but that was a lie, I haven't even STARTED it, and I hope that doesn't do her head in, my betrayal of her on the issue of Chaucer, etc. LOL. I doubt it. She probably knew all along.

And tell Federico I'll catch up with history in the afterlife. LOL. And ah, tell anyone else whatever you want.

Your daughter,

Belle

Madeleine looked up, blinking.

"We should call the police," she said.

"Come," smiled Olivia. "We must consider the situation."

She ushered them into the house and down the hall.

"Not the kitchen," she decided. "The sitting room. For this is a special occasion."

"It's not a party," murmured Jack.

The sitting room was even darker than it had been the last time Madeleine visited, at night.

"I will not open the curtains," Olivia said. "Out of respect for this sombre occasion. As Jack points out, it is *not* a party!"

They could hardly see one another and the clutter in the room formed small dark hills and curious shapes.

"Madeleine's right, we have to call the police," Jack said. His voice was lined up ready to shout.

"Pfft!" said Olivia. "We are not to bother them with her pranks and games. This letter, it is full of jokes. What would they even do? Laugh?"

"Well," Madeleine said carefully, "she says she's fallen in love — and it sounds like she and this man have a sort of plan. . . ." She had a sense that finding the right words here was important, but they were lost somewhere in the dim light. "I think we should — open the drapes," she said.

Olivia laughed again.

"Fallen in love with a man! A *man*! She is a child! She does not know love, nor does she know men!"

"It must be one of the four guys she was seeing," Jack said to Madeleine. "But which one? Or what if she's gone and met someone else?"

"Four!" exclaimed Olivia, her voice trilling out into the shadows. "Perhaps she *does* know love? I hope not. She is only — what is she? Is she fourteen years old?"

"Fifteen," Jack said coldly, and he spoke to Madeleine again. "There's the tyre fitter, the baker, the student, and the machine operator. Two of them live in other cities. They come here on weekends to catch up with friends at pubs. That's how she met them."

"Four," repeated Olivia, mystified and proud. "It is as if she is *orbited* by men! But they do not sound especially wealthy. This machine operator. This tyre fitter."

"Do you know their names?" Madeleine asked Jack.

"I am thinking," Olivia said, and she stood. They both looked up at her, trying to make out her face. "I am thinking that I must prepare a *platter* of fruit and cheeses. To help us with our conference." She moved across the room, stepping between shadows. As she passed the window, she brushed against the curtain so it shifted slightly, letting in a thin beam of sunlight.

The light crossed the darkness. It hit a pale pink shape sitting on a pile of books.

Jack and Madeleine stared at this.

"It's a sugar mouse," said Madeleine. "The kind you put on cakes."

They both spoke at once. "It's the baker," they said.

The curtain fell back into place, the room into darkness once again.

"You know this how?" Olivia said, her lips forming an upside down smile.

"She said she'd never accept a gift from a boy," Madeleine explained, "unless she was in love with him."

"What a strange child!" cried Olivia. "Such an absurd policy! No gifts!"

"And the baker makes sugar mice," Jack finished. "But he lives in Norwich — he's one of the out-of-towners. I don't know the name of his bakery."

Olivia moved towards the door again. "Leave her to play her games until she grows tired and feels foolish and comes home. You are both looking *much* too solemn. Come. I have been this morning to that little cheese shop in All Saints Passage, the name of which I always forget, but which —"

"Do you remember *his* name, Jack? Did Belle tell you that?"

"No."

"We should look in her room." Madeleine stood. "See if we can find any more clues up there."

"Oh, now!" Olivia smiled again. "Leave her be! Respect her privacy! You are, what, the child detectives?"

Jack squinted at Olivia.

"Even if it is just a cry for help," he said, "shouldn't we *answer* the cry?"

Olivia shook her head firmly. "It is as when she was a small child — a toddler — this is called a temper tantrum. If you want a sweet, you stamp your feet and wail? No. We ignore you if you do that. So. Too. If you wish for help, you *cry* for it with threats to take your life? Ha! She must learn that *this* is not the way."

Jack and Madeleine stared.

"Is it all right if we look in her room?" Jack asked.

Olivia shrugged. "As you like. It is up the stairs."

"Yes," said Jack. "I know."

There was another pause.

"We're off, then," Jack said eventually.

Madeleine followed.

They left Olivia standing in the middle of the room, still smiling her odd smirk.

3.

It seemed easy at first.

Elliot had followed the slope of the land until he was up on an elevated plateau, looking down on his farmhouse. From here he watched as the Sheriff's car drove down the driveway and away. He watched the WSU chopper land. Five or six officers running at a crouch toward the house. Agents Tovey and Kim sauntering across the field to meet them. The WSU officers straightening.

There was some kind of an exchange as the chopper engine cut.

Now the officers were walking across the field with Tovey and Kim. Their mood seemed different: still brisk, but calmer. One of the WSU officers was talking, and Tovey and Kim were listening, nodding, their pace still leisurely.

They all reached the front of Elliot's house, and there was another pause. From here, the wind blew pieces of their voices way up to Elliot:

not the words, but the tenor and tone. It seemed casual, even touched with laughter now and then.

Next thing, they had all disappeared from Elliot's view. They'd either stepped up onto the porch to talk, or gone inside the house.

He rocked back and forth on his feet, while slow plans formed and unformed in his mind. There was Jimmy's idea of cutting through the woods to Sugarloaf, and then taking a train someplace, and hiding out. But that seemed complex. He caught a glimpse of the sun on the river, which was full and high after last night's rain. Now that was appealing. Just get on the Chokeberry and ride its current south, out of town, all the way through Golden Coast.

He'd need a boat, of course. He couldn't think, just now, where one might be. There'd be people fishing. He could ask someone politely to hand over their boat.

And if they said no, he could just swim on over, and tip them out. Scramble aboard, start the motor while they flailed in the water —

No. That was getting complex again. Not to mention unkind.

Better just to build his own boat. A raft would be simple. Cut down a few saplings, strap them together —

He smiled at himself. He was being a fool, he knew, but he also knew that things would work out fine. The WSU would never catch him. He was going through the motions of being "on the run," and it was interesting enough, figuring out a "plan," but nothing to get bothered about. He was indestructible.

This feeling was familiar, and now he remembered why. He'd had it the weekend after the agents told him his father was a genius and would soon be home. Fantastic news or terrible news: In a way, they were the same.

They put you outside of the rules.

He started walking. Here's what he'd do. He'd hide out in a friend's barn until the WSU left. Country town full of friends and barns he had here. There'd be hay, water, light through the cracks, maybe animals to keep him company. His friends could bring him food in secret.

He walked along Acres Road. In the middle of the road. Eventually, he'd have to cross through the woods — Nikki's farm would be the easiest to reach from here — but for the moment, it was all so quiet. May as well get some space and air.

There was a thin, distant clapping sound. He looked up into the blue, and saw nothing — and then, in the distance, three or maybe four black specks.

Choppers, he realized.

There were more of them coming.

Not much Tovey and Kim could do about *five* WSU choppers.

He took a jump over a puddle in the road, hit the edge of it, and watched the sunlight catch the spray.

The pieces of a broken ceramic bowl sat in the grass on the side of the road. He'd always wondered, how did things like that get there? Did someone drive by and throw out their ceramic bowl? But why would anybody do that?

Here was Olaf Minski's property. He could see Olaf's hives lined up at the edge of the field there, like packing boxes propped on bricks. That was an idea. He'd find some kind of stick. The branch of a tree. A *tree trunk* itself maybe. And he'd hook a hive onto the trunk and brandish it at those choppers. The bees would swarm. Sting the officers until they turned the choppers around and flew away.

Olaf might be sad, though. He'd miss his bees. They'd come back, sure, once they'd done the job, but their honey would taste weird. From the stress.

Ah, it wouldn't work anyway. The choppers were swinging in closer now, growing bigger, louder, angrier. There were six of them, in fact, and already they were stirring up a wind at the tops of the trees.

The bees would just get blown away.

Elliot kept walking. It had occurred to him that he couldn't stay in a friend's barn, after all. Six WSU choppers — seven if you counted the one that had landed at his place — meant a whole bunch of WSU officers. They'd swarm out across the town like bees themselves, searching everyplace. He'd get his friends arrested.

No. He'd have to go back to Jimmy's idea. Woods. Sugarloaf. Train.

His feet took their steps, one after the other. Woods. Sugarloaf. Train.

Woods. Sugarloaf. Train.

A chopper flew right over his head, and blew his hair about a little.

Woods. He needed to get into the woods.

He had a feeling that he was standing at a ticket machine at a train station, say, and reading the instructions, slowly and methodically. Running his finger along the words, then turning to the buttons to figure out each step. While, at the same time, another Elliot was waiting in line just behind him, impatient, frustrated, jiggling on the spot, cursing under his breath, wanting to give the guy at the machine some kind of push or shove, wanting to lean over his shoulder and press the buttons himself.

But the Elliot at the machine was implacable. He kept right on taking his steps one at a time. Slow and careful.

There was that buckle in the road. His eyes swung left.

This was the spot where he'd found his uncle's body. Over a year ago. He'd been out running in the dawn light. He'd had that jogging high, the sweat on his back and running down his chest, a good ache in his arms and legs, his body strong and loose. The surprise of his father's truck on the side of the road, door open, lights on. Blood in the grass. Uncle Jon, the color of his skin, the color of his blood, his eyelids —

Another chopper swung low above him.

Elliot looked up. He saw an open door. Faces looking down. Two different people swinging their arms to point directly at him.

He turned into the woods, and started running.

The noise was ferocious. It set up a clamor in that line behind the Elliot at the ticket machine. There were a whole *bunch* of Elliots waiting now, and all of them shouting that he had to get a move on. He had a rising feeling that they were right, but now that he *wanted* to rush, he couldn't do it. His body had a big, clumsy feel — his hands couldn't work the ticket machine — no, he had to let go of that ticket machine idea and catch up with himself. His actual self. Here. Running in the woods, except that he *couldn't* run.

Of course you can run, he told himself. You run all the time. You leap over furrows. You sprint. You fly. You're a deftball champion. You're a *hero.*

Hero. The word slipped down his throat, as small as words can be. It was like a piece of candy he'd been sucking on so long that it was just a touch of nothing now — used to be big and sweet and round, now it was just stale old sugar. Wafer-thin, soft-edged.

He was no hero. His father was dead, his mother alone, and he'd done nothing. He'd been nothing. Running around the Kingdom searching Purple caverns for his dad, chasing nothing. Those days in the front room of the Watermelon Inn watching Tovey and Kim eat their waffles, watching nothing.

The ground here was slick with mud and damp. He kept tripping, catching at trees, the bark slippery or tearing away in his hands. Wet leaves slapped against his face, and got themselves caught up in the cuffs of his jeans. His jeans were getting stiff and heavy.

He couldn't even remember which direction he should run. They knew where he was, the choppers, he could feel them, taste them, all around him. They must have called one another, there was such a roar and bellow of them. Sending trees and branches sideways, lifting the leaves in damp flurries. He'd been thinking of the woods as safe, but they were much more sparse than he remembered. Great gaps and clearings between little clumps of trees.

He looked up as he ran through one clearing, and the choppers were dancing away up there, leaning in, moving back. Faces and guns. A cracking sound, then another, and he thought maybe there was a problem with a chopper's engine, and hoped it wouldn't crash into the woods, then he ran a little farther and there were another two cracks. Gunshots.

That looked like an old shed in a clearing up ahead. He could take shelter in that. But he got closer and saw it had caved in on itself, nothing but a rotting pile of mulch.

Seven choppers. He skidded, nearly tripping over a tree root, and stopped to catch his breath. That's a serious waste of resources. Seven choppers, one boy.

The crack sounded again.

He remembered himself standing on the hill above his house just half an hour back. Very, very good news, and very, very bad news put you outside of the rules, he'd been thinking. They make you indestructible.

Now clarity came slicing through his mind.

They don't *really* make you indestructible. They give you that illusion, but they don't. Even if your father's been dead for more than a year — even if you've wasted that time searching for him — a sky full of choppers will still kill you.

He had no idea where he was.

This part of the woods, he didn't know.

He stopped, pressed himself against a tree trunk, and checked the sky. They were hovering now, quivering in the air. Four choppers in a careful circle. Strange how silent those faces were in all the noise. Strange how he could see them behind their weapons, those silent faces watching him.

They could get him right now, against this tree.

Beyond him was another clearing, but past that thicker woods, trees pressed closer together. The ground there seemed to slope down a little, as if it might slip into a valley.

He took a chance, and ran.

The air cracked once, a pause, and then again.

He reached the trees, pressed through them — and swung both arms in circles, around and around, his body blazing hot and cold, hot and cold.

He'd hit a cliff edge.

A narrow ravine, sheer-edged, tumbled below him, directly beneath him, plummeting down into a deep, cavernous darkness.

The choppers waited. Clearing behind him, cliff edge before him.

One more step and he'd be over it, falling to his death.

Keira's voice spoke round and clear, sensible in his head: *Sometimes you have to let go. Let yourself fall. Give up.*

His mother was crawling on the floor of a Big Wheel carriage. His father was immobile in darkness.

There was nothing left except to let go. He felt the arms of that idea curling around him. Right here, on this muddy edge. He didn't even need to take a step, he just needed to shift his weight a little.

One of the choppers adjusted its position, inching closer, engine changing key.

It sent arrows of light though his body, that change. A rush of defiance. He swiveled, ready to face them, fight them, and that swivel was enough to break the edge. The ground crumbled beneath him.

His shout swept up behind him, became a scream of horror and of pure revelation: the enormity of falling.

4.

They found Belle leaning against the Delectable Bakery and Pie Shop.

She was facing the street, her elbows pressed back against the glass. She wore sunglasses they'd never seen before.

"Nice shades," said Jack.

Belle regarded him. She looked past his shoulder at Madeleine.

"Hiya," she said. There was a long pause, then she pushed herself off the glass and straightened up. In her hand was a glossy tourist brochure.

"Thought you were going to off yourself," Jack said.

Belle chuckled. "Just messing with my mum. How'd you find me?"

Paper bag on the floor of Belle's bedroom, they told her, pastry crumbs still inside, the bakery's name and address printed down the bottom.

Belle's mother had thrown back her head and laughed when they showed her the bag. "No wonder she is getting those plump cheeks!"

she had chortled. "Those plump arms! No, no, you surely do not plan to take a train to Norwich now? At this moment? In this day? But it will take you an hour and a half to get there!"

They didn't tell Belle that part.

The Delectable Bakery and Pie Shop was on London Street, a busy pedestrian shopping street, between the River Island Clothing Co. and Russell Bromley Shoes.

"Is he in there now?" Madeleine asked. "Your baker?"

"Yeah. Can't see him from here, though. He's out the back. It's his lunch break soon, that's why I'm waiting here."

"Have you just come for the day," Jack asked. "Or are you planning on living in Norwich now? With the baker?"

Belle shrugged. "Staying, I guess."

"Didn't pack much," Jack said. "All your stuff was still in your room."

"Couldn't pack, could I? That would have undermined the messing with my mum."

Jack and Madeleine nodded, seeing her point.

"It was a cry for help," Jack suggested.

"No, you tosser, if I'd wanted help I'd have asked for it."

They looked in through the bakery window, watching customers' mouths move and hands point, while the people behind the counter shifted around one another, held tongs over cakes, hovered, selected, packed paper bags.

"Well," said Jack. "Let's get you out of Norwich."

"Nothing wrong with Norwich," Belle said. She held up the brochure. "It's loaded with medieval charm. The Norwich Cathedral boasts the second-tallest spire in England, which I admit I'm a bit bothered by. I mean, if it had the *tallest* spire, all right, go ahead and boast. But second. Not sure boasting's called for."

"You've been reading tourist literature," Jack said, impressed.

"Been waiting here awhile. I thought his lunch break was twelve but it's one. The most impressive thing about Norwich, though, as I see it, is they've got a museum of mustard."

"You haven't lived," Madeleine agreed, "until you've seen a mustard museum."

"And there's the Cow Tower," Belle added.

"What's a cow tower?" Jack asked.

"No idea. Sounds brilliant, though, doesn't it. Cow Tower."

"It does."

"It got three out of five stars on TripAdvisor. As a tourist destination. The Cow Tower."

There was a thoughtful pause.

"That's not that good actually," Madeleine said.

Belle nodded. "No. Might give it a miss."

Another silence.

"Come on, then," Belle said. She stepped into the crowd of pedestrians.

"Don't you want to tell the baker you're leaving?" Jack called.

Belle turned back, and considered the question.

"Better to stay mysterious," she decided. "It'll keep what's-his-name interested."

"Have you forgotten his name?" Madeleine asked.

"Not a good sign, is it?" Belle agreed.

She started off again.

Jack and Madeleine looked at each other.

"I think I should call my mum and let her know Belle's okay," Madeleine said. "She was worried. Can I borrow your phone?"

Jack handed his phone to Madeleine.

They walked slowly into the crowd, keeping Belle in sight ahead of them.

Belle's shoulders were back, her head was high and she moved quickly. People walked towards her and away from her. A man in a business suit peeled a banana. They watched Belle see this, and look away again. A woman reached into her handbag, rummaged around, and spilled tissues to the ground. Again, they watched as Belle glanced down at the tissues and then carried on.

Madeleine held the phone in her hand, but didn't use it.

Belle was striding, her head turning this way and that, and then she was crumpling. It was so smooth a transition from striding to falling that it didn't register with Madeleine and Jack at first. They were walking and they were watching Belle as she folded quietly downward. People glanced towards her and away. People stepped around her. A man turned to look, his spectacles catching the sun. Belle's hands flew up and around her head, but the rest of her collapsed to the ground.

5.

Elliot fell with such speed that the fall became its own force, became everything: his scream, the chopper roar, the brutal wind, his flailing arms, this blackness, that jagged streak —

Then his feet hit the ground at a run.

He skidded, nearly colliding with a bald man in jeans and a red sweater.

"Where'd you come from?" said the man.

Elliot looked up. The sky was placid and dim blue.

There was a faint sun.

No cliff edge. No ravine. No woods. No choppers.

He looked around. He was at a gas station, only not a familiar chain. This one was done up in greens and golds, and called itself *BP*. Under the *BP* there was the word *Shop* with a swirl as if the "shop" wanted to run somewhere. Beneath that, in red, *Off-Licence*, and under *that*, emphatic with diagonal blue stripes, *BP Ultimate*.

Cars moved or stood about. They had a small, busy look to them, the cars, and neat little black-and-white licence plates. A handful of people also moved about and they had a neat, busy look to them too. Their eyes were all on their own thoughts, rather than on other people.

The man in the jeans carried on walking. He stopped at a car just beyond Elliot, and fumbled with keys. He had a newspaper pressed under one arm and a can in the other hand.

Elliot tried to read the newspaper sideways.

Daily Mail, it said, in an elaborate print that made Elliot think of Olde Quainte. But they didn't have cars in Olde Quainte. Didn't have cans of drink like that either. This one was green and said *7UP*.

"Excuse me," Elliot said to the man. "What province am I in?"

"Province?" The man squinted.

Elliot paused.

"I'm not in Cello anymore, am I?" he said.

"Kansas." The man chuckled. "Not in Kansas. That's what you meant to say, yeah?" He looked at Elliot, suddenly intent and wary.

Elliot tried again. "What — Kingdom am I in?"

Now the man nodded sharply. "The United Kingdom of England, Scotland, Wales, and Northern Ireland, or whichever bits haven't absconded on us yet. Ha-ha." He pressed his car keys and there was a *beep* sound.

"England," Elliot repeated. "Are you saying I'm in the *World*?"

"Now there's a question." The man laughed again, but looked a little annoyed at the same time. He climbed into the car and slammed the door.

6.

They pushed through the crowds to Belle, and crouched beside her.

"I'm okay," she murmured into the path. "Just. Couldn't seem to stay upright anymore."

"That's all right," Jack said. "We'll carry you."

Belle laughed, but stayed where she was.

"You will not," she said.

"Of course we will," said Madeleine. "What do you think we're doing here in Norwich?"

"Here," said Jack. "You take her legs, I'll get the top bit."

"I don't come in bits," Belle said to the path.

PART 15

Maximillian Reisman should be feeling cheerful.

He is walking to Schwartz's for a smoked meat sandwich with fries, coleslaw, and pickles. This is his Friday treat. Celebrating the impending arrival of the weekend and so on.

But he can feel himself scowling at other pedestrians, especially at people who walk slowly, or stop to pick up something they've dropped. He glowers at anyone who laughs with friends, or who smiles at some secret thought.

The buzzer had woken him early the day before: a courier with an overnight letter from the UK. Those "kingdom-of-cello" people again. This time they were instructing him to be at the corner of St-Catherine and St-Denis on Saturday at 2 P.M., ready for his "transfer" home. He was to pack a small overnight bag, bringing any personal possessions he didn't want left behind "in the World."

In addition, they suggested he start "preparing himself" for his role as "Candlemaker" at the "Namesaking Ceremony" in Aldhibah, as he'd have to travel there as soon as the "transfer" was complete. It might even be a good idea to write a draft of his speech now, although, of course, his speech writers were working on it around the clock.

Of course they were. His speech writers.

There was also a P.S., scrawled in blue ink.

P.S. Listen, if you're still not sure that you're really from the Kingdom of Cello, you should squeeze some lemon juice onto your inner elbow. If you see something unexpected, you'll know it's true.

The whole thing has stopped being funny. It stopped when they referred to his wife's singing. It's not an advertising campaign after all: It's somebody who knows him, and his wife's beautiful voice, and possibly knows how much he, Maximillian, regrets the fight he had with her the night he left. Maybe even knows that he gets migraines almost every night now, thinking of the cruel things they both said in that fight, remembering the kinder, sweeter, comical things they'd said in all their years together — not to mention the memories of their children.

Maximillian assumes it's a former band member who has finally fried his or her brains. Drugs. But did the frying have to take on this bizarre "kingdom" angle?

Across the road, a boy with dreadlocks is leaning on the railing of a balcony, smoking a cigarette. The boy's pants are splattered with white paint.

As Maximillian watches, the boy stubs out the cigarette, grabs a broom and begins sweeping the balcony: fast and furious, *clang! clang!* against the rails.

That's exactly how it feels inside Maximillian's chest.

This is the first time Sasha Wilczek has seen a doctor since she arrived in Taipei, Taiwan.

She takes painkillers for her rheumatoid arthritis, and otherwise never gets sick. She can't afford to.

But today she is frightened. She can't find a single reference to anything like this on the net. People have itchy inner elbows, and they get hives there. They have purple rashes on their inner elbows, and they ache there after doing chin-ups — but, as much as Sasha searches, *nobody* has a spray of multi-coloured specks.

She's in the waiting room, staring at the colours. The doctor might laugh and say it's nothing. Or he might tell her she needs an X-ray, or a CT scan, which she won't be able to afford. Or he might know immediately that this is a form of jaundice, and her liver's shot to hell.

Or — and this is the most likely — he'll say that is something that her gang leader ex-husband injected into her bloodstream while she slept, just before she left, just after their fight, and it is, in fact, a tracking device. He's using it as she sits in this empty waiting room, tracking her down wherever she is in the world.

Those letters she's been getting about the "kingdom-of-cello" — they must be gang-related. She hadn't thought of that possibility because they'd always had English stamps and postmarks. And since they sounded more like a children's book than gangster talk, to be honest.

But now she sees that this is the gang's way of telling her they're on their way. They're everywhere. They know where she is.

She should maybe go to the police instead of the doctor, but she needs a diagnosis.

It's fading.

That's all right. She's brought along some sliced wedges of lemon in a little plastic bag. She'll squeeze some more while the doctor watches.

Monty Rickard and his buddies are all squeezing lemon juice onto their inner elbows. They've taken Interstate 84 west to Nampa so they can eat burgers at Starvin Marvin's Blue Sky Café, and celebrate the fact that Monty has a rainbow of colours in both his inner elbows that only shows up under lemon juice.

Nobody else has the same thing.

They all swear they have nothing to do with the letters he's been getting from the UK, nor with the latest, which came by courier, nor with the trick his elbows can do. Also, they're all planning to come along to the meeting place on Sunday, so they can see what happens when he gets "transferred" to the Kingdom of Cello. They want to get transferred to Cello too, they say.

He doesn't believe them for a moment, but he's having a blast.

In Berlin, Ariel Peters is doing tequila slammers, only instead of sucking the lemon, she's squeezing it onto her inner elbow. Each time she does this, and sees the beautiful colours, she has a searing, magical sense that she is going home. That her entire confusing life is about to make sense.

At Avoca Beach, there's a storm rattling the doors and the windows. At the same time, the upstairs shower has started leaking, and the clattering of water in the bathroom seems to be conversing with the rain splatters against the windows.

Prince Tippett has already packed a plastic bag. He's taken a few of his favourite DVDs from the living room, his driftwood collection, and the chart of local frog species that he took from an old science magazine. That's it. Everything else belongs to the owners of his holiday house. The whole time he's been here, the house had only been used by three different groups of vacationers, each for a weekend at a time.

He slept on the beach at that time, until they packed up and drove away. As far as he could tell nobody seemed to notice he'd been living there and eating all the tinned and frozen food. He supplemented these by swiping leftover fish and chips from tables outside the takeaway.

Cleaners arrived the day after each of the vacation groups left. The first time it happened he had to hide in the pantry while they mopped and vacuumed.

He doesn't need to do the lemon juice trick. He knows exactly who he is, and where he's going at 3 P.M. tomorrow afternoon. He'd been thinking he was a runaway named Finn Mackenzie — and even finds himself slipping back into that idea sometimes. But he just needs to hold the piece of blanket, and Finn fades into what he is: a story he invented, a movie in his mind.

He is Prince Tippett of the Kingdom of Cello, and he's sitting at the kitchen table now, plastic bag on the floor beside him, watching the clock.

PART 16

The Royal Youth Alliance posed for photographs in the Reception Room of the White Palace. They drank glasses of GC teakwater and ate crackers with cheese or smoked oysters.

Then the Princess stood on the raised platform, and confirmed the rumors that their missing member, Elliot Baranski, was either dead, or presumed dead.

She could never remember which was which, she said, and added that he had perished, or presumably perished, again she could never — the reporters shook their heads as they scribbled notes — while being pursued by the WSU, because, it *turned out* — and this news, she explained, sent the Princess's head into a spin faster than a roulette wheel, but a *bigger* sort of spin, so maybe a spin like a *Big Wheel*, except that those things spun fairly *slowly*, which would *not* be representative of how her head — anyhow, the Princess shivered, and confirmed that Elliot Baranski had, it seemed, been communicating with the World.

Which, quite obviously, if she or anyone in the Palace or the royal family had *known*, well, there was no *way* he would have been on the Royal Youth Alliance! Are you kidding?! No, sir. So, it was maybe better that he was dead now, so he wouldn't have to be thrown off the RYA in disgrace, but sad, and that.

"However!" The Princess swung her lips upward, into a beam. "Let's not let a sad and that situation turn a starspin to a slug! Because that's what today is! A starspin! Because guess what, the whole gang — well, what's left of the gang — is about to embark on a *tour* of the total Kingdom! Well, a lot of the Kingdom! Because *that* is what Alliances are all *about*! Travel, right? And getting to know the *people* and that. So, applause all around is what I'm thinking! After which, we'll need to get cracking with our packing!"

There was applause, a few more smoked oysters, then they fared the reporters well, and withdrew to their rooms to get cracking with the packing.

"We have ten minutes to get to my little brother's room and open the crack," the Princess said as they strode along the corridors together.

Sergio appeared around a corner, and joined them. His eyes were bloodshot.

"It is not true," he said. "Is it true? Is Elliot dead?"

"From what I hear," said the Princess, walking faster. "He fell off a cliff while the WSU were chasing him. They haven't recovered his body yet — they're bringing in special equipment. It's a steep, narrow ravine he fell into, too rugged for the choppers to get down. They need abseilers. Mountain climbers. I don't know. But he did fall. And he could not have survived. So yes. He's dead."

Samuel staggered a little.

"Hurry up," said the Princess. She glanced back at Samuel. "What's wrong with your skin? It's flaking off in pieces. You look like crap."

"As to a —" began Samuel, his voice hoarse. "I cannot say that I am altogether in the greatest of health, your highness. But this news of Elliot, it —"

"Well, get sick later."

"There was nothing you could do?" Sergio said, his voice breaking. "My warning came too late?"

"Have you got the detector?" Princess Ko demanded, looking back at him, but then she slammed into Keira, who had stopped still in front of her.

"You're telling me," Keira began, "you're saying you *knew* the WSU were coming for Elliot, and you did *nothing* about it?"

"Keep *walking*," cried the Princess, stepping around Keira. "Of course I did nothing. The monarchy has no authority over the WSU. It's a separation of power thing." She had reached Prince Tippett's room, and stopped by the closed door. "You think I *wanted* Elliot to die? He hadn't even told me how to open up a crack yet!"

Keira was a few steps behind.

"He told *me* how," she said, staring at the Princess. "You need a mirror and a light."

"Well, that's something."

"You are unimaginable," said Keira.

The Princess threw open the door.

"It's something," she repeated, "but it's also nothing, unless Sergio has the detector." She ushered the others into the room, and they were quiet for a moment. The room was exactly the same. Clothes and toys on the floor, racing car track on rumpled bed, frogs of all shapes and sizes.

The Princess spun around and spoke to Sergio.

"You haven't answered me, Sergio," she said. "You *must* have the detector. Your hands are empty, I see, but you *must* have it somewhere."

"As to a . . ." murmured Samuel. "Of course he hasn't got the detector, Princess. Might I lie down somewhere? I feel as faint as a . . ."

"My princess," said Sergio sadly. "Ko, I am very sorry. I cannot tell you . . ."

"There it is," said Keira.

Her hand was raised.

"Just next to the chest of drawers there — just to the right of the TV screen. Can nobody else see that?"

They all looked to where she was pointing.

"See what?"

"It's so obvious I just can't believe you can't — but it must be the crack." Keira stepped over the toys. "It's like a thin line of brightness in the air, but it's been tangled up somehow. I guess that's how they seal it. But I can unknot it easily now I can see it. I just —" She reached up, and they watched her hands moving about oddly, her fingers twisting and turning, tracing patterns in the air. "I don't understand why I couldn't see it last time we were in this room. It's perfectly clear."

"Are you serious?" whispered Samuel. "You are unknotting a crack — unsealing a crack — as we speak?"

"It's weird," said Keira. Her voice was excited, her anger gone. "I can see it but I can't feel a thing. But it's coming — I can see the knots coming loose. I'll be done in a minute."

"Then we need a mirror and a light," breathed the Princess.

Sergio picked up a night-light. It was shaped like a bullfrog.

"It's battery-powered," he said.

"Someone catch Samuel," Ko said, unhooking a small mirror from the wall. It was framed in blue with white ceramic stars and moon. "He's about to faint."

Samuel swayed back and forth. The others took no notice; they were gathering around Ko.

"Done," said Keira, dropping her hands from the air. "I'll point to exactly where it is. Keep ahold of that mirror and night-light. You might need them to get yourself back through."

"Will it work?" Samuel breathed.

"How will she see the crack to get back through in this direction?" Sergio asked.

Samuel leaned up against the wall, and then slipped toward the floor.

"Excuse me," he murmured, crawling toward the door.

The Princess adjusted the mirror and angled the light.

There was a long pause, minutes passed, then there was a thud, the air itself seemed to tumble, and Princess Ko tumbled with it.

She was gone.

In her place was a kind of empty space of panic: a smearing of glassy streaks and smudges in the air, as if unseen fingers were frantically splashing dirty water at window panes.

Seconds later, there was a showering displacement, and the Princess stepped toward them.

She was grasping the hand of a small, dark-haired boy. He had a plastic bag pressed beneath his arm. He gazed around, solemn and frowning, with large, dark, critical eyes, then breathed a small sigh and smiled.

PART 17

1.

It turned out that Elliot was at a BP petrol station just outside of Harrogate in Yorkshire, England. Cambridge, he was told, was a three-and-a-half hour drive south down the A1 and the A1(M).

Elliot thanked the people who gave him this information and set off to walk to Cambridge. He had no car. He had a handful of Jimmy's cash but doubted this was legal tender in the World.

As he walked, he tried to figure out what had happened. There must have been a crack in the air above the ravine, he decided. He must have "stumbled" through it — he remembered Samuel mentioning that people sometimes "stumbled" through a crack without using any technique.

Seemed impossible, but he accepted it like a fine, fine line of truth from here to home.

Another thing that seemed impossible was the translation effect. He was supposed to lose his memory now? Translate himself and his past into Worldian?

How could he be anybody other than Elliot Baranski?

That's who he'd been all his life.

But Samuel had insisted it affected everyone, sometimes right away — and Samuel had been right about "stumbling" — so he had to take it seriously.

If he did translate himself, he'd be lost here forever.

I am Elliot Baranski of Bonfire, the Farms, he said, taking one step after another along the grassy bank that lined this part of the highway. *And that's the truth.* Trouble was, another truth kept clawing at the inside of his skin.

All this time he's been dead —

He set that aside with that logic he'd been using: *If he's dead, that's no different to his being gone, so what's the difference? Who cares? Don't even THINK about it.* And when something seemed to buckle inside him at that, he'd say to himself: *Don't think: Just get to Madeleine.*

Madeleine had held his hands in the darkness and she'd spoken in that voice of hers. *It's going to be okay*, she'd said, *your dad is coming back.*

She'd promised. All he had to do was get to her.

* * *

It didn't take long to realise that walking the A1 was not going to be possible. It was a huge, dual carriageway, without any sidewalk. He'd walk through the adjacent fields but kept hitting hedgerows and ditches and barbed-wire fences. He was going to need to find some kind of cross-country route. He'd ask at the next town.

From this point on, his journey to Cambridge became complicated. Strangers in shops had conflicting advice, although everybody agreed that walking to Cambridge was preposterous. An old man with a collie sketched a map of England for him on the back of an old paper bag, but it turned out he was only doing it to point out exactly *how* preposterous it was, to try to walk that distance.

A friendly middle-aged couple bought him a sandwich, while the man told him to take the "Roman roads" ("straight as an arrow') or to follow the canals ("get yourself a bike and you'll whistle along the towpaths") and the woman said that he was such a handsome lad he ought to go on home to his mum at once, and here, why didn't he borrow her mobile phone and give his mum a call?

Eventually, an efficient woman in a business suit turned from her plate of lettuce and croutons, and instructed him to go to the local library.

"Look up the 1 to 50,000 maps," she said. "They've got pink covers. There'll be a wall of them just inside the door. On the back of each, there's a map of the UK with a grid that'll show you which ones you'll need. They'll show you walking routes."

This turned out to be true, although it also turned out that he was going to need about thirty of the maps to cover the route.

He stole a handful, and set off.

England, he couldn't figure out. Sometimes it seemed exactly like home — farmhouses, barns, cows low in the valleys and sheep on the hills, double-decker cattle trucks lowering their ramps — but next thing you knew he'd arrive at a village that was straight out of Olde

Quainte. Pubs with thatched roofs and names like the Red Lion or the White Hart; wooden signs with coats of arms; red postboxes; duck ponds with reeds.

Except that the villages all seemed to have been invaded by Jagged-Edgian technology and Golden Coast billboards and set into rolling-hill landscapes that were borrowed from Nature Strip.

It was wet, boggy, and blustery. Sometimes he'd find himself lost in low clouds, or slipping on scree. For a while the buildings were made of a light, sandy limestone, but then there was a grim patch of dark, gravelly material, in a region that reminded him of the northern industrial part of the Farms.

He stole something called a Jaffa Cake from a little shop in one town, and a wrapped chocolate called a Mars bar from a giant supermarket called Sainsbury's. Later, he stole a chicken leg wrapped in plastic, and an apple, from a place called Marks and Spencer. In the early mornings, he borrowed milk and bread from deliveries outside cafés; and in bigger towns, he found "food courts" where people abandoned trays of barely touched pastas, or pastries wrapped around meat.

Farther south, there were orchards, and he stole fruit.

He slept by the side of the road or in barns, only it was more half-wake dreaming than sleeping. Once, he dreamed that darkness was tendrilling towards him, getting knotted in his hair, tugging on him. He woke himself, then right away fell into the dream of a great, gusting wind. He knew he had to tether himself — his essence, his soul, the Elliot Baranski of him — to a post or the branch of a tree, but he felt too weary to do so.

At other times, he dreamed a charcoal darkness, fingers pressing into the darkness then hovering over his body, ready to plunge down on him, press that darkness deep into his flesh, his bones, his organs, his heart.

Once, he woke from this dream in such a panic he forgot how to breathe.

Then a pair of memories came to him, side by side. One was the memory of Keira, telling him how she'd thrown her mother's necklace into a snowbank; the other was Madeleine's tale of going out into the street to search for her mother's lost ring.

Strange, he hadn't connected the stories before, but now the contrast soothed him. Keira discarded; Madeleine saved.

And here he was, on his way to Madeleine.

He carried on with his journey and the cracks kept opening — *your father is dead* — he could feel them forming all over his body. But he kept on patching them up, sealing them, rolling out pastry dough, and smoothing it again, running his palms over his face, keeping himself in place.

I am Elliot Baranski of Bonfire, the Farms, Kingdom of Cello.

2.

Behind Madeleine's closed eyes, she saw Belle falling.

That crowd of people, the hurry in their footsteps and their eyes, and Belle was falling. It was the opposite of everything. A decision to stop being. Falling as a way of choosing not to stand.

Or maybe it was the opposite of deciding? Gravity wants us to fall, so every moment we *don't* fall is a choice to defy gravity.

A clattering sound opened her eyes.

She was sitting on a couch. Belle was tipping corn chips into a bowl, and Jack was on the floor across the room, hooking up his iPod to the stereo.

They were in the baker's flat. Belle hadn't wanted to go home yet, and the various parents, and Jack's grandfather, had agreed they could stay a couple of days — although they'd wondered about things like the state of their education, and how the baker felt about three houseguests.

The baker had turned out to be friendly, distracted, and sleepy. He'd offered them the living room floor for as long as they wanted, then headed to bed himself. His flatmates were brooding and scrawny. They'd looked a bit dark about houseguests in their living room, then headed down the pub.

The living room was almost empty except for the couch, a coffee table, and the stereo, which sat on a plank of wood, held up by a couple of bricks. A piece of red tinsel was tacked to the wall, and fell across the window, which looked over a busy street.

The Only Place For Eyelash Extensions in Norwich! exclaimed a neon sign across the road.

Something soft started up on the stereo: acoustic guitar and wandering vocals, and Jack landed on the couch beside them and took a corn chip.

"Do they mean they're, like, *the* place to get eyelash extensions?" said Madeleine. "Or the only place. Like, literally, nobody else extends your eyelashes."

"That's exactly what I was just thinking," Belle said.

They leaned back, the three of them in a row, staring at the sign.

"I think what happened was," Belle said, then stopped.

The others waited.

There was a long silence, and eventually they turned to Belle. She seemed lost in thought.

"What?" Jack prompted.

"What?" repeated Belle.

"What happened was?"

"Oh, right. Well, it's like this. There are a lot of cruddy auras around, see? A lot of muddy, cracked, ruptured auras; a lot of worn, feeble, wounded auras; a lot of auras just *crammed* with rubbish. And each time I see one of these, it's like it gets *loaded* on top of my own aura. So mine gets too heavy to carry. So I have to lie down in the street."

Madeleine and Jack waited.

"Or maybe not," Belle reflected. "That could be bollocks. I mean I don't physically go around picking up other people's auras. This is like metaphor talking. And as it's the first time I've ever had to lie down in the street, I'm just speculating."

The music played. Jack put his feet up on the coffee table, and the girls did the same. They lay back against the couch.

Belle shrugged. "It is what it is."

"Ah." Now Jack sounded miffed. "Don't start with that pseudo-Buddhist tosh. *It is what it is.* That's just more *close your eyes and trust the force.* Works very nicely for the establishment, I'm sure, cause everyone's sitting around meditating instead of starting a revolution. Also works nicely for people like your mum who do crap jobs of being a mum. They never have to fix that or say sorry, they can just go, *It is what it is. What will be will be.* Bollocks."

Madeleine brushed corn chip crumbs from her lap.

"Isn't that the opposite of astrology?" she said to Jack. "Don't the stars say what will be? So how can you change that?"

"Of course you can change what's in the stars," Jack said promptly.

Belle and Madeleine looked at each other across Jack.

"That," Belle said, "is totally inconsistent with your whole world view."

"No, it's not," Jack said easily. "You're forgetting how time happens all at once. So if you change things, you change the stars retrospectively. I've explained this to you both on multiple occasions."

Belle considered this. "I might stop listening sometimes," she admitted.

"Me too," Madeleine agreed. "You've gotta take a break from Jack sometimes."

There was another pause. Jack sighed philosophically.

They leaned back on the couch and closed their eyes, all of them watching the image of Belle falling.

"I'm thinking," Madeleine said, "if you've got all that extra junk in your aura, Belle, you should give some of it to us. Kind of like, share your aura with us."

"So we can air it out for you," Jack said, somewhere towards sleep.

"Profound," murmured Belle. "You think my aura's a cupboard." She yawned and spoke into the downside of the yawn: "Very nice of you both, thanks, but that's okay. I don't want your help. No offence."

There was a long quiet.

Their eyes were closed.

"Are you in love with the baker?" Madeleine said.

"Seems unlikely," Jack put in. "She can't even remember his name."

"But she accepted the sugar mouse from him," said Madeleine.

"Well," Jack began, ready to argue.

"She's not in love with him," Madeleine said, almost talking in her sleep, her words slipping away from her as she spoke. "The sugar mouse was a message to us. So we'd know where to come and get her. She's lying when she says she doesn't want our help."

Jack chuckled sleepily.

Belle was silent.

The music drifted across them. Their heads tilted towards one another, a slowing in their breathing.

"This music," Madeleine said, "is not a lie."

"That's the truth," mumbled Belle.

"The main thing is not to — *don't* just close your eyes — and let yourself —" Jack's words fell, then he started again. "Except now," he said. "Now you can."

They slept, and the music played on behind their quiet.

PART 18

The Royal Youth Alliance had half an hour to get from the White Palace to the airfield, but Princess Ko did not want to leave.

Her little brother had curled himself into her for the first few minutes, winding his arms tightly around her neck. Then he had sprung away and flown around the room, picking up toys, frogs, games, switching on the TV, switching it off again, turning over his pillows, until a thought had filled his eyes, and the Princess had handed over his blankie. He had exclaimed, buried his face in it, danced with it, then looked up and realized he was in a roomful of strange teenagers, and he'd dropped it casually to the floor and kicked it aside.

The security guards had been summoned, along with the Prince's nanny, who lost her voice in her hysteria, and the room had been filled with questions from all directions, about his abduction, and the year he'd spent in the World. He'd ignored all questions and asked his own, specifically about various pets, Palace foods, and then his other sister, Jupiter, his brother, Chyba, and his mother and his father.

"They're all in the World," Princess Ko explained, "but we're getting them back today and tomorrow."

"Starting with King Cetus," Agent Ramsay reminded her. "Princess, we need to leave at once to make the flight to Ducale."

"Where's Samuel?" someone asked as Samuel crawled back into the room.

"What's wrong with him?"

"As to a strong coffee," mumbled Samuel.

"There might be delays," Agent Nettles said. "Word is, there's a spate of Color attacks across the province."

"Across the *Kingdom*," Agent Ramsay corrected. "And some have mutated, apparently: sharper version of themselves. Shutters are still working but the protective clothes are useless now. Not strong enough."

"Colors," smiled Prince Tippett, his dark eyes lighting up. "I remember Colors!"

"Welcome home, kid," said Keira, sounding wry.

Then the members of the RYA were running down corridors and leaping aboard the sleigh.

The sleigh spun to a stop just short of the airfield. Warning bells filled the air.

"That's a sixth-level Orange," shouted the driver, pulling on levers so that shutters flew up, enclosing them in darkness.

Almost at once, the Orange pinged and clanged against the shutters like raining pebbles or a hailstorm.

The Princess looked at her watch.

"Is the plane on the runway?" she shouted, above the noise.

"Yes."

"And the pilot's aboard, ready to go?"

"Should be."

Outside, the Orange intensified, and they all instinctively flinched, hunching forward.

The Princess looked at her watch again.

"We need to risk this," she yelled.

"Oh, Princess!" yelped Samuel. "A sixth-level Orange? Isn't that an Excoriating Orange?"

"No, Excoriating is seventh-level. This is just Slashing. Won't kill us. Might hurt a bit."

"A lot," corrected Agent Ramsay. "But she's right. If we don't go now, we miss our chance. Open the shutters."

The driver chuckled. "You haven't even got your protective gear on," he said.

"I command you to open the shutters," the Princess shouted. "Gear won't help if it's sharpened anyway. We'll just run. Be ready," she told the others.

The driver looked at her, amazed, then shrugged and pulled another lever.

The shutters swung back.

At once, the sky crashed down on them, tiny pellets of Orange, sharp as razors, slicing at their faces, striking their shoulders, arms, coats, gloves, legs.

They stumbled from the sleigh, and ran, slipping, dropping their bags, and fumbling their way to the fixed wing.

The pilot threw open the door, dragged them inside, and slammed the shutters closed again.

"You're mad," he said.

"You can fly in this?" the Princess said. She pulled off her gloves and touched her face, then glanced, surprised, at the blood smears on her hands.

"Shutters on fixed wings are transparent," the pilot said. "So I can. But I still think you're mad."

The Princess looked at him.

"With respect," he added.

The flight was almost silent, except for the sounds of scissors cutting bandages, the lid of the first aid box opening and closing, disinfectant being poured into basins.

Samuel's right eyelid had been cut open; there was a fine line of blood from Keira's chin to her collarbone. The agents dabbed cloths at each other's cheeks and noses. Mostly, the Oranges had not penetrated their clothes, only ripping the material here and there, and bruising the flesh, but Sergio's jeans were threadbare, and his legs were crisscrossed with nicks.

The pilot turned back and called to them: "There are reports of Color attacks everywhere. Charcoal Gray covering Brighton. Lemon Yellow in Northbridge. I need to detour around Melphintown. Okay?"

"Whatever," the Princess said, pressing her palm hard against the wound on her cheek. "Just get us there."

Twenty minutes later, the pilot called again.

"We can land at Ducale," he said. "But you won't be able to disembark. They've got a Magenta."

The fixed wing circled a few times, then lined up to land.

Samuel moaned. He had reclined his chair to almost horizontal, and was lying back, his hands over his face.

"You have to put your seat up when we land," the Princess snapped.

Samuel ignored her.

The fixed wing bumped and thudded onto the runway.

There was another silence. The window glass seemed to have a deep pink coating.

"The Magenta," Agent Nettles said, amazed. "It's everywhere."

Abruptly, the Princess unbuckled herself and stood.

"We need to go," she said.

Both agents unbuckled too.

"We survived the Orange," Agent Ramsay said. "We can cope with this."

Everybody stood, and there was a slow staggering down the aisle. Samuel stumbled, fell against a seat, then dragged himself upright again.

"Seriously," complained the Princess. "What's *wrong* with you, Samuel?"

Blood leaked from underneath the bandage on the Princess's cheek.

"You need to get that stitched up," Keira said. "And, Princess?"

"Open the door," the Princess commanded.

"You're out of your mind," the pilot replied. "With respect."

"Princess?" Keira repeated. "Listen. All the letters that you've written to your father in the World: Has he answered a single one?"

The Princess ignored her, fixing her glower on the pilot.

"He hasn't, has he?" she persisted. "You think maybe Samuel might be right? That your dad has forgotten who he is, and letters won't make a difference? In which case, he won't *be* at the crossover point? So this is all for nothing."

"I think Samuel *is* right on this one," Samuel murmured faintly.

The two agents pushed to the front, and turned to address the group.

"A Magenta will give you the mother of all headaches," Agent Nettles said. "If flecks get in your eyes, they stay for good: chronic headache and permanently bloodshot eyes. In other words, a permanent hangover. So if anyone prefers to stay here, do." Her gaze drifted over the group. "But we need you, Keira. To see the crack and unseal it." She touched the pilot's shoulder. "Open the door."

The pilot sighed, leaned across, and rested his hand on the door. "Welcome to Ducale. Enjoy your stay. Kindly disembark *at lightning speed*!" Then he threw it open, bellowing, "Go! Go! Go!" before slamming it behind them.

They stopped on the runway, and stood in a huddled group.

It was empty and silent. The Magenta misted damply around them.

It seemed harmless enough.

Nearby the aerodrome hummed behind its shutters.

"Run," Agent Nettles ordered.

They jogged around abandoned luggage trolleys, past empty trucks, past the side of the aerodrome building to the street, where they slowed and stopped.

The street was silent too. Empty cars stood about at odd angles. A half-open suitcase lay on the sidewalk. An ice cream melted in the gutter.

"They didn't have much warning of this one," Agent Ramsay observed.

The Magenta's deep pink haze gave everything a dreamy prettiness. Its touch against their skin was light and soothing.

"How do we get to the Sandringham Convention Center?" Princess Ko asked. "I guess the limousine's not coming. Should we just borrow a car? I think —"

The headache got them all at once. It was like being kicked

repeatedly in the forehead, while fists beat at the insides of their skulls, trying to shove out their eyeballs.

It was like discordant, high-pitched feedback from a microphone while cigarette lighters set flash fires in their brains.

"We need to go," Keira moaned. "I'll hot-wire a car. Get up, Samuel."

Samuel was on his hands and knees, swinging his head wildly like a dog under a hose.

"I can't," he cried, hysterical. "I'm going to throw up in this mud."

"Come on!" Princess Ko staggered toward an abandoned car. "If we stay any longer — mud? What mud?"

They looked down, squinting through the pain, which intensified now in their confusion. The ground beneath them was a rich red-brown — polished like wet mud, but dry and hard. This substance ran across the pavement and curled up the side of the aerodrome building. In the other direction, it covered the street and opposite pavement, running up the sides of shops there. About a block away, they could see where the edges met regular asphalt.

"That wasn't there a moment ago," Sergio said, mystified.

"Why would they have *mud* here?"

"This isn't mud," Keira said abruptly. "It's a Clay Brown. We're standing on a Clay Brown. In less than five minutes we'll all be dead." She laughed aloud.

PART 19

Maximillian Reisman is having an existential crisis.

His apartment is crowded with friends. It's a warm fall afternoon. There's a plate of crackers on the table, spilling at the edges, alongside a tapenade and a smoked-trout dip. There are glasses and bottles on every surface. Music is playing. Conversation and laughter are swaying.

He opens a window and wonders what he's doing here.

His existential crisis has narrow boundaries: Specifically, he's wondering why he's here in Montreal.

Why did he leave his band, his wife, his children, his life in Europe?

Two daughters. Two sons. What was he thinking?

He looks at his watch. It's ten to two. At two, he's supposed to be at the corner of St-Catherine and St-Denis for the "crossover." For a moment, in the night, he'd considered going there. To confront whoever was behind this, and give them a taste of his right hook. But when he woke this morning, he remembered that he didn't really have a right hook. He'd never punched a person in his life. He'd always got along with people. He liked people. He liked to chat with them and have a drink.

So he'd invited the office over for drinks instead.

He tips back his whisky.

Montreal is great. That's why he's here. He likes ice hockey. He likes *poutine*. He likes how Montrealers call convenience stores *deps* and blueberries *bluets*.

Down below, an SUV pulls up at the curb. A couple gets out and begins to argue, in English, about the parking signs. That's another thing he likes. The complicated parking rules in Montreal.

"You can't park there," he calls down now. "You'll get a ticket."

Nearby party guests step over to him at the window and look down too.

The couple squint up.

"You can't?"

Maximillian shakes his head.

The woman calls, "Thanks."

The man stares a moment, then turns away.

That's another thing he likes: the complicated reactions of strangers to his parking advice. Grateful, suspicious, resentful. They *want* to park here.

The party guests are talking, making jokes about parking and English speakers, and he smiles and nods, and drinks from his whisky.

He likes how the guys at the office call him Max instead of Maximillian. He laughs suddenly, and the people talking to him laugh too, thinking they've pleased him with their stories.

But he's laughing at the idea that he could squeeze lemon juice on his inner elbow and turn out to be somebody else.

That his memories of his past could be invention. It does your head in, thinking like that. Because how can you know for sure? You can't. His own memories, for example, are always getting tangled with dreams he's had about people or places. So they slip around, his memories. Change shape.

It's like those toy dispensers where you put in a coin and twist the handle, then the handle springs back and a toy comes out. Each time he tries to lean into a memory, it springs back like that handle.

But everybody has that, right?

His phone buzzes in his pocket.

He looks at it.

It's an email.

He gets an odd, excited feeling. This email. It could be *the answer.*

It's from Air Canada. Discount Flights to Halifax.

Nah, that's not the answer. He doesn't want to go to Halifax.

He tips back his whisky, but it's empty. He pours himself another.

His phone buzzes again. *The answer,* he thinks again, but less enthusiastically.

It's a phone call this time. That tech guy from the office. What is he doing inside Maximillian's phone? He should be at the party!

Maybe he forgot to invite him. Who knows with memories these days?

He shrugs, and answers.

"Hey," says the tech guy. "Remember that weird audio thing you gave me?"

The kingdom-of-cello again. He'd forgotten he gave the tape to the tech guy.

"Come to the party!" Maximillian says.

"What party? Anyhow, it's not a regular audiotape like you thought, but I figured out how to get sound off it anyway. It's a woman singing. You want me to play it to you now? I'm only saying cause I'm not sure I'll be able to get it to work again on Monday. The technology is super out-there weird."

Maximillian shrugs again.

"Okay."

There's a shuffling, some static, then the singing starts.

Maximillian listens. He keeps listening, pressing the sound so close it hurts his ear.

Then he disconnects the call. Puts the phone in his pocket.

Puts the whisky on the window ledge. Pushes up his shirt sleeve. Calls to his party guests, "First person to get me a lemon can have this apartment."

PART 20

At first, the Clay Brown was perfectly still, but then movements began to catch the corners of their eyes.

It was shifting beneath them like a deep, slow ocean. There was something almost tender in its billowing.

"I can't think through this headache." Agent Nettles gritted her teeth, hunched her shoulders. "Princess Ko, follow me. We'll get you off this thing. Ramsay?"

Agent Ramsay was bent forward, hands on his knees, eyes squeezed tight.

"You can't escape from a Clay Brown," Keira said.

"Follow me, Princess," Agent Nettles repeated, but the Princess's arms were wrapped around her head. She was rocking back and forth on the spot.

Agent Nettles slipped and slithered until she reached the edge of the Clay Brown where it crawled up the side of the building.

"Come on, Princess," she called. "We'll climb." Using her knees, elbows, and fingernails, she clambered up until her hands were touching the brickwork of the building. At once, she slid back down. She tried again. The same thing happened. Each time, the edges would tilt slightly, tipping her gently back.

"It plays with you, see," Keira called, then she pressed her hands into her hair, moving them around her scalp, her face crumpling with the pain.

Samuel lay flat on his stomach, now and then rolling from side to side and moaning.

Sergio wandered about, his eyes wild, tripping and falling as the Clay Brown surged beneath him like a theme park ride.

The edges rose higher. Agent Nettles continued clambering up the sides, and tipping back in. She screamed suddenly, and Keira laughed, then her laughter caught another flare of headache and turned into a wail.

The Princess dropped her arms from her head.

"The Magenta's getting worse," she said. She could hardly make out the others' faces through the mist, but their mouths, eyes, and noses were outlined now in dark pink. It was underneath her own fingernails and spotting her knuckles like a row of scabs.

She staggered along and nearly tripped over Samuel, who rolled over and saw her.

"Princess," he said. "I will always love you."

"We're not dead yet," she said, absentmindedly, but the Clay Brown was moving steadily. Its edges rising higher and tipping inward now. The billowing had increased too, like whales surfacing, or like a giant sleeping body moving underneath a blanket.

Sergio appeared beside her, his face creased with headache.

He took her hand.

"We will take a run at the edge," he said.

"It'll just tip us back in. Then it will start to crush us."

"I know."

He held her hand anyway, and started to move.

"Wait, wait," she said, pressing her fists to her eyes. "I can't see through this headache. I can't —"

Sergio waited, then she held his hand again.

She was crying openly.

The Clay Brown was rising like cake mix folding beneath beaters, forming mounds that lay down and then reformed.

They slipped toward the edge, passing Keira whose eyes were closed. She was deep inside her headache. Her cheeks were wet with tears.

The ground tipped and slid them about, its sides rising, wrapping slowly around them. As if someone were gathering the edges of a picnic blanket, and they were all the plates and utensils, sliding toward the middle.

Sergio had stopped. His face was twisted with pain.

"Come on," the Princess said.

She pulled at his hand. Sergio staggered two more steps, and then his steps moved upward and into the air.

He was just above her.

He was leaning sideways, his legs at an awkward angle, as if one of his dance twirls had gone wrong. He was hovering. He looked down at himself, and saw the air between his feet and the ground.

He frowned, scraped at the air with his free hand, scooping at it.

He rose a little higher.

He adjusted his grasp on Princess Ko's hand, and gave an experimental tug. Her feet lifted off the ground.

He scraped his way even higher, grinning, and Princess Ko followed.

Agent Nettles looked up.

"Holy crap," she said. "He's an Occasional Pilot."

Then she was stumbling toward them, grabbing Princess Ko's hand for herself, and waving at the others: "Join hands — join hands —" which they did, one at a time, until they were all lifting, rising, slow and steady, like a chain of paper dolls being dragged into the air.

They rose out of reach of the Clay Brown. They soared above the Magenta, breathing the sky, headaches blowing free, hands joined, Sergio riding the wind ahead, his eyes as bright as the buckles of a harness under sunlight.

PART 21

Maximillian Reisman approaches the intersection of St-Denis and St-Catherine in a taxi.

He's fifteen minutes late. There are better intersections in Montreal than this, he thinks. Those brown brick buildings, they might be part of the University of Quebec or Montreal or whatever it's called, but they're nondescript and hulking. The other corners are just shops.

JACOB, he can see, and a little green sign that says VUE. Glimpses of Hotel St-Denis in one direction, and that's a nice church. Chapelle Notre-Dame-de-Lourdes, he remembers. Otherwise, it's just your regular lampposts, bare trees, trash cans, bike stands.

NO PARKING signs, phone booths, and patches of unfinished roadwork: toppled barriers and witch's hats.

People walking. Cars driving.

His wife's voice sings in his mind. He's still carrying his whisky. It sloshes over the edges of the glass as he pays the cab fare, and opens the door.

He turns a slow circle. Which is the southwest corner? Does it matter? He's looking for familiar faces in the crowd, somebody come to get him and take him home. Usually, directions make sense to him, but his wife's voice is singing more and more persistently through the haze in his mind, so nothing else matters. The whisky sloshes again. He licks the spilled drops from his hand. He smiles at everybody.

Then there's a blink of blackness, a streak of something jagged, the glass falling, a smallish hand clutching his hand, fingernails cutting, and here he is, somewhere else.

How about that.

High ceilings. Carpet. Chairs. A crowd of strangers, mainly teenagers it seems, pressing in at him, their eyes wild, clothes disheveled.

They're a bit much.

He looks away from them and around.

It's a conference room.

The Sandringham Convention Center, he remembers.

Ducale. Golden Coast.

Memories shoot at him: ping, ping, ping. It's a pleasant kind of pinging. He grins and lets them keep on shooting.

"I'm the freakin' King of Cello!" he says.

"Indeed you are," says a grim-looking woman in a uniform of some kind — she's an agent. She's a *security agent.* She's talking fast to another agent beside her, a guy, also familiar: "The WSU have issued a press release," she's saying. "They give a list of places where major cracks have been reported. Local law enforcement are setting up barricades right now, the release says, and WSU officers are on their way. It's all the crossover points. Someone's leaked it to them. We won't be able to get the others through."

He ignores all this. He's waiting — it will come —

"Agent Nettles!"

She looks back at him.

"That's your name, right?"

"It is. Welcome home, sir."

Now he looks down at the figure beside him, the one still clutching his hand, with the fingernails.

It's Ko. His daughter. She returns his gaze.

She looks like hell. Dried blood and bandages streaking across her face, hair in knotted tatters, clothes torn and mud-splattered, eyes and face all lit up with that beautiful, self-important, self-conscious, knowing, cranky smile of hers. He lets go of her hand so he can lift her off the ground into a bear hug.

PART 22

By the time he walks into Cambridge, the soles of his feet feel like they're pressing into lava.

There's no room in his mind to look around. There's just that thin white line: *I am Elliot Baranski. Bonfire. Cello. Madeleine.*

He has to follow that line.

He gets glimpses in his peripheral vision. Bikes. Bells. Turrets. People eating cake. A clock eating time. A kid kicking a ball along the path. A man shouting at the kid: "Oy, this is not a park!" People glancing at Elliot as he passes them. He stinks, he realises vaguely. He's filthy. He's coated in stains.

He turns back to the thin white line.

Elliot Baranski. Cello. Madeleine.

It's getting thinner.

He remembers a story Madeleine once told him, about an astronomer who lost his nose in a duel. He had a new nose made out of gold and silver, Madeleine had said, and affixed to his face with glue.

Outside that thin white line it's just a dark space now.

He needs to glue new memories in, made of gold and silver.

Only how did that astronomer breathe through the gold? How did he smell?

Elliot. Madeleine.

He stops and someone brushes against him. He can't look up. He has to close his eyes and remember.

He knows her address here in Cambridge. She's told him.

The street name comes to him. He says, "Excuse me," to a passerby, and they ignore him. Do they speak a different language here? He tries again, twice more, until someone stops, and tells him how to get there.

He follows the directions.

He remembers the number of the house.

He remembers that Madeleine lives on the top floor.

There's a line of buttons down the side of the door.

4, 3, 2, 1.

He guesses 4 might be the top floor, and presses the button. There's a lightening at once. That's all he has to do. Press that button.

Now she'll come to him.

He waits.

There's a great, gaping silence.

He presses it again, hears the shrill, and again the shrill, and nothing.

She's not home.

He leans against the door, thunks his head gently on the wall.

Elliot.

He remembers she has a friend who lives downstairs. *The computer guy downstairs.*

Denny. Her friend's name is Denny. He'll ask Denny where Madeleine is.

Does downstairs mean one floor down, or all the way? Another memory comes to him: Denny hits his ceiling with a broom, Madeleine says, when he wants Holly and Madeleine to come down to him for a chat.

He presses the buzzer for 3.

He straightens. It occurs to him that the people in the street might have ignored him because he looks like a tramp. They probably thought he wanted money. This Denny guy might turn him away.

Block him from seeing Madeleine.

He runs his fingers through his hair.

He can hear footsteps from inside. Thudding footsteps, and a smaller pattering, a panting sound. A dog. There's a man and a dog coming downstairs.

The door opens.

A dog pours out, and just behind, a man with a wheeze, an unshaven chin, grey-specked hair.

The man catches his breath, lets the wheeze fade, looks at Elliot.

Elliot looks back.

There is a long moment of looking.

Then Elliot grins his crooked grin, his famous grin, his *Elliot Baranski* grin.

"I knew you weren't dead," he says, and loses the grin because all those cracks are splitting open, and from the sound that his father is making as he reaches for Elliot, lunges at Elliot, the same thing is happening to him.

PART 23

They stayed in Norwich for three nights and then came home.

On the train, Madeleine closed her eyes and fell into a daydream in which Belle's parents were waiting to welcome Belle at the station.

Belle's mother would be carrying a bunch of wild freesias (Belle's favourite flowers) and a golden mango (Belle's favourite fruit) — no, she'd have a straw basket. She'd have a basket over her arm, laden with flowers and mangoes, which she would have tracked down somewhere, even though neither was in season.

As the train pulled into the platform, Belle's mother would throw out her arms (being careful not to spill the basket), joyful tears spilling down her cheeks as she showered Belle with promises: that she would unburden Belle of her sadness; that she would clear away the clutter from her own aura so that Belle could see the glow of her love for her daughter; that she would never again laugh unless something was genuinely funny.

Then, Madeleine imagined, her own eyes would move farther along the platform, and there would be *her* father, her mother beside him, swinging a hat in one hand, holding his arm with her other. Both of them radiant to see each other and see her.

And Belle would glance over from her own tearful reunion and say, "Look at that. Your dad's aura is totally clear! His substance-abuse issues have been washed out of him!" — while meanwhile, in another reality, Elliot Baranski would be sitting on his farmhouse porch with *his* parents, the rescue from the Hostiles having proceeded smoothly — and then, soon, she would reach out her hands and carry Elliot across the space between — out of the darkness — and into her world — where —

The daydream faltered because someone was slapping her knee.

She opened her eyes. They were pulling into Cambridge, and Belle was watching her shrewdly.

"They won't be there," she said, and Madeleine turned to the window. The platform was empty except for a woman with a baby in a sling across her chest.

Belle reached to grab her bag.

"Some things you just have to take," Belle said. "My parents. Your dad. They'll keep on letting us down. Nothing we can do about it."

"There you go again," complained Jack, and he and Belle argued their way out of the train, onto the platform, and out to the bike racks, where they switched to an argument about whether Jack would take Belle home.

"Ya tosser," Belle said. "I know the way."

Jack quoted a line from a Byron poem which seemed completely inapplicable, as Belle herself pointed out, and Madeleine left them arguing, standing close together in the afternoon light, the shapes of their shadows jittering, bickering, swaying.

She rode straight to the parking meter.

There was a thin line of white but when she pulled it out, it seemed faded and worn, and it was not in Elliot's handwriting.

WEDNESDAY, 2 P.M.

TO WHOM IT MAY CONCERN,

IF YOU'RE THE PERSON IN THE WORLD WHO'S BEEN WRITING TO ELLIOT BARANSKI, THIS IS TO IMPRESS ON YOU THAT YOU'D BETTER STOP DOING

THAT. YOU MAYBE DON'T KNOW THIS BUT IT'S A CAPITAL OFFENSE TO COMMUNICATE WITH YOU PEOPLE, AND IT SEEMS SOMEONE HAS REPORTED ELLIOT TO THE WSU. I CANNOT THINK WHO'D HAVE DONE THAT, AS HE'S A POPULAR BOY, AND TO BE HONEST, WHOEVER DID HAD BETTER HIGHTAIL IT OUT OF TOWN IF THEY DON'T WANT TO GET LYNCHED. ANYHOW, THAT ASIDE, THE WSU ARE RIGHT NOW, AS I WRITE, IN PURSUIT OF ELLIOT. SEVERAL CHOPPERS IN THE AIR ABOVE ME. I'M JUST HOPEFUL THAT ELLIOT WILL GET AWAY, AND IF HE DOES, WE CAN'T HAVE ANY INCRIMINATING LETTERS ABOUT. SO PLEASE DO NOT WRITE BACK TO THIS. IF YOU HAVE ANY INTEREST IN KEEPING ELLIOT ALIVE, FORGET ABOUT HIM. STARTING NOW.

ONCE I POST THIS, I'M TEARING OUT THIS TV SCULPTURE AND DESTROYING IT, SO MAYBE THERE WON'T BE A CRACK ANYMORE TO WRITE THROUGH. MORE LIKELY, THOUGH, THE CRACK WILL STILL BE THERE, JUST NO "POST BOX" SCULPTURE TO CATCH IT, SO IF YOU DO WRITE, YOUR LETTER WILL END UP FLOATING AROUND IN THE BONFIRE HIGH SCHOOL GROUNDS FOR ANYONE WHO LIKES TO FIND.

SO KINDLY CEASE AND DESIST, ELSE I'LL FIND MY OWN WAY THROUGH AND WRING YOUR NECK.

APOLOGIES FOR THE SCRIBBLE, WRITING FAST.
JIMMY HAWTHORN, DEPUTY SHERIFF

A thread of fire ran through her.

That Elliot was being chased by choppers was one thing. That seemed so surreal and unlikely that it didn't really bother her much.

It was the idea that this Deputy Sheriff was about to rip away the TV sculpture. He seemed to think that the crack would still be there, but what if he was wrong? What if he had ripped away the only route between them?

She looked at the letter again. Wednesday, 2 P.M. That was days ago. What had happened to Elliot since then?

The flames twisted. Was he *actually* in danger? Choppers chasing him. A capital offence. Was that *real*?

She walked home through the darkening streets, her backpack thumping slowly against her shoulders, Jimmy's note folded in her hands.

When she arrived, Denny was sitting on the front step of their building, Sulky-Anne by his feet. He was holding a small, tattered notebook.

He looked up, and his eyes seemed almost to have vanished, they were so squinty and red.

"Sit a moment?" he said to her. "Strangest thing happened today, and I'd kinda like to tell you about it."

PART 24

The storm of Colors poured across Cello until late into the night. Meanwhile, teams of WSU officers swooped on all the crossover points, reinforcing the bindings on the cracks, erecting barriers, installing guards.

In the penthouse suite of the Lillian Hotel, the Princess stood at the window looking down at the empty streets and flickering lights of

Ducale. Her hair was loose. She wore a white bathrobe, tied at the waist, and when she turned away from the window, the scent of spearmint bath products washed across the room.

"I know you are all sleepy," she said. "I will keep this brief, and then you may retire to your beds. The tour of the Kingdom has been officially canceled on account of the Color storm. In the morning, you will all be taken by shuttered vehicle to the aerodrome and flown to your respective homes."

The members of the Royal Youth Alliance sat about the room in their pajamas: Sergio on the desk chair, Keira up on the leather-covered desk itself, and Samuel on the edge of the bed. Agents Nettles and Ramsay leaned against the wall, alongside the minibar.

"As you will have heard, our plans have been thwarted. It appears that the Hostiles must have learned of our success bringing Prince Tippett back through, and, ingeniously and drastically, have leaked the crossover points to the WSU. As we speak, they are resealing the crack at the Harrington Hotel just a block away. Meanwhile, my mother, sister, and brother Chyba remain trapped in the World."

Samuel moaned gently.

"Quite," agreed the Princess. "Moreover, in losing Elliot Baranski, we have lost our source in the World."

There was a sharp tapping sound. Keira had picked up the hotel pen from the desk and was clicking the end with her thumb repeatedly.

"Thank you, Keira," the Princess sang. "You make a good point. The loss of Elliot himself is a severe blow too. He was a fine, brave young man — a hero — and he gave his life for his Kingdom. His memory will be honored forevermore."

"Except," said Keira, "that this whole thing is a total secret, so I'm not sure I see how it *can* be honored —"

"And there is still no news of Elliot?" Sergio interrupted, dragging his chair across the carpet a short distance as he spoke. "Has his body been recovered?"

"Eeeow," murmured Samuel, tilting slightly.

"Not yet," the Princess replied. "And the search may be abandoned as too dangerous — apparently, the ravine into which he fell is sheer and brutal. It has been confirmed, however, that he could certainly not have survived the fall."

Samuel made another mewing sound.

"I have also heard," the Princess continued, "that a high-school physics teacher named Isabella Tamborlaine packed her bags and ran away from the town of Bonfire the day that Elliot was killed. It seems clear that she is the one who reported him."

"She is a *terravixtiol*!" cried Sergio.

"A serpenttooth," agreed Keira, narrowing her eyes.

"Oh!" said Samuel.

"All right," the Princess sighed listlessly. "No curse words. Even Maneeshian and Jagged-Edgian curse words. You're upsetting Samuel's sensibilities." She shook herself. "The town of Bonfire is in mourning, I understand. Elliot was a favorite, and Isabella, although new to town, was also popular. She was dating the Deputy Sheriff, Jimmy Hawthorn, apparently, and I understand that he is taking this turn of events very hard, which — Samuel, what *is* the matter with you?"

Samuel had pulled his legs up onto the bed, curled his arms around his knees, and was making low humming noises.

"Oh," he said. "As to a — call yourself my — I apologize — but it is . . ."

The Princess took a step across the room. Sergio and Keira both stood and moved too.

"He is like a horse with the tetanus infection," declared Sergio.

"His skin is a disaster," said Keira.

"His *skin* looks like a horse with the rain rot," Sergio agreed.

"He's sick," said Princess Ko. "What *is* this illness, Samuel? Is it something from Olde Quainte? I've never seen anything like it."

"Hope it's not contagious," Keira observed.

There was another low moan from Samuel.

"He reminds me of the drug addicts I've seen while touring hospitals," Princess Ko said. "It's a little like withdrawal from —" She breathed in sharply. "Wait," she said. "Oh, Samuel, no. Is this a Turquoise Rain thing? Have you been chasing Turquoise Rain around the Kingdom since that night? Are you an *addict*?"

Samuel turned a slow circle on the bed, winding himself around like clock hands, his own hands pressed to his stomach.

"It's not that," Keira said, and her voice had an odd, slow lilt to it, so the others turned to look at her. "Turquoise Rain doesn't do this. But when we were in Olde Quainte, I remember seeing an old man on a street corner. His limbs were wound together like plaited bread. His eyes were leaking pus. His skin, I remember now — his skin was exactly like this. Somebody told me he'd be dead within a week. They said it was caused by —"

She stopped, then started again.

"Somebody told me the guy had used Olde Quainte magic."

There was a loud exhalation from the Princess, and she stamped her foot.

"Oh, do *not* tell me," she half shouted at Samuel. "Do not *tell* me that you've used Olde Quainte magic."

Samuel whimpered again.

"Call yourself my — but, Princess, I had to use just a little —"

"I told you *not to tell me that*!" the Princess screamed.

". . . to get access," Samuel continued, "to the archives for you — and a deal more — to try to see through the blocked parts . . . of those reports — although that came to naught — and then *more* to steal . . . the originals — so you see . . ."

His body arched oddly, then fell back onto the bed.

"It has ailed me for some time — the symptoms, I mean — that Turquoise Rain gave me — some beautiful relief — but now, I see not what . . ."

The Princess raised her hand as if she was about to slap him, but stopped herself.

"Get an ambulance," she barked at the agents, who had both stepped forward from the wall. "He will need a blood transfusion, but it won't save him. Do you hear me, Samuel? A blood transfusion will keep you alive a little longer, but *nothing* can save you now. You ridiculous boy. You stupid, utterly ridiculous boy. *Nothing* can cure an infection of Olde Quainte magic."

Samuel began to sob quietly. "It was only for you," he sobbed. "I did it for —"

"I don't want to hear it," the Princess snapped, and she retreated to the window, and stood with her back to the room while calls were made, Samuel writhed, Sergio murmured soothing words, Keira swore, paramedics knocked, and Samuel was hooked up to oxygen and lifted onto a stretcher.

"Princess," he called thinly as the paramedics navigated the stretcher through the hotel room door. "Call me your forgiveness! I know I was foolish as to a candied orange peel in whale brine, but my — but my heart was in the right place."

The Princess swung around from the window.

"It won't be for long," she shot back, and then Samuel was gone, the door closed.

There were faint noises from both Sergio and Keira.

"Well, it's true," the Princess countered, her eyes flashing. "An infection of OQ magic contorts your limbs, peels off your skin, and tangles your internal organs. His heart *won't* be in the right place soon. Shall we continue our meeting?"

A resigned, gloomy, appalled shrug seemed to blow across the room. Sergio returned to the chair. Keira leaned up against the desk, her arms folded, breathing loudly through her nose.

The Princess waited.

"The news is not all bad," she said. "We have successfully rescued my little brother. I understand that he has already skated on the moat and snowboarded the steep hill behind the Palace. We have also rescued my father. I understand that *he* has arrived safely in the Kingdom of Aldhibah, and is already delighting the dignitaries there with his high good humor. The relations between our Kingdoms have been saved. War has been averted. The Hostiles, presumably, have gone back underground. For this, you all deserve the Kingdom's gratitude and recognition. Keira, your vision found the cracks for us. Without that, we —"

"Yeah, about that," Keira unfolded her arms. "I don't get it — I mean, I'd been in your brother's bedroom before and it wasn't there that time, so what, the crack was new, or what?"

The Princess shook her head.

"No. The crack was always there. It is only now that you can see cracks because your vision has sharpened. Have you not noticed any other improvements? Those exercises I have been giving you these last months —"

"Exercises?" Keira frowned, then opened her mouth. "You don't mean those piles of documents? You *don't*! They were *exercises*? I thought you were just giving them to me to punish me — for my mother — I thought they were meant to *hurt* my eyes."

The Princess hesitated.

"I found an obscure study," she said, "that suggested that Jagged-Edgian vision could be dramatically improved in this way. Of course," she scratched her cheek and frowned a little. "Of course, there were also studies showing that some had been permanently blinded by the exercises, but the risk of that seemed . . ."

"Worth taking," Keira supplied dryly.

"So, for risking your vision — albeit unknowingly — and completing the exercises to triumphant effect, Keira, I hereby thank you."

Keira shook her head.

The Princess pressed her lips together, and turned to the agents.

"Agents Nettles and Ramsay," she said. "I must also thank you. You have been loyal, patient, and brave. You have stood by us —"

Here, Agent Nettles cleared her throat. "I guess we should say —" she began, but the Princess interrupted.

"Yes," she said. "Quite. You should say that you owe me an unreserved apology. You doubted me. You were *wrong.* You doubted all of us. You were *utterly* wrong. You failed to show respect. In particular," she hesitated, her eyes narrowing, "you failed to show respect to Sergio."

Both agents readied to speak, and the Princess raised a hand.

"Let me finish. You owe *him* an abject, pleading, desperate apology," she said, her voice strengthening. "He is an *Occasional Pilot.* He saved *all* of our lives. You do know, I take it, that Occasional Pilots must, of necessity, be courageous? And I suppose you two have been asking yourselves how it is that a *slight, dancing* stable boy from Maneesh could possibly have courage enough? Let me *tell* you something you do not know about Sergio!"

"Princess," murmured Sergio.

The Princess ignored him. "This is Sergio's life to date: When he was eight years old, his entire family was wiped out by the Maneeshian plague. Before they had been buried, the Maneeshian civil war broke out, and the eastern forces rode into town — did you hear me? *Rode* into town. The *horsemen* of the eastern army took Sergio prisoner — he escaped, found his way onto a ship bound for Cello — arrived in our Kingdom suffering from a *profound terror* of horses. And do you know what he did?" She paused. The room waited. "He found a *job* as a stable boy — working with horses! — do you know why? Stop shaking your heads like children! Of course you don't know. He did it because his father had always said that one must *take one's greatest fears and hold them close to one's chest*. One must *embrace* those fears *like a lover*! That's what his father always said! And now he *does* love horses! And he embraced them so strongly that he ended up working his way north until he was in the finest stables in the land, the stables of the White Palace of the Magical North! Because he had enough courage to *devour* a Kingdom!"

She flung her final words across the room like a whip.

"We didn't know," the agents murmured.

"Well, you shouldn't have *had* to know! Even if Sergio *hadn't* demonstrated such courage — even if he *wasn't* an Occasional Pilot — what are you *thinking* disrespecting a person just because he's *slight* or *feminine* or *comes from Maneesh*? Where did you *find* those absurd, narrow, comic-books ideas of yours about what a *hero* looks like?! And *where do you get off disrespecting my best friend?!*"

The agents blinked.

"Now you look like a pair of horses who are deeply ashamed about the fact that they have worms," the Princess added.

"I am not sure that horses feel shame about such —" began Sergio thoughtfully, but the Princess was swinging around to face Keira, picking up her tirade again. "As for you, Keira, if you think I *liked* risking Sergio's life by asking him to go undercover at the

WSU — if you think I *like* the fact that Elliot is dead because I instructed him to communicate with the World — if you think I *enjoyed* risking *your* vision, and threatening you with your mother's execution — and if you think I *relish* the fact that *my* demands have caused Samuel to *destroy* himself with Olde Quainte magic — that stupid *child*, that . . ."

Keira was watching her skeptically; Sergio's face was profoundly sad.

The Princess, seeing their reactions, stopped abruptly and resumed her calm.

"In any case, once my father returns from Aldhibah," she said, "he will assume responsibility for the Kingdom and for the rescue of my family. Perhaps he will call on your help again? Likely not. Either way, I will invite him to reward you all generously for your efforts to date. For now," she sighed, and her eyelids lowered slightly. "For now, you may sleep, and, in the morning, you may return to your lives."

She sank down onto the bed, and continued, almost chattily: "As for me, I'm going to fly home to the Magical North, hang out with my little brother, read novels in a hammock, take long bubble baths, and go for many, many horse rides across the wide snowy fields with you, Sergio."

There was a pause in the room.

"Did you not *hear* me?" The Princess threw herself onto the bed, bouncing once, and propping a pillow beneath her head. *"Return to your lives!"*

PART 25

Shafts of evening sunlight caught patterns of dust and dog hairs.

There was the usual rubble of toolboxes and motherboards covering the floor, the two workbenches rising majestically above this, remnants of steam misting from the open bathroom door, that soapy, heady smell of aftershave or antiperspirant or whatever it was that boys used when they showered, and, across the room, dim in shadows, the shape of a boy beneath the blankets of the bed.

Madeleine stood by the window, watching him.

Elliot lay on his side, an arm reaching beneath the pillow, dark blond hair, eyelashes. He was perfectly still, deeply asleep. If she caught her own breath and concentrated, she could hear him breathing.

Half an hour earlier, just off the train from Norwich, Madeleine had sat beside Denny on the front doorstep.

"Here's the news," he'd said. "My son, Elliot Baranski, is sleeping upstairs. Says he's been writing to you awhile. Seems he's walked here from Harrogate."

"*Walked* here?" she'd said. "From Harrogate?"

"I know. For seventeen quid or so he could have got the National Express Coach and got here in an afternoon."

"A long afternoon," Madeleine said. "I think it's about six hours by coach. But *still*. Walked! It must have taken him *days*!"

Denny leaned down and rubbed Sulky-Anne's belly.

"Our focus might be a little displaced here," he said.

"We could be straying from the point," she agreed. "You're not seriously Elliot's father."

Denny lifted the notebook he was holding in his left hand.

"I surely am," he said. "Came through myself more than a year ago now, at the exact same place my boy came through. I wrote these notes in the first couple of days I was here, knowing I'd be losing my memory. Might be best if you read them yourself — if you can — my handwriting's not great at the best of times, and I was in a bad state then."

Madeleine had turned the notebook over, then handed it back to him.

"I should tell Mum that I'm home first," she said. "Just wait a moment."

When she returned, he was sitting in the exact same position, Sulky-Anne lying beside him, her chin on her paws.

She read his notebook.

I am ABEL GAREK BARANSKI. I come from BONFIRE, THE FARMS, KINGDOM OF CELLO. I have a wife, Petra, and a son, Elliot. My brother is Jonathan Baranski. He's married to Alanna. They own the Watermelon Inn. They have a daughter, Corrie-Lynn. I own an electronics repair shop. I MUST NOT BELIEVE ANYTHING ELSE ABOUT MYSELF.

Here's what happened to me.

Mischka Tegan came to Bonfire not long back — high-school Physics teacher — she recruited Jon and me to her organization — told us it was a Loyalist Network branch — working against the extreme terrorist arms of the Wandering Hostiles — she wanted our help developing techniques for constructing cracks thru to the World — as method of resistance against Hostiles / escape route for royals under threat — we started development of a revolutionary technology for this purpose — experimented with listening devices and transponders — great success — first effort at actual crack thru to World was underway in back of a broken TV when Jon grew suspicious of Mischka — watched her closely — discovered she is in fact a Wandering Hostile herself — things turned ugly fast — other Hostiles with attack dogs — they were hunting me and Jon — truck got waylaid by a Purple — shutters failed — Purple got Jon — Mischka's group pursued me thru the woods — chased me to edge of a ravine — fell into ravine — must have "stumbled" thru to the World thru a crack in the air —

Note: Why did I come thru?

Jon and I had theorized that "stumbling" occurs when acute emotional intensity is combined with powerful "absence" — but did the emotion / absence "construct" a crack in the air, or propel me thru a preexisting crack? Does it matter?

Do intense emotions jostle reality and THEREBY open cracks? Space contracts when you move. Did the speed of my fall / adrenaline cause the universe to contract and thereby crack?

Plan: make way to a university town. Find professors of Quantum Physics and consult on issues of crack construction. Consider replicating conditions of extreme emotion / absence. Can a missing bike wheel replicate the sudden absence of a brother?

Note: one of attack dogs also came thru with me — shock seems to have rendered her harmless — also seems loyal/clings to me — take care tho —

Madeleine closed the notebook.

She looked down at Sulky-Anne.

"I'm sorry about your brother," she said.

Denny nodded. "Miss him every moment. And Petra. And Elliot. Only, I've been remembering them all with different names in different places in a different story. But the same. If you see what I mean."

Madeleine's gaze was still on Sulky-Anne.

"Wait," she said. "Don't tell me *this* is the dog that came through with you? Please don't tell me Sulky-Anne is a Hostile attack dog."

Denny shrugged. "I clipped her claws."

Madeleine sighed deeply.

"And your name is Abel, not Denny? And you and your brother were working on *cracks*, and *that's* why the TV in the schoolyard sculpture had a crack in it?"

"Ah, just keep calling me Denny for now if you like. By the time I got to Cambridge, that's who I'd become — my brain had translated everything." He took back the notebook, and held it up. "Thought I must have got drunk and scribbled notes for a novel, which" — he paused, thoughtful — "struck me as odd, seeing as I've never shown a particularly literary bent."

"Did Elliot tell you about him and me? And the missing royals and everything?"

"Kinda," Denny said. "He was on the verge of incoherent, but I think I got the gist. And he mentioned your mirror-and-light trick. I've been trying to figure how that could work. Just thinking aloud here, but you know that if you shine light on certain metals, it blasts some electrons out of the metal? And mirrors are made from metal, of course, although —"

Madeleine interrupted him.

"I feel like it's not so scientific as that," she said. "I think when two people in two realities have a serious connection — reflect each other's essences somehow — it sends a shot of energy between those realities. And *that* opens a crack. And maybe the mirror and light replicate that? Like a sort of literal reflection of the other person's light. Like how you were thinking that a missing bike wheel might replicate an absence."

Denny raised his eyebrows. "Could be," he said, "that your theory matches up with mine. A mirror might be an absence in a way — it's waiting for something to reflect. And light could be like an emotion — that flow of energy."

"The most powerful force in the universe is human emotion," Madeleine said, remembering what Belle had said, "especially when it's brought on by an absence."

"Well," said Denny. "Seems you've given this a lot of thought yourself. And I surely hope you'll help me and Elliot figure out how to get home. We need to keep working on that crack in your parking meter."

"We can't," Madeleine remembered, and she took out the letter from Jimmy. "They'll have taken away the sculpture by now."

Denny read Jimmy's letter, then held it to one side, and stroked Sulky-Anne in long, slow, thoughtful strokes.

Eventually he stopped. "I don't think it's relevant," he said. "The TV sculpture being gone. There'll still be a crack right there in the schoolyard that connects to the parking meter here. Whatever I did to the back of that TV must have been more or less right, but the crack formed when it got into the schoolyard. Maybe the way it was moved or positioned on the sculpture? The point is, the crack's not literally *inside* the TV, the TV's just been catching the things that come through."

He picked up Jimmy's letter again, curling it into a scroll.

"Can you do me a favour?" he said. "Can you post a letter through the parking meter right away?" He tapped his fingers on his knee, suddenly urgent. "Because who knows what she's thinking right now?"

"What who's thinking?" Madeleine asked.

But Denny was tearing a blank page from the notebook, swearing about how there was never a pen when you needed one, and running inside. He reappeared ten minutes later, holding up an envelope.

Cody Richter said the envelope.

"Cody Richter," Madeleine read aloud, then: "Wait, that's one of Elliot's friends. The artist?"

Denny's face broke into a grin. "You sure do know my son," he said. "I'm thinking this letter will just float into the schoolyard when you post it. And I'm hoping it'll find its way to Cody. I *think* he's the most reliable of Elliot's unreliable friends. Then Cody can deliver it to her. She needs to know where we are and that we're safe."

Madeleine looked at the envelope, then up at the third-floor window.

"He's still asleep." Denny sat on the front step beside her again. "If you like, you can wait in my flat for him to wake? Not sure he'll know who you are — his memories were in a slipping, spinning phase before he fell asleep. They'll probably be all gone by the time he wakes. Reassembled into who knows what."

Madeleine stood up. "But you want me to post your letter first?"

"Please," he said. "It's important."

She reached to take it, but paused, looking down at Denny.

Not Denny.

Abel Baranski.

"Can I ask you a question?" she said, and before he'd replied: "Were you planning to run away with that woman? The teacher? Mischka Tegan?"

Denny began to scratch under Sulky-Anne's chin so closely and attentively, that she thought he was not going to answer.

"Mischka was a goddess," he said eventually. "Sharpest mind. Beautiful smile. Jon and I were both smitten. We should've seen much sooner who she really was, but . . ."

He continued scratching, and Sulky-Anne shifted a little, indicating she'd had enough and was just enduring it now, out of politeness.

"But were you planning to run away with her?"

There was a long pause.

"The honest answer," he said, "is absolutely yes, and absolutely no. Both at once. I don't *think* I would have, but . . ." and he left it there, his hands in the air.

She looked at him: thin shoulders, inhaler half slipping from his pocket, bloodshot eyes, helpless hands.

Then she took the envelope, got on her bike, and rode away to deliver it.

Now, standing in Denny's flat, and looking down onto the street, Madeleine was thinking: *absolutely yes and absolutely no.*

She turned from the window, and looked across at the kitchenette, where an upturned muffin tray sat beside a pair of coffee mugs.

The duality, she realised, is inside us. We are all composed of absolutely yes and absolutely no, of north and south, dark and light; we are all both heroes and the opposite of heroes; we can all fly and we can fall.

A strong wind can blow us away, or we can ride it.

There are two sides to everyone, and two sides to everything, and then there's the infinite space that's in between.

Dusk was falling fast.

She wondered if Denny was still sitting outside on the step, waiting to be Abel Baranski again. She wondered if her mother was sewing upstairs, or watching TV, or standing at the window like Madeleine, waiting.

You wait to find out where the truth will fall — at hope or at despair — but until it falls — even while it falls — it can be both.

It *is* both, until it's measured.

She touched the window. It was smudged with her breathing and with fingerprints.

There was a polite cough behind her, and she turned.

The flat was dark now, but she could make out his figure, standing by the bed, white T-shirt and boxers that he must have borrowed from Denny, his hair sticking up in tufts that caught fragments of light.

He took a step towards her. Now he was closer to the window, and she could see him more clearly. His eyes were bright and his expression suggested a person who is utterly baffled — but also amused by his own bafflement, and up for the challenge of sorting the whole thing out.

"Maybe I could introduce myself," he said, and then paused and chuckled. It was that deep, wicked chuckle she remembered from the space between. "*Maybe* I could introduce myself," he repeated. "Not sure. Seems to me that I am Alexander Krol, and I —"

"No, you're not," said Madeleine. "You're Elliot Baranski, of Bonfire, the Farms."

Now Elliot grinned, and it was a grin that made her think it could prise you right open and let the light come rip-roaring in at you.

"If that's who you'd like me to be," he said, "that's who I'll be. As for you, I have absolutely no idea who you are, but two things — one, you're gorgeous, and two, I think I know you absolutely."

He paused. "That sounds like a line, doesn't it? Fact is, it's the truth."

He reached over, put his arms around her, pressed a kiss onto her forehead, and stepped back again, studying her.

"Absolute magnitude," she said, "means the intrinsic brightness of an object."

"Is that a fact?" The grin returned.

The kiss was still there on her forehead. Inside the kiss was the essence of everything.

PART 26

In Taipei, Taiwan, Sasha Wilczek lies on her narrow bed and waits.

The doctor had been fascinated by the coloured specks inside her elbow, but had nothing in particular to say about them. When she'd asked if they could indicate a tracking device, secretly implanted by a New Zealand–based gang called the Death Bears, his eyes had narrowed carefully, and his words had crept towards issues of mental health.

She'd come home, and shut herself in her room.

Now she looks at her watch. It is several hours since the designated meeting time. Obviously, they know her address, so she expects them any moment.

Outside her door, her flatmates are setting up for their card game.

She hopes, half-heartedly, that she has not put them in danger. They're just kids, really, and it might have been more heroic for her to go to the meeting point, only she hadn't *felt* like being shot down by a passing, speeding car.

Now, though, they might storm in and put bullets between the eyes of the flatmates. She can't bring herself to care all that much. If they played something *other* than gin rummy now and then, or if they'd even *once* made her laugh, things might be different.

Still. Maybe they have unexpected ninja skills? She'll completely forgive their lack of humour if they save her life.

She falls into a fitful sleep and dreams she finds a trapdoor that leads her to a palace.

In Boise, Idaho, Monty and his friends pull up at the corner of West Jefferson and North Sixth Street, as instructed, and wait a full thirty seconds.

Almost at once, another buddy of theirs walks by on the opposite side of the road, arms around a big brown paper bag.

They all shout through the windows at once, and the buddy runs across the road, and leans in the window, saying hey. They talk and laugh at him, and he has no idea what they're on about, or where the Kingdom of Cello is, or what it has to do with anything, but the brown paper bag's full of booze, he says, and he's heading to a party at another buddy's place, and they all ought to come along.

They tell him to jump in the car, and they speed off right away, all of them still hooting about cellos, and about this being *the* most elaborate party invitation ever concocted, the letters to Monty and the Prince Chyba thing and the whole mad lemon juice thing.

The buddy has even less of a clue what any of it means but he laughs hard, thinking he'll figure it out eventually.

Monty, crammed in the backseat, has only a single moment in which he wonders if they might be missing the real thing — and inside that moment, there's a sudden certainty that he *is* missing it, and an astonishing, terrifying plummet of loss — but then he's outside the moment again, and shouting to the driver that he should take a right here, at which the driver's shouting back that Monty wouldn't know the best route if it crawled out of his shirt and sucker-punched him in the chin, and the car drives on and swings left.

In Berlin, Germany, Ariel Peters has been waiting on this corner for almost five hours. It's dark but she's still wearing her cheap sunglasses, the ones she stole from a petrol station. Her duffel bag is over her shoulder.

She's pacing in small circles to keep warm. There's plenty going on. She's on the corner of Friedrichstrasse and Unter den Linden, a very fancy corner. An upmarket corner. Too upmarket for a girl like her, whose gloves are fraying at the fingertips. They're not cutoff gloves; they're frayed.

A couple walk by with wet hair. They're fully dressed, but have towels hanging over their arms, and both are laughing, excited about something. From behind, Ariel sees a shiver run down the girl's back.

Ariel pushes up her sleeve, and peers at her inner elbow in the fading light. She can't see the colours anymore. Her pacing circle is changing shape, stretching out, turning into a line that leads her home.

She has in mind a new tattoo right there on her inner elbow. A spray of coloured specks. An imitation of the lemon juice effect.

A permanent reminder of the time when, for just a few brief weeks, she got to be Princess Jupiter of the Kingdom of Cello.

In Bonfire, the Farms, Kingdom of Cello, Petra Baranski sits on the edge of her porch, waiting for nothing. She thinks lists of words like rows of pots.

Raspberry. Quince. Beehive. Fertilizer. Pest.

You can start with a random word, she's found, and follow it along. Or get triggers from things you see or hear.

The main thing is to keep the words coming.

A bag of wet cement is slammed at her, now and then, and it knocks her off her feet, on account of having lost her husband and her son in a single day.

But she's found that, so long as she follows her rows of words, she can keep it from swinging too often.

There's the smooth rustle of a bicycle wheel in the driveway.

Here comes Cody Richter, his wild head of curls, riding toward her.

Bicycle. Axle. Spokes. Rust.

That's sweet of him to come, she thinks, but she sure hopes he won't expect a cup of coffee.

She'd have to stand up then, and the words might slip.

White fly. Thrip. Downy mildew. Powdery mildew. Gray mold.

Cody leans his bike against the wall of the house. He's walking toward her. He's got an envelope in his pocket. She can see a white square of it, sticking up.

Square. Circle. Triangle —

It's slipping.

"Hexagon," she says aloud, relieved.

"Octagon," Cody counters, and he sits beside her, reaches into his pocket, and hands her the letter.

Acknowledgments

I am enormously grateful to all those at Scholastic, and at Pan Macmillan, who have contributed such insight, energy, and artistry to this book, especially Arthur A. Levine, Emily Clement, Elizabeth B. Parisi, Sheila Marie Everett, and Lizette Serrano (in the US), and Claire Craig, Samantha Sainsbury, Cate Paterson, Julia Stiles, and Charlotte Ree (in Australia).

For answering my questions and sharing thoughts, ideas, and expertise, thank you so much to Rupert Baker (Library Manager, the Royal Society), Mark Staples, Steve Menasse, Robert Guthrie, Rob Summers, Douglas Melrose-Rae, Robert Travers, Alistair Baillie, Tim and Julia Smith, and Andrea Nottage.

For reading drafts and for suggestions, inspiration, and the distraction of a small child, thank you so much to my Mum and Dad, to Liane Moriarty, Kati Harrington, Fiona Ostric, Nicola Moriarty, Michael McCabe, Rachel Cohn, Corrie Stepan, Erin Shields, Jane Ecccleston, Lesley Kelly, Gaynor Armstrong, Libby Choo, Henry Choo, and Kirrily Agus.

For being a consistently delightful small child, thank you to Charlie.

This book is dedicated to my friends, Corrie Stepan and Rachel Cohn who, between them, took an impossible journey and reshaped it as a dream holiday.

This book was designed by

Elizabeth B. Parisi.

The text was set in Adobe Caslon Pro,

and the display type was set in Carolyna Pro Black.

Tippett's handwriting by Max Ferrante.

The book was printed and bound at

R. R. Donnelley in Crawfordsville, Indiana.

Production was supervised by

Starr Baer,

and manufacturing was supervised by

Angelique Browne.

ML 1/2015